SEEING
FIREWORKS

SEEING FIREWORKS

Elaine Coffman
Victoria Barrett
Ashland Price
Trana Mae Simmons

St. Martin's Paperbacks

SEEING FIREWORKS

"Playing with Fire" copyright © 1997 by Elaine Coffman.
"Summer Fling" copyright © 1997 by Vicki Hinze.
"One Star-Spangled Night" copyright © 1997 by Ashland Price.
"Showers and Sparks" copyright © 1997 by Trana Mae Simmons.

ISBN: 0-312-96258-4

Printed in the United States of America

St. Martin's Paperbacks edition / July 1997

10 9 8 7 6 5 4 3 2 1

Contents

PLAYING WITH FIRE

Elaine Coffman

Chapter One

Susan Klein had been warned about cowboys. She hadn't paid the warning much mind until the man who showed up to drive them from the airport spit a wad of chewing tobacco on her shoe.

"I hope this isn't an indication of how the next two weeks are going to be," she said to her three friends as the four of them stared down at her shoe.

A car door slammed, then a voice said, "Beg your pardon, ma'am."

Susan and her friends looked up to see the cowboy who had driven up just moments before he spit out the window and it landed on her shoe. The man stood next to a white Suburban with the words SPLIT FORK GUEST RANCH written on the side of the door.

He brought his hand up to the brim of his hat. "You ladies waiting for a ride to Split Fork?"

Susan nodded. "Yes. Our bags are over there," she said, nodding toward the spot where their bags waited.

The man tipped his hat again. "Sorry about your shoe, ma'am. My aim ain't what it used to be." He pulled out a soiled handkerchief and offered it to her.

Susan eyed the handkerchief. "No thank you," she said, and plucked a tissue from her purse. She gave her shoe a couple of swipes.

"My name is Fish. I'll be driving you ladies out to

Split Fork Ranch,'' he said and began loading their luggage.

Inhaling a lungful of air, Berny exclaimed, ''I never knew what pure, clean air smelled like. I think I'm allergic to it. I'm getting dizzy.''

''It's the altitude, stupid,'' Audrey replied. ''The air is thinner up here. It'll take you a few days to adjust to it.''

Berny Goldman ignored her and gave her attention to Fish. ''Did you say your name was Fish . . . the kind that swims in water?''

''Yes, ma'am, I shore did. 'Course my real name is Fisher . . . George Fisher, but everybody here abouts just calls me Fish.''

Susan looked Fish over. He was the first real cowboy she had ever seen. She was hoping for Antonio Banderas. She got George Fisher—short, squat, balding. He had to be at least sixty-five.

Fish helped the four of them into the Suburban. Susan climbed into the far back seat. A moment later Beth Ann Wallace took the seat next to her. ''It's hotter than I expected,'' Beth Ann said, then removed a rubber band from her purse and pulled her straight blond hair back into a ponytail.

Audrey O'Malley, whose red hair and freckles bespoke of her Irish descent, took the seat in front of Susan. Berny fell into the seat next to Audrey, ran a hand through her short brown hair, and said to Beth Ann, ''I wish my hair was long enough to pull back like yours.''

''It would be if you'd stop whacking it off everytime it touches your shoulders,'' Audrey replied.

Fish climbed into the driver's seat and started the engine. ''Where are you gals from?''

''Audrey is obviously from Boston,'' Berny said, doing her best Boston accent when she said, ''Park the kaah . . . Beth Ann is from Alabama. . . .''

''Mobile,'' Beth Ann interjected.

''Susan is from Richmond, and I'm from New York, but we all live in Washington, D.C., now.''

"You're gonna be here for two weeks. Is that right?"

Audrey's nod was enthusiastic. "Fourteen days of bliss. Just smell that fresh air. Not a trace of bus fumes anywhere."

"What made four city gals like you pick a guest ranch for a vacation?" Fish asked.

"We gave the trip to Susan for her birthday," Beth Ann said. "She turns forty next week."

"Why don't you put a sign on the side of the door so everyone in the state of Montana will know about it!" Susan said.

"Susan's a little touchy about her age," Audrey said, and everyone laughed. Everyone, save Susan, that is.

"Turning forty ain't so bad," Fish said. "There are a lot of things worse than being forty."

"Yes, like losing your job, or having your boyfriend dump you for a younger woman," was Susan's reply.

Susan glanced up and saw Fish was watching her from the rearview mirror. She made a face and turned to gaze out the window. While her friends were busy talking to Fish, Susan leaned her head against the window and watched the Montana landscape as it passed by. If this vacation was supposed to make her forget her woes, it wasn't doing the trick. And turning forty was the least of her worries. Losing Joel, whom she had dated for four years, had been a real blow. And if that wasn't enough, two days after Joel walked out of her life, Susan learned her job with Senator Milford Claiborne was in jeopardy since the senator announced that it was highly probable he would be retiring and would not seek reelection.

If she had been the mushy sort, Susan might have given in to the urge to cry, but since she wasn't, she wallowed in a few sentimental thoughts about how lucky she was to have the kind of friends she had.

Bad things might come in threes, but not when it came to friends. Susan had three of the most wonderful friends in the whole world and that just seemed to balance things a bit. Not that she didn't have every right to have a nervous breakdown. A week ago, Susan thought her world was coming to an end, but that was before her three friends came to her rescue.

"We're giving you a two-week trip to a real, bona fide guest ranch in Montana," Beth Ann said to Susan in her most sympathetic voice, her sugar-coated Alabama accent as comforting as the warmth in her blue eyes.

"A guest ranch?" Susan repeated slowly.

"You said you wanted to enter your forties with a bang," Berny said. "What better place to get banged than at a ranch with all those horny cowboys around?"

"She said with a bang, idiot, not get banged," Audrey said.

"Bang . . . get banged, what's the difference?" asked Berny.

"Depends on the length of the gun barrel, I would imagine," Audrey said, and everyone laughed. "Anyway, the part about the guest ranch in Montana is for real. We want you to have two weeks there as our gift to you."

Stunned, all Susan could say was, "Oh, I couldn't. . . ."

"You don't have any say in the matter," Audrey said. "We've already paid for the four of us to spend two weeks at the Split Fork Ranch and there will be no backing out."

"You mean we're all going?" Susan asked.

This time it was Berny who said, "You don't think we'd let you go alone, do you? As if we didn't know you'd mope around and feel sorry for yourself for the entire time. What kind of birthday gift would that be?"

"It's too much, really. I appreciate your concern, but I couldn't let you do something like that. It's way too expensive."

"It's already done," Berny said, her tone saying the subject was dismissed.

Susan put up one last bit of resistance. "I don't think

I'm up to a vacation right now. In a few months, perhaps.''

Beth Ann had obviously anticipated Susan's words. ''You aren't in any condition to make that decision. As your best friends, we have made it for you. Now, we have four tickets to Montana, and come Monday there are going to be four of us on that plane.''

And so, here we are, in Bane, Montana, Susan thought as the Suburban turned off the highway and drove beneath a sign that said WELCOME TO SPLIT FORK GUEST RANCH. She looked at the pile of moose antlers stacked in a pyramid next to the entrance. How very, very far away Washington, D.C., seemed. Maybe her friends were right. Perhaps this is what she needed.

Not one to jump to conclusions or rely too heavily on first impressions, she would reserve judgment. After all, she could not imagine what could possibly happen way out here in the middle of nowhere that would change the outcome of the things in her life that were already set in motion. The facts were clear: She would turn forty, Joel was gone, and more than likely her job would be too by the time she returned home. Nothing could change that.

Susan had not planned to like the owner of Split Fork any more than she had planned to like this trip, but after a few days she found she liked both. Andy Whittaker was friendly, down to earth, and much, much younger and better looking than any of them expected. Beth Ann had dibs on him before the Suburban had come to a complete stop. When Berny suggested that Susan should have the right of first refusal, since it was, after all, her birthday, Susan refused—on grounds that although Andy was definitely nice looking, he was not her type. ''Besides, I've sworn off men.''

''Yeah, yeah, yeah,'' was Berny's reply.

The first two days passed uneventfully, with the four of them relaxing and catching up on their sleep. After two afternoons of sleeping in the sun by the pool, the circles were gone from beneath Susan's eyes and her face had a healthy tan. Beth Ann declared, ''Honey, you sure are looking good . . . for a woman who's about to turn forty.''

The dreaded day arrived on Wednesday, which was also the day they were scheduled to go horseback riding. When it was announced, Susan and Berny were the only ones who admitted to being complete novices when it came to horses, although Beth Ann and Audrey didn't show any signs of proficiency in that department once they were mounted.

Susan's horse was a buckskin brute named Tommy. Fish said Tommy was a gelding, and since Susan didn't know what a gelding was, she did the appropriate thing and asked.

''Well, you might say he's had his personality altered,'' Fish said, ''so now he isn't all that interested in girls.''

''It's like he's been neutered,'' Beth Ann said.

''Don't let Tommy hear you say that,'' Fish said with a chuckle. Then to Susan he said, ''Don't you worry none. Tommy's a good, sturdy mount. He'll get you where you're going.''

Susan learned later that she should have asked if he would get her back from where she was going, because after riding for an hour, they decided to take a rest and dismounted. Susan tied Tommy to a bush, which didn't seem to matter, because when Tommy decided to leave, he wasn't about to let any bush stand in his way. One moment he was standing there placidly switching his tail and the next thing she knew he snorted and sat back on the reins until he unearthed the bush. Before anyone knew what he was about, Tommy took off running as if someone had mentioned he would be going to the glue factory.

Susan watched him go, feeling not all that disappointed. Already her backside was sore and the seams of her jeans had rubbed the insides of her legs raw. A nice long walk didn't sound too bad, actually.

"Aren't you going to go after him?" Beth Ann asked Fish.

"He'd be back at the barn before I could get mounted."

"Susan can ride behind one of us," Beth Ann said.

"You can ride behind me," Audrey volunteered.

"I'll walk, thank you."

"Can't let you do that, missy. You'll have to ride behind me or one of your friends."

Susan started to climb up behind Audrey.

"You're mounting on the wrong . . ." Fish didn't get to finish what he was going to say before Audrey's mount bucked once and tossed Susan in the dirt.

"I don't think he liked the idea of carrying two of us," Susan said as she climbed to her feet, rubbing her backside.

"What he didn't like was you trying to mount him from the right side. Remember, I told you to always mount from the left."

"I bet she'll remember now," Berny said.

"How wise you are," Susan said, then made a big to-do about going around to the left side of Audrey's horse. "Okay, brute, let's try this one more time." The horse turned his head and looked at her when she put her foot in the stirrup, but that was about it.

Susan swung up behind Audrey and they started off.

Once they were back at the barn, Susan went straight to her cabin and fell across the bed. She slept until Berny woke her.

"Wake up. It's time to start getting ready for dinner. We've got a real birthday party planned for you."

After a dinner of barbecue chicken, Andy brought out a birthday cake that had so many candles on it, Beth Ann exclaimed, "Why, I declare, if your cake doesn't look like the burnin' of Atlanta!"

Susan, who had barely touched the chicken, ate only

a couple of bites of her cake. She was too tired and too sore to think about food. So, she opened her presents: a pair of Calvin Klein panties and a knit top, a bottle of Fendi perfume, a leather photograph album that was engraved SPLIT FORK RANCH, 1996.

"That's for all the pictures we're going to take," Audrey said.

After hugging each of her friends, Susan gathered up her gifts and announced her intention to return to her cabin, which she did—accompanied by Berny, Beth Ann, and Audrey, who carried two plastic gallon jugs of margaritas Andy made special for the occasion.

After a couple of margaritas, Susan forgot about being sore and tired. She was really getting into the spirit of things when Berny pulled out a box of fireworks. "Freddy gave me these. They were left over from the Fourth of July. He said they'd be a great way to celebrate your birthday."

Susan looked down at the box of fireworks. "Tell your brother thank you."

"Come on," Audrey said, "let's go outside and light up the sky."

"We can't light these here," Susan said. "It might scare the livestock, or at least wake up all the ranch hands."

"Why don't we go down the road and find a place to light them?" Beth Ann asked.

The foursome set off down the road, carrying the box of fireworks and the two jugs of margaritas, which they drank as they walked. By the time they found the perfect, isolated spot, Susan was definitely inebriated. "I think I'm drunk," she said.

"So am I," Beth Ann said.

"So what?" Berny said. "I'm feeling a little tipsy too, but we aren't driving, so what's the harm?"

They stopped at a clearing along the side of the road and Berny gave each of them a punk—a long stick that smoldered when it was lit—enabling them to light their firecrackers. Without a worry to her name, and feeling quite jovial, Susan was getting into the spirit of things and began to dig into the box of fireworks. Soon the sky was flashing with color as skyrockets exploded in brilliant cascades, flares, and starlike sparks. Those were followed by Roman candles, cherry bombs, Catherine wheels, sparklers, and serpents, which writhed like snakes while burning.

Laughing, Audrey said it was a good thing they had chosen a spot away from the ranch house, since they were making a lot of noise.

"Not to mention smoke," Beth Ann said, waving her hand in front of her face.

Susan, who was bending over the box of fireworks, had just located a long string of jumping jacks, which she gathered in her hands. About that time, Berny looked up and stared across the fence into the pasture beyond. "Speaking of smoke," she said, "I think something is on fire. Look at all that smoke over there."

They all stared in the direction Berny pointed. They saw the pasture and noticed at the same time a small orange glow that soon became a creeping, thin red line of flames that burned an irregular path across the dry grass. "Oh, my God," Beth Ann exclaimed, "is that a prairie fire?"

"I don't know about the prairie part, but a fire I recognize and that is definitely a fire," Susan said. "Come on, we need to stop it before it spreads."

"Stop it?" Beth Ann squeaked. "How?"

The four of them climbed over the fence and ran toward the line of fire, stomping and kicking dirt across the creeping flames. It was at this moment that Susan realized she still had the jumping jacks still clenched tightly in her hands. The fire was burning dangerously close to the fence now and Susan had a vision of burning down some rancher's fence and them finding their sooty faces hauled before some hick magistrate who had no empathy for city girls. With renewed vigor, she began stomping even faster.

They were fortunate that they were able to stop the fire just a few feet from the fence, but in giving all their attention to that side of the pasture, they had neglected the other side, which now burned out of control down the side of a hill. Berny was breathless when she ran up to Susan. "What should we do? We can't stop it on this side."

"There isn't anything we can do. We'll just have to let it burn. It will stop when it reaches that pond down there."

Berny looked toward the pond. "Gosh, that's a long way."

Exhausted, sweating, and covered with cinders and soot, the four of them stood together, watching the fire burn its way down to the pond, then die out. They stared at the blackened and charred pasture, unable to believe so much grass had burned. "Well, we might as well start back. There is nothing we can do now. At least the fire is out."

Audrey shook her head. "Some rancher is going to be really pissed when he wakes up in the morning and discovers his pasture is a charcoal bed."

The words had no more than left Audrey's mouth when a speeding pickup came tearing down the road, looking for a moment like it might plow right through the fence. Suddenly, it came to a screeching halt, throwing dust and gravel all about, the headlights shining in the women's faces, blinding them and making it difficult to see.

Susan brought her hand up to shield her eyes. "I think that pissed rancher decided not to wait until morning."

The pickup door opened and a very furious man stepped out. The moment he did, two dogs jumped out of the back of the pickup and started barking.

The four women huddled together.

Amid barking dogs and furious curses, the four of

them watched in horror as the angry man walked toward them. Susan remembered the jumping jacks in her hand and afraid to be caught with the evidence red-handed, she put her hands behind her back and tried to stuff the jumping jacks into the back pocket of her jeans without being noticed. She opened her hand, then realized the braided fuses had somehow become entangled in her ring. As she struggled to disentangle herself, her three friends did a remarkable job of lying, proclaiming themselves blameless, claiming their innocence with a bald-faced lie that Berny told with unbelievable aplomb.

"Why, we were just walking by and saw the fire and decided to do what we could to keep it from spreading. It's lucky for you that we happened by when we did."

"Oh, I'm lucky all right."

"Don't worry about thanking us, sir. We were glad to be of help," Beth Ann added.

"And you expect me to believe that you just happened up on this fire?"

Berny said, "I swear, it's the gospel truth," and Susan wanted to roll her eyes.

Audrey then did her bit by saying, "We wouldn't know how to start a fire if someone held a gun to our heads. We are terrified of anything that even looks like fire."

The angry man looked on the verge of believing them when misfortune struck.

A breeze stirred, then became a gust of wind that stirred a few cinders and brought them to life as they swirled about them. Some of the cinders had drifted around Susan and unbeknownst to her, one of them landed on the braided strand of fuses entangled in her ring.

The cinder ignited the fuse.

The fuse burned down to the jumping jacks.

The string of jumping jacks went off like a Gatling gun in a rapid round of exploding firecrackers, spinning and smoking, their colors changing from pink to blue and all the colors in between.

And then, all hell broke loose.

"Yeee-ow!" Susan shouted and began dancing around, shaking her hands, trying to disentangle the jumping jacks.

The tall stranger swore, then grabbed her. He pulled the string of fireworks loose from her ring and tossed them onto the charred ground. "Of all the stupid. . . ."

"It was an accident," Beth Ann said. "We. . . ."

"Don't say another word," the stranger said in tones hot enough to blister paint. He grabbed Susan by the arm and propelled her to the front of his pickup, forcing her into the light. Taking her chin in his hand, he looked her over. "Who in the hell are you?"

Susan looked up, stared into eyes of the most unholy blue and received a jolt—the kind you'd get if you sat on an electric fence. A second later, she was reduced to a quaking, quivering idiot. Her heart, which should have soared at the sight of him, sank like a lead pigeon. A romantic to the core, Susan had waited all her life to look into a pair of eyes like his and now that the opportunity presented itself, it was screwed up before she had a chance. Life could be so unfair.

"I asked you a question. Who are you?"

"Nobody."

"I wouldn't press my luck if I were you. You have broken the law, trespassed and defaced property, not to mention endangering the lives of my livestock. I could have you arrested," he said in tones that went beyond angry.

It was a dirty trick, she had to admit, but when all else fails, a woman has a definite advantage: She can act like a woman. Susan started to cry.

He wasn't moved. "Who are you and what are you doing out here this time of night . . . and I want the truth this time."

Susan intended to cry. She had not planned to blubber

like an idiot, but for some reason when she started crying, she couldn't seem to stop. She cried for meeting such a dreamboat under the worst possible conditions, not to mention the fact that it happened when she was forty and over-the-hill. She cried for Joel's abandoning her. She cried for her lost job and the new wrinkles that were bound to appear now that her birthday was here.

"Why didn't you try that when it would do some good?" he asked. "Save your tears. The fire is out and I am impervious to tears. You are wasting my time and yours."

As far as an incentive to stop crying, that did the trick. She gave one last, long, loud sniffle and resigned herself to her fate. Before she could say anything in her defense, Berny, who could never resist a chance to talk, spoke up.

"If you're going to call the sheriff, then do it and hurry up. It's ten-fifteen and Susan's birthday is almost over."

"Which one of you is Susan?"

"I am," Susan said.

"Don't ask her how old she is," Beth Ann said, "because she is sensitive about turning forty."

If there was a vein of humor in his six-foot frame, Beth Ann's blunder seemed to bring it to the surface, for the anger he had shown earlier seemed to settle, and for a brief moment she thought he might actually smile. "Are you trying to tell me that you set my pasture on fire with forty candles?"

"It wasn't the candles," Audrey said, "although they did melt the icing on the cake."

"Why don't you tell him *everything*?" Susan said.

"It was the firecrackers," Beth Ann said.

"Firecrackers in the middle of August?"

Berny explained. "They were leftover from the Fourth of July. My brother gave them to me. I thought they would be appropriate. . . ."

"Appropriate?" he said. "For what? Mass murder? Burning down half the county? Don't you realize someone might have been killed, or did you even consider that?''

''Susan said she'd like to enter her forties with a bang,'' Berny explained. ''That's why I thought they were appropriate.''

''But we didn't mean to set your pasture on fire,'' Beth Ann added. ''It was an accident. You should be grateful that we stayed to put out the fire, instead of running away and letting it burn.''

''I should be grateful? Grateful that you stupidly set off fireworks in the middle of a pasture with dry, brittle grass in the middle of one of the worst droughts in the history of Montana?''

''We aren't well versed in Montana's weather history,'' Susan said.

''You aren't versed in much of anything except tears. What were you doing out here?''

''We came out here to celebrate,'' Audrey said.

''From where?''

''We're from Washington, D.C.,'' Berny said.

''Figures. Where are you staying?''

''Split Fork,'' Susan said. ''Have you ever heard of it?''

''I've heard of it.''

''Do you know the owner?'' Audrey asked.

''Andy is my brother.''

''Poor Andy,'' Susan said.

''You might want to temper your words a bit. You aren't off the hook yet.''

Susan's hands were burning and she wanted to go home. She did her best to ignore the pain while accepting full responsibility for what had happened. ''Look, we're sorry about what happened. It was an accident, and since it was my birthday, I'll take full responsibility. We were stupid, foolish, naive. . . .''

''You should have stayed in Washington.''

''I have never agreed with anything more,'' she said. The pain in her hands was getting the best of her now, and she couldn't stop the tears that welled in her eyes any more than she could stop the tears that rolled silently down her face.

He did not look sympathetic. "Now, why are you crying?"

"She's crying because it's good for you," Berny said. "According to Dickens, tears open the lungs, wash the countenance, exercise the eyes, and soften the temper. . . ."

"You," he said, pointing at Berny, "would do well to remain silent." He turned to Susan. "Tears won't work and they're not the right response for a disaster like this. It didn't work before, so why try it again?"

"I'm crying because my hands hurt," she blurted out.

"If you don't want to get burned, don't play with fire."

"Thank you. I'll try to remember that."

"Let me see your hands," he said in the gruffest of tones that went beyond impersonal.

She didn't care how unholy a blue his eyes were. Susan had had enough of him and his witty adages. Without a word, she turned away.

She had no more than reached the edge of the light, when she felt his hands on her shoulders and found herself propelled back into the light of his headlights. With a grunt of irritation, he reached for her hands and turned them over, inspecting them in the light. He must have seen no real damage, for he dropped her hands and said, "You'll live."

"That's encouraging," she said, trying to sound as sarcastic as she could.

"Don't move," he said and turned around. He took something out of his pickup. When he returned, she saw it was a first-aid kit. A moment later he was smearing aloe-vera ointment over her palms as he told her she would be lucky if the burns weren't deep enough to cause blisters.

"The only blisters I have were raised by your caustic words."

He ignored her and looked around. "Where's your car?"

"We walked."

"Get in. I'll take you back after I have a look around."

The four of them climbed into the back of the pickup, while he called his dogs and walked across the pasture. As soon as he left, the four of them sat there looking at the reflection of his white shirt in the headlights. "I don't know about you," Susan said, climbing out of the back of the pickup, "but I don't intend to grow bunions on my backside waiting for him."

Berny followed her. "Where are we going?"

"Back to Split Fork."

"What if he finds us?" Beth Ann asked as she climbed down.

"He won't. He's driving a truck, remember? If we hear him coming, we'll disappear."

"Wait for me. I'm coming, too," Audrey said.

The four of them walked down the road toward Split Fork Ranch. As they walked, Susan wondered if he would come looking for them.

"Do you think he'll come after us?" Beth Ann asked.

"Of course he will," Audrey said.

Susan found herself half-wishing he would come looking for them. In spite of his angry countenance, he was as handsome as the devil, and those eyes of his were something she would never forget. Yes, she hoped he would come after them.

But he didn't.

Chapter Two

Wwhen Susan arrived at the big house for breakfast the next morning, Andy was in the kitchen, pouring a cup of coffee. The table was set, but Andy was alone.

He looked up when she entered. " 'Morning."

"Good morning." She glanced around. "Where is everyone?"

"So far you're it." He turned around and offered her a cup.

Susan reached for it, then remembered the blisters on her fingers. "Just put it on the table."

He smiled. "How are your hands?"

"How'd you hear about my hands?"

"Wyatt called last night to make sure you gals made it back okay."

"I'm surprised. I would have thought it would have pleased him immensely to hear we disappeared from sight."

Andy laughed and pulled out the chair next to her. He cupped his coffee in his hands. "Wyatt has always taken being the big brother too seriously . . . just like he takes everything too seriously."

"Yes, he has all the personality of a gargoyle."

"He leads a life that is what you might call unfettered."

"He isn't married."

Andy's brown eyebrows raised. "You aren't surprised, are you?"

"Definitely not." She studied Andy for a moment. "You and your brother aren't close, are you?"

"We're getting better, but we still have our differences."

"He lives close by, I take it?"

"His land adjoins mine. After our parents died, we couldn't agree on what we wanted to do with the ranch. Our relationship has been somewhat strained ever since."

"How long ago was that?"

"Twelve years."

"Who won, you or your brother?"

"We both did, I guess. I had always dreamed of turning the place into a guest ranch. Wyatt wanted to keep it a working ranch. When we couldn't reach an agreement, we split the land, each of us taking half. Now, I have my guest ranch and he works his butt off. . . ."

"As long as you're both happy. . . ."

"I'm happy and I suppose Wyatt is as close to happy as he will ever get."

Susan shrugged. "I guess some people are destined to be unhappy."

"I don't know that Wyatt was destined to be. His mostly came from bad choices and unfortunate circumstances."

She didn't say anything, but she was curious. Still, it wasn't her way to pry, and she figured if Andy wanted to tell her about his brother, he would.

"What did you think of Wyatt?"

She finished the last of her coffee and got up to pour another cup. "I didn't meet him under the best of circumstances, you understand, so my opinion of him is bound to be colored somewhat by our run-in."

"His bark is worse than his bite."

"He seems to go out of his way to be unpleasant . . .

not that he didn't have a reason to be upset. We did a foolish thing.''

''Yes, it was foolish. It was also a reminder of something very painful in Wyatt's life. I'm sure that made him be a little harder on you than he would have been ordinarily.''

She gave him a questioning look, but said nothing.

''You're a strange woman, Susan.''

''What do you mean?''

''Most women would have been dying with curiosity by now.''

She laughed. ''I didn't say I wasn't.''

''No, you didn't say anything, and that's unusual.''

''I don't pry.''

''If you did, I wouldn't have told you, but since you didn't. . . .''

''Your brother's business is your brother's business.''

''True, but you may run into Wyatt again before you leave. A little understanding of him might make things easier . . . for both of you.''

''Why are you telling me all of this?''

''Because I know my brother and I find it strange that when he called he asked about everyone but you.''

She was amused by that. ''I don't find that strange at all. I was the one who gave him the most trouble.''

''And that's why it's strange that he didn't mention you. Unless I miss my guess, I'd say ole Wyatt met the first challenge he's had in a long time and I'll lay you odds that his overlooking you was intentional.''

''Why would he do that?''

Andy smiled, and Susan saw in that smile that Andy knew something she didn't know, and that he wasn't going to share it with her. ''A minute ago I told you Wyatt wasn't married. That isn't exactly right. He was married once.''

She shrugged. ''It happens to the best of us.''

''You too?''

"It was a long time ago. It didn't last very long. We married in college. We were too young."

"Like you, Wyatt married in college. In fact, he married his college sweetheart. They were both law students at Columbia University. Megan was from a wealthy Connecticut family. She lasted two years out here before she left Wyatt and their infant son to return to New York. When their son was eight years old, he was killed in a range fire. Some hunters didn't do a very good job putting their campfire out. Apparently, Jeremy saw the smoke and went to investigate."

"I'm so sorry. No wonder he was so upset with us."

"Fires are a nightmare out here. They can come from nowhere and spread so fast, leaving nothing but devastation after they're gone."

"Susan, are you in here?"

It was Berny's voice.

"I'm here."

Berny walked into the kitchen with Beth Ann. "We went by your cabin to see if you were up," Berny said.

"I woke up early," Susan said. "Where's Audrey?"

"She's not a morning person, remember?"

"That's why I'm glad we have our own cabins. We have enough tight schedules back home. It's nice to relax."

Berny and Beth Ann sat down and Andy got up. "I've got breakfast warming in the oven. Help yourself to the coffee."

They poured their coffee and had just sat down when Audrey walked in, her red hair frizzed all over her head. "I can't do a thing with my hair up here."

"Have you thought of mowing it?" Berny asked.

Audrey ignored her and poured a cup of coffee. She took a seat next to Susan. "How are your hands this morning?"

Susan looked down at her hands. There were only a couple of small blisters. "Better than they should be, considering."

"I'm just thankful you were holding jumping jacks and not something more powerful," Berny said.

"Me too," Susan said, just as Andy put a platter of pancakes in front of her. Susan helped herself to two.

"What are we doing today?" Beth Ann asked.

"I thought we'd let you try your hand at fly fishing," Andy said.

"I saw *A River Runs Through It*," Berny said. "It doesn't look all that hard."

"I distrust anything that can get tangled up," Beth Ann said.

Andy laughed and Susan found herself joining in.

Soon they had finished breakfast and after a jeep ride down to the river, they were outfitted with waders, rods, flies, and too many instructions.

"We'll practice casting, or angling. That's when you try to get the fly as far across the river as you can," Andy said.

"Why?" Audrey asked.

"So you will have plenty of room to angle for a fish," Andy said. "Now, watch me." Andy took the long, flexible rod and with a few flicks of the wrist had the long fishing line whipping like a long snake over his head. Then he extended his arm and the long line with the fly on the end went sailing out over the water to land on the water's surface with a slow descent.

"It's floating on top of the water," Berny said. "Why won't it sink?"

"It's what we call a dry fly. That's one that floats on top of the water."

"How are you going to catch a fish like that? The fish are all in the water. Doesn't the fly need to be in the water, too?" Beth Ann asked.

"No. If a fish sees the fly on top of the water, he'll strike."

"What's a fly that sinks in the water?" Susan asked. "Do you call it a wet fly?"

Andy raised his brows. "Good guess. That's exactly

what we call it. Sometimes the fish strike a wet fly better, sometimes a dry fly is best. You just keep trying different things until you find something that works.'' Andy reeled his fly in. ''Now, let me see you do a little angling with your rod . . . one at a time.''

Audrey went first. Disaster struck on the first try when Audrey let go of the rod and threw the whole thing into the river. After Andy waded out and retrieved it, Beth Ann did something terribly wrong with the reel and tangled all the line up in a wad the size of a softball.

For a moment it looked like Berny had gotten the hang of it. But then, she cast so far that she went over the river and tangled her fly in a tree on the opposite bank. She let go with a barrage of curse words—three of which Susan added to her vocabulary.

There wasn't much left of Andy's good humor by the time Susan's turn rolled around. ''There isn't much you can do to screw things up that hasn't already been done,'' he said to her. ''Okay, give it a try. Remember to keep your wrist flexible.''

Susan held the fishing line in her left hand as she began angling the rod over her head, back and forth in a snakelike pattern just as Andy had done.

''Good. Good. Great!'' Andy said. ''You've got a lot of natural rhythm.''

''That's what Joel used to say,'' Berny blurted out, then blushed and said, ''Sorry.''

Susan made a mental note to strangle Berny when she finished, then gave her attention to what she was doing.

''Okay, take it back a little further on the next round, then let her sail out over the water.''

Susan did as Andy instructed. And then, the darnedest thing happened. She made a sweeping motion that somehow went wrong and the fly sailed out over the water and landed with a loud splash.

The loud splash wasn't because the fly was heavy, but because there was a straw cowboy hat hooked onto the end of it.

"Where in the hell did that come from?" Berny asked, turning around. "Holy moley, would you look at that? Susan has gone and caught herself one fine-looking fish."

Andy burst out laughing, just as Beth Ann, Audrey, and Susan turned around.

Susan let out a gasp of recognition.

Audrey picked up on it immediately. "Do you know him?"

"It's the firecracker man," Susan whispered.

"Him? That was *him* the other night? He was the ogre with the two dogs? How could you recognize him?"

"By the way my hair stood on end. I'd know him anywhere," Susan replied.

"Looks like you've done it again," Audrey said. "First with fire and now with water. Your meetings are beginning to look like an astrology chart. Wonder which element will be next? Earth or air?"

"She's got a head full of air," Berny said.

"Well, what brings you over here on such a fine morning?" Andy said. "I hope you aren't going to be angry about your hat. It was an old hat and a little large. Maybe a good dunking will shrink it a little bit."

Wyatt's gaze was fastened on Susan and she noticed everyone else looking at her like they were trying to figure out just what was going on here, as if she had any more inkling than they did. "I came to see how your hands were doing."

"They're fine," Susan said. "Thank you for asking. I'm sorry about your hat. I would like to pay you for it."

"Forget the hat. I've got several. As Andy said, it was an old one."

Susan couldn't think of anything to say, so she turned and began reeling in the fishing line, then waded out and retrieved his hat. When she returned, she handed it to him. "I'm afraid it's ruined. It's soaked through and through."

He took the hat and held it in his hand.

She glanced up to see how he was taking all of this and her gaze seemed to get stuck there. She felt like a fool, just standing there looking at him. All that jet-black hair and those hairy arms and those legs that were longer than a wet summer. Her heart was thumping in her head and her breath seemed to be searching for a new way out. She knew she looked like an idiot standing there with that stupid grin on her face and she wished someone would thump her up beside the head and knock some sense into her.

That didn't happen.

All she could think about was the fire she and her friends had started and the way his son had died. She was amazed that he was nice enough to check on her well-being at all. She wished there was some way she could make amends . . . for the pasture and the hat.

Wyatt paused a few feet from the group, his gaze still on Susan. "You're sure your hands are okay?"

She held them up for him to see. "Good enough to throw your hat in the water," she said.

He laughed.

Oh, Lord, that smile and those eyes. Whoa and wait a minute. Just what do you think you are doing, Susan? Will you get a grip on yourself. Just because he has blue eyes, that isn't a come-on. For God's sake, he can't help the color of his eyes.

"Well, I guess I'd better be going," Wyatt said. "I just wanted to make sure everything was okay."

"Your pasture . . . is the damage bad? I mean real bad?" Susan knew was stammering like an idiot.

"Only a few fenceposts were charred. The rest of the damage was to the grass. It will grow back . . . next spring."

"I am very sorry."

"Forget it. No harm done." Wyatt looked at Andy. "See you around."

"Why don't you come over for supper tonight? Trying to ride herd on four women is a real chore . . . especially these four women. I sure could use a little help.''

"I'll give it some thought," Wyatt said with a quick glance in Susan's direction.

For an instant a feverish current seemed to shoot through her and Susan wondered what he would do if she threw caution to the wind and grabbed him, cavewoman fashion, and dragged him into the bushes. But she did the sensible, contemporary thing and said, "Thanks for checking up on me."

"You're welcome," he said, reaching up to tip his hat. He realized what he'd done and he changed the movement to a short wave, but not before Susan noticed a slight blush of red across his cheeks. "Maybe I'll see you all at dinner tonight."

"I'd like that," Susan said, but Wyatt had already turned around and was walking back to his pickup. She wasn't certain if he had heard her or not.

Chapter Three

Everyone was seated at the big table in the dining room that evening at half past seven, waiting for the meal to be served. There were spots of conversation about the table. But Susan didn't join in. She was silently wondering if Andy's brother would show up when he walked into the room, looking as brushed, starched, and polished as a six-year-old on his first day of school. Adorable man.

This was just the kind of bang she needed for her fortieth birthday. Good choice, Montana.

Andy slapped Wyatt on the back. "Have a seat, big brother. Fish is grilling some steaks. Harriet will be in with the baked potatoes and beans. Salad and bread is on the table. Eat all you want, but save room for the cherry cobbler."

"I never could resist Harriet's cherry cobbler," Wyatt said.

"Harriet didn't make it, Susan did," Andy said.

Wyatt gave her a look that said he didn't think she had the gumption to find her way to the refrigerator, let alone bake a cobbler, but he didn't say anything.

Susan wasn't so gracious. "There are a few things I can do besides have birthdays and pop firecrackers."

"I didn't think city girls knew how to bake a cobbler."

"I grew up in Richmond. Learning to cook is a prerequisite in the South. You don't have to worry. I think you'll find it edible.''

"The proof is in the pudding," Beth Ann said.

"Then I'll withhold my judgment until after dessert," Wyatt said.

Susan was surprised when he pulled out a chair and sat down next to her. She felt a wave of something that lay between ecstasy and disappointment. The ecstasy was because he chose to sit beside her——never mind that it was the only chair vacant——and the disappointment was because she would have loved to have him sitting across from her so she could lose herself in those blue eyes. She wondered what he thought about her eyes. Had he noticed they were green?

Conversation picked up after that. Susan joined in somewhat, but she found herself reluctant to talk much in front of Wyatt. Starved, she concentrated on eating and left the conversation to the others. Wyatt didn't seem to mind, for he said very little to her. Before she knew it, Harriet was bringing in the cobbler and serving up big bowls with homemade ice cream on top.

Susan picked at hers, trying to see out of the corner of her eye if Wyatt was eating his because he enjoyed it, or out of politeness. She couldn't decide.

But then he said, "I didn't think anyone could top Harriet's cobbler, but I'll have to be honest and say you managed to do just that."

Susan felt her face grow warm. "Why, thank you. My grandmother always said it was all in the crust."

"Delicious," Andy said.

"Light as a feather," Beth Ann said.

"Flaky," Berny said.

"What's left for me?" Audrey said and everyone collapsed with laughter.

It was just the ice-breaker they needed and conversation picked up after that. Soon Andy stood and said, "It's a beautiful evening. Why don't we go out onto the back porch for coffee or after-dinner drinks?"

Once they were outside, Susan took the porch swing, surprised once again, when Wyatt sat next to her. She saw his big frame lowering itself into the swing and couldn't resist saying, "Are you certain it will hold both of us?"

"My grandfather gave this swing to my grandmother on her fortieth birthday. It's managed to hold up for over fifty years. I think we're safe."

When Wyatt lowered himself into the swing, it shot backward and Susan felt a rush of remembrance. "It's strange that you said this was your grandmother's swing. I remember one very much like it at my grandmother's house in Charleston. In fact, she had two on her porch and my sister and I spent many an hour there."

"Where is your sister now?"

"She's in Atlanta."

"Married?"

"With children. Five boys."

"And you?"

"I . . . I don't have any children."

"You don't wear a ring, so I assume you aren't married."

"No, I'm not married."

"Not ever?"

She smiled wistfully. "I was married such a long time ago and for such a short period, it almost feels that way."

"How old were you?"

"Eighteen. I was a freshman in college. Richard was a sophomore. Our marriage lasted six months . . . until I came home and found him in bed with a sorority sister of mine. End of marriage."

"I'm sorry. I ask too many questions."

"I had a friend tell me once that when you first meet someone, you are allowed three questions about your ex, then it's a taboo subject."

"I suppose you want to ask your three?"

"Andy told me about your marriage . . . and your son.

I am terribly sorry. I understand now how you must have felt when you saw what we had done.''

''I was angry at the time, but it's forgotten now.''

''Do you ever practice law?''

''No. I'm a rancher, but there are times when my law degree comes in handy.''

''Have you ever considered running for congress?''

''I served two sessions in the Montana State Senate. I was approached a few months ago about running for the U.S. Senate.''

''Have you decided?''

''Yes. I've decided not to run. Capitol Hill isn't for me.''

''It may not be for Susan much longer either,'' Berny said.

Wyatt gave Susan a questioning look. ''Why does she say that?''

''I've worked for Senator Claiborne since I graduated from college. Just before we left, he announced that he would not be seeking another term, that he would let us know soon if he intended to finish out this one. His wife has been in poor health and they're both getting up in years. I may be out of a job when I return home.''

''Something will turn up,'' he said. ''It always does.''

''I don't know. Good-paying jobs in Washington are at a premium.''

''I didn't necessarily mean a job,'' Wyatt said, and before Susan could speculate on that, he changed the subject. ''What are you scheduled to do tomorrow?''

Susan groaned. ''Ride horses.''

''Maybe I'll come over and join you,'' he said, and gave the swing another shove.

She turned to look at him. ''Why on earth would you want to ride with a bunch of novices like us when you don't have to?''

''Maybe I'm only interested in riding with one of them.''

''Why?''

"Because I haven't had much fun or laughter in my life for a long time, and you have managed to bring a little of both since you've come here."

She gave him a narrow-eyed look. "Why would you say something like that when all I've done is deface your property? First your pasture and then your hat."

"I always did have a weird sense of humor."

"He is telling the truth, there," Andy said. "I can vouch for it."

"Well, you will be wasting your time tomorrow," she said. "We rode horses the other day, so we're all experienced at it. I doubt there will be anything fun or amusing as far as we're concerned."

"Oh, I wouldn't say that. Horses are as unpredictable as women. Sometimes when you mix the two. . . ."

Susan found out what he meant the next morning.

The weather had turned cool and the horses were as frisky as the devil, at least that's what Jasper said. Jasper was one of the ranch hands who was going to ride with them today, since Fish had something else to attend to.

"Yes, sir, they sure are feeling their oats this morning," Jasper said.

That made Susan eye the corral full of horses with mounting trepidation. He might call it "feeling their oats," but to Susan they looked downright wild, kicking, snorting, and bucking. She wished there was some way she could get out of this.

Since there wasn't, she did the next best thing. She went back to her cabin and located a bottle of bourbon. She took two big shots, screwed the lid back on, and felt fortified. Then she returned to the corral.

While Jasper helped the others get their horses saddled, Susan wandered around a bit, stopping by a corral with only one gray horse in it. The horse came up to the fence and poked her head over the top. Susan scratched her between the ears. This horse was smaller than Tommy . . . and friendlier, too.

Susan walked back to where Jasper was just finishing up with Berny's horse. He turned to Susan. "Do you want to ride the same horse you rode the other day, or would you like a different one?"

"I want to ride that gray one in the pen over there."

"That's Power Surge. She's for an experienced rider."

About that time, Wyatt rode up on a sleek and sturdy sorrel. Susan didn't look at him, but she saw him out of the corner of her eye. She wasn't about to act like a tenderfoot in front of him, so she said, "I'm experienced," figuring that wasn't such a big lie, since she had ridden Tommy for a whole hour the other day. Besides, she liked the idea of riding a girl horse, not to mention she had a feeling the gray was ten times gentler than Tommy ever thought of being.

Jasper shrugged and told one of the hands to saddle Power Surge. A moment later, he helped Susan into the saddle. "Power Surge can be a little nervous and edgy, but she's a smooth-gaited little mare."

Susan's head was buzzing. She looked at Jasper and saw twins. That made her think that maybe she should have had just one shot of bourbon. "She's a smooth-gaited little what?" she asked, trying not to slur her words.

Jasper gave her a strange look. "Mare . . . a female."

"Oh . . . well, of course I know what a mare is," she lied, "I just didn't hear what you said."

"Just hold a tight rein on her until she gets warmed up a bit and then everything should be okay."

Jasper mounted and rode up to where Wyatt waited. They talked as they turned their horses and headed up the road. Susan and her friends followed. Susan had not the remotest idea what a tight rein was and with two shots of bourbon under her belt, she really didn't care, but the gray mare seemed to be every inch the lady Susan suspected her to be, so Susan relaxed and tried to check out the scenery, but found it a bit blurry.

About that time, Fish drove up and took one look at

Susan on Power Surge, jumped out of the pickup, and
began to wave his arms and yell at Jasper. The minute
he did, Power Surge lived up to her name and bolted,
dashing wildly off the road and across open country. Susan, who managed to get a death grip on the saddle horn
with one hand and a fist full of mane in the other, was
hanging on for dear life. She didn't have a chance to see
if Jasper and Wyatt had noticed her or not. She tried
looking for a nice soft spot to throw herself onto, but the
countryside was passing with such a blur and her head
was spinning so fast she couldn't make out anything she
saw.

Susan's hat fell off and her ponytail came down. Her
hair was blowing out behind her like a calvary flag, but
she hung on. Once, she had the sensation of being air-
borne and felt a jolt when they landed. When she felt a
splash of water on her face, she figured they must have
gone over a creek. It didn't slow Power Surge down one
bit though, for they were thundering over the grass-
covered hills at top speed. Once, Power Surge took a
sharp turn and they shot through a field that was dotted
with haystacks. The mare misjudged one haystack that
loomed up in front of them. Trying to avoid crashing into
it, she tried to jump over it, but the haystack was bigger
than she realized and they made a soft landing, then tore
through one side with Susan still on board. Susan's face
was covered with hay and she couldn't see a blooming
thing, but soon the sheer velocity of the wind blew the
hay away.

Jasper and Wyatt were riding at full speed after her,
but they were riding cow horses. Power Surge was bred
for speed. When Susan burst out of the haystack, Jasper
shouted, "My God, she's still on board. I ain't never seen
anybody ride like that."

With Susan still hanging on, Power Surge left the hay-
field and charged through a field of cornstalks that rustled
and slapped Susan in the face. She closed her eyes for
protection and when she opened them she saw a wide,

sparkling river coming up ahead. Power Surge acted like she didn't see it, or if she did that she was planning on sprouting wings and flying over it, for she headed straight for it, tearing up a hill and running breakneck toward a bluff that overlooked the river.

Susan braced herself, and just as she did Power Surge made a sharp right turn.

Susan did not.

Instead, she sailed out of the saddle and disappeared over the bluff.

When Jasper and Wyatt came running, hell-bent for breakfast, up to the river's edge, Susan was wading in water up to her chest. When Wyatt dismounted and started toward her, she said, "Stand back! I made that ride by myself and I'm going to finish it by myself."

Wyatt stopped and had an amused look on his face but said nothing. Jasper still had that same bewildered look on his face that he had when she left the barn. They waited for her to reach the bank. When she was on dry land, she made it as far as a stool-sized rock and sat down, completely exhausted. She only had enough wind to say, "Hell and double hell. I've ruined my damn hundred-dollar boots."

Later that night, there was a celebration of sorts, with Andy throwing what he called a shindig, complete with the Longnecks, a popular country-and-western band, lots of barbecue, and Andy, speaking with the aid of a microphone, outlining every detail of Susan's spectacular ride. He spent an inordinate amount of time, Susan thought, talking about her outstanding seat, which she thought terribly impolite. He then went on to discuss her mettle and her bottom, which was in such bad taste she was tempted to march up on the platform and tell him.

Instead, she told Wyatt, who was standing next to her. She was acutely disappointed to hear him laugh. She was on the verge of leaving the party altogether when Wyatt kissed her softly on the mouth, then said, "Sweetheart, he was referring to the way you sat your horse, not to the attributes of your posterior.''

Before the dance was over, she had six invitations to attend the Calgary Stampede and three to ride in the parade.

When Andy announced the last dance, Wyatt led her to the dance floor. ''Would you like to go for a ride with me tomorrow?'' he asked.

''No. I've learned all I need to know about horses.''

''And what have you learned?''

''That they are deadly at both ends and damn uncomfortable in the middle.''

Just before the song ended, Wyatt drew her closer and kissed her again. She leaned against him and kissed him back.

When her head had stopped spinning, he whispered, ''I know damn good and well that you had never ridden a horse in your life, but what I can't figure out is, how did you manage to stay on? That took a lot of courage.''

''No, it took half a bottle of bourbon and a good grip.''

Chapter Four

Susan went to bed thinking about Wyatt.

She woke up thinking about today being the day Andy said they were going whitewater rafting. Then she thought about Wyatt again and wondered if he would take Andy up on his invitation to go rafting with them.

Susan had seen a special on TV once about whitewater rafting and had vowed then and there that no one was ever—absolutely not, don't even mention it, forget it, no way, when hell freezes over—going to get her in a tiny rubber raft and send her shooting down a churning, foaming, rushing, icy river that probably still held the bodies of the idiots who tried to make their way over those same rapids the summer before.

"What do you mean you aren't going?" Audrey asked when she came to tell Susan it was time to leave.

"I have something to confess. I am not a brave person. I am a lily-livered chicken, afraid of my own shadow, and I have not one dram of adventure in my blood. My idea of excitement is defrosting a chicken breast with my hair dryer. I get out of breath going outside for the morning paper. I am definitely, positively, in no way, shape, size, or fashion curious about anything that has to do with animals, elements, or Mother Nature. I love polyester, artificial lighting, diet colas, plastic fruit, and silk flowers. Even the zebra rug on my floor is a fake. The closest to nature I have ever been is playing my tape of English garden birds. And on top of that, I love hot, soaky baths, so why would I choose to freeze my tush off in a rubber boat, being showered with icy water that was solidly frozen snow a few hours ago?''

"It'll be fun and Wyatt might be there."

"First off, I wouldn't go rafting if they had Brad Pitt sitting next to me in the raft . . . and Tom Cruise on the other side . . . with Kevin Costner sitting behind me and Antonio Banderas sitting on my lap. Secondly, fun for you has an entirely different connotation than it does for me. My idea of fun is getting a good love story and situating myself in the porch swing with a glass of iced tea and staying there until I am in danger of becoming petrified. You go rafting. I'll stay here."

"If you don't come, none of us will go. We did this for *your* birthday, remember?"

As far as guilt trips went, this was a pretty good one. With lead-footed reluctance, Susan picked up her windbreaker and followed Audrey down to the jeep, but her heart was not in it—it was lying in the porch swing on the front porch.

It took them a little over an hour to reach the place on the river where they would meet the rafting company employee who would go down the river with them. When they arrived, they were met by a guy who introduced himself as Doug, without ever looking up from what he was doing on the raft.

The term "whitewater" doesn't really have anything to do with water. It gets its name from the fact that the entire time you are sitting in that tiny rubber raft, you are holding on so dearly that your knuckles are white. The only part the water plays is that it is the catalyst that makes you have white knuckles. For her part, Susan thought rafting might not be so bad if the rapids weren't located right in the middle of the river. This was an opinion she expressed. "What happens if you fall out?"

Someone threw her a life jacket. She glanced up to see

it was Doug, who looked like he had heard every excuse in the book—and had an answer for each one of them.

"Oh, this is great," she said, trying to figure out how to get the life jacket on. "Now I'll be able to float long enough to freeze to death."

"The water isn't that cold," Berny said.

"Have you been in?" Susan asked. "It is melted snow and yesterday it was part of a glacier."

Susan got the life jacket on, but ended up with two cords that didn't seem to have a purpose.

"You've got it on wrong," Doug said. "The straps go between your legs."

Horrified, Susan looked at the two straps. *Between her legs*? No, thank you. She took the jacket off and watched Berny, Beth Ann, and Audrey put theirs on, straps between their legs.

"Those straps go between your legs, like this," Beth Ann said.

"You think I'm going to wear something with two straps between my legs when I can't even stand to feel floss between my teeth?"

"It isn't uncomfortable," Berny said.

"I hardly feel it," Beth Ann added.

"Once you're in the raft, you'll forget all about it," Audrey said.

"I think I'll just go without one."

"You don't get in the raft without a life jacket on," Doug said.

Susan stepped into the life jacket. "Wonderful. Just what I've always wanted . . . a thong life preserver."

The sound of laughter reached her ears and Susan looked up to see Andy and Wyatt leaning against a tree a few yards away. She scowled at them. "How long have you been there?"

"Long enough to get an education," Andy said.

"Oh, and what did you learn?"

"That men and women sure are different."

"Oh, really. Next, I suppose you'll discover the world

isn't flat.'' Susan turned around and walked toward the raft. ''Where do I sit?''

''Anywhere you please,'' Doug said, but this time, he turned and looked at her.

While Beth Ann, Berny, and Audrey found their places in the raft, Wyatt and Andy walked toward them, talking softly.

Straining to hear, Susan made out every word they said.

''I don't know when I've seen anything so damn funny,'' Andy said. ''I don't know what she wanted us to do about that life jacket.''

''I don't think she wanted us to do anything with it,'' was Wyatt's reply.

''If she didn't, she sure did put up a fuss for nothing. However, I've never been able to understand a woman.''

''Only thing you need to understand is that they have feelings we don't have. That is something I say to myself every morning when I shave. You also need to remember that a woman will react to her feelings in a way that is totally foreign to a man. The worst thing you can do is to respond to either her feelings or her reactions to them. Try it and you'll go stark-raving mad.''

''Why?''

''Andy, when a woman has feelings and reacts to them, it doesn't mean anything except she has feelings. She is simply feeling. That's it. It is not a signal that a man has to do something. If you get involved; if you try to fix things, you will only end up more confused. A woman's feelings aren't something you can understand, fix, smooth out, tie down, or get rid of. You've got to remember that when a woman gets emotional, when she is feeling, it is something like a book—it has a beginning, a middle, and an end. It will pass and she will feel better, regardless of whether you do anything or not. A man has to learn that a woman's feelings are her feelings. She will iron everything out by herself and in her own way and timing. Your role, if you have one, is to listen, to empathize. But don't ever try to understand. The worst thing you can do is to try to change her feelings, to sugar-coat them.''

''Where did you learn all of this?''

''I was married, remember?''

''You also got divorced, so it must not have worked.''

''I didn't understand it then, that's part of the reason why we got divorced.''

''When it comes to women, all I understand is that women are different.''

''Yes, but what a difference.''

''Well, with all that understanding you've got, it's a real shame you don't have a woman to use it on.''

''Maybe, and maybe not.'' Wyatt glanced toward the raft. His gaze captured Susan's.

Beth Ann sighed. ''That is the most romantic thing since Clark Gable said, 'We will always have Paris.' ''

''That was Bogart,'' Susan said. ''Not that it matters. This isn't anything like the movies. The props are all wrong. Nothing romantic would ever come out of a place with a name like Bane, Montana.''

Susan survived the outing with a good soaking, but she decided that riding the rapids was definitely not for her. She also decided she was probably the first person in history to get seasick boating on fresh water.

When they finally reached tranquil waters and the end of their journey, Susan stepped on dry land and vowed she would never again get around water that was any deeper than her bathtub.

''That shade of green becomes you,'' Berny said when she reached the tree where Susan waited. ''Are you feeling any better?''

''A little.''

Audrey and Beth Ann walked up. ''Andy said there's a great gorge near here where we can go rappelling,'' Audrey said. ''Wanna come?''

''No. I've had enough movement for one day. I need to feel solid earth beneath my feet for a while. A shower and clean clothes sound great. I think I'll go back."

"If we take you back, we won't have time to go rap-pelling," Audrey said.

"I'll check with Andy," Berny said, and dashed off.

A few minutes later, Berny came back. "Andy called Wyatt on his mobile phone. He isn't very far away, so he's going to come over here and take you back home."

Susan felt a ripple of pleasure shoot up her spine.

Wyatt saw her sitting on a rock, her elbows resting on her knees, her hair tucked up under a baseball cap that said RALPH LAUREN USA. He didn't know why the sight of her sent a warm sensation through him and made him think about doing more than just giving her a ride home. Nope, he couldn't understand it at all. She looked more like a drowned rat than a seductress.

He pulled to a stop next to her. "Need a ride?"

"I didn't expect to get taxi service out here in the wilds of Montana."

"We're trying to become a progressive state." He climbed out of the jeep.

"You need to do something to offset your militia im-age."

"Be nice or I'll start saying bad things about Wash-ington, D.C." He opened the door.

She laughed and hopped in. "You couldn't say any-thing I haven't said . . . or heard before."

He closed the door then went around to the driver's side. He put the car in gear and turned around. "Do you need to get back right away?"

"Do you have a better offer?"

He had several, but to tell her would get his face slapped. He had learned a long time ago that men were creatures of action and women were creatures of inter-action. If a man wanted to be happy with a woman, he better learn to focus more on interacting and less on ac-tivities. Take right now, for instance. In typically male fashion, Wyatt wanted to make love. Just as typically, Susan was probably wishing he was a man she could talk to and do things with, a man who would cuddle and tell her sweet things.

What it all boiled down to was something as basic as: Women are different from men. That was it. Period. In a nutshell. No ifs, ands, or buts. Not even a maybe. End of discussion. If Wyatt had learned anything in his forty-five years, it was to stop thinking of women as men with breasts and childbearing capabilities, and to understand they were different creatures entirely. "I thought you might like to drive over to my place and see my cows."

She raised her brows. "Is that the same as asking me up to see your etchings?"

"It's basically the same, just updated a little from the forties."

They drove along in silence, with Wyatt occasionally pointing out a sight or two. Susan, he noted, was a little on the quiet side, almost pensive. As they passed by a stand of charred lodgepole pine, he knew she must be thinking about the night they first met and the fireworks that had gotten out of hand. To get her mind off that, he pointed out an elk that was feeding on a patch of grass that had escaped the flames.

He turned the car off the paved road and traveled down a gravel road. Below ice-carved peaks they traveled along the river where slivers of sunlight turned a stand of spruce and white pine to silver.

"It's so beautiful out here. I guess you never see all there is to see."

"Even if you did, it's constantly changing. Each season is different and the ecosystem is in delicate balance. It doesn't take much to throw it off."

"Like fires, you mean?"

He shrugged. "Fires, droughts, severe winters, insects . . . I remember one year when mountain pine beetles killed off more acres of lodgepole pines than the two previous fires."

"It must be difficult to watch such destruction."

"It's part of nature. When trees die, they make room

for grass and other vegetation. That, in turn, feeds the wildlife.''

She stared out the window for a while, then turned to look at him. ''Do you ever miss it . . . the city, I mean. Living around other people.''

''No, and there are people up here.''

''Only if you hunt for them.''

''Maybe that's the part that suits me.''

''I don't think I could live like this. I mean, what do you do in the wintertime?''

''Pretty much the same thing we do in the summer. Life goes on.''

''Yes,'' she said softly. ''Life goes on.''

They drove through a gate and she noticed a small sign that said WHITTAKER RANCH. ''We're on your property now?''

''Yes. I thought I'd drive you around a bit, then we'll stop by the house.''

A red fox ran along the road, then darted into the trees. ''A fox,'' she said. ''We have them in Virginia.''

''That's a kit . . . a young one. His mother is probably close by. By late fall, he'll start hunting on his own.''

They drove for over two hours, through meadows and over streams teeming with cutthroat, then along the cleft of a long canyon with its heat-tinted walls. Once, he handed Susan his binoculars and pointed out the golden highlights of grizzly fur as a mother and her scampering cubs meandered across a meadow.

''I wish we were closer,'' she whispered. ''They're so beautiful, so free.''

''A grizzly with cubs is also very dangerous.''

She continued to watch through the glasses. At times the cubs would stop and stand on their hind legs as if they were looking for their mother in the tall grass, then they would strike off running toward her. When they reached her side, one of the cubs rolled over. He watched the expression on Susan's face when she laughed at seeing its legs in the air. He studied her as she watched the gleaming golden sides of the bears until they turned away, leaving nothing to look at but a round brown rump. Soon they disappeared from sight altogether. She put the glasses down. "I can see why you love it here. The beauty, the wildness . . . it's breathtaking."

"It is now, but soon the river and valley will start looking weary, the grasses well munched and well trodden, the stream running slow and low with weeds marring the surface.

"I wish you had more time. There are places like nothing you've ever seen, but they're accessible only by horse."

"I'm not much of a horse person, if you remember."

He gave her a frank look, wondering what she thought about him. She was a strikingly lovely woman, even as she was now, without a hint of makeup on her face. "I could teach you."

She glanced at him and he saw the color rise to her face. She wasn't indifferent to him. At least that was something. "You would have your work cut out for you, I'm afraid. I don't think I have any cowgirl blood in me."

He turned off the road and stopped. "Then let's see how you are at gathering wild raspberries."

She followed him out of the car and went traipsing behind him as he ambled along a line of broken-down fence. Raspberries grew in profusion, trailing over bits of wire fencing and broken stumps. "Can we pick them? Are they good to eat?"

He picked a few and held them in the palm of his hand. He put one in his mouth. "This is as good as it gets," he said, picking up another one. He brought it up to Susan's mouth. "Try it."

She opened her mouth. He tossed the raspberry inside. Her eyes grew round. "Why, they taste just like raspberries . . . I mean they taste like the kind you buy in the store."

"Better than that, I hope. Here. Try another one." He

tossed another one at her and then another. Soon, her mouth was full and she held up her hands, trying to tell him she wanted no more. He understood this, of course, but he didn't let her know that. Raspberries kept coming and she was trying to chew, back away from him and laugh all at the same time.

She backed against the trunk of a pine tree. Her startled gaze flew to his face.

"I was going to give you another raspberry," he said, looking down at her with her mouth all red and sweet with raspberry juice, "but I've got a better idea." Before she had time to figure out what he was saying, Wyatt brought his mouth against hers. He kissed her firmly, forcing her mouth apart and tasting the sweetness inside. When the kiss ended, he stood looking down at her mouth, tracing the shape of her berry-stained lips with his finger. "You're a lot like these raspberries," he said. "A bit prickly, but if one can get past the thorns, there's a sweetness that makes it all worthwhile."

She looked down. "No one has ever accused me of being sweet before."

"No one probably ever took the time to learn about you before," he replied, his arms going around her.

She didn't pull back or push him away, but she seemed a bit self-conscious, so he released her. She glanced around. "I . . . I wish I had a bucket," she said.

"There's one in the back of the jeep," he said, then headed that way.

A few minutes later he was back. He handed her a galvanized bucket. "You pick the berries and I'll make a cobbler."

"You cook?"

He grinned. "Among other things. How about you?"

"You mean, can I cook?"

"Among other things."

A teasing light danced in her eyes. "I'm better at warming up leftovers."

"That's something else I've got to teach you," he said, wanting to kiss her again.

"Then you better hurry. We have less than a week before we go home."

He put his arms around her and drew her against him. "I can hurry, when I want to."

"And do you want to?"

"I want to," he said. "How about you? Do you have any feeling for me?"

"I don't know. My heart is pounding . . . really pounding. And I feel tingly all over." She brought her hand to her head. "I must have some feeling for you . . . or else I've gotten into poison ivy."

Chapter Five

On the way back, he showed her the golden, unblinking gaze of a great gray owl scouting for prey, the active pursuit of a coyote bounding through tall grass in search of food, and the drowsy contentment of a yellow-bellied marmot dozing in the summer sun. He drove her through a herd of cattle and stopped to let her observe the awkwardness of a newborn calf trying to stand for the first time. As she sat there beside him, she found herself feeling a bit awkward, too. She could identify with that calf. She really could.

It was almost dark when they reached the ranch house. "If you don't have to get back, I'll show you around and then we can have a bit to eat." He rested his hands on the steering wheel and turned toward her. "How does that sound?"

"It sounds great. I don't have anything special going on tonight and, as for dinner, I'm starving."

"There's one catch."

"What's that?"

"My housekeeper is on vacation this week. We'll have to cook our own dinner."

"I'm a great can opener," she said, glancing at him. "What do you excel at?"

"I can peel potatoes."

"That's a start," she said and caught the way he was

looking at her. A lump bigger than the national debt formed in her throat. That was the most penetrating, I'd-like-to-get-you-naked-in-my-bed look that she'd ever seen.

She was wondering what he was thinking when he up and said, "I'd like to think of it as more than a start."

She was so thrilled, little arias seemed to be trilling up and down her spine, and she was certain her heart was pumping blood in 4/4 time. He wants it to be more than a start, her mind was singing. He wants it to be more than a start! Oh, joy! Oh, thrill! Oh, elation! Oh, my God! What am I thinking? I'm leaving here in a few days . . . going all the way back to Washington, D.C., if you please, which happens to be halfway across the United States. Nothing could come of this. Nothing! Absolutely nothing! He is here . . . I'm going to be there . . . I'm a city girl. I love Kennedy Center, Wolf Trap, sailing on the bay, jogging along the Potomac. He's a cowboy, and that probably means he has a strong inclination to be the boss and treat his women like his cows. He's probably into marathon football watching, beer drinking, country music, and training his horses and his dogs.

She followed him into the house.

He showed her around. It was much bigger than it looked on the outside. Eight bedrooms. "Were you planning on a large family?" she asked, then remembered his son and felt like kicking herself. Thankfully, it didn't seem to bother him.

"No, my parents did, though. This is the house where Andy and I grew up. My parents wanted a big family, but Andy, Ruth, and I were it."

"Ruth?"

"My sister. She was killed in a car wreck when she was eighteen."

"Oh, I'm sorry."

"It was a long time ago. Come on. I'll show you the kitchen."

The kitchen was as big as a football field, complete

with an enormous fireplace at one end that was tall enough for Susan to stand up in. "Two dishwashers? You must do a lot of entertaining."

"My parents did," they said in unison and then laughed.

"Want a beer?"

"Do you have a margarita?"

"I can in a couple of shakes," he said, and began filling a glass with ice. He must have made quite a few margaritas in his lifetime, for he didn't have to stop and think about what he was doing. A moment later, he handed her a margarita. It was a good one.

"This is the pantry." He opened a door and she stepped into a small room that was lined with shelves. Boxes and cans and sacks and bottles of things were arranged neatly on the shelves. "Feel free to open cans to your heart's content."

"Something to go with potatoes, right?"

"It's not like I've got my heart set on peeling potatoes." He opened the refrigerator and stood back a little bit, looking everything over.

She took advantage of the opportunity and checked him out, deciding she liked what she saw. Well, I was always a sucker for a long-legged, lanky build, she thought, but didn't have time to think further, for he said, "We've got hamburger meat, lettuce, tomatoes, onions, cheese, eggs." He turned to look at her. "Sounds like a hamburger, doesn't it?"

"Or an omelet." She was feeling a bit nervous, so she downed the margarita.

He raised one brow. "Like margaritas, do you?"

"On certain occasions," she said, but she was thinking: Like when I'm having a nervous breakdown, or someone that looks better than a year's vacation is paying me some attention, or I win the lottery.

He laughed. "This must be one of those occasions."

"Oh, believe me, it is definitely that."

They ended up making an omelet. It started out with

Susan beating the eggs, then adding cheese. Wyatt suggested they Southwestern it up a bit and tossed in onions and tomatoes. Susan opened a can of refried beans and Wyatt found a bag of tortilla chips, which he crushed up over the top of the omelet and beans.

Susan sat at the kitchen table and eyed the plate before her. She had to admit it didn't look too appetizing.

"Go ahead. It tastes better than it looks."

"Does it have a name?"

He studied his plate for a moment. "Not to my knowledge. It's sort of a cross between migas, huevos rancheros, and potluck."

She took a bite, surprised to discover it was really quite good. Even the refried beans were good. She saw he was watching her. "Good," she said. "Surprisingly so."

"Did you doubt my culinary abilities?"

"No," she said with a laugh, "I doubted mine."

Once they finished, Wyatt made her another margarita and told her to sit at the table while he cleaned up the dishes. He was almost as fast at cleaning the dishes as he was a making margaritas. When he finished, he picked up his beer and her margarita, then led her into a large room with tall, raftered ceilings and a huge stone fireplace. She was about to sit down on the sofa when Wyatt took the margarita from her and put it down on the coffee table. "Ordinarily I'd spend a lot more time getting acquainted, but we don't have much time, do we? You'll be leaving in a few days.

"We don't have much time for what?"

"This," he said, and took her in his arms.

His mouth was soft and warm, touching hers with just enough pressure to entice her to kiss him back, and she did. She melted against him, wishing he would do more than kiss her; knowing she would stop him if he tried. "I think I should go back now."

"Why?"

"This can only serve to complicate things. I mean, what can come of it? I'm going home in a few days and you will stay here. Long-distance romances are doomed from the start.''

"What's wrong with enjoying the few days we have left?''

She felt her blood getting warm. "You mean a temporary liaison?''

"Those are your words, not mine. I'm not the kind of man who goes around seducing women.''

Her heart fell down to her feet. He wasn't interested in anything more than getting her into his bed while she was here. She figured women were a little on the scarce side out here in the wilds of Montana, so he had to take advantage of every opportunity. That she might be the opportunity didn't sit too well with her. "And I'm not the kind of woman who goes around getting seduced, so we're evenly matched and going nowhere. Why don't you take me back now?''

"Not while you're angry,'' he said, pulling her against him.

"I'm not angry,'' she said, her words becoming muffled against his mouth.

"Yes you are, but you won't be in a minute,'' he said, and kissed whatever thought she had of resisting right out of her head. Her head was spinning and she wasn't certain if it was him or too many margaritas. At least she wasn't nervous anymore, but now she was worried that she might have gone too far in the other direction. It wouldn't do to start dancing on the table. The words to Jose Cuervo started echoing in her mind.

He was such a distraction. He was such a good kisser. She tried to think of the way she should act, but she found she couldn't keep her mind on anything but the warm closeness of him, the feel of his arms around her, the way he made her feel. He kissed her and kissed her and she kept kissing him back . . . until he tried to get her on the sofa, then she balked. She knew if she ever let him get her on that sofa it would be all over. If she had learned anything tonight, it was that as far as Wyatt

Whittaker was concerned, she had no resistance. Nada. Zilch. Zero. "Look," she said, pushing him away.

"What's wrong?"

"Nothing. There is simply no point in pursuing this."

"Why?"

"Why? What do you mean, why? I am speaking English. I am sorry you find that confusing. Is it your second language?"

"It must be, so explain it to me. Why pull back now?"

"I told you. I'm leaving in a few days."

"So we spend a few days together."

"Nothing can come out of it."

"Except a few days of pleasure for both of us. You want it and so do I, so what's the harm?"

She broke away from him. "There is no harm because nothing is going to happen. You're looking for a one-night stand, something I am not. Your overstuffed confidence has clouded your judgment. I am not in the market for a fling. I just turned forty. My biological clock is ticking and the way I see it I have two choices: marriage, or be an old maid."

"That's very cut-and-dried, isn't it?"

"Perhaps, but that's the way I feel. I don't want to wake up an old woman who has been used and discarded. I think more of myself than that. I have values."

He frowned. "I know you were married, so don't try to act the virgin."

"That was such a typical male comment, I am tempted to laugh. Virgins or whores. There are only two categories for women, aren't there? Well, for your information, I'm not a virgin, but I haven't spent my life on my back either. I've been married briefly and since then I've had two relationships, and both of them ended up on the skids after several years. If I've learned anything, it's that there is something to all this talk about good old-fashioned values. I've been burned before. I won't set myself up for heartache again. If there is a next time, it will be done right, or it won't be done at all."

"I didn't mean to insult you."

"Well, you did, so there is nothing to be done except to take me back." She picked up her jacket and turned to look at him. "And I thought you were different. I thought you understood women."

He looked properly shamed, but she wasn't about to be moved by that. "I misread the signals and for that I apologize. It wasn't my intent to insult you . . . to the contrary."

"I accept your apology. Now, take me back."

Chapter Six

Susan walked into Berny's room.

Berny was drying her hair. Beth Ann and Audrey were sitting on the bed talking. They looked up when Susan walked in.

"Uh-oh," Beth Ann said.

"What happened?" Audrey asked.

"Don't ask," Susan replied.

"Susan, you have to tell us. We're your friends, remember?" Beth Ann reminded her. "Now, tell us."

"A major disappointment. That's all."

"What kind of disappointment?" asked Audrey.

Susan sat down on the bed. "I can't believe I misjudged him so much, but the kind of things he said, the way he behaved—prior to this evening, that is—made me think he was a man who was different . . . a man who understood women."

"He doesn't?" Audrey asked.

"Nothing could be further from the truth," Susan said.

"What a disappointment," Audrey said.

Beth Ann sniffed the air then, leaned toward Susan and sniffed again. "Have you been drinking?"

Susan nodded, still feeling a bit wobbly. "Margaritas."

"Maybe you should stick to margaritas and lay off men," Beth Ann said. "They're a lot more predictable."

"Yes," Audrey said, "having a man in your life is like having an electric blanket when you don't have electricity."

Susan stood up.

"Where are you going?" Beth Ann asked.

"To my room to have a good cry," Susan replied, then left.

Berny turned off the hair dryer. She looked at Audrey, then at Beth Ann. "What's wrong with her?"

"Too much margarita and not enough Wyatt," was Audrey's reply.

Chapter Seven

The sound of someone knocking on her door woke Susan the next morning. "Susan? Are you up?" It was Beth Ann's voice.

Susan raised her head and blinked. Shafts of sunlight wedged its way through the closed draperies. "What time is it?"

"Half past ten."

Susan raised her head and feel back to the bed with a moan. "God, what a headache."

"*He's* here."

"Who?"

"Wyatt Whittaker."

"Bully."

"He wants to see you."

"Bully."

"Susan, is that all you're going to say?"

"Tell him we don't always get what we want out of life."

"He's pretty persistent."

"So am I."

"He looks awfully contrite. He's even apologized to all of us. Won't you reconsider?"

"No."

"But he's such a dream, and *soooo* nice."

"Then you talk to him."

"He doesn't want to talk to me. You could get him if you played your cards right."

"If I played. . . . Listen, I wouldn't want him if he was dipped in gold dust . . . if he had a diamond in his navel and one up his. . . . Never mind. Just tell him I don't want to see him again. Ever."

"Okay. We're going down to the barn. Andy is going to show us how to milk a cow. Do you want to come?"

"No. I'm through with cows and I'm through with cowboys."

"Can I get you anything?"

"A gun or an Alka-Seltzer."

"Do you feel that bad?"

"I'm trying to remember when I felt worse."

"I'll check on you when we get back. Maybe you'll be feeling better then."

"I'll be better or dead, and they sound equally attractive to me at the moment."

Susan heard the sound of Beth Ann's footsteps going across the porch and down the steps. She rolled over and pulled the pillow over her head, which was pounding. She swore off margaritas for the rest of her life and closed her eyes, praying for sleep.

"I believe you ordered an Alka-Seltzer," a masculine voice said.

"Dear God!"

"Guess again."

It couldn't be. Susan peered out from beneath the pillow. It was. Wyatt Whittaker stood there bigger than Dallas, wearing a blue shirt which did absolutely everything wonderful to his blue eyes. She hated the man. How dare he come in here looking good. "How did you get in here?"

"In the usual manner . . . through the door. Now be a good girl and drink this before the fizz is all gone." He thrust the fizzing glass in her face. "Down the hatch."

"Take a long walk off a short pier." She reached for the pillow, but he was faster.

He tossed the pillow out of the way. "Stubbornness like that goes beyond all logic. *You're* the one with the hangover, remember? Refusing to drink this won't do a thing to me, whereas drinking it might do a lot for you."

"I hate a wise-ass," she said, taking the glass and drinking it down.

"So do I." He took the glass from her and put it on the bedside table.

She closed her eyes and lay back against her pillow.

"Lie here for half an hour, then take a shower. I'll be back to pick you up."

"For what?"

"A picnic. I'll drive you up into the mountains. We can eat lunch there."

She opened one eye and looked at him. "Why are you being so nice?"

"I'm always nice, but if you are thinking about yesterday, I plead temporary insanity, and if you don't believe that, then try the fact that I was under a lot of pressure."

"Pressure? What kind of pressure?"

"Your going back to D.C. kind of pressure. Two weeks isn't a very long time for a courtship. However, I should have known better than to assume you felt the same sense of urgency that I felt."

"Sex is always more urgent from the male point of view."

"I know. I learned a long time ago that when a woman says she feels something, it means something completely different from what a man thinks he feels. I knew it, but I allowed by own selfish thoughts and desires to overshadow my common sense. I'd like the chance to make it up to you."

"Why?"

"Why?"

"Why would you go to all this trouble. I mean, I'm leaving soon. Why bother?'

"I don't know. I keep having this strange feeling that

there might be a second chapter after this first one is over.''

''And after the second chapter?''

''Maybe a third . . . maybe a whole book.''

''It won't work.''

''What won't work?''

''A whole book with the two of us as the protago-nists.''

''How do you know it wouldn't work?''

''Okay, for starters, can you see yourself coming to D.C. and starting up a law practice?''

''Not in my wildest imagination.''

''And I would go insane out here with nothing but trees and cows for companionship.''

''I thought you liked it out here.''

I love it, she thought, but it would never work. Never in a million years. I'm just getting over one heartbreak. I'm not ready to have my heart broken again. It's too soon. We're too different, our lives are too different. It would never work. I'd just end up getting hurt. Better to stop it before it gets started. ''I do like it out here . . . for no more than two weeks. After that, I'm ready for civilization. What can I say? I'm a true-blue, dyed-in-the-wool, till-death-do-us-part, liberated, can-take-care-of-myself career woman . . . a bona fide city girl.''

''I see.''

No, you don't see, she thought. If you really knew, you'd come over here right now and you'd take me in your arms and tell me that I'm being ridiculous, that love is where you find it. But you won't, because you really don't see.

''Well, I hope you enjoy the rest of your vacation, he said, then left.

How come doing the right thing feels so wrong, so absolutely rotten, she wondered?

Then Susan rolled over and started to cry.

*   *   *

The door opened and Beth Ann walked in, followed by Berny and Audrey. "Are you feeling worse? Beth Ann asked.

"No."

"Then why are you crying?" Berny asked. "Did Wyatt say something upsetting?"

"No," Susan sobbed, "I did."

The three of them sat on the bed at the same time. "What did you say," they asked in unison.

"All the wrong things."

"Well, it's not like it's written in stone. What was said can be taken back," Beth Ann said.

Susan shook her head. "But it was the right thing to say."

"What did you say?" Audrey asked.

"I said I could never be happy out here, that I was a city girl through and through."

"But that's a big lie. You're always talking about leaving D.C. and going to a smaller town," Berny said.

"It's Joel, isn't it?" Beth Ann asked. "You're afraid of being hurt again."

"It's Joel . . . it's me . . . it's the distance . . . the differences . . . everything."

"And that's a great reason to throw away a chance at happiness," Beth Ann said.

"I was being sensible."

"Just where is it written that a woman should be sensible?" Berny asked. "When you're in love, that's the one time in your life you are expected to be anything but sensible."

"I'm not in love. I haven't known him long enough for that. I'm in like."

"Maybe he's in love," Audrey said.

"Hardly," Susan said. "He just had me pegged for an easy mark."

"That was cruel," Beth Ann said.

"I know what goes through a man's mind. He saw me as a vulnerable woman. I was an easy target. He thought he'd give me a little attention and then get me in his bed. It's the typical thing. Take a woman out, show her the sights, feed her, give her a few drinks, and then seduce her. Once it's done, he lies there wondering how long she is going to lie there before she gets up and goes home."

"I think you should give him the benefit of the doubt," Berny said.

"I have spent my life giving men the benefit of the doubt. That's why I'm forty and an old maid."

"You can't be an old maid. You were married once."

"That doesn't count. Now, I'll let you in on a little secret. If anyone ever gets me even close to committing, he's going to have to do something spectacular like being shot out of a cannon, or kiss me until I see fireworks."

"So what are you going to do now?" Beth Ann asked.

"Get a cat and a parrot, plant a garden and raise tomatoes, and live alone in peaceful, blessed silence."

"Gee, that sounds like a lot of fun," Berny said, then she turned to Audrey and asked, "Wouldn't you like to be Susan, with all that excitement waiting for you at home?"

"No."

"All right," Susan said, "lay it on with a trowel. For once in my life I've done the sensible thing in order to save myself a lot of heartache later, and what do I get?"

"Nothing but a parrot and a cat and a few frigging tomatoes," Berny said, and Susan's friends turned and filed out of the room.

Chapter Eight

Susan didn't have time to get the parrot or the cat when she returned home. She was too busy looking for a job.

Sitting in a booth at California Pizza Kitchen on Connecticut Avenue, Susan was eating a half order of Oriental chicken salad, discussing her plight with Audrey. "I can't believe Senator Claiborne decided to retire *before* Christmas. I'll never find a job this time of year. Fall is the absolute worst time to be job hunting."

"You've been offered at least six jobs since you started looking."

"They weren't right for me."

"It wouldn't matter if it was summer, winter, or spring. You wouldn't find a job anytime." Audrey bit into her pizza.

"What do you mean?"

"I don't think you'll find a job because you don't want to find a job."

"That's ridiculous. Why wouldn't I want to find a job? So I could move in with you and let you support me?"

"No, so you could go to Montana and let Wyatt support you."

"I hardly think about Wyatt any more."

"Good, then take the job with Senator Pellman."

"I don't know. . . ."

"Pellman or Whittaker, what's it going to be?"

Susan took the job with Senator Pellman, but her heart wasn't in it. It was still in Montana.

December passed uneventfully. January was filled with too much snow. February was worse. March was rainy and cold. April was when Wyatt called.

"You're going to be in D.C.?" Her heart hammered and she could barely get the next word out. "Why?"

"Nothing glamorous, I'm afraid. I'm coming up to testify before the Senate on the issue of ranchers leasing federal grasslands."

"When are you coming?"

"In two weeks. Susan, I'd like to see you. Would you like to have dinner?"

"I'd like that."

"Where's a good restaurant?"

"Where are you staying?"

"The Ritz-Carlton on Massachusetts."

"You can't beat the Jockey Club."

"I'll call you when I get there."

"I look forward to it."

"I'm glad I have this chance to see you. I've thought about you a lot."

"Me too."

"Really?"

"Really."

"Good thoughts, I hope."

"I can't seem to conjure up any other kind."

"I'm going to be in town for two days. Maybe we could have dinner both nights . . . that is, if you're available."

"I'm available."

"Good. I'll see you in two weeks."

"I'll be here."

" 'Bye."

"Good-bye, Wyatt."

*   *   *

The next two weeks passed at a snail's pace, but on Tuesday morning Susan got a call from Wyatt.

"I've got dinner reservations at the Jockey Club for seven-thirty. Where do I pick you up?"

"I've got to work late, so I don't know when I'll get home to change clothes. How about I meet you there. If I'm a little late, you can have a drink and I'll find you in the bar."

Even in a crowded, smoky bar, Wyatt was easy to find. He was sitting at a table in the corner, looking better than her last two raises. "Hi. Sorry I'm late."

"Hi yourself," he said, standing up. "You aren't that late. Only ten minutes." He gave her a kiss on the cheek. "You look beautiful." He pulled out her chair.

She sat down. "You always know what to say."

He laughed. "Not always, if I remember right."

She found herself laughing, too. "Times change."

His tone turned serious. "I hope so. I'd like to think I'd get another chance."

"I'm in a charitable mood."

"Then I don't need to get you drunk?"

"Nope, but I'll take an Absolut martini, up, with a twist."

He ordered her a drink and when it came, she sipped it slowly, listening to him tell her about Andy, the ranch, and things in Montana.

"So, how's it been going for you?"

"Nothing spectacular, but I'm optimistic."

"So am I. Shall we go to dinner?"

Dinner was delicious, but she was so entranced she hardly noticed what she ate. When the Grand Marnier soufflé came, she ate it with one hand. Wyatt was holding the other. After dessert, she had a glass of Port, then they went into the Fairfax Club and danced until midnight.

"I'd love to invite you up to my room for a nightcap, but I know better, so I'll get a taxi and take you home."

She wanted to tell him to invite her up, that she wasn't

as pig-headed as she had been before, but they were already outside and a taxi was pulling up.

Once they were inside, Wyatt put his arm around her and drew her close. "It was good to see you again. I hope we can do this again tomorrow night."

"What time?"

"Seven," he said, kissing her softly on the mouth.

"What. . . ." He kissed her again, deeper this time and Susan felt her arms sliding around his neck.

"That's better," he said, just as they pulled up in front of her town house in Georgetown.

He helped her out, then said to the driver, "Wait here. I'll be right back."

Susan felt a wave of disappointment. Well, what did she expect? She had been insulted before when he suggested more, and now that he was being the perfect gentleman, she was wishing he would suggest more.

He walked her to the door and kissed her once again. She kissed him back, leaning into his arms, feeling weak at the knees.

"Mmmmm, you make it hard to remember my manners."

She wanted to tell him to hell with your manners, but she said she'd had a wonderful evening instead.

Once inside, she stood in the hallway and watched through the window until his taxi drove off. Then she went to bed, wishing she wasn't alone.

The next night they dined at The Prime Rib, then went to the River Club to hear jazz. Afterward, they went to the Ritz and had a drink in the bar. As he had been the night before, Wyatt was a perfect gentleman, much to her frustration. Once again, when they left the bar, he said, "I'd love to invite you up, but I'll get a taxi and take you home."

She stopped in the middle of the lobby and turned toward him. "What if I said I didn't want to go home?"

He hugged her. "That's what I've been wanting to

hear ever since I got here." He kept his arm around her as they walked to the elevator. "The bad thing about being from out of town is there isn't really anyplace you can go to be alone. I've been dying to kiss you all evening."

The moment the elevator doors closed, he did just that, and didn't stop until the doors opened on his floor.

Once in his room, he opened a bottle of champagne, took off his jacket and his tie. Then he sat next to her on the sofa. She took a few sips of champagne, but soon his kisses got in the way, so she left the champagne on the coffee table and devoted herself to kissing him back, which gave her a better high than champagne ever did.

She had forgotten how good it felt to be held with a pair of strong arms. His body was strong and warm and enveloping her with a comforting ease. He was kissing her face, her neck, whispering words to her, words she couldn't completely comprehend, but that made her melt against him. "Make love to me, Wyatt."

"Hell!"

It wasn't exactly the reaction she expected. There must have been something funny about the way she looked for he burst out laughing and took her in his arms, smothering her face with kisses. "You are adorable, you know that?"

She pushed at him, trying to break his hold.

"Sweetheart, don't be angry. I didn't mean it the way it sounded. What I meant was, I don't have any protection . . . I never dreamed you would consent."

She kissed him, whispering against his mouth. "Don't worry. I'm not going to let a little thing like that stop me."

"You shouldn't be so trusting. . . ."

"I'm not. I went to the drugstore at lunch. I've got all the protection you need in my purse."

He threw back his head and laughed. "I like a woman who's always prepared."

"I was a Girl Scout. One of the first things we learned was to be prepared."

She didn't say anything after that, for by the time she finished speaking, he was removing her clothes, then he carried her to the bed, stopping just long enough for her to pick up her purse.

Where did he learn to do everything he did, in the way he did, that drove her crazy? How did he know to kiss her and kiss her until she was aching for him? When he finally did make love to her, he did it so exquisitely and with such ardor, she had no doubt that he had wanted this every bit as long as she had. Making love had never been like this. She never knew there were so many ways he could position her, each of them driving her to the edge, so that when release did come, it was so shattering, she could only lie in his arms gasping for breath, weak, and wanting to be held like this for the rest of her life.

She fell asleep in his arms. Sometime during the night, she thought she heard him say "I hope you realize that what we have here isn't lust, it's love." But when she awoke the next morning, he was gone. When she called downstairs, she was informed that Mr. Whittaker had checked out.

As she sat in the taxi on her way home, she kept hearing the words "What we have here isn't lust, it's love." But he had left her, without a word of good-bye. By the time she reached her town house, she knew Wyatt had not whispered those words. She had dreamed them. She had dreamed the impossible.

Chapter Nine

"I'm worried about Susan," Berny said to Audrey, while they waited for Susan and Beth Ann to meet them for lunch. They were sitting outside, at Cafe Deluxe on Wisconsin, soaking up the June sun and talking about what they could do to get Susan out of her slump.

"She's lost weight," Audrey said.

"She never goes out," said Berny.

"I know. She's done exactly what she said she would do," Berny said.

"What's that?"

"Think about it. In April, Susan got a cat. May came and she bought a parrot. When June rolled around, she dug up one flowerbed in the back yard. . . ."

". . . She planted tomatoes," Audrey finished.

"Exactly."

Beth Ann came rushing up to the table and sat down. "You will never believe what happened."

"What?" Audrey and Berny asked in unison.

"Wyatt Whittaker called me."

"You?" Berny said. "Why would he call you?"

"That's what I wondered . . . until he explained that he wanted our help."

Berny scowled. "Doing what? Kidnapping Susan so he can go off and leave her again?"

"He's coming to town over the Fourth of July," Beth Ann said.

"Whoopee," Audrey said. "What does he want us to do, set off fireworks?"

"Don't be so hard on the guy."

"You want us to be nice to him?" Berny asked. "To the man who dumped our friend?"

"How could you even talk to him?" Audrey asked.

"Will you listen? He wants our help."

"Not in this lifetime," Berny said. "I wouldn't give him all the hay he could eat."

"He wants us to bring Susan down to the mall on the Fourth. It's to be a surprise."

"Everything he does is a surprise," Audrey said. "What's he going to do this time, shoot her out of a cannon?"

"I believe he's going to propose."

"Propose what?" Berny said.

Beth Ann rolled her eyes. "Marriage, you idiot."

"Marriage!" Once again, Berny and Audrey spoke at the same time.

"That's generally what a man does when he falls in love and wants to spend the rest of his life with someone."

"I always knew he was a gentleman," Berny said.

"It was obvious he was in love with her from the moment he first saw her burning up his pasture," Audrey said.

"Shhh," Beth Ann said, "here comes Susan. Not a word about this, you hear?"

"Our lips are sealed," Berny said.

"Wild horses couldn't drag it out of me," Audrey added.

"Hi," Susan said, "What's happening?"

"Nothing much," Audrey said.

"We're just sitting here listening to the blood pumping through our varicose veins. How 'bout you?" Berny asked.

Susan sat down. "Nothing much here, either. I was thinking I'd make tomato sauce tonight. You won't believe how many tomatoes I've gotten off of three vines."

"Gosh, what an exciting life you lead," Beth Ann said.

"Don't make an issue out of being an old maid," Susan said. "You may be one yourself."

"I know," Berny said, "that's what I hate about being a liberated woman. You have to learn to lose."

Chapter Ten

On the morning of July 4th the phone rang at half past seven. Susan picked it up. It was Berny.

"Don't forget we're picnicking on the mall this evening."

"I won't forget."

"We'll pick you up about four."

"Okay. I'll be ready."

" 'Bye."

" 'Bye." Susan hung up the phone and went back to sleep.

Half an hour later, the phone rang again. Susan picked it up. It was Beth Ann.

"Just wanted to remind you that we're going to the mall this afternoon."

"I know. Berny called half an hour ago."

"Oh, did she say we'd pick you up?"

"At four."

"Okay. See you then."

" 'Bye." Susan hung up the phone and went back to sleep.

Fifteen minutes later, the phone rang. Susan picked it up. "Yes, I know we're going to the mall today. I know you are picking me up at four."

"Is this the lady who placed the ad about the lost parrot?"

"Oh, yes . . . yes, it is. I'm sorry. I thought you were someone else."

"Obviously."

"Did you find a parrot?"

"No, I just thought I'd call about your ad. Yes, I found a parrot in my back yard."

"Did you catch him?"

"No, he looks like he might bite."

"He won't bite. Just go out there and hold out your hand and say, 'Hi, George.' "

"Okay. Just a minute."

Susan waited for about five minutes.

"Hello? Are you still there?"

"Yes. Do you have my parrot?"

"No. I did like you said, I went out there and said ' 'Bye, George,' and he took off."

Susan let out a breath. She wasn't even going to explain. "Well, thanks for trying."

"If he comes back, I'll call you."

"Yes, please do. Thanks."

Susan hung up the phone and tried to go to sleep. Five minutes later, the phone rang. She picked it up. "Did my parrot come back?"

"I don't know? Did he?"

"Oh, hi, Audrey."

"No word on ole George?"

"One call, but the parrot flew off."

"Well, maybe you'll get another call. Don't give up. I just wanted to remind you that we'll pick you up at four."

"Thanks. I'll see you then."

"Okay. 'Bye."

" 'Bye, Audrey."

They were there, at Susan's town house right at four o'clock. When they honked, Susan picked up her Mexican blanket and three bottles of Chianti and a duffel bag filled with tapes, a small radio, her camera, and a sweat-

74 ELAINE COFFMAN

shirt. Once she was in the car, they headed toward the Key Bridge.

"I thought we were going to the mall?"

"We thought it would be better to be on the other side of the Potomac," Berny said.

"We could get a spot down by the water," Beth Ann added.

Audrey agreed. "It would be a lot cooler."

Susan nodded. "Okay."

They parked the car, then found a great spot down by the water. Soon they had their blanket spread and the picnic basket opened. Inside were cucumber sandwiches, sliced rounds of Italian sausage, a chunk of Parmesan cheese, grapes, a container of melon and strawberries, crackers, and a baguette.

Susan opened the wine and soon they were eating and laughing, talking about old times. When it started growing dark, they put everything but the wine back in the picnic basket. Susan poured another glass of wine and leaned back against her duffel bag.

Beth Ann, Berny, and Audrey stood up.

"Where are you going?" Susan asked.

"We're going to take this stuff to the car," Audrey said.

"Now?"

"It will be easier now, while there aren't any crowds to contend with," Beth Ann said.

"Want me to help?" Susan asked.

"No, you stay here and hold the blanket down. We'll be back in a flash," Berny said.

Susan watched them leave, then took another sip of wine. The weather was remarkably nice, not hot or humid. There was a small breeze blowing in across the Potomac. Perfect weather to be outside.

When her friends didn't return by the time the fireworks were ready to start, Susan wondered what their meaning of 'back in a flash' was. She sat up and looked for a place to set her wine cup, intending to go look for them. She stashed the cup, then stood up, just as someone came up behind her.

"Where have you been?" she said.

"Going crazy without you."

Susan turned around and saw Wyatt standing there. "Wyatt. What are you doing here?"

"I came to ask you something."

"What?"

"Will you marry me."

"Why?"

"Because I love you. Isn't that the usual reason?"

She opened her mouth, but he stepped closer and took her in his arms. "Shut up and kiss me," he said, not waiting to see if she would do as he asked.

He kissed her with all the feeling she could ever hope for. "Well, what's your answer?" he asked. "Will you marry me?" He kissed her again.

Susan heard a loud boom and opened her eyes just as a huge burst of color lit up the sky. It rained down in hues of lavender, pink, gold, and blue.

If anyone ever gets me even close to committing, he's going to have to do something spectacular like being shot out of a cannon, or kiss me until I see fireworks.

"Yes, oh yes," she said, unable to believe she had really gotten what she wished for that day so long ago in Montana.

SUMMER FLING

Victoria Barrett

Chapter One

Y ou can never go back.

No matter how desperately you want to, or how hard you try, things happen to change you from the person you were into the person you are, and you can never go back to who you'd once been.

That simple truth, whether blessing or curse, had proven itself inescapable to Adam Weston and Anne Hayden. They'd kissed and caressed and made love a thousand times—in Anne's dreams. In her fantasies. In those darkest niches of her heart where her deepest desires and most cherished wishes hid secreted from the rest of the world.

From first glance between them it'd been fireworks. All sparks and sultry sizzle. Sheer magic and pure temptation. But anything between them had been forbidden.

Now, six years later, it still was. And that they had parted then without once kissing or touching or making love still haunted her, still fed her fantasies, still flooded her dreams.

With a little sigh of remorse-laced regret, Anne replaced the telephone receiver on its cradle, disconnecting the link to Adam now as she had then. With that final click, she tried to bury the lingering memories and futile wishes that things between them could have been different. *If only* he hadn't been her college roommate

Maxine's lover. *If only* Anne hadn't taken one look at him and proven true that "old rubbish" about love at first sight. *If only* she could meet her eyes in the mirror when she swore to herself that breaking the connection to him in these phone calls didn't hurt, didn't remind her of the pain she'd suffered in walking away from him six years ago.

Why couldn't she convince herself that reality *could* hold a candle to her fantasies of him . . . and to his fantasies of her?

Get a grip, Anne. That can't happen. Things are what they are, and nothing that matters can change.

Oh, but she'd be wise to listen to herself. So what if Adam and Maxine had parted ways a year ago and she'd married Adam's best friend? Aside from their phone calls, Maxine's marriage hadn't impacted Adam and Anne's relationship. The facts had to be faced. She had to accept that their chance had come and gone. Adam had become a neurologist and built a life in New Orleans; Anne, a physical therapist, had done the same in Mississippi. But far more than a state line and a scant sixty miles separated her and Adam, and it always would.

She slumped down in an overstuffed chair in the two-bedroom apartment she shared with her younger sister, Janese. They could never go back.

"I'm late. I'm *sooo* late!" Janese breezed through the living room in a lacy bra and peach panties, looking like a leggy blond bundle of sex straight off the latest catalogue pages from Victoria's Secret.

Obviously Janese had a date. When *didn't* she have a date? Nearly choking on a cloud of her sister's perfume, and on an absurd knot of envy, Anne mentally prepared for another exciting night of TV and her own company. "Why do you do this? You know Rick's anal-retentive about time."

"He's not. He's just punctual. But that was last night—or maybe the night before." Her eyes lost focus, as if she were trying to remember, then she shrugged. "Whatever. Tonight I'm seeing Jay."

"Another new one?"

"New and yummy. Six solid feet of tall, dark, and handsome."

Weren't they all? "What does he do?"

"Mmm, I don't know." Dismissing that tidbit as unimportant, she let out a wistful sigh. "But he fills out a great pair of jeans."

"God, Janese. There's more to life and relationships than—"

"Don't start, okay? I'm going to settle down to one guy . . . eventually. Well, glare if you want to, but I am. Just as soon as I'm ready. Until then, I intend to have a good time." She bent down to dig through a mountain of clothes they loosely referred to as her ironing pile. Taking up a good chunk of corner in the dinette, it more realistically resembled a hill. "Maybe once in a while you should try having a little fun."

"I have plenty of fun."

Janese snorted. "Earth to Anne. This is your sister you're talking to. You can lie to yourself, but you can't lie to me."

She couldn't. But she wouldn't admit the truth either. More than not wanting Janese to hear it, Anne herself didn't want to hear it.

"Seriously. Men *are* fun. They're interesting and stimulating." Janese's voice went husky. "And *sooo* sensual."

"All those assets and yet you still find keeping track of them separately a challenge." Droll, and catty. Anne didn't like sounding either, much less both. Maybe she'd just forget TV, fix herself a Scotch-and-water and sit on the balcony.

A year ago, she could have seen the Mississippi shoreline of the Gulf of Mexico from there. Now, the view was of a casino's parking garage. She sighed. TV might be the better option, after all. With nothing to look at, she'd think, and she didn't want to think. Not so soon after talking with Adam. They were friends, but. . . .

"Keeping track is only the nicest kind of challenge." Janese laughed, low and throaty. "Now you, on the other hand—" She glanced over, sobered, then winced. "Ouch."

Toeing off her sneakers and shrugging out of the lab jacket covering her jeans and blue silk blouse, Anne frowned. "What?"

"You've got that look."

"What look?"

Janese flung aside a slinky black jumpsuit, rifled through the pile, then pulled up a hot pink halter dress. "That I-wish-I'd-damned-my-conscience-and-Maxine's-feelings-when-I-had-the-chance-and-jumped-Adam Weston's-bones-so-I-could-quit-wondering-what-it-would-have-been-like look."

Anne had wished it countless times, and had damned herself as forty kinds of fool for ever wishing it. But her pride wouldn't let her admit it. Not now, not ever. "That's not my style."

"But it is mine, hmm?" Janese smiled, her green eyes twinkling without shadows or remorse, or even a shade of guilt. "It's okay. I'm first to admit I'm a firm believer in going with my gut instincts. If they say go for it, I go." A pair of purple slacks flew across the pile to the carpet. "Though, I have to say, my instincts don't go for it nearly so often as you think they do."

"It wouldn't have been right between Adam and me." Anne studied her nails, wishing they were long and painted a soft pink like Janese's. But they were practical for her work; neat, trimmed, and buffed, but not ultra-feminine. "Nothing good can come out of a relationship born in someone else's pain." How many times did she have to say it?

"Honey, please. Unless we're talking prepuberty here, *everyone* is in pain. Nobody gets through adolescence without it, much less all the way to adulthood." Janese pulled a lemon-colored sheath from the pile, gave it a visual once over, then tossed it back onto the heap. ''Besides, Maxine's married to someone else now, and that leaves the door wide open for you and Adam. You still have the chance—''

''Don't even think it,'' Anne interrupted. Six years was far too long. They were different people now, and their fantasies of each other surely would crumble under reality's unforgiving glare. No human being could measure up to fantasy's perfection, and Anne had no intention of falling short and disappointing Adam. Obviously, he had no intention of risking disappointment or failing either.

Janese wrinkled her nose. ''But if you really want the man—''

''I don't.''

Janese went statue-still. A black blouse draping over her hand shimmered, and she cast Anne a shrewd look. ''Are you honestly going to sit there and tell me you don't regret not jumping Adam Weston's bones?''

How did the woman *always* know? Anne resisted squirming by sliding the gold hoop earrings from her earlobes then plopping them down on the table, next to the telephone. ''I'm not telling you anything.''

''You don't have to tell me. I know you, okay? And I know you're wishing you'd jumped—''

''Would you *please* stop saying that?'' Anne gritted her teeth. ''How do you know what I'm thinking? Can you read my mind or something?'' If Anne could figure that out, she could hide whatever evidence Janese picked up on and stop these infernal inquisitions. They were really wearing thin, rattling her nerves—probably because they forced her to look too closely at things she'd rather not see at all.

''Aside from it being a safe guess—the man has called you every night since Valentine's Day, for God's sake— you're flushed and your boobs look like dart tips. It doesn't take a mind reader or a rocket scientist to figure out you're attracted to him.''

Anne glanced down to the blue silk and saw the telltale evidence. Her face burned red-hot. Too agitated to sit, she got up then headed for the kitchen.

Tiptoeing through a gap between the clothes littering the floor, she spotted her forest-green skirt. It'd been missing for a month. She scooped it up, wrapped it over the back of a bar stool, then went on around the end of the bar and into the kitchen. One day she'd get brave enough to dig through her sister's ironing and gather up all the items Janese had borrowed. But not tonight. Tonight Anne felt fragile. Mostly because her too-observant sister was dead right when Anne wanted her to be dead wrong.

Janese tossed the pink dress onto a chair, reheaped the rifled articles into a semblance of a pile, then grabbed the ironing board from its closet in the corner of the kitchen. Near the dining room table, she cranked the board open, plugged in the iron, then flicked it on. ''When are you guys going to quit talking about which brand of paper towel is most absorbent and get to the good stuff?''

''We aren't.'' Anne filled a glass with ice at the fridge, then poured tea into it from the crockery pitcher they'd inherited from Grandma Hayden. Why was her blasted hand shaking? ''But, for the record, we have some serious talks, too.''

''Ah, yes. Your 'life, death, and the universe' debates. Your 'God, what a lousy date I just had' discussions. Your 'this job is really getting to me' sessions. I know all about them, but, Anne, this thing between you two is still crazy.'' Janese reached over the board and grabbed the pink dress. ''I know what you've said about your jobs, but Adam lives in New Orleans, for God's sake. Not on Mars. You could get together any weekend.''

Putting the pitcher back into the fridge, Anne debated making a sandwich, decided against it, then snagged a slice of cheese. "We like our independence."

"Bull." Janese plunked down the iron, then furiously swiped at ironing the pink fabric, muttering something godawful, Anne felt sure, under her breath.

"We do." She frowned, held it so Janese wouldn't miss it, then sat down on a stool and unwrapped the cheese. The cellophane wrapper crinkled. God, but she loved the smell of cheese. And hot bread. And baked apples. And Adam's cologne. It'd taken her two weeks of exploring scents in Gayfer's to peg it as Obsession.

Obsession. She chomped down on a bite of cheese. How fitting.

"I know you both prize your independence—why, only God and you know—but that wasn't what I meant." Janese flipped the dress to press its skirt. "What you guys are doing isn't healthy. Seriously. I mean, you've been talking to each other on the phone for a year. Why the heck don't you ever see each other?"

"Janese, don't start. You know Maxine was my friend and Adam belonged to her."

"Operative word there, Sis. *Belonged.* As in, past tense. She married another man. All bets are off now."

"Who she married doesn't matter. And there are no bets." Anne nibbled at the edge of the smooth, creamy slice. "We did what we had to do then, and it's too late now. You can't go back, Janese. You just . . . can't."

Janese grunted, rolled her gaze ceilingward, then leveled Anne with an I-can't-believe-you-expect-me-to-swallow-this-tripe look. "What, she's still got dibs on the man—in case she ever gets a divorce?"

"No." The cheese stuck to her teeth. Anne rubbed her tongue over them. "It's not like that."

"Well, how is it, then?"

Anne wished to heaven she knew. She squeezed her eyes shut, then swallowed a long draught of tea. Condensed droplets of water trickled down the outside of the glass and made a perfect circle under its base on the beige bar. "Adam and I are just friends. That's all we've ever been, and all we'll ever be." Her voice sounded as weak as a beggar's. Was she convincing Janese, or trying to convince herself? Unsure, Anne's chest went tight. "We just like to talk. Let's leave it at that."

"Let's not. You were in love with the man in college, and I think you're still—"

"Don't say it." Anne's heart thudded against her ribs. "I mean it. Just . . . don't."

"All right, I won't." Janese shrugged, looked down at her ironing, and lowered her voice. "But not saying it doesn't make it any less true."

"Those days are over." Anne took another bite of cheese, then chewed it slowly to steady her nerves. "I was in love with him, but we're different now. We don't love each other anymore."

"You might be different, but you're both still block-headed—and too blind to see the truth and it right before your eyes."

"Janese, I'm warning you—"

"Okay. Okay. Don't have a spasm." She flipped the dress off the board, then pressed down the halter ties. Steam lifted from the iron. "I have to say this, though. Quit glaring at me, Anne. You're my sister, okay? When you're being stupid, it's my duty to tell you."

For all her fun-loving sass, Janese took her sisterly duties damn serious. And the only way to get her to shut up was to let her have her say. Once she had, she'd be over it, and then Anne could get some peace. "Whatever. Just no long-winded lectures. I had a rough day at the hospital—two burn victims—and I'm really not in the mood for it."

"I'll keep it short." Janese turned off the iron, then stepped into the slinky dress that hugged her every lush curve and ended abruptly mid-thigh in a flattering flair. "You and Adam talk about everything and nothing. But you never talk about getting together in person. Why do you think that is?"

Anne knew exactly. She opened her mouth to tell Janese, caught herself, and said nothing.

"I think it's fear."

The glass of tea in Anne's hand shook. Ice clinked against the sides and tea splashed over the rim, down onto the counter. She swiped at it with her hand, then brushed her wet palm over her jeans. "That's ridiculous." And, God help her, true.

"Maybe. But I think you and Adam don't want to risk changing your lives. You've got these ideas about each other, and you're scared stiff you won't measure up in real life. This phone relationship of yours doesn't threaten anything. It's safe." She paused to slide into three-inch strappy heels that matched her dress. "I can't speak for Adam, having never met the man, but you're a warm and loving, sensual woman who's living like a sexless hermit. It's not natural, for God's sake."

"Okay, that's enough. I said I wasn't in the mood, and I'm out of patience." Anne set down her glass with a firm thunk. "Besides, you're wrong. Adam and I both date. And we both like dating."

Janese crossed her arms over her chest.

Tall, lithesome, and blond, she was the pretty sister. Dating came as natural as breathing to her. Janese was bright, an extrovert with great legs that perfectly matched her great face who was out for a good time and had no intention of settling down before she hit thirty. Anne was shorter, about five-six, slim rather than curvaceous, quieter and more intense. They were as different as night and day and, in relationships with men, those differences became glaringly apparent. Janese fell in and out of love at least twice a month, and seemed to welcome the emotional roller-coaster rides that went with it. Anne had fallen in love once. With Maxine's Adam. The experience stung and scarred, so she'd backed off and avoided letting it happen again.

Why was the woman just standing there, arms akimbo, staring at her? Anne grimaced. "What?"

"You *date*?"

"You know I do."

"An occasional dinner with a man you know will bore you stiff doesn't qualify as dating, Anne. Where's the fun? The excitement? Where's the romance?"

"I don't only date boring men."

"Yes, you do."

Did she? Of course not. Well, sometimes. "Not always," she stubbornly insisted, shifting on the bar stool.

"Always." Janese grabbed her purse, then slung its strap over her shoulder. "You need to take a few risks. Find yourself a summer love." Janese shrugged. "Hell, why not go all out and have yourself a summer fling?"

Anne shuddered. "Don't be ridiculous."

"I'm serious."

"A summer fling?" Anne guffawed. "Me?"

Janese hiked her brows and nodded.

Good grief. Her arms were folded over her chest again. Janese was dead serious. Wondering how long it'd take them to get past this discussion, Anne set the iron on the counter to cool, then let down the ironing board. It creaked, grating at her raw nerves. "I can't imagine a man I'd want to have a fling with, not that I would—"

"I can." Janese tilted her head and the light caught her chin-length hair. Swinging over her cheek, it shone like spun gold. "Ordinarily I'd suggest a suitable stranger—a girl has to be careful these days, you know—but you're far too stuffy to go for a stranger. So why not Adam?"

Anne's knees threatened to buckle. She crammed the ironing board back into its cabinet then slammed the door shut. "No."

"Why not? He'd be perfect. No chance of you falling in love with the guy again, right? And you'd get to find out what jumping his bon—er, what he'd really be like."

Anne went pier-post stiff. "He wouldn't be perfect, and it wouldn't be perfect. It'd be a disaster."

"Fear." Janese grasped the front door's knob. "Just

like I said. And some serious doubt too, I think. You really should—"

"Shut up, Janese."

"Certainly. Just as soon as you give me one good reason why you shouldn't have a fling with Adam Weston."

Why—*oh, why*—had she chosen now to nag? "I said, no."

"Good grief, Anne. I'm not talking about chaining yourself to the man forever." Janese struck a be-reasonable pose, her hands uplifted, her shoulders hiked. "I'm talking about having a fling with the guy. One weekend. That's it."

The thought alone had Anne's blood thrumming, her pulse pounding in her temples, heat swirling low in her belly. She clenched her muscles and talked from between her teeth. "You don't understand. Neither of us ever has mentioned meeting in person. We have an unspoken agreement."

Pursing her pink-tinted lips, Janese strolled over, propped her elbow on the bar, then leaned low and dipped her chin to her hand. "Well, dear heart, if the agreement is unspoken, then I'd say the sucker doesn't exist."

Anne gripped the edge of the countertop, held on so tight that her fingers ached. "I can't just ignore it and ask him to do this, Janese."

"Why not?" She arched a brow, defiantly challenging, and her gaze never wavered. "Afraid he'll say no?"

Anne's stomach flipped over. She forced her gaze up to her sister's, then slowly shook her head. "I'm afraid he'll say yes."

Chapter Two

Temptation proved unrelenting.

Anne couldn't focus, couldn't think, couldn't go ten minutes while awake or asleep without thinking about Adam Weston and wanting to see him again.

For the hundredth time since she'd come in from work, she eyed the phone next to the overstuffed chair and debated picking up the receiver and just calling and asking Adam away for the weekend.

Maybe Janese was right. She had made some valid points. Since Anne and Adam had begun this phone relationship last Independence Day, Anne *hadn't* exactly radiated contentment. Adam *hadn't* actually said he didn't want to see her, and Anne *did* want to see him again.

Want to?

Bending double on the chair, she buried her face in her hands. Okay, she craved seeing him again. Craved it. Soul-deep.

What *would* be the worst that could happen?

He could say no. Could stop calling.

Maybe that'd be for the best. Maybe if they actually saw each other, whatever still simmered there between them—after all this time, it had to be illusion—would finally be put to rest and they could get on with their lives. Separately. Independently. Maybe a fling would get him out of her system.

Smelling a "soothing food" chocolate cake baking in the oven, Anne again reached for the phone receiver.

But what if he made her feel all she'd felt before?

She grimaced, again jerked her hand back. Dangerous, that. He'd captivated her, and no man she'd seen before or since ever had lured her like Adam. He didn't discriminate. Her mind, body, and heart, he mesmerized them all.

She tensed against the memories, against the heat. It was time for this to end. Time to get over the man. Janese had been right about that, too. But Anne wasn't going to get over him unless something changed. Unless she quit wading in the safe surf and plunged in for a swim.

The thought alone made her queasy.

She forked her fingers through her hair, pressed their tips against her scalp, and gave herself a good lecture that ended with her grousing. What was she getting so worked up about? She'd ask, Adam would refuse, Janese would quit nagging, and Anne would quit fantasizing. The matter would finally be closed.

Before she could again lose her nerve, Anne grabbed the receiver. Against her palm, the phone rang.

Oh, God. It was him. It had to be him. Her heart thumped against her ribs, and she lifted the receiver to her ear. "Hello."

"Anne?" he asked, his voice soft and uncertain.

Adam. She broke out in a cold sweat. "Hi."

"You must have been right by the phone. I didn't hear it ring."

She curled her legs up beneath her and ran a fingertip over the edge of the polished wood table at her side. Could she do this? "I'd just reached for it to call you."

"What's wrong?" His voice tensed. "You sound upset."

Upset? *Ha!* Scared stiff. "I'm fine," she lied. Well, it was now or never. Though the air-conditioner blew a steady blast of cold air over her right shoulder, the room temperature seemed to spike ten degrees. "Adam, what do you have planned for the July Fourth weekend?"

He hesitated, clearly wary. "Nothing."

He wasn't making this easy on her, but then why should he? He hadn't once mentioned them getting together, and that she had mentioned it probably knocked him off-balance. At least, she hoped it had. The idea of her going through this agony and him sitting there unaffected seemed too unfair to contemplate. "Janese is going out of town."

The soft, soothing huskiness she'd grown accustomed to returned to his voice. "So you'll be alone, too."

Her palms went clammy. She crooked the phone at her shoulder, then rubbed her hands hard against the thighs of her jeans. Perfect opening. All she had to do was to take it. But her throat seemed dust-dry. She swallowed hard, then pushed the words out through her lips. "I was thinking maybe we could be alone together."

Good God, she'd actually said it. She'd actually gotten the words out without tripping over her tongue. *Bravo, Anne.* Now he'd refuse, and they could call this craziness done.

Silence.

A trickle of uneasiness slithered up her spine. "Adam?"

Still no answer.

She stared at the ceiling. No choice now but to brazen this out. "A friend of mine has a cottage on the beach in Florida. She's selling it and, before she does, I want to see it."

"And you want me to spend the weekend there with you?"

He sounded positively shocked. Anne frowned at the receiver, then replaced it at her ear. "You can stop with sounding as if I've just invited you to your own execution." Good thing she wasn't in this to feed her ego. "If you don't want to go, just say so."

"I didn't say I didn't want to go."

Her heart rate doubled and her stomach muscles clenched. Impossible. Ridiculous. Wasn't it? "Are you saying you do want to go, then?" Good grief, now *she* sounded shocked. She squeezed her eyes shut. So what if she was stunned senseless, did she have to sound like it?

"Yes, I do." He paused, then dropped his voice, letting her hear his concern. "But I don't want to start something we're not prepared to finish."

What did *that* mean? Ah, ground rules. Adam didn't wade in unchartered waters, nor did he swim in them. Well, she'd opened these floodgates. It seemed only fair that she define their perimeters. What was the difference, anyway? He'd refuse before they finished the conversation. She just had to stick out the worst of it and get from here to there. At least then he wouldn't consider her a fool *and* a coward. She plucked a loose white thread from her sleeve. "I'm suggesting a weekend, not a life-altering relationship."

"A weekend."

He seemed as unsure as she felt, and about as enthusiastic as a dead stump. Just how was she supposed to feel about that? At some level, it irked the bejesus out of her. Why didn't the contrary man refuse and get it over with and done? "A weekend," she repeated. "That's it."

"Just so I understand, are we talking being together, or being *together*?"

Every nerve in her body tingled, and her throat muscles spasmed. "I'm asking you to have a summer fling with me, Adam. That's it, okay? So say no, and then we can chalk this up to a lousy idea and get past it." Geez, how did any woman ever survive this asking business? It was sheer hell.

"A summer fling." Adam's voice went whisky-soft.

She could almost smell his relief, and despite her agitation and fit of nerves, that relieved her too, knocking out a ton of tension. She swiped a damp palm over her thigh, then wound the phone cord around her finger. "Exactly. No more."

"And no less."

The time had come to be perfectly frank. "Look, we obviously don't want to change our lives or we wouldn't have waited a year to even talk about seeing each other again. But I've been thinking about it, Adam, and I do want to see you." There. She forced her shoulders to relax, her eyes to open. That was as honest as she could get—as honest as she dared to get, even. with herself. "We could just have a quiet weekend together, and then go home. That's all I'm suggesting."

"Do you invite men away for the weekend often?"

This wasn't going at all as she'd envisioned it. "You know I don't."

"Just checking."

Staring out the window at a palm frond blowing in the breeze, she grunted. "I listen to this from a man who took Mary Jane skiing in Aspen for a week last winter?"

"Mary Jean," he corrected, a smile in his voice. "And you know it was awful."

"Jane, Jean—whatever. And how awful it was is beside the point. You went."

"You're right." His sigh crackled through the phone. "Okay, Anne, give me the directions to your cottage. You want a summer fling, we'll have a summer fling."

Her face went hot; a mix of honest temper and acute embarrassment. She gave him the directions, then added, "I want you to want this too, Adam."

"Do you?" Doubt laced his voice.

It wrapped around her heart and, suffering a tender tug, her own voice dropped a notch. "Yes, I do."

"I want—"

A beeping noise sounded in the background on his end.

"Damn. I've got to go," he said. "I'm on-call tonight and the hospital's already tagging me to come in. I'll see you about three, Annie."

Dear God, he was going to come. "Three," she croaked out, breathless and pseudo-dizzy.

Shaking like a leaf, she hung up the phone then stared at it in disbelief. What had happened here? He was supposed to refuse. *Why hadn't he refused?* What had he meant by that "You want a summer fling, we'll have a summer fling?" And what did *he* want?

If his bloody beeper hadn't gone off, she might be able to answer that. Now, she feared she'd never know.

Something else he'd said came back to her. Just before he'd hung up, he'd called her Annie.

Annie.

A fragment of a memory flitted through her mind. *Don't leave, Annie. Please.*

I have to, Adam.

Seeing him with Maxine had been too hard. It'd hurt too much.

The old pain rolled over her in crushing new waves.

"Oh, Janese," Anne mumbled, swiping at her stinging eyes. "What have I let you con me into?" She was plunging in for a swim, all right. In shark-infested waters. "He's going to break my heart again. I just know it." And damn fool that she was, she'd asked him to do it.

When would she learn?

Even when temptation proves unrelenting, you can never go back.

Chapter Three

Pastel-painted cottages dotted the Florida coast.
Most were built up on stilts, had parking beneath
them, and wooden stairs that led up to multilayered decks
that overlooked sand dunes, clumps of sea oats, the whispering surf, and sugar-white beaches.

Anne turned off the palm-lined Island Boulevard, glad
for the break from bumper-to-bumper traffic, then drove
down Tropic Avenue, looking for 231. Finally, she spotted it, fairly separated from the other retreats and cottages, at the end of the cul-de-sac on a jut of land
protruding out into the Gulf.

Sun-drenched, stilted, and weathered pale blue by constant exposure to the sun and salty sea air, the cottage
looked rustic yet welcoming, and the reason she was
there had fantasies traipsing through her mind, heat swirling low in her stomach. After six long years, in just a
few hours, Adam would be here. Adam. . . .

Shivering with anticipation, and a healthy dose of fear,
she turned into the sand-swept driveway, drove past a
crooked "For Sale" sign staked in the yard next to a
lonely-looking palmetto, then pulled her Saturn out of the
blazing sun and between the pilings underneath the cottage. Lord, how she hoped that coming here didn't prove
to be the biggest mistake of her life.

Stop it. She couldn't allow herself to think that way.

It was a weekend. No more, no less. They'd laid out the ground rules—and she couldn't afford to forget them.

She filled her arms with bags of groceries, her luggage and purse, then bumped from side to side up the wooden stairs to the cottage door, the key dangling from her hand. Juggling the mess in her arms, she attempted to fit the key into the lock. A grocery sack tipped and an apple rolled out then plunked down onto the deck with a flat *thump*.

"Maybe I can help." A man's warm breath fanned over her neck. He reached around her, his chest brushing against her back.

Every muscle in her body clenched at once. She snapped her gaze to his, and suffered that old rush of joy and desire. Denying either reaction had been triggered by seeing him, she felt her lips curve into a smile. "Adam."

He smiled back. "Hi, Anne."

Her heart flipped, then thudded. Subtle changes, but he looked so much the same. Khaki slacks, white shirt with sleeves baring his forearms, midnight-black hair needing a decent trim, broad forehead, winged brows, and feather-soft gray eyes twinkling a happiness at seeing her that arrowed straight into her heart.

He studied her much as she'd studied him, and she had to force herself not to reach up and smooth her wind-swept hair. She'd come early so she could have a few minutes to rid herself of road grime, put on some makeup, and change into a summery dress. Instead, she stood in white shorts and sandals and a "Therapists Know All the Right Moves" T-shirt, barefaced, and wilted-haired. "God," she whispered before she could stop herself. "I look awful."

He laughed, deep and throaty, took the sacks out of her arms, then dropped a peck of a kiss to her lips. "You look beautiful."

Before she could react, he swung the door open, then nodded.

She stepped inside. Outside, it was hot, but the constant breeze off the Gulf helped create an illusion of comfortable temperatures. Inside the cottage, the air was hot and still. Sultry. Muggy. And the cottage itself was a wreck. Newspapers lay sprawled over the upholstered, contemporary furniture. A toppled chair rested legs up with stiff towels, long since dry, draped over it, and an inch of dust covered everything in sight. Anne resisted an intense urge to cry.

Adam walked straight through to the kitchen, then deposited the sacks on the counter. "I hope you've got cleaning supplies in here." He turned to look out a patio door that led to a deck littered with white wicker chairs and a table, and Adirondack chairs that overlooked the sand and surf.

"Cleaning supplies? I vote for a demolition crew." The more Anne looked around, the deeper her spirits sank. "Melanie said it needed a little perking up. Not that it was a disaster area."

Anne dropped her purse into a chair near the front window. The impact stirred up a cloud of dust that sparkled in the sunlight streaming in through the window, tickled her nose, and set her to sneezing. That was the last straw. Tears brimmed in her eyes, and Anne blinked furiously to keep them from falling.

Adam came over, took one look at her, and his smile faded. "Don't be upset. It'll be fine." He cupped her face in his hands, and his expression turned tender. "It's got a great view."

How like him. Soothing. Caring. Still wearing Obsession. Her chin trembling, she met his gaze. "But I wanted everything to be perfect."

"It is." He stroked her jaw with his thumb. "We're finally together, Annie," he whispered, then claimed her lips.

Her heart swelled, then seemed to burst, and sparks of brilliant light showered behind her eyelids. She lifted her hands to his chest, let them explore and glide over his soft shirt to his shoulders, down beneath his arms to his wide back. Their lips parted, tongues swirled, and a little moan vibrated deep in her throat. Finally, after all this time, she was really touching him. Really touching him, and really kissing him, and—''

On a shudder and a sharp breath, he broke their kiss, then looked deeply into her eyes. ''I've missed you.''

A tear trickled down her cheek. ''I've missed you, too.''

The tension in his face drained and he smiled, then stepped back. ''Do you want to stay here and shovel out the place, or find a good hotel? The island is full of them.''

He'd first kissed her here. First held her in his arms here. Stupidly sentimental, and a direct violation of their defined Fling Rules, but she wanted to stay. ''I'd rather shovel.''

A teasing light lit in his eyes. ''Don't want to share me, eh?''

''Not exactly.'' If their kiss was any indicator, within five minutes of entering that hotel they'd be in bed. She wasn't quite ready for that. She needed to come to terms with this rush of old feelings—and to decipher the new ones inspired by his kiss. She had expected it to be tender, exploratory, not a searing surge of raw power. Cleaning would give her time to get over the initial flood of feelings that seeing him again, and finally touching him, had conjured. ''The hotels will all be booked for the holiday.''

''Ah, I wasn't thinking.'' His gaze slightly unfocused, he let his thumb drift over her cheekbone. ''You start in the kitchen. I'll take the bath—after I find the air-conditioner and get it going.''

''The bath?'' She grinned. ''I always did have a soft spot for you nervy doctors.''

''Glad to hear it.'' He slid a fingertip down over her collarbone to the swell of her breasts, following the words printed on her T-shirt. ''Therapists who know all the right moves bring out the best in us.''

Feeling too much, too fast! Her breath swooshed out. "We'd, um, better get this place habitable."

"I agree." The look in his eyes warmed, telling her blatantly there were other, more pleasurable things he looked forward to doing. "But there's a lot of work to be done," he said, closing her within the circle of his arms. "I need another adrenaline kick to get through it."

As his lips came down on hers, Anne tiptoed to meet him, leaned against him, reveled in the feel of his strong body aligning with hers, and denied what she knew to be true.

Something definitely still lay between them. What exactly, she didn't know, but it sure as certain wasn't an illusion. And, God help her, it burned even stronger and with more intensity than it had six years ago.

She cleaned the kitchen.

He scoured the bath.

While she dusted and ran the vac, he shuttled the bed linens down to the corner Laundromat. A short time later, he returned with them, a mysterious white box, and a dozen peach-scented candles. He placed one in each room—living, kitchen, and bath—and two in the sole bedroom, then lighted them all.

The air-conditioner had whirred constantly, and now the cozy cottage felt crisply cool. The musty scent had fallen first to that of Lysol and now, thanks to Adam's candles, to that of sweet, ripe peaches.

As dusk neared, they met up in the living room then inspected their handiwork.

"Who would have believed it?" Anne let her gaze skim over the pretty teal and peach pastel sofa and low-slung chairs, certain no self-respecting dust bunny would be caught dead in such a pristine place.

"Not me." Adam flipped an arm over her shoulder. "We make a good team." Dirt smudged his chin.

Some team. He'd been assaulting her senses all afternoon. She grinned up at him, and thumbed off the smudge. "So, when are you going to tell me what's in the box?"

He caught her hand then touched her knuckles to his lips, his eyes twinkling mischievously. "What box?"

She elbowed him in the ribs. "The one you snuck in under the sheets and bedspread when you came back from the Laundromat and then stashed in the bedroom."

"Oh, *that* box." His lips twisted into an irresistible, mysterious smile. "Later. I need to get cleaned up." He nuzzled her ear. "Care for a shower?"

"Um, you go ahead." She sucked in her breath, unable to meet his gaze. Her being embarrassed seemed silly, considering she'd initiated this weekend. But silly or not, it was there, and she had to deal with it. "I want to sweep the deck first."

His eyes full of promise, he stroked her chin with his fingertips. "Next time, then."

She was stalling, and he knew it. "Next time."

Nipping at her earlobe, he whispered, "Don't peek, Annie."

"I wouldn't do that." She frowned at him, righteously indignant. "What kind of woman do you think I've become?" Obviously one so desperate she had to settle for cheap thrills, spying on men showering.

He chuckled and tapped her nose. "I meant, don't peek into the box."

Heat crawled up her neck, and she silently cursed, knowing she was blushing to the roots of her hair. "Oh."

Still smiling, he headed toward the bath. "Just so you know, you're welcome in my shower, any time."

The images that remark conjured ignited a wildfire in her belly. Anne grabbed the broom, then attacked the deck. Sweeping was safer than attacking Adam—and they both knew it. He'd made that remark deliberately, of course. Just as he'd made others like it the entire time they'd spent cleaning the cottage.

Anne sighed. The truth was the man had been taunting her all afternoon. Flings were supposed to be like that, she supposed, dragging the broom between white wicker chair legs under the table. Grains of sand pattered against the wooden slats. But Adam's obvious experience at this fling business irked her, and with whom he'd gained that experience didn't bearing thinking about. Anne was a novice, a rank amateur, and making the transition was tough. Six years of fantasies kept getting in her way.

To the sounds of water lapping at the shore, she finished sweeping what seemed a ton of sand from the deck, then from the stairs leading down to the beach and surf. The warm constant wind and glare from the sun had her shielding her eyes to watch a cawing gull swoop down to the water, chasing a fish. Down the beach, a mixed group played volleyball, and strains of their laughter and distant rock music drifted on the wind to her. A body could get used to this relaxed atmosphere.

She climbed back up the steps, then slid open the patio door to the kitchen. A rush of cold, peach-scented air whisked over her, and she breathed in deeply.

"Anne?"

Hearing but not seeing him, she called out. "Yes?"

Adam walked out of the bath, wrapped in a white towel that rode low on his narrow hips. "Where's the soap?"

He looked as guilty as sin. Another intentional temptation maneuver that worked as well as all the others. Confronted with his broad chest, covered with fine black hair that spiraled down his middle and disappeared beneath the towel, with the muscles that created ridges in his thick arms, heat rippled through her, her breath caught in her throat, and she forced her gaze up to his. The gleam in his eyes proved he knew his effect, and was pleased by it. She'd be crazy to attempt to deny it. But he expected her to; she could see that he did in his eyes.

Of course, she wouldn't do it. Instead, she grabbed a bar of soap from the little closet in the narrow hallway, then slapped it into his hand. "There you go. Soap."

"Thanks, sweetheart." He planted a chaste kiss on her cheek then turned away.

Wishing he'd forgotten chaste and done the job right had her frowning at his back. "You ought to come with your own warning label, Weston."

"Glad to hear it." He gave her a grin she should want to smack off his face.

That she found it adorable and charming infuriated her with herself. She was blowing their Fling Rules again already.

Just before he slipped back into the bath, he dropped the towel, exposing his backside. She gasped instinctively.

He laughed, and closed the door. "Sorry."

"Sure you are." She frowned at the white wood. "Make that a 'Wicked Man' warning label, Weston."

"We nerve doctors are far too conservative for wicked, Annie."

The man oozed sensuality: smelling as tempting as sin, moving like a sleek, surefooted cat. And he'd done everything humanly possible to lure her into a sensual fog. Smoldering looks, little unnecessary but oh-so-delicious touches. Too conservative? Ha! "The heck you are."

"Truly." He cleared the lingering remnants of laughter from his throat. "It's a good thing I trust you, or I'd have to insist you come in here with me."

How could he trust her? She didn't trust herself. Not when it came to him. She wanted to abide by their rules, knew she should abide them, but, from her physical and emotional reactions to him, she had serious doubts she could do it. That too was his fault, and she positively refused to feel guilty about it.

"You did give me your word you wouldn't peek inside the box, right?"

"Technically, no. I didn't." She paused for a second, thoroughly enjoying wrinkling her nose at him even though he wouldn't see it—unless she goaded him too far and he strode back out into the hallway nude. Gulping, she hastily added, "But I will."

"Will peek? Or will give me your word you won't peek?"

"I won't peek."

"Don't sound so put upon. You were going to peek and we both know it."

"I was not." She glared at the door.

"Yes, you were. You always have."

He remembered. Her heartstrings suffered a fierce tug, and she leaned back against the wall, needing its firm support. Bags or boxes, and wondering what was inside them, always had intrigued her to the point of insanity. He used to tease her by bringing a sack into the apartment and putting it on the bar. Maxine had found the teasing cute. And Anne never had failed to eventually give in and look to see what was inside, at which point Adam would chide her, and—She grimaced. He knew her too well. "Okay, I was," she confessed, pretending to be irritated when she felt anything but.

"Of course you were, darling," he said, interrupting her thoughts. "But now I expect you to keep your promise."

Darling. She might just melt. "All right, Adam." Warmed from the heart out, she turned toward the bedroom, half smiling, half grumbling.

It was a welcoming room. Spacious, with a long dresser and mirror on the west wall, a king-size bed draped with a soft teal bedspread, fluffy pillows, and natural wicker nightstands flanking the matching headboard. A candle burned on each of the stands and, though it was far too warm to light a fire, logs lay stacked in the glass-front stove tucked into the corner. A patio door that led out onto the deck took up nearly all of the south wall, and Anne wondered. How many couples had lain in bed, gazed out the window onto the moonlit gulf, and whispered their lovers' secrets, their hopes and dreams? Would she and Adam be one of them?

Fear and longing blended with guilt, resentment, and desire, then hit her all at once. Weak from the onslaught, she clenched her hands and pivoted her gaze to the ceiling. "You're in deep trouble here, Anne. Deep trouble."

Above the bed, a ceiling fan's paddles whirled, softly thumping, and the room's subdued colors of peach, a tranquil green, and an almost opaque blue soothed her. Adam had made the bed, and turned down the covers. Thinking of what could happen in it had her hot and cold, yearning, and fearing she'd disappoint him.

She turned away, saw his clothes hanging in the closet. He'd stowed his suitcase, too.

Unpacking her own things rated far wiser than filling her head with fanciful thoughts that knotted her stomach and set fire to the rest of her. She squatted down to the floor, then unlatched her case. It snapped open.

Nearly empty? How could it be *nearly empty?* A slinky lemon sheath. A diaphanous white nightgown that might as well be Saran Wrap film. And a minuscule black bikini. That was it? *Where the heck were her clothes?*

Surprise faded to suspicion, and she groaned, then cursed. "Damn it, Janese!"

And tucked into the black bikini, Anne found a note from her interfering sister.

Fling Rules require ammunition, dear heart.

Fire at will!

Love,
Janese

Wadding the paper in her fist, Anne vowed. "I'm going to murder you. Just as soon as I get home. No jury in the world would convict me."

"You look beautiful."

"I feel like a damn fool, Adam." Anne frowned across

the deck's candlelit wicker table at him, resisting an urge
to tug at the hem of her dress.

"Janese didn't mean any harm. She just has a flair for
the dramatic."

"When I get home"—Anne jabbed the air with her
fork—"she's going to have a knot on her head."

A smile tugged at the corners of his lips. He dragged
a boiled shrimp through a spicy horseradish sauce, then
popped it into his mouth. "I like it."

"You're not going to spare her scalp. She's gone too
far this time, and that's that." Anne looked through the
darkness to the surf she couldn't see but could hear, then
plucked at the lemon sheath clothing her. "There is no
back to this contraption, and not much of a front. And if
it were half an inch shorter, I'd be arrested for indecent
exposure."

He laughed, and began apologizing for it in nearly the
same breath. "All right, sweetheart. We can fix this." He
wiped his hands on a napkin, slid back his chair, stood
up, and then began unbuttoning his shirt.

"You're not going to sidetrack me by stripping, Adam
Weston. And I mean it."

"I wouldn't dare to deprive you of your snit, darling."
The last button came free from its hole and the shirt
gaped, exposing his chest. "Even if you do have to look
away—to keep from getting sidetracked."

"I'm sure this is extremely amusing from your point
of view, but I'm not at all good-natured about her swiping my clothes, Adam. She even stole my damn toothbrush." Anne risked looking up to make sure he wasn't
still smiling and her gaze riveted on his bare chest. Big
mistake. Her throat went tight. God, but he was gorgeous.
Perfectly sculpted.

"I got you a new one." He came around the table,
draped his shirt over her shoulders, then pressed a kiss
to her nape. And then another, warm, wet, lingering one
to her neck. An enticing third followed, to the soft spot
behind her ear. "And just so you understand, I'm not

amused by anything that makes you uncomfortable.''

As tender as ever. Too tender by half. "Thank you.''

"Any time.'' He raked her earlobe with his teeth, his spicy breath fanning her face, her neck, then he returned to his seat.

Trapped somewhere between sizzling and melting, Anne finished dinner, certain this fling with him was doomed. He meant too much to her; this couldn't be just physical. And it being anything more violated the terms of their agreement. A sickening feeling spread like hot lead in her stomach. What was she going to do?

Adam began clearing the table. Anne helped him. When they were done, they returned to the deck with fresh glasses of wine. A radio from the kitchen piped soft, dreamy music through speakers onto the deck, and lights from distant boats out in the gulf twinkled.

Sitting side by side in the Adirondack chairs, Adam stretched out his legs then crossed them at his ankles. Bathed in tawny candlelight and that cast down from the sickle of moon, his bare chest taunted her.

"Are you content, Anne?''

Loaded question. The gentle breeze tugging at her hair, she looked down at the wine, swirling in her glass. "Most of the time.''

"Really?'' His head lolled back, he cranked open one eye.

Why bother lying? They knew each other too well, respected each other too much. "No.''

"Me, either.''

"I want to be.'' She glanced his way from under her lashes. "I even thought I was for a while, but I'm . . . not.''

"Same here. A successful career just isn't enough.''

That truth stung. It'd taken a long time to accept it, but she'd known it on a lot of levels for what seemed forever now. "It appears that it's not.''

"We were such smart-asses back in college, weren't

we?'' He laughed, but there was no humor in it. ''We thought we had life all figured out.''

''We *did* have it figured out.'' A bug buzzed near her ear. She swatted at it. ''Back then.''

''So what changed?''

''We did.'' She leaned back to stare at the stars and picked out the Little Dipper first, just as she always had. ''Having a successful career was all we wanted then. Now, that success alone just isn't enough to fulfill us. We want . . . more.''

''What would be enough?''

Something in his tone tugged hard at her. She gave him a sidelong look, but he too was stargazing, his chin lifted to the sky. Still, even not looking into his eyes, she didn't dare to be honest about this. He really didn't want honesty. He wanted to be talked into being satisfied with what they had. She knew that as well as she knew the roar of the surf was constant and endless. She knew, because she felt that way, too. ''I don't know.''

''Me, either.''

They'd both lied, and they both knew it. Survival instincts had kicked in, and Anne was grateful they had. This was a weekend. No more, and no less.

''Do you want to find out, Annie?''

Did she? Her heart screamed, *yes*, but her logical side shouted, *no*. At odds with herself, she gave him the only answer she could give him. ''I'm not sure. Do you?''

''Maybe.'' He gripped the arm of his chair and rubbed at his temple. ''I think we're going to have to decide.''

Oh, but she feared him right. Her insides felt as stable as gelatin. ''Not yet.''

''No, not yet.'' He looked over at her, his eyes serious. ''Dance with me?''

She nodded, set down her wine, then took his outstretched hand and stepped into his arms. Their bodies fitted together, aligning, and she rested her head against his chest, then let her fingertips drift over his warm skin.

How many thousands of times had she dreamed of being held in Adam's arms?

He let out a content sigh that flooded her heart with joy and, knowing it would be wise to diffuse some of their turbulent emotions, she teased him. "Neurologists aren't supposed to be so fit." The man was hard all over.

"They're not?" Swaying in rhythm with the soft ballad, he looked down into her upturned face.

"No. They're supposed to be flabby and soft and stooped—from all those hours of being locked in surgery. And they're not supposed to be tanned, either." His skin looked like sun-washed bronze, far too natural to have been acquired on a tanning bed.

A frown furrowed his brow. "Are you complaining about my looks, Annie?"

"Damn right, I am." She feigned a grunt, and let him see the longing in her eyes.

He rubbed her fingertips with his thumb. "I love it when you're grumpy."

What he loved was her finding him attractive, and she couldn't be miffed about that because she loved knowing what she thought mattered to him. "You hate it."

He stopped dancing, held her to him, let his hands slide down her back to her hips. "I don't hate anything about you."

The breeze, warm and sweet, lazily swept over their skin. "I don't hate anything about you, either."

He rubbed the tips of their noses. "I'm glad."

"I'm not sure." She'd known it on their first kiss, and everything since then only had reinforced her fears. If she listened to her body, she'd be in bed with the man now, but her heart and mind agreed that she'd be breaking every single one of their rules. They needed to discuss this, to get it out in the open before someone— namely, her—got hurt.

She let her hand glide up then down his arm. "Adam, it's not going to work between us, is it?"

A cloud slipped in front of the moon and a shadow

sliced across his eyes. "The summer fling?"

Not at all surprised that he intuitively deduced her meaning, she nodded.

He looked down, letting her see the tangle of things he was feeling. "No, Annie, I'm afraid it's not."

Tears threatened her throat, stung the back of her nose, and she swallowed hard. She'd have to live with regret after all. With never knowing what loving him would have been like.

"Sex would have been safe," he said, then dropped his voice a notch. "But we both know, we wouldn't be having sex. We'd be making love."

They would. She tightened her arms, looping his waist, hating the distance between them, and having no idea how to span it. "And then we'd convince ourselves we're in love and—"

"That would produce complications and dilemmas neither of us want nor need." He eased his hand under his shirt, then wandered from her shoulder to her bare back.

"Yes, it would." His fingertips grazing her skin aroused delicious tremors, and she had to remind herself to breathe, to fight for coherent thoughts. "We have successful careers and lives. Success isn't enough, but neither one of us wants to walk away and lose that, too. We don't want to start over with nothing."

He flattened his warm palm on her back, drew her closer still. Breasts to chest, he tilted her face with a thumb to her chin. "We're independent."

"Yes." Feeling fluid, she looked at him through heavy-lidded eyes, wishing he could just absorb her, or her him. "And we like being independent."

Adam searched her face, her eyes, then touched light butterfly kisses to her temples, her eyelids, the tip of her nose. "We love it," he whispered thickly, his erection pressing hard against her belly. "Which is why we'd be smart not to sleep together."

Relieved and disappointed, Anne nodded. Making love

would definitely breach Fling Rules. So why didn't she care? Why did she want to be reckless and fickle and to sleep with him anyway? It wasn't just physical. It'd simplify matters if it was, but it wasn't, and she couldn't pretend otherwise. "Do you think we're going to be smart?"

"I think we should do our best to be, unless. . . ."

Not at all sure asking was wise, she prodded him. "Unless?" She shouldn't have pushed. God, why had she pushed? She would have been so much better off to have just left the question alone.

He melded their chests and thighs, splayed his fingers low on her back. "Unless we're ready to finish what we start."

Life-altering. It was happening too fast. They were getting in too deep, too quickly. "We're not ready, Adam, and we know we're not. We're different people now."

"Logical, but I don't think logic is going to help us much, Anne." He let his hand skim down her side, rib to hip. "I think we're doomed to hormones and hearts."

Unfortunately, she agreed. "We need to cool down, to start thinking with our heads instead."

"Let's give it a shot," he said, though his expression directly conflicted with his words. He clearly didn't hold much hope for success.

"Okay." She pulled back, creating distance between them, then changed the subject. "Do you like parades?"

"I live in Parade Central," he reminded her, sounding as relieved as she felt, and again moving to the music. "Love them."

"Mardi Gras in New Orleans is something else," she said, tempted to kiss that bit of skin between his collar and neck. "There's a parade here tomorrow. Downtown." She settled for caressing the spot with her thumb. "It isn't as grand as the ones you're used to, but it should be fun."

"With you, it can't miss." He squeezed her gently. "I don't want to wait, Annie."

Instinctively she knew he meant he didn't want to wait to make love and, knowing it, thickened the provocative haze of being in his arms. She stepped closer, and nuzzled that spot near his collar with the tip of her nose. "First, I have to buy some clothes."

"Not to please me." His gaze warmed and enticing silver flecks glittered in the depths of his irises.

Tingling head to toe, Anne flushed from the bone out, and shifted in his arms. "The things you make me feel with a simple glance should be illegal."

"Glad to hear it." He dipped his chin and stroked the cove of her neck. "I'd hate to think I'm going through all this alone."

Her heart lurched and her knees seemed to turn to water. She leaned more heavily on him, sure as certain that if they were going to get past their hormones and hearts and physically abstain until they could commit to finishing what they started, then they'd better stay out of the cottage. The intimacy and electricity between them carried a megawatt charge, making it highly unlikely either of them would remember the wisdom of good intentions and logic. When Adam had been nowhere in sight, temptation had proved unrelenting. But with him this close, she didn't stand a chance against it. Oh, yes. They'd be far wiser to immerse themselves in crowds. So why in the world did she want, more than her next breath of air, to be foolish?

He dragged his fingertips up her spine to her shoulder. She shivered.

"Cold?" His chest rumbled against her breasts.

"I'm afraid not." Oh, how she wished she were cold. Wished she were doing anything except refusing to bet herself even a nickel that their Fling Rules would survive the night.

Chapter Four

Police barricades detoured ten blocks of downtown traffic, allowing only pedestrians access. Vendors lined both sides of Main Street, displaying cases of pewter jewelry; shelves of pottery, slung by local high school students; oil and watercolor paintings by local artists; and a menagerie of craft items. On the seventh block, booth after booth offered the crowd oysters, crab, fried fish, shrimp, and crawfish; french fries and hush puppies; lemonade, colas, beer, and frozen strawberry daiquiris.

Sitting at a concrete table beneath a canopy of moss-draped oak limbs, Adam looked over at Anne and groaned. "God, honey. No one eats strawberry sno-cones and raw oysters simultaneously."

"They do now." Anne swallowed the last oyster, then slid Adam an evil grin.

He smiled indulgently, the wind teasing his hair. "You should be a little more sympathetic. Six feet of man on five feet of sofa doesn't do wonders for a nerve doctor's attitude."

"You need therapy." Suppressed laughter brimming in her voice, Anne stood up and extended a hand to him. "A walk will fix you right up."

"Not exactly the kind of therapy I had in mind, but it'll do—for now."

Flushing, Anne skirted around someone dressed in a

sparkling sequin "Uncle Sam" costume then fell into step with Adam, pleased he'd shortened his stride so she could easily keep up with him. Stabbing at her sno-cone with the straw, she sipped at the strawberry nectar. "You still haven't told me what's in the white box."

Twirling his sunglasses between his forefinger and thumb, he glanced over at her, the skin beneath his eyes crinkling against the glare of the sun. "I haven't, have I?" he asked, positioning the glasses on his nose.

Baiting her. Again. She grunted. "You're a wicked man, Weston. Down to your toenails."

He curled an arm around her shoulder, then hauled her to his side. "And you love it."

"I guess I do." Their hips bumped, and feeling his body heat, a memory flashed through her mind. One from the last morning she'd been roommates with Maxine.

The movers had cleared all of Anne's things from the apartment and, on her last look around, she'd double-checked her empty bedroom for forgotten articles. On the bare floor, she'd seen a long-stemmed white rose.

No card.

No note.

Only the rose.

Adam had put it there; Anne had known it, just as she'd known that regret and resignation had fueled the choice they'd been compelled to make about their relationship. They had to either acknowledge their love and forfeit their self-respect, knowing that doing so would tear them apart, or to deny their love and retain that respect. Lost and lonely and empty inside, Anne had sat down on the floor, curled her knees to her chest, and rocked back and forth. She'd cried, long and hard, holding the rose petals against her cheek, letting them absorb her tears until there were no more tears. And, knowing she didn't dare to take the rose with her, didn't dare to keep the memory of what couldn't be alive, she'd left the flower there, on the carpet.

Many times, she had regretted that. With what had

come afterward—a total separation for five years that did nothing to diminish her thinking of Adam—she could have taken the rose with her. But she hadn't realized then that it wouldn't matter. That, either way, she wouldn't stop thinking of him or caring for him. She couldn't have realized that then.

"Anne?" Adam stopped at one of the booths and pointed at a keg. "Want one?"

"No, thanks." Beer and sweet strawberry nectar didn't sound at all appealing. Neither were her memories. They'd done the right thing. So why doubt their decision now?

A family of clowns snagged her attention. They passed out miniature plastic American flags on sticks, drawing a large group of parents and kids. Center-circle, the clowns entertained everyone with amusing antics, and the sounds of laughter grew loud. Bright orange, electrified hair, size fifteen shoes, red bulbous noses; if Adam had an ounce of compassion, he'd look like one of those clowns for a while and give her senses a break. So attuned to him, she noticed every inflection in his voice, his every nuance and expression. The strong set of his jaw when he was determined, the laugh lines on his face that only were visible when very close. The smell of his skin—a hundredfold more enticing than his cologne. And even his habit of looking away when a topic in the conversation cut too close to the bone.

But the man had no compassion whatsoever. He taunted her. It seemed second nature to him, as if him teasing and tempting her happened unaided, automatically. How could something so alien to her seem so natural to him?

She let her gaze drift to the man serving the beer from behind a long plywood table. The mermaid on his T-shirt advised readers to "Fish Naked," and his dark sunglasses sported lime green Croakies. He pushed down on the beer keg's spigot and looked at the woman working at the next table. "Sally, you guys gonna watch the fireworks tonight?"

Melanie, the cottage owner, had told Anne there'd be a spectacular fireworks display from a barge out in the Gulf at midnight.

"Wouldn't miss it," Sally said.

Adam paid for his beer, then sipped at it. Tiny bubbles of foam speckled the right lens of his sunglasses. "Want to head to the beach?"

Ready for a little quiet and a little space from the jovial crowd, Anne nodded. "We'll have to watch the fireworks from the deck at the cottage tonight. It'll be gorgeous. No lights from town competing with the sparkles."

"Sounds good to me." Adam stepped off the wooden pier and down onto the sand. "The deck's got to be more comfortable than the sofa." The wind clipped his shirt collar, lifting it.

Anne smoothed it back down. "Would you quit griping about the blasted sofa? I refuse to feel guilty about you sleeping on it, Adam. Remember, I did offer to share the bed."

"Yes, you did." He clasped her hand, then pressed the back of it to his lips. "But we couldn't promise to behave."

Wishing he'd taken off his sunglasses so she could see his eyes, she shrugged. "I figure our odds were fifty-fifty."

"You're generous." He bent down and removed his sandals. They dangled from his hand by the straps. "Or else you have no idea how you affect me."

How could she not know? Anne grabbed his arm and removed her shoes. "I trust you."

"Don't."

Now why did that remark have her smiling up at him when she should be scared stiff? On second thought, maybe she was better off not wondering about that just now. His heated breath still warmed her hand—and far more than the skin he'd touched.

"Another night on the sofa and I'm going to need a physical therapist."

Was this his back-door way of telling her that he was prepared now to finish what they started? Couldn't be. "Magic-Fingers-R-Us." Anne wiggled her fingertips at him. "At your service, Mr. Weston."

He flashed her a sexy grin. "Hold that thought, darling."

Anne ditched her sno-cone cup in a trash barrel that was doing double duty as an anchor for a huge balloon shaped like a firecracker, then returned to Adam. They linked hands and walked down the edge of the curling surf, talking about nearly everything and nothing, and watching the sun sink low in the sky.

When it dipped down nearly to the horizon, they stopped and sat down in the sand, back to back and knees bent. For the past two hours, they'd watched fishermen check their traps, skiers slice through the water, artists compete in a creative sand sculpture contest. They'd laughed and teased and talked nonstop, but neither of them had mentioned altering their Fling Rules. Actually, both had avoided that topic as if it carried plague, and Anne wasn't sure how she felt about that. She should be happy. And maybe she would be, if she weren't bombarded with smoldering, sensual input with her every glance at Adam. The man had the hottest eyes and the sexiest mouth she'd ever seen. Simply put, logic fought a good fight and fell hard. Hearts and hormones triumphed.

"Did you like the parade?" Adam stared over his right shoulder at the sparkling water.

"I did. Especially the Air Force marching band." Anne lifted her lashes to look at him. He was smiling. How she loved Adam's smile. It warmed her from the inside out.

"You liked seeing all those men in uniform."

"That, too." She rocked, bumping her back against his. "What did you like best?"

"The clowns." He dragged a fingertip in the sand, drawing something. "When I was a kid and we went to parades, I always loved the Shriners in their little cars best. I guess I still do."

Letters? Doodles? What was he drawing? "Mmm, and what about the baton twirlers?"

"Annie," he chided her. "Those girls are just kids."

"True. But the Fishing Rodeo Queen sure wasn't." She swallowed hard and looked from the sand to the surf. He'd drawn a cracked heart. God help them both.

"Do I hear a sliver of envy in your voice?" He turned toward the water to look at her.

"Envy? Me?" If it stained skin she'd be appropriately costumed for St. Patrick's Day. "I don't think so," she lied. "But it is kind of absurd, watching you drool, Adam."

"I didn't drool."

Anne buried her toes in the warm sand, digging down until it turned cool. "You wanted to drool."

He pivoted and fitted Anne between his thighs, then rested his chin in the cay of her neck. She leaned back against his chest and looped her arms over his bent knees, flanking her hips. "If I drooled," he whispered low, the tip of his nose brushing her ear, "it was for you." His hand drifted down from her waist to her thigh, then settled against her bare, sun-heated skin. "I love those shorts, Annie."

"You love my legs," she corrected him, sounding shamefully smug.

"Mmm, I do." He splayed his fingers and nibbled at her nape.

Little bursts of pleasure rippled through her body. In a near drool herself, she tensed against them. "You're doing it again, Adam."

"Driving you to distraction?"

Now he sounded smug, and as if he were honestly trying to hide it. "Don't play innocent, Weston. Fling Rules—"

"Okay. Sorry." He gave her neck a final throaty growl, then put his hands back at her waist.

"Sure you are," she chastised him. Her senses filling with the scent of his skin, his Obsession, his body heat, she closed her eyes and arched her neck, giving him greater access.

"I had to say good-bye, Annie. I wouldn't want your neck to feel abandoned. Good-byes always should be handled face to face, don't you think?"

"Face to face. Always." Her entire body felt abandoned—and on fire. But she didn't dare to douse the flame. "Consider the job done, then."

"Can't handle the heat, sweetheart?"

"I can." She gave him a siren's smile and arched her back to rub against him. "Can you?"

A shudder shimmied through him. "You're a heartless woman." He clicked his tongue, but his eyes twinkled. "I'm seeing a whole new side of you."

"And you're loving it."

"True. Especially your modesty."

"Oh my, yes." She bit the smile from her lips, dragged her fingertips from his knee to his hip. "And I'm so humble. Don't forget that."

He flicked a curl away from her face and stared at her lips. "I think you're punishing me for tempting you."

"That, too." She shrugged. "Fair's fair."

The teasing lilt in his voice died. Sadness replaced it, and a faraway look came into his eyes. "Very little to do with us has been fair, Annie."

It hadn't. "No, but we survived." The weight of that truth smothered her lighthearted feelings, and she went quiet.

They sat there, staring out onto the water, silent and still and lost in deep thoughts of all the things they'd never share. Memories they would never create, never have to comfort them in their twilight years. They wouldn't be together. Wouldn't have children. Wouldn't share their lives, their joys and sorrows, or their love.

And watching the sun spangle the water, the curls of froth and foam constantly creep ashore, then recede, Anne feared that they'd never even know life's greatest joys. Never know fulfillment. Or be content. Apart, how could they? How could she?

When the last traces of twilight faded to darkness, Adam helped Anne to her feet. With gentle swipes of his hand, he brushed at her calves, her thighs, her bottom. The fine grains of clinging sand splattered on her feet, lightly stinging.

"Thanks." She tried her darnedest to sound normal, but failed. Her heart felt ragged, her spirit wounded. And she hurt in places so deep inside she couldn't say where exactly they were, only that they ached, left her feeling hollow. Isolated. Empty.

He clasped their hands, and they walked back to the cottage.

How in the name of heaven she was going to sleep tonight—any night—knowing she would never love another man as she loved Adam? Knowing that this night he'd be one room away on the sofa he hated? Knowing that for the rest of her life she would regret not making love with him? How?

She had no idea. But she couldn't, wouldn't, go through another night like the last one. Asleep or awake, all her thoughts centered on him. But despite their teasing, she well knew if Adam had any inkling of the path of her thoughts, he'd be in his Porsche in ten seconds flat, speeding toward New Orleans, getting away from her.

And then she'd be even more devastated than she'd been six years ago. Much more devastated. Because, in losing him now, she knew more of what she'd be missing.

"Hurry up, Anne. It's five minutes until midnight."

"All right." Anne stepped back out onto the deck, flipped off the light inside the cottage's kitchen, then shut the patio door. "Don't have a cow, Weston. I was just getting some more chips." She dropped the bag on the blanket, right by Adam's shoulder, vowing she'd never admit she'd been cooling down again. Adam, wearing only swimming trunks, left too little to the imagination.

He looked up, let his gaze rove over her, head to toe. "Nice bikini."

His gaze was hot, and feeling her body flush, she grunted. "This scrap of a swimsuit hardly qualifies as a bikini. It's more like a G-string with an attitude." She pulled at the front of his shirt, closing it over her breasts, then sat down beside him.

Stretched out, he rolled over onto his side, and pulled her back against him, snuggling her hips against his stomach. "Careful, Annie. I'm getting used to you snitching my shirts."

"Complain to Janese. She stole my clothes."

"Janese, I'll thank." He ran his hand up under the hem of the shirt to her bare back, around her side, then over her ribs. "To you, I'll complain."

She looked down at him. "What for?"

"Two reasons." He lifted his chin and moonlight spilled across his jaw. "First, I'm not convinced you don't love flaunting your body, tempting me. And I'm sure you like keeping me bare-chested. No, don't bother denying it, darling. I've seen how you look at me."

"Oh, I'm not denying it." She let her lids drop to half-mast, then gently scraped her nail over his nipple. "I do like looking at your chest."

Tension flooded his face and he tightened his hold on her. "You're still the same sassy bit of baggage you were in college."

He hadn't wanted her to be the same. Hadn't wanted to feel all those feelings for her now that he'd felt then. She understood completely. But he did feel them, and so did she. Should they celebrate, or mourn?

More than likely, they'd end up doing a fair amount of both.

He clasped their hands and pressed their palms flat. His tone turned serious. "I loved you, Annie."

"I know." Her chest went tight. "I loved you, too." Why did this have to hurt again now? After all this time, why couldn't it not matter anymore? *Why?*

"You never asked me why I didn't leave Maxine, or what happened to us."

"Maybe I didn't want to know." Anne looked away, afraid he'd see too much in her eyes. She hadn't wanted to hear that he'd loved them both. "It wasn't any of my business," she said softly, staring out into the night.

"I didn't love her, Anne." He let his hand wrap around her waist. "I thought I did then, but now I know I didn't."

"You had to love her." A burst of anger shot through Anne. Intense and raw. "Don't you dare tell me we threw away what we could have had for nothing, Adam. Don't you dare!"

"Don't ask me to lie to you. Please, Annie." Regret and recrimination laced his voice. "I wanted to love her. I didn't want to love you. You scared the hell out of me."

Anne rubbed at a dull throb in her forehead, not at all sure she understood anything anymore. Then the light dawned. "Maxine was safe. She didn't threaten your heart. Is that what you're telling me? That you stayed with her because you could control how you felt about her?"

"Yes." He looked out, over the surf.

Anne's emotions rioted. How could she feel anger and relief simultaneously? Joy and grief? Elation and guilt? It didn't make sense. "So why didn't you marry her?" She risked a glance back at him, and the pain etching his face nearly crushed her.

"I didn't love her. I thought that's what I wanted. I really did, Anne. But after you left, well, I couldn't make myself marry her."

He'd loved Anne as much as she'd loved him. Putting

herself in his place, she knew she wouldn't have been able to marry anyone else either. Valid or not, she'd have felt unfaithful. "So Maxine finally got tired of waiting and married your best friend."

He stroked Anne's arm with gentle sweeps of his fingers. "I guess."

"Don't you know?"

He looked down at the blanket, clearly wanting to avoid her eyes.

"Adam?"

No answer.

"For God's sake, Adam, you were with the woman for nine years. You had to ask her why she was marrying your best friend."

"I didn't." He rolled onto his back, then shielded his eyes with his arm. "I guess I'd just been waiting for her to go."

Anne twisted around and faced him. "You should have had the decency to tell her."

He lowered his arm from his eyes. "I never lied to Maxine. Never. Not once."

"All right. All right. I'm sorry for judging you." Anne calmed her voice, softened her tone. "I just find it hard to believe that, after all your time together, you didn't ask her why she was leaving you."

"Give her some credit, Anne. Maxine isn't a stupid woman. Don't you think she knew I didn't love her? Don't you think she knew I loved you?"

Anne gasped. "I never said a word. Not one word."

"I know you didn't, honey. Neither did I. Yet I knew you loved me, and you knew I loved you. It's arrogant of us to think Maxine wouldn't have picked up on it, too."

It was. Anne stilled, absorbing. But if Maxine had known the truth, then why had she stayed with Adam? Maybe she'd loved him, and she'd hoped he'd get over Anne. Logical. Possible. And maybe on seeing things weren't going to change, Maxine had accepted that Adam had no interest in marriage, and she'd moved on.

Adam lifted a hand midair then let it fall back down to his side without touching her. "Why did you ask me to come here?"

"You know the answer to that."

"I know only that we came for a fling we're not having. I don't know why you chose me." His fingers stilled on the nubby blanket. "Are you wanting to punish me, Anne?"

"Punish you?" Of all he could have said, that she hadn't expected. She frowned her confusion at him. "What for?"

"For not walking away from Maxine back then. For not walking toward you."

"Oh, Adam. No." Anne stroked his cheek, felt the rough stubble of his midnight shadow. "I understood. You didn't want to hurt her anymore than I did. It wouldn't have been right."

"Instead, I hurt you both." He clasped Anne's upper arms, his eyes anguish-ridden. "I never wanted to hurt you. I swear, I didn't. I'm sorry, Annie."

"We were young." She smiled, hoping to ease some of the strain between them. Adam was hurting, and so was she. He'd left her out of fear. Fear. And, as sorry as she was to have to admit it, that too Anne completely understood. "Besides, things worked out fine. We both have great careers and lives, right?"

He stilled his hands on her arms. His fingers seemed to burn her through the sleeves of his shirt. "Are you happy right now? I mean, being here with me?" He sounded so uncertain.

It tore at her heart. "Yes, I am." Tender, she dipped her chin and kissed him.

His lips were soft, enticing, welcoming, and, wanting to deepen the kiss, she pressed at their part with the tip of her tongue.

He held her back, separated their mouths, and touched his forehead to hers. "This isn't a good time, sweetheart," he whispered on a ragged sigh. "I want you too much."

He wanted her. *Wanted her.* Her heart felt too big for her chest. She laced their fingers, squeezed until their hands rested palm to palm. "You loved me, Adam, and I loved you. We never expressed those feelings. Just once," she whispered. "Just once, I want to show you."

He tensed, let out a groan. "We can't go back, Anne."

God, didn't she know it. She stroked his jaw, let her fingertips thread through his hair, smoothed a hand over the ridges and planes of his bare chest, down his center to cover his placket, the hard essence of him beneath it. "Then let's go forward. Just this once, Adam. Just for tonight."

Trembling inside, she wet her lips with her tongue, then again fused their mouths, kissing him deeply, lovingly, longingly, reveling in the feel of her hands on his bare skin, in the sure and gentle touch of his hands and mouth on her body. Reverent and greedy, scorching and soothing—oh, but he was good at this. So very . . . good at this.

Roman candles and bursts of colorful sparks exploded in the velvety night sky, kindling the magic ignited between them. The distant sounds of fireworks fell silent to the thrum of hearts beating in tandem, of blood roaring through their veins and, when neither could bear being parted a moment longer, they joined their bodies as they had joined their hearts.

Chapter Five

"It's dawn." Half-draped over Adam's chest in the big bed, Anne stared out the patio door to the Gulf and lazily stroked his calf with her toes. The sky lightened from violet to lavender tinged with wisps of pink and gold, and the sun lifted over the horizon.

Anne's heart sank below it. She and Adam had had their night together. Now it was over. And that he too stared out through the glass, his expression a study of abject misery, told Anne they'd made love, yes—three wonderful and gloriously enriching times that proved fantasy could dim to reality—but they'd also paid the price.

With reality's light comes its balancing darkness. And that darkness, in its own way, was as poignant and powerful and potent as their lovemaking had been. They both had lives, obligations and responsibilities, and people depending on them. People they couldn't let down, not without losing their own sense of self, their self-respect. So while they'd made love, and reality's light had shone blindingly bright, reality's darkness had proved equally strong. Had proved that this weekend had indeed been their summer fling.

"Yes." Adam tightened his arms around her, his tone mirroring all the anguish churning inside her. "It's dawn."

The sheet cool against her bare skin, she gripped his

arm, felt his muscles stiffen, and her heart rebelled. Six years ago they'd forfeited love because it'd been the right thing to do. They'd gone on apart, and had continued to do what was right. Why couldn't it be their turn now? *Why couldn't it ever be their turn?*

"Are you okay with this, Annie?" His chest vibrated against her cheek.

She heard his worry, his uncertainty. He didn't know what she expected from him but, like her, he knew what he was and wasn't capable of giving. She wasn't okay, but she'd endure hell itself to keep him from regretting what had happened between them. It wasn't their turn, would never be their turn, but they'd had last night. This weekend. She'd always treasure it, and she wanted him to remember it fondly, too.

"Annie?"

She hurt, and she would hurt for a long time—inside. After she got home. "I'm fine, Adam." Pushing aside the bunched sheet, she kissed his chest, over his heart, then forced a smile into her voice and rocked back to look up at him. "I guess we had our fling after all."

His fingers on her back went stiff, and he stared at her for a long moment. A hard glint flickered in his eyes and he masked his expression, shuttering his feelings from her. "I guess we did."

Had she said something wrong? No. That glint had to be relief, not resentment. Adam was distancing himself. Of course, that's what he was doing. Until now, being in his arms, in his bed, had felt so right. So perfect. Now, though he still held her, she felt suddenly alone. Closed off from him. And she hated it. God, how she hated it. "Why, Adam?"

He ignored her question, rolled out of bed, snatched up some clothes, then headed for the bath. "I need a shower."

Her heart shattered. Tears burned her eyes, and she blinked hard and fast. Nothing had changed. He'd wanted to make sure she understood that. And she had. His message had been loud and clear. Why hadn't he understood that she'd known it without being reminded? Why couldn't he have just continued to be Adam, the tender and thoughtful lover, the man she had loved and would always love, until they'd gone home? Wouldn't that have been soon enough to let her fantasy of them and forever die?

Evidently not. Anne sat up in bed and stared out the window at the brilliant sun mocking her. It was dawn.

They ate breakfast, packed, and straightened up the cottage with barely a word or a glance between them. The tension rattled Anne. Why were they tense? It was time to go home, and neither of them had suggested staying over nor meeting again. That should alleviate tension, shouldn't it? So why did she feel as if a two-ton weight bore down on her chest? Why did he look at her as if she'd wronged him? And why did her heart ache so much she doubted it could hold all that pain being inflicted on it without bursting?

In jeans and a pale yellow shirt, Adam walked into the living room, carrying his black suitcase. Never before, not even around Maxine, had his expression appeared so guarded.

"I've got to go, Anne."

Anne. Not *Annie.* "I know." She looked up at him, stared deeply into his beautiful eyes. Eyes she'd never tire of looking at, of dreaming into, if ever given the chance to look and dream. A flash of hunger flitted through their depths, then disappeared. Maybe she'd imagined it. Maybe she'd wanted so badly to see it that she had imagined longing for her there. She blinked, and checked again. But it was gone.

Adam hesitated, then dropped a kiss to her lips. He cupped her chin, his hand trembling. "We set the rules. A fling, not a relationship." He let her see his regret, his frustration. "But if I could—"

Her heart slammed into her throat. She palmed his hand on her chin. "What, Adam?"

He stared at her for a long moment, then let his hand slide down from her face to his side. "Nothing."

Her heart beat hard and fast. She should push him; her instincts screamed it. But she couldn't make herself do it. What would they gain? She could wish for more, want it, crave it, but she couldn't risk losing what small part of him she had by suggesting more. He'd turn away. Completely. She'd lose him. She'd loved him for six years. Knew innately she'd always love him. Only him. And because she did, she couldn't push. She had to let him walk away.

His knuckles white on the handle of his suitcase, he paused at the door, looked over his shoulder back at her. "I'll call."

He would. But it'd never be the same. Before this weekend, they had loved without knowing all they were missing. Now, they'd glimpsed what could have been. And that glimpse would taint what they'd had before, and what they could have after it. How could it not? And that left them stuck, unable to go forward or back to what they'd once been to each other. She dredged up her courage and pasted on a brittle smile. "For a nerve doctor, you do a good fling, Adam."

Letting out a little grunt, he smiled back. It didn't touch his eyes. "Yeah, well, you therapists make it easy, knowing all the right moves."

A bittersweet laugh gurgled in her throat, and she pecked a kiss to his cheek. "Be safe."

He nodded. "I will." Then he turned away, walked down the wooden steps, and out of her life.

Leaning against the doorjamb, she heard his Porsche roar to life beneath the cottage, saw him back out of the driveway, pass the "For Sale" sign, and then drive down the street until he disappeared from her sight.

He was gone.

Her eyes hot and dry, Anne woodenly turned off the air-conditioner, checked the locks on the patio doors in the bedroom and the kitchen, then took one last look at the deck where they'd watched the fireworks and had made love for the first time. Bruised and tender, she turned out the lights.

Their party was over. Adam had accepted it; she'd seen it in every line in his beloved face, in the tense set of his broad shoulders. And soon Anne would accept it, too.

Downstairs, she walked between the pilings, and remembered the white box. He never had shown her what was in it. "Hardly matters now," she told herself, then unlocked the Saturn and tossed her case into the backseat.

But it did matter. Everything that had anything to do with Adam mattered.

She jerked the car door open. Heat gushed out, stealing her breath. Smoothing down her floral skirt, she got in, then cranked the engine. She had to stop this. Had to accept that it was over. And she would accept it. Really, she would. She was a survivor. She'd hurt before and had gotten through it and, by God, she'd get through it again.

Right after she had herself a Class-A cry.

By the time Anne crossed the Mississippi state line, she'd cried herself out, cursed everything and everyone, including Cupid for his lousy timing, and Uncle Sam for having the audacity to celebrate independence when interdependence sounded so damn good and proved about as easy to grasp as a pipe dream.

She dragged herself out of the Saturn and into her apartment, weary to the bone and brokenhearted, blaming herself for being such a fool, and Adam for still being irresistible to her. He should have let himself go, become an arrogant jerk, or done something godawful. Instead, the sorry soul had become a more mature version of her personal vision of Mr. Perfect. She might just hate him for that.

Janese stood in the living room, holding a vanilla wafer in one hand and a half a glass of milk in the other.

She took one look at Anne and let out a moan that would cinch an Emmy. "Oh, geez. You're gonna kill me dead."

"Bank on it." Anne dropped her suitcase by the door. "Later. Right now I hurt too damn much. No way could I face ironing something black to wear to your funeral."

"Seriously?"

"Don't I look serious, Janese?" Anne slung her purse onto the sofa. Her keys jangled, spilled out onto the cushion.

"Oh damn, honey." Still holding the cookie and the glass, Janese hugged Anne. "Did he show up?"

Her perfume nearly knocked Anne to her knees. "Oh, yes. He was there."

"So you're gonna kill me for the clothes thing, right?"

"Wrong. I'm going to lecture you for that." Anne pulled away to give her sister a reprimanding look. "It was a cheap shot, Janese."

"But was it effective?" Her smug look said she knew Adam hadn't minded.

He hadn't, and remembering the warm look in his eyes then, knowing she wouldn't see that look again, sent another wave of pain pulsing through Anne. "It ticked me off."

Janese crunched down on the vanilla wafer. "Well, if he showed up, and the clothes thing was effective, then why are you going to kill me?" Her mouth dropped open and she sucked in a little gasp. "Oooh, it's the fear thing, right? Reality didn't measure up to the fantasy?"

Reality surpassed fantasy. Hands down. Anne's jaw trembled, and her vision blurred. She couldn't cry anymore. She just couldn't.

"Anne? Will you talk to me, for God's sake?"

"I don't want to talk to you."

"If you're going to kill me, you owe it to me to tell me why."

She plopped down into the overstuffed chair, then looked up at her sister, a tear trickling down her cheek. "Oh, Janese. M-My . . . f-fling . . . f-flopped."

Janese stared at her for a long minute, swallowed down a gulp of milk, then laughed.

"Did you hear me?" Anger roiled in Anne, burned like acid in her stomach. "Damn it, Janese. Stop laughing. Look at this face. Does this look like the face of a woman who wants to hear laughter?" She'd lost her ever-loving mind. Had to have. Janese never had been cruel. Or an idiot. So why was she laughing while Anne's heart was breaking?

"I'm sorry." Janese literally wiped the smile off her face, along with a couple cookie crumbs. "It just never occurred to me that you wouldn't realize. I mean, you're so smart about everything else, Anne. Seriously, you are. But when it comes to the heart—"

"Will you stop with this garbage and just get to the point?"

"Of course." She cleared her throat. "Naturally, your fling flopped."

Anne clenched her hands into fists, wadding her floral skirt against her palms. "Excuse me?"

Janese sat down on the sofa, then looked up at Anne with a clear blue gaze free of guile. "Honey, your fling couldn't not flop. You love the man. A woman can't have a fling with a man she loves."

That bit of wisdom hit her like a sledge. Love. So simple. So damn simple. She'd thought of feelings, but never love. Why hadn't she thought of love? More anger heaped onto the mountain of it already inside her. "Well, you might have mentioned *that* Fling Rule before you conned me into this, Janese. Damn it, you knew I had no experience with this stuff!"

"Don't be absurd. If I'd told you, or given you time to think of it on your own, you'd never have gone." She curled her feet up under her and licked the milk from her lips like a content cat. "Now, tell me what Adam said when you told him you love him."

Anne slumped back into the chair. She'd been manipulated and outmaneuvered, pure and simple. Bristling, she let her gaze slide to the floor. "I didn't tell him."

"What?" Janese sounded mortified.

"How could I tell him?" Anne lifted a hand then let it flop back onto the arm of the chair.

Janese stood up. Her toenails were wet; cotton balls had been stuffed between her toes. "I'm going to fix you a nice cup of Lemon Zinger tea," she said, walking to the kitchen on her heels, "while you tell me everything."

"Why should I?"

"Because you're hurting. Because I'm your sister, and I love you. And because you know if you don't I'm going to nag the hell out of you until you do. Why? Because I have a gut-wrenching feeling that you're being stupid again, and I'm dying to save you from yourself."

Janese went into the kitchen, and Anne began relating events. By the time she finished, Janese had returned with the tea and put the hot cup into Anne's hands.

"Makes perfect sense," Janese said. "So then you two very logically decided you couldn't sleep together because it wouldn't be sex, it'd be making love."

"Right." Anne inhaled the steam from her cup, smelling tart lemon and tangy orange. "But then when the fireworks started—oh, they were so beautiful without any lights around to interfere, Janese. Just burst upon burst of color, and showers of sparks that. . . ." She closed her eyes to remember, to again savor. "Well, it was magic. Like anything was possible. Even for me and Adam."

"And then the fireworks really started."

"Yeah." Anne sipped at her tea. It warmed her throat, and remembered sensations warmed the rest of her. "It was absolutely the most beautiful thing I've ever experienced in my whole life."

"So what went wrong?"

"Dawn."

"I'm sure that makes some kind of sense, but I don't get it. Dawn?"

"It came." Anne sighed, then set her cup on the table beside the phone. "I tried to reassure Adam that nothing had changed. He looked scared to death I'd bare my soul and start spouting talk of love and forever after. That's why I couldn't tell him I loved him. I do, and I wanted to tell him, but I just couldn't.''

"Well." Janese smoothed a hand down her sea foam green silk slacks. "You might be smart, sister dear, but you're also a damn fool.''

Anne grimaced. "Tell me something I don't know.'' She pointed a finger at her sister. "But part of this is your fault. I mean, he looked so good, Janese, and I kept hearing you inside my head saying what you did about me wondering what making love with him would be like. I knew things would be different between us after this weekend, and I'd never again have the chance to find out. And I didn't—'' She stopped suddenly, unwilling to go on.

"You didn't want to regret not knowing,'' Janese finished for her. "But you didn't jump his bones, did you, Sis?''

"I just told you—''

"You told me you made love with the man. That's not jumping his bones. Jumping bones is sex, dear heart. And it's just not in you to have sex with a man you're not in love with. I was so sure you'd realize that and tell Adam how you feel about him. But I underestimated you. Adam, too. I knew you two were blockheaded and blind, but I thought that in making love you'd get past it.''

"What the hell are you talking about?''

"I thought you'd make love, share your feelings, and finally do what you should have done six years ago.'' Janese glared at her and leveled her with a frown. "Instead, you're even bigger fools than I thought. I'm damn disappointed in you both.''

"You're *disappointed*?'' Flustered, Anne rolled her gaze ceilingward, swearing her sister needed some serious counseling. "You're the last person I expected would advise me to break Fling Rules. What prompted this big swing in your feelings?''

"You can't have a fling with a man you love. Damn it, Anne. You know that. Why didn't you remember it while the two of you were together?"

Why hadn't she? She opened her mouth to answer just as the phone rang. She stared at it, but didn't reach for the receiver, not sure if she'd be relieved or devastated that it wouldn't be Adam calling.

Janese stood up. "You need to get that. It's bound to be Adam." Then she walked into her bedroom and slammed the door shut.

On the third ring, Anne lifted the receiver. "Hello."

"Anne?"

Adam. Her heart swelled. "Are you home already?" He must have flown. He should have another hour's ride.

"Not yet. I'm at the Slidell exit. I just wanted to make sure you'd gotten home okay." He sounded miserable.

She felt misèrable. "I'm fine."

They chatted for a few minutes, and she reluctantly accepted that neither of them were going to do a thing to change their relationship, or to suggest anything different between them. Until now, in the corner of her heart where she hid her fantasies and deepest wishes, she'd harbored a sliver of hope that things would change. But not anymore. And for the first time in the year she and Adam had been talking again, the conversation felt uneasy. Stiff and stifled. He clearly didn't want to hear what she wanted to say, and she didn't want him to say what she most wanted to hear. Either way, and they'd be forced to act. And they'd lose.

"We're doing the right thing, Anne."

Anne, not Annie. She'd been right about that, too. Pain sank deep in her chest, and she squeezed her eyes shut. How could anything that hurt so much be anything but wrong? "Yes, I'm sure we are."

"Independence is right for us."

He wanted reassurance, to offer and to receive it. "Absolutely." Her voice shook with the lie. "It's the best of all possible worlds."

He hesitated, then blew out a breath that hissed through the phone. "But I won't regret what happened between us."

"Never." Her throat and chest went tight. She stared at the flowers in her skirt until they all blurred together. Damn it, she would *not* cry. Not again. Not anymore. "I've got to go."

"Me, too." A sad finality crept into his tone. "Goodbye, Annie."

And down deep in all those secret places of wishes and dreams and desires she knew this really was goodbye. The changes between them were irrevocable, permanent. Knowing she'd never again feel his hands on her face, his lips against hers; fearing she'd never again hear his voice on the phone, she mumbled the words she'd once said to him and had prayed she'd never have to say again: "Good-bye, Adam."

How in the name of God would she bear it?

For the next three days, Anne functioned. Focused on getting from moment to moment, from hour to hour. Even a single day seemed too long, too hard to deal with at one time.

Adam hadn't called. She'd known that he wouldn't and yet she'd still foolishly prayed for a miracle. But after she'd cleaned the apartment, pressed every single piece of clothing in Janese's ironing pile—which had Janese worried sick, and Anne disgusted with herself for not getting a better grip on her emotions without resorting to the dreaded drastic: domesticity—Anne still hurt. Yet she had accepted that there would be no miracle for Adam and her. That was progress, and she had to take it where she could get it. Even if the corner of the dinette now looked as empty as she felt.

She mopped the kitchen again, though it hardly needed it again so soon, wrote down a grocery list, then cleaned out the fridge.

"Okay," Janese said. "I've been worried, I admit it.

But now I'm terrified for you, Anne. Seriously."

Anne dumped a container of yogurt with an expired "sell by" date into the trash, then scoured the sink with pungent cleanser. "I'm fine."

"The hell you are." Janese glared at her, then softened her gaze to let Anne see her concern was genuine. "Look, honey. I know you're working through this thing in your own way. And that's fine. But I'm telling you, Anne, you start cooking and I'm committing to you to Memorial Hospital for mental evaluation. I'm your sister, and I can do that."

She could. Once. For thirty days. Anne positively, unequivocally detested cooking, but the temptation was there, and she'd be lying to herself if she denied it. "Desperate women do desperate things to get past the curve balls life hurls at them. But don't worry. I'm not going to cook."

"Good." Janese swung her purse strap over her arm. "I'm, er, going out for a while. But if you don't want to be alone—"

"Thanks, but I don't need a keeper. I really am fine."

Looking unsure, Janese studied her, then walked toward the door. More than anything Anne wanted to be alone, and her sister had picked up on that. Thank God.

"I'll be at Jay's if you need me, okay?"

Jay again? That was twice in five days. Love appeared imminent. "Okay."

Janese left and, relieved, Anne lay down on the sofa, then stared at the ceiling. A palm frond just outside the living room window cast a shadow on the white ceiling. A breeze made the shadow dance. It'd been easy enough to admit to Adam that her career wasn't enough to fulfill her anymore. That she wanted and needed more. But what she hadn't admitted was that she wanted that closeness and sense of being connected to someone special outside herself. She'd dated a lot, but she'd felt those special feelings only with Adam. Only for Adam. And a world full of cleaning and ironing and long hours of overtime at the hospital weren't going to change that. She'd always want that closeness and connection to him. Desperately. But Adam didn't want it and he wouldn't come to want it. Theirs was a lost cause.

She folded an arm over her stomach, her other over her forehead. Her eyes drifted closed and she remembered him at the cottage. Glimpsed them dancing on the deck, teasing and laughing. Sitting back to back on the sandy beach, talking as if they'd never run out of words. Eating sno-cones and raw oysters, and him sauntering out of the shower swathed only in a towel and asking her where he could find the soap, deliberately taunting her physically and emotionally with his body and that mysterious white box. Them making love on the deck beneath the stars and bursts of fireworks; in the big bed, beneath the whirling paddles of the ceiling fan where, in each others' arms, they'd cuddled and watched the coming of dawn. And on parting. That flash of hunger and longing for her in his eyes that might, or might not, have been no more than her own imagination. Earthy and elemental, sweet and hauntingly beautiful, that had all been real. The cottage had been real.

The cottage.

Anne snapped her eyes open. Of course. The cottage.

She couldn't have Adam and, for her, there'd never be another man like him, but she could keep her memories of him within reach. She could have that much. And she would.

She reached across the overstuffed chair, lifted the receiver, and then dialed the phone.

A woman answered on the fourth ring.

"Melanie, this is Anne Hayden. I want to buy the cottage."

Chapter Six

"Have you lost your mind?" Arms akimbo, Janese stared at Anne as if she'd sprouted two heads.

Why—*oh, why*—had she told Janese she'd bought the cottage? Stabbing a fork into her salad, Anne held a cracker midair. "Aren't you late for a date, or something?"

"I'm going." Janese's chest huffed up beneath a pale blue silk blouse. "But I'm warning you, this thing with you and Adam is the real thing. If you let him just walk out of your life without lifting a finger to stop him, you're a damn fool." Janese gripped the back of a chair, glared across the table. "Don't turn your back on forever. You'll regret it. I swear, you will."

The intensity in Janese's voice spiked into Anne's heart, and she innately knew that, at some point in time, Janese had turned her back on forever. And she regretted it. Was that why she dated so many different men now? Why she fell in and out of love so often? Could it be that she refused to allow herself to care beyond the superficial for any man because she'd been hurt? Or because, for her, there could be only one man—like Adam for Anne? "A damn fool," Anne repeated. "So you've said numerous times. But what you're forgetting is that this isn't just about me and what I want. It's about Adam too, and he doesn't want forever."

"How do you know that?"

"We made an agreement." Anne put down her fork, then lifted her hand. "I can't change the rules in the middle of the game. It wouldn't be fair."

"I know, I know. You have to stick by your word." Janese let out a sigh that ruffled the fine hairs clinging to her cheek. "But this isn't a game, it's your life."

"Janese, please, don't start again. We've been through this so many times it's become cliché."

"Yes, we have. But there's this thing about clichés, Anne. They get to be clichés because there's an underlying truth in them. One truth in particular comes to mind. All's fair in love and war."

"I'm not at war with Adam," Anne said. "Only with you."

Janese slid her a that's-debatable look, then snitched a cracker from the pack on the table. "Something else you still haven't accepted is worth mentioning here."

She glared up at Janese. "What?"

"The reason you bought the cottage."

"I bought it because—unlike my home these days—it's peaceful."

Janese crunched down on the cracker. "I could call you a liar, but I won't."

"Thank you so much," Anne speared a slice of carrot, "for that consideration."

Her shoulders slumped, and Janese walked to the front door. "Anne?"

"Mmm?" God, but the woman was exasperating.

"Will you just think about something for me?"

A quiet pleading in Janese's voice had Anne getting out of her chair and walking into the living room. Janese stood near the door, her eyes stretched wide, wounded. "I'll think about it," Anne said, then waited for Janese to disclose what exactly she'd agreed to think about.

"Flings and fireworks fizzle." Tears filled her sister's eyes. "But love never dies."

Janese walked out, then closed the door.

Anne just stood there, the words washing through her mind, echoing over and over again. Careers, patient loads, medical practices—none of that was more important. None of it.

Terrified but determined, she picked up the phone and dialed Adam's number. With her luck, he'd be on call tonight. If he was, then she'd just call him at the hospital. No excuses.

He answered.

"Hi, Adam." Her heart nearly stopped, then thudded like a jackhammer. "I thought I'd better check and see if you're still alive." It'd been two weeks since they'd talked. Two long, seemingly endless, weeks.

"I'm alive. More or less."

She sat down. "Business must be booming at the hospital."

"It is. I've been there more than at home."

"Exhausted, huh?"

"Yeah."

They talked about little nothings, and she settled into the chair, wondering how she could work the conversation around to say what she wanted to say without just dropping it on him like a bomb.

He dropped a bomb of his own. "I, um, thought we might go to the cottage for Labor Day, but when I called to rent it, the realtor said it'd been sold."

Anne sat straight up in her seat. "You called the realtor?" She sounded stunned but, Lord almighty, she was stunned.

"I take it you're not enamored with the idea."

"No, I'm—" She paused to catch her breath. "I just didn't expect this."

"I didn't either." A slapping sound carried through from the background, as if he'd whacked his thigh. "I guess the idea of a fall fling doesn't much appeal to you."

He'd tried to rent the cottage. He'd really tried to rent the cottage. For them. For Labor Day. Why? Anne wasn't sure if she should laugh or cry. What did it mean? "It appeals." She had to tell him. "I bought the cottage, Adam."

"You what?" Surprise riddled his voice, then it turned sober, suspicious. "Why?"

So I could go there alone and remember being with you. No, she couldn't tell him that. Hearing it would only make them both uncomfortable. "I like the relaxed atmosphere."

"But you wanted to call in a demolition crew."

Naturally, he'd remember that and call her down on it. "Only until we cleaned it up. Afterward, it was charming."

"Is that the only reason, Anne? The relaxed atmosphere?"

Anne. Not *Annie*. She told herself to forget that. To stop wanting it. "No," she admitted, half-wishing she'd lied.

He let out a groan that almost sounded like relief. "Look, we need to talk. Face to face. Can we meet somewhere?"

Face to face. At the cottage, he'd said that severances deserved to be handled face to face. He knew why she'd bought the cottage. He knew and, God help her, he wanted to sever things between them. Her lips felt parched. She wet them with her tongue. "I'm going to the cottage this weekend. If you like, you can meet me there."

"Fine. I'll see you Friday at four-thirty."

Anne hung up the phone then wrapped her chest with her arms. Her nerves were shot. Adam had to have figured out the truth.

She stared at the blank TV screen. Six years ago she'd lost him without so much as a whimper. Two weeks ago, she'd let him walk out of her life without even a token protest.

And he'd called to rent the cottage.

Primed for a fall fling ... until he'd learned she'd

bought the cottage. Then he'd done a one-eighty. Ready to bail out, he'd asked to meet, face to face.

The odds stacked high that he intended to make final a break between them. And she very well could lose him. She lowered her hands to the chair arms and curled her fingers into fists. But if she did lose him, this time, it wouldn't be without a fight.

Chapter Seven

Four-thirty and still no Adam.

Anne frowned at her watch, then shoved aside the living room curtains and looked down the street for the hundredth time. Why was she doing this to herself?

Maybe he'd decided a face to face finale wasn't essential, after all. Maybe he'd gotten tied up at the hospital. Maybe he'd gotten into an accident. . . .

A loud knock on the door jarred her, and Anne jumped. "Adam."

Swinging open the door, she stepped aside. Relief sluiced through her and, on its heels rode a different kind of fear: severance. "I was about to call out the National Guard."

"Sorry." He didn't smile. "I had a couple stops to make." Drifting down her length, his gaze warmed. "I see Janese packed your clothes again."

"Not this time." That flicker of hope reignited somewhere deep inside, and she refused to let the fact that he carried only that infernal white box and no suitcase douse it.

He didn't quite meet her eyes. Probably giving her time to absorb that he wasn't planning on staying. She gave herself a two-second lecture on courage and going after what she wanted, then pecked a kiss to his cheek, resolute. "I made some margaritas. Want one?"

"Sure." He stepped away from the door.

Gray slacks, not jeans or shorts. No sandals or sun-glasses. A crisp white shirt, still cool on the sleeve from the steady blast of the air-conditioning during the ride over. A tie, for God's sake. Gray and blue silk. Freshly shaven, and not one gorgeous strand of glossy black hair out of place. No, he wasn't planning on staying. And he'd come armed to the teeth for formality in leaving. Power clothes. I-mean-business clothes. Clothes that murdered her flicker of hope.

Anne stiffened her shoulders. She needed a moment to regroup, to remind herself of all the reasons she *should* change her entire future. Armed and dangerous herself in that backless, nearly frontless, lemon sheath he'd been so enamored with, she still feared she'd seriously miscal-culated. Maybe the black bikini would have been—

Oh, stop it! You love him, you idiot. That's the only reason worth changing a thing for, especially your life. Bikini or dress, what the hell is the difference? Either he loves you enough to want to spend his life with you—making the changes he has to make—or he doesn't. It's as simple as that. As terrifying and as simple as that.

Her voice not quite steady, she looped her arm through his. "Let's talk out on the deck."

Outside, Adam sat down at the table, then put the white box on top of it, between them.

Anne passed him a salt-rimmed glass without so much as glancing at that blasted box, then took a seat opposite him. Sipping from his glass, he stared out onto the water. Just now, it shone a brilliant green, as fiery as a precious gem, which is why, she imagined, the area was called the Emerald Coast. From Adam's expression, he was a million miles away, and that hurt. He was distancing him-self emotionally. Already. Before the finale discussion even had taken place. Should she offer a penny for his thoughts? Was she that brave?

His chest lifted then fell, and he turned his gaze to her. "I thought you'd have this deck filled with plants by now. The apartment used to look like a jungle."

She smiled. "Give me two weeks." He didn't sound like a man of a mind to dump a woman who'd foolishly fallen in love with him twice. Yet something significant preyed on his mind. He had that look, as if he were wrestling with a weighty issue—and losing. It had to be severance. What else could it be?

His gaze lost focus. "I remember mostly that ficus. I used to swear it was an octopus."

"You nearly killed it, tripping over the thing."

"You kept moving it around."

"To keep you from running into it."

"I remember." He lifted his gaze from his glass to her. So steady. So serious. "You said they're very fragile, sensitive to touch."

"Aren't we all?" She downed a healthy swig of tangy margarita, her nerves strung so tight she had to release or explode. "I can't stand anymore of this, Adam."

"Me, either." He set his glass aside, leaned forward in his chair, then laced his hands atop the table and looked her straight in the eye. "Why did you buy this cottage, Anne?"

This was it. Coming out of the gate, they'd reached the point of no return. She stood up, began pacing the deck. Realizing she was wringing her hands, she made herself stop. Still, fear clawed at her stomach and *what-ifs* plagued her mind.

"Anne?"

She stiffened her shoulders and made herself look at him. "I'm probably going to goof this up, Adam, but, well, just don't say anything until I'm finished, okay?"

He nodded, radiating wariness. His fingertips clenched, bleaching his knuckles white.

"Six years ago," she began, "I fell in love with you. When we were here last, you admitted you'd fallen in love with me, too. I knew it inside, but hearing you say it meant a lot to me, Adam."

No expression change. No softening of the hard lines,

the sharp angles, of his face. "It couldn't work for us then because of Maxine. We know all that, and there's no sense in rehashing it now. We did what we had to do. And as much as it hurt, I still believe with all my heart that we did the right thing."

God, but this was hard. So hard. She paused to look out over the deck, to the steady ebb and flow of the tide coming in, curling on the sand. "When we came here, I thought we could have a summer fling and then go back to our lives. At least, I told myself I believed that. But, regardless of our responsibilities and obligations, that wasn't true." She turned to look back at him, steeling herself to see his condemnation of her in his eyes. "I lied to you, Adam. And I lied to me."

Shaking, she crossed her chest with her arms then rubbed them furiously. "I think I knew I was lying even then, but I didn't want to know it because I was afraid."

"Anne." He stood up.

She held out a staying hand. "No, please. Don't." She lifted her chin and met his gaze. "If you stop me, I'm not sure I'll have the courage to try again. Please, Adam. Let me finish."

He frowned, then lowered himself back into the chair.

Her heart pounded hard. "When we were here, we admitted that our successful careers just weren't enough. We weren't fulfilled." She walked across the deck and stopped beside his chair. "We were right about that." The stiff breeze blew her hair over her cheek, and she tilted her head, needing to see his face, his expression, his reaction, to what she was about to say. "You asked me then what would be enough, and I lied again.

"The truth is, I don't want to grow old alone, Adam. I don't want to sit out on this deck forty or fifty years from now and look at an empty chair beside mine. But I don't want just any man. I want to grow old with you. I want to see you in that chair. I want you in my life like you're in my heart."

"Anne, wait."

"Please!" Tears filled her eyes. "I know how you feel about your independence. I used to feel that way, too." She lifted a finger. "But I have to tell you once, Adam." She swallowed a sob. "Otherwise, when I'm old and sitting here alone, I'm going to make myself crazy, wondering if I'd had the courage to tell you, it would have changed things."

She backed up a step, looked down into his turbulent eyes. "I don't want to start over in my job. I don't want to leave my friends and the things and people who matter to me. I don't want to put my trust and faith in someone who has the power to hurt me." The fight seeped out of her voice, and a surge of tenderness rushed to the fore. "But I will, Adam. For you, I will. Because even more than I don't want those things, I do want you."

He sat there. So still. So quiet. Too many emotions flashing through his eyes to decipher them singularly. Afraid her knees would give out on her, she slid back onto her chair. "I-I'm finished now."

"I see." He rubbed at his jaw, a furrow creasing the skin between his brows, and leaned toward her. "Just so I understand, you bought the cottage because you love me, right?"

Hadn't she just told him that? "Yes."

He slid the white box across the table to her. "Open it."

Nervous, emotionally spent, she fumbled with the inserts to get the box opened, then looked inside. On a bed of shredded white tissue lay a rose, browned by age and time. The rose he'd left on her apartment floor, whose pure white petals had absorbed her tears. The rose she'd left lying there in her empty bedroom when she'd walked out of his life six years ago.

Her eyes clouded, and she lifted her gaze to his. "You kept it."

He nodded. "I love you, Annie. I've always loved you."

"Oh, Adam." He stood up and she flew into his arms. "I love you, too."

He lifted her to him and they kissed, branding, marking, claming, for the first time, holding nothing back. And when their fused mouths finally parted, the joy of loving and of being loved had seeped through to Anne's soul. A brilliant smile welled straight from her heart and curved her lips.

Adam smiled back, his eyes suspiciously moist. "If you'd peeked into that box during our fling, you could have saved us a lot of heartache."

She sniffed, and nipped at his neck. "If I'd known what was in there, I'd definitely have looked."

He kissed her again, then asked, "So will you?"

She loosened the loop of her arms around his neck so she could see his face. "Will I what?"

"You didn't read it?"

What in the world was he talking about? "Read, what?"

Without letting go of her, he grabbed the box, then pointed to some writing on the inner lid. "Will you marry me, Annie?"

"Good God!" Her heart skipped then thudded and skipped again. "I missed seeing *that*?"

"Ahem." He made a production of clearing his throat. "I'm dying here, waiting for an answer."

She cupped his face in her hands and punctuated her words with pecked kisses. "Yes. Yes. Yes."

"Thank God." Adam let his knees fold and fell back into the chair, pulling Anne with him, onto his lap.

She settled in, then smiled against his neck. Unless she was very much mistaken, her darling Adam, who never waded in unchartered waters much less swam in them, had a plan he wanted to share with her. And, in his arms, she was quite content to let him talk for hours. Days. Even weeks.

"I've been thinking we should both start over, Annie." He curled his arm around her, and drew lazy circles on her bare back with his fingertips. "I was late today because I met with the local hospital administrator. They're eager for another neurologist and a physical therapist here—if you want to do that."

Anne frowned against his neck. "You'd leave your practice?"

"You're leaving yours."

"Yes, but—"

"No, buts." He flattened his palm on her back. "I want us to grow in a life we've built together. For us. I love you, Annie."

They couldn't go back. But they could go forward. Different, and yet much the same. "Me, too." Anne dipped her chin, closed her eyes, and claimed his lips. Behind her lids, she again saw fireworks burst in a velvety night sky. With Adam, she always would. Content, she whispered a silent good-bye to her summer fling and joyfully embraced love.

ONE STAR-
SPANGLED NIGHT

Ashland Price

Chapter One

"You're going to love this vacation, Alison. I'm telling you, you're just going to love it! The hotel we'll be staying at is even said to be haunted! Isn't that great?"

Alison Kimball flopped back on her French provincial couch and scowled over at her longtime friend Molly Miller. "Haunted, huh! What a crock! Who told you that?"

Molly shrugged, not taking her eyes from the Williamsburg travel pamphlet she was perusing. "I don't know. The reservation-taker person at the front desk of the place, I guess. It's an 'inn.' You know, one of those Colonial American renovations, and the management claims it's sometimes visited by Revolutionary War ghosts. Isn't that cool?"

"Oh, don't tell me you actually believe that nonsense. You're a psychologist, for heaven's sake! You're supposed to know better. People pay you one hundred and fifty dollars an hour to help them separate fact from fiction, and you're going to sit there and tell me you're buying this 'quaint haunted inn' business?"

Molly straightened in her chair, the expression in her large brown eyes turning rather defensive. "I'll have you know that psychiatrists have been regressing patients back to past lives since the time of Sigmund Freud, and, if people can remember previous existences under hypnosis, it makes a very strong case for disembodied souls inhabiting two-hundred-year-old inns. Now stop being such a poop about this trip and start getting into the fun of the thing! It took a lot of juggling for me to clear my schedule for the next week, and if you spoil it with that relentless skepticism of yours, I swear to God I'll never speak to you again!''

Alison couldn't help flinching a bit at this threat. She'd known Molly for well over twenty-five years, ever since they'd met in the second grade, and Alison was well aware that Molly meant every word of what she'd just said. With a laid-back temperament, which would have made her as adept at teaching drivers' education as she was at counseling neurotics, Molly was rarely visibly riled; but she certainly was now, and Alison knew that she had to do her best to smooth things over.

''All right, look, maybe I haven't been the best of company lately. Maybe I really have let Stan and the divorce get to me more than I should. But I—it's not about you, Moll. I mean, it's not your fault that I'm not as enthused about this trip as I probably ought to be.''

As always, Alison's effort to match her friend's eloquence with some of her own had bombed terribly. But Molly, true ally that she'd always been, met this pathetic attempt at an apology with an understanding smile.

''That's the spirit,'' she praised. ''Just because Stan proved himself a total back-stabbing, money-hoarding sack of manure doesn't mean that his whole sorry gender doesn't deserve another chance. You don't want to displace that anger at your ex—now, remember, no transferring it to your old friend Molly, right?''

''Right,'' Alison agreed with a resolute nod. ''But please don't expect me to be a bouncing blow-up clown on this trip either. Okay? I haven't been on a vacation in ages. I don't have the nerve to try on the one swimsuit

I own, because I know I'm going to look like two tons of marshmallow creme in it. I can't imagine eyeing men again, to say nothing of letting them eye me in this— this gelatinous state I've fallen into.'' She gave her head a discouraged shake. ''I don't know, maybe Minnesota is and always will be the best place for me, since the cold weather gives us an excuse to be bundled from head to toe nine months of the year.''

''Oh, God, you're a whiner. You know that?'' Molly punctuated this by rolling her travel pamphlet into a long tube and raising it to her lips to serve as a mock megaphone. ''I'm telling you for the last time, Alison Kimball,'' she said loudly, ''you do *not* look fat in summer clothes. And you're not 'gelatinous.' And don't worry about not having a tan. If you hadn't spent the past several years of your life working double shifts at the hospital, you'd realize that no one bakes in the sun anymore. As you well know, it's far healthier to let yourself stay the color of marshmallow creme—your term, mind you, not mine,'' she concluded, dropping her rolled-up pamphlet to her lap.

That's easy for you to say, Alison thought. Molly possessed the sort of golden complexion that made her look like a professional tennis player year-round; whereas Alison's fair skin seemed to threaten to catch on fire after just a few minutes in the sun. ''Yes, you're right,'' she conceded nonetheless. ''I'm putting myself down again for no good reason, just like Stan always used to. I'm more than just a frumpy R. N. in white orthopedic shoes. Inside the body of this bill-paying drudge is a female libido waiting to have its fuse relit.''

''Well, we'll be celebrating the Fourth of July over our vacation, what better time for letting someone put a match to you?''

Alison laughed and shook her head in wonder at her companion's unflagging optimism. Molly Miller—for whom everything had always come so easily. Molly Miller—who had grown to a model's willowy height, had never had to diet, had been blessed with sleek, shiny blond curls and hadn't once battled the horrors of frizzy hair or cellulite-ridden thighs or finding herself tongue-tied with the opposite sex. Molly Miller—who had aced her way to a Ph.D. in psychology in far less time than it had taken Alison to become a garden-variety nurse. In fact, were Molly not her best friend, Alison was convinced that she would have grown to hate her beyond all belief.

"What is it?" Molly asked, apparently having noticed how her companion's amused expression had slowly sunk.

"What is what?" Alison returned innocently.

"What's the matter *now*?"

"Oh, nothing. It's just that it's going to be hard for me to put this whole nurses' aide battle out of my mind while we're gone. Just be glad *your* job security isn't being threatened by a pack of inexperienced, under-trained schmoes willing to work for minimum wage."

Molly threw back her head and issued a dry laugh. "The heck it isn't! The whole counseling industry is constantly giving way to every tarot-card reader and two-bit phone psychic who happens down the pike. Soothsaying was around long before we 'shrink' types came into being, so don't be telling me you're the only one with competition out there. Do you know how many patients I've lost to televangelists alone in the last few years? . . . Now stop worrying about the politics at that infernal hospital and start focusing on what a great time we're going to have in Virginia. I've been to Williamsburg and I promise you'll love it. Just wait until you see all those guys from the College of William and Mary dressed up in their fife-and-drum-corps uniforms. With those white knee socks and breeches and those black buckle-topped shoes they wear!" She unrolled her makeshift megaphone and started fanning her face with it. "Honestly, I get hot just thinking about them."

"Lord, you're shameless! College boys, no less. May

I remind you that we're practically old enough to be their mothers?'' Seeing how her friend scowled at this remark, Alison decided to amend it slightly. ''Well, their much-older sisters, in any case.''

''Speak for yourself, dearie. But the truth is that men have been dating younger women for eons, and you don't see them being criticized for it.''

''Since when are men our role models in life?''

''They're not. I'm simply pointing out that age is really just a number in the end. Once you crawl between the sheets with a younger guy, you'd be surprised how the generation gap melts away. Besides, most men are looking for a mother in their lover anyway. It's one of the tenets of psychology. And, since I'm looking for the oversexed variety of male, it's usually a pretty good match.''

''Well, you can do as you please on this trip. Heaven knows, you always do. But you'd better not try setting me up with some twenty-two-year-old! I'm only interested in the mature sort.''

''Yes, yes. The 'mature' sort. Like Stan, right? The kind of guy whose every mood is dictated by the rise and fall of the stock market. The sort who can't even walk out to get the morning newspaper without a cell phone planted in his ear.'' Molly paused to blow her a raspberry; her great animation with friends, she claimed, was the result of having to repress so many of her personal responses while with her patients. ''God, what a colossal bore he was. You can't tell me you're not just a little bit hungry for a more adventurous, lively type after six years of that.''

Alison sighed, then fell silent for several seconds, contemplating this question. ''I don't know. I'm not sure what I want anymore. Maybe just to change my name and my profession and get the chance to start all over somehow. Do you ever feel that way?''

''Are you kidding? With that parade of loonies I treat? Of course I do. You would, too, if half the patients you

saw spent the first five minutes in your office wiping
down your waiting-room magazines and the arms of the
chairs with moist towelettes for fear of 'catching germs'!
I mean, at least yours is a truly tangible profession. You
honestly know you've helped to ease some people's suffering at the end of each day. Whereas I'm not so sure
that all those Post-it notes I keep sticking on my patients'
wrists reading 'I won't die, if I leave my apartment' and
'Dating married men is self-destructive behavior' are
sinking in. . . . Look, have you ever gone without eating
for so long that you became almost nauseated with hunger?''

"Sure. A few times.''

"Well, that's how it is now for you and taking a week
off from your job. It's been so long since you have that
you're sort of repelled by the idea of it. But, believe me,
it's high time you quit focusing on healing everyone else
and started treating your own wounds, even if they are
only emotional ones. And I promise you that once we're
on the plane to Virginia, you'll realize it's the best thing
for you. I have kind of a sixth sense about stuff like this,
and I feel very certain that you're finally going to meet
Mr. Right on this trip.''

Alison ran a hand back over her thick black hair, her
palm moist with her misgivings. "Yeah. All right,'' she
returned; but uneasiness was all she really felt. Though
she knew that Molly was not particularly given to whimsical claims where romance was concerned, a "haunted''
inn at Williamsburg certainly didn't seem a likely place
for it.

The recently reconstructed Wetherby Inn was a white
columned manse with black shutters and eight dormers
protruding from the front of its long roof. Although it
looked as soundly built as any modern structure, there
was an ancient scent to it which bespoke its two-hundred-
year-old origins. It was a cedar-chest–and–antique-
upholstery smell, which even the huge fresh floral

arrangements on the tea tables about the lobby and corridors could not seem to mask. And this was all the proof Alison needed that the place was as authentic as the Williamsburg brochures had claimed. ·

After checking in, she and Molly were shown upstairs to their neighboring second-floor suites by a young bellboy who was clad in Colonial garb and whom the front-desk clerk had referred to as a "footman." Alison bit her lower lip, fighting the urge to laugh out loud when she noticed Molly ogling his tightly breeched posterior. ·

As he kept pressing forward, with their heavy suitcases hanging from each of his hands, the psychologist shifted her gaze to Alison and raised a comically suggestive brow. "What do you say we lure him in with the promise of a big tip, then jump him?" she whispered, as they continued walking. "I'd get him first of course, since it's my idea."

"Leave the poor guy alone," Alison hissed back, elbowing her. "It can't be pleasant, having to be dressed up in all those clothes in this heat."

"So we'll just relieve him of some of them," Molly continued under her breath. "Besides, he can't be that miserable. It's air-conditioned in here."

She fell silent, as the bellboy stopped at what was, apparently, the first of their doors and turned back to them with an unsuspecting smile. Actually looking ruffled at so nearly being caught in the act of leering at his physique, Molly immediately began digging through her purse. After dredging out her wallet, she handed him a five-dollar tip.

"Thank ya, my lady," he replied, his Texan drawl being all that could have kept one from truly believing that he actually was an American Colonist. With that he slipped one of the keys, which hung from a large ring about his lace-covered wrist, into the suite's lock and swung the door open for their perusal.

"Oh, God, *neat*," Molly declared, pushing into the room before him and pivoting to take in the details of its luxurious, eighteenth-century décor. "Isn't this place cool?"

Alison, noting their escort's subtle smile at Molly's enthusiasm, sidled in past him as well and joined her friend in studying the furnishings. There was a beige canopied bed centered against the long wall to their right, and several yards from the foot of it were two gold satin-striped wing chairs. Between these was a French writing table which, like the room's dresser, armoire, and night-stands, was made of lustrous cherry wood.

"Yeah. It's nice all right."

"See, I told you you'd like it here. . . . She was a little concerned about the place being haunted," Molly added, as an aside to the footman.

He moved their luggage over to the right of the door, then entered as well. "Oh, does that scare ya?" he asked Alison with a soft laugh.

She glared over at Molly for putting her in such an embarrassing spot. "No, of course not. I don't know what she's talking about. I don't even believe in ghosts."

"Suit yourself," he returned evenly. "To each his own, I guess."

"What are you saying?" Molly inquired playfully. "Don't tell me you've actually seen them here."

"Sure. Everyone who's worked at the Wetherby for any length of time has. Even after the renovation last summer, the spirits make appearances from time to time. I think it's just some sort of residual hauntin', though, if you want my opinion."

Molly cocked her head. "Residual?"

"Well, yes. The sort where they simply go about the daily activities they once did when their original house stood on this spot. Because every time one of 'em is seen, they seem to be sweepin' a floor or combin' their hair or doin' somethin' else that's borin' and repetitive. So I guess it's not really an active kind of hauntin', like ya sometimes hear about. You know, where apparitions are tryin' to drive the new occupants out of their former home. These ghosts don't seem to have any interest in doin' that. In fact, I think they kinda like the staff for dressin' as they did in their day.''

''I'm sorry, but this all sounds pretty farfetched to me,'' Alison couldn't help protesting. ''I mean, I'm not trying to be rude, but I'm sure this ghost business is just something the management has told you to pass on to visitors so the place will seem like more of a novelty.''

''Well, as I said, suit yourself, Ma'am,'' he concluded, with an aggravatingly insouciant shrug. ''You probably won't see any of 'em if ya don't expect to. Now, which suitcase should I carry to the next suite?'' he inquired, turning back toward the door.

''I'm taking this one. I'm already in love with it,'' Molly declared with her usual decisiveness.

''Okay. Mine then,'' Alison said to the servant. ''The blue bag, please.''

''Very good. And y'all have a nice stay with us, ladies,'' he replied in parting.

''Now there, you see?'' Molly scolded in a hushed voice, once he'd stepped out of view. ''That's just what I meant about you being such a poop. Why didn't you play along with him? Take the opportunity to flirt a little. Ask him what *other* everyday 'activities' he'd seen the ghosts engaged in. Initiate some repartee.''

''This may surprise you, but I have absolutely no desire to run off with a twenty-something summer bellboy from Texas.''

''So who said anything about running off with him? That's the whole point of flirting. It's not supposed to be taken seriously. It's just for fun. You know, simply getting a little bing-a-bing-a-bing going, so you're sure you're still alive. Offer him a couple inviting glances, a girlish smirk or two. It would do you good to lighten up a bit. Help you prove to yourself that the Walrus didn't succeed in wringing every drop of amorous juice out of you.''

''The Walrus'' was her nickname for Alison's ex-husband, an epithet she'd assigned to him because of his ever-widening five-foot-seven form. Weight control had never been Stan's long suit.

Alison waved her off with a laugh. "Ah, Lord, let's not start that again. I'm going next door to unpack and I suggest you do the same, with the dinner hour so close upon us. Gosh, I'm starving. I hope the food is good here."

"Well, look at it this way: Can it be any worse than that flavorless slop you usually get stuck with at the hospital?"

Alison shook her head, continuing to smile. "Nope. Not a chance."

With that, she proceeded to her suite to begin the ponderous task of emptying her overloaded suitcase. The now unlocked door of her room swung open for her with ease, and she stepped inside to find it furnished in much the same way Molly's was, except that all of the curtains, bedding, carpeting, and upholstery were in blue tones.

After locking the door behind her, she walked over to one of the regally draped windows and looked out at the cobblestone street below. It was filled with the cool greenish shadows cast by the many towering trees that lined it, and, if not for a few tourists, who were strolling about it in modern dress, it could easily have passed for an eighteenth-century road.

The phone rang, causing Alison to start, and she turned about and spotted the source of the intrusive noise resting upon the night table to the right of the king-sized bed. It had to be Molly. No one else knew where she was. As she crossed to it and picked up the receiver, however, the uniquely strident voice saying her name on the other end made her realize that she had, indeed, specified her vacation plans to one other person.

"Mom," she greeted, sinking down on the edge of the bed. "How are you?"

"Fine," Mrs. Kimball snapped. "It's not me I'm worried about. It's you, out there on that crime-ridden coast!''

"Honestly, I'm okay. Molly's here with me and—''

"What sort of comfort is that?'' her mother interrupted. "That girl has been leading you into trouble for as long as you've known her.''

Alison laughed. "Mom, stop. We're not girls anymore. We're grown women; and you should see this place. It's absolutely beautiful. In fact, the concierge here told us that Churchill and the Queen of England and a whole bunch of other royalty have stayed at the hotel just a couple doors down. So, you see, we're safe as babies. Stop worrying. I know you mean well, but it's really not necessary.''

"Well, what about all the drive-by shootings out there? Just stay off the freeways, that's all I have to say!''

"We're pretty well removed from the freeways. It's like a resort, see. There are golf courses and tennis courts and things like that all around us.'' Although Alison was making the best case she knew how in order to put her mom's mind at ease, she could tell, from the dubious clucks on the other end, that extricating herself from this call was going to be tough. She, therefore, focused upon the gilt-framed mirror, which hung above the dresser to the far right of the bed, and she began studying her travel-disheveled reflection in it.

She pressed her lips together, in an effort to redistribute what little lipstick remained from her last application hours earlier. Then she began running the fingers of her free hand through her windblown hair.

"So, anyway,'' she heard her mother droning on, "I would have been a lot happier if you two had decided upon Scottsdale or Mazatlán or some more normal place for a vacation—''

Blah-blah, blah-blah, blah-blah, Alison's mind finished for her. After thirty three years of fretful lectures from Mildred Kimball, mother of four and secretary to the senior pastor of Shepherd of the Light Lutheran

Church, one simply couldn't help tuning her out. The best course, Alison had learned from experience, was to let her talk until she couldn't think of a thing more to say. It was much like allowing a wind-up toy to waddle and flail about the floor until it ran itself down to a standstill.

Molly had once referred to this prattling from Mrs. Kimball as "pathological." It was a term which Alison wasn't altogether clear on, in anything but a physiological sense, and she'd always been far too proud to ask her friend to define it. Nevertheless, she'd taken it to mean that her mother wasn't truly certifiable. She was just one of those fairly functional neurotics who posed endless annoyances, yet no real danger to the rest of the human race.

Alison inwardly groaned, sadly aware of how quickly this one precious week of vacation would fly past and how soon she'd be returned to her increasingly joyless existence in Minneapolis. It was a life filled with the wreckage of a nasty divorce, growing fear of career loss, and, of course, the perpetually nagging Mildred Kimball. How things had managed to fall into such a pathetic state, after so many years of hard work and sacrifice on Alison's part, she wasn't entirely sure. She only knew that more and more she truly wished to escape it all permanently.

Continuing to look into the mirror, as her mother yammered on, she noticed the sadness and vulnerability which shone in her big blue eyes. Then, suddenly, inexplicably, her reflection began to take on a rosy, romantic glow, and, instead of running into unbrushed tangles, as her fingers went on combing through her thick hair, her sense of touch met with an odd silkiness which offered no resistance. Blinking in disbelief, she saw that the top of her head was now crowned with some sort of white linen cap and her face was framed with a flood of glistening, perfectly arranged ringlets!

She froze in horror. Was she simply daydreaming? Or

was what she was seeing real? Her gaze at her reflection moved downward and she acknowledged that, far from the high-collared tan dress she'd worn for traveling, she was now in a daringly low-cut garment. It was a white-ruffled light-blue gown that appeared to be made of taffeta.

She was just overly tired, she tried to tell herself—exhausted by both jet lag and rushing about to get ready for their trip. But, as one of her hands slipped upward and confirmed that the linen cap she saw in the mirror was *actually* perched upon her head, she couldn't help letting out a gasp.

"What is it?" her mother demanded in response. "Don't tell me someone is breaking into your room! I've warned you time and again about keeping your door locked in hotels!"

In spite of her efforts to stay calm, Alison could feel her heart racing with panic. She sprang from her bed, then saw in the mirror, an instant later, that she was again dressed as she had been upon leaving home and that everything about her image had returned to normal.

"No, no," she said into the phone, doing her best to sound composed. "It's nothing, Mother. No one's trying to break in. I just—just pricked myself with a safety pin is all—while unpacking my things," she stammered, realizing that a fib was her only recourse, given the unbelievable experience she'd just had.

"Hmm," Mildred returned, somewhat skeptically. "Well, you should be more careful then, shouldn't you. I don't know why you'd have anything in your wardrobe pinned anyway. I've told you countless times how important it is to mend and alter your clothes with a needle and thread. . . . You young women and your sloppy shortcuts these days," she added with another disapproving cluck. "Is it any wonder you can't keep your marriages together?"

Although Alison would ordinarily have offered some protest to this last barb, her only desire now was to get her mother off the phone, so she could try to collect her wits once more.

"Listen, Mom, I hate to cut you off, but Molly's at my door and we're about to go down and catch an early supper," she fibbed again, the little white lie having become one of her key coping skills with Mildred. "Maybe I can call you back later."

"Yes, all right, dear. If it's not after nine o'clock. You know how early to bed your father and I are."

"Yeah. Well, if not tonight, sometime later this week then. Love ya. Good-bye," she blurted in conclusion, setting down the receiver before Mildred could say more than " 'bye" in response.

With that finally behind her, Alison flopped back upon the bed, exhaling the huge breath it seemed she'd been holding since the mirror had begun playing that bizarre trick upon her.

A *ghost*, she surmised, with a horrified chill running through her. Perhaps the Wetherby was every bit as haunted as the staff claimed.

But no, another voice within her countered. It hadn't been an apparition she'd just seen. Indeed, it was, unmistakably, her own image—only attired as she would have been had she lived some two centuries earlier.

Bizarre, she thought again. And, yet, for as frightening as it had been, she had to admit to herself that the Alison she'd spotted in the mirror looked to be a much happier one than she presently knew.

Dear God, it had come to this, she inwardly lamented. She'd let herself grow so worn-out by the tensions of her day-to-day life that she'd actually started hallucinating!

Or had she? 'Daily, repetitive' activities, the bellboy had claimed. Such as 'combing their hair.' Another shiver ran over her as she recalled that she'd been attempting to do just that when the image had appeared to her. Too far from where she'd left her purse to get a comb or brush out of it while on the corded phone, she'd spread her fingers to move teethlike through her travel-tousled hair and, bang, there it had been: a spirit from Colonial times seemingly superimposed upon her reflection.

She exhaled again. She was still shaken by what she'd experienced, yet she was determined not to let the mere power of suggestion con her into believing the absurd claim that the place was haunted.

There was a sucker born every day, as the old saying went; but, after being played for a fool by the likes of her smooth-talking ex-husband, she was determined to never let it happen again.

With a discrediting laugh, she pushed herself back up to a sitting position. Then she rose, hoisted her suitcase up onto the bed, and crossed to the dresser to dig her luggage key out of her purse.

"Utter nonsense," she muttered, stopping just long enough to offer the mirror a glare. "Parlor tricks or something. But certainly not reality," she continued to grumble, as she began hanging her clothes in the nearby armoire. "All done with smoke and *mirrors*," she concluded, chuckling at her unintended pun. "But reality? Nope. You'll never get me to buy it!"

She wasn't one for talking to herself normally, but she had to acknowledge that, given what she'd just seen— or, more rightly, what she *thought* she'd seen—the sound of her own voice was strangely comforting now.

Upon finishing her unpacking, she walked back over to the mirror, again hell-bent on proving to herself that what had seemed to occur minutes before was all simply a figment.

She stood before the gold-framed glass, combing her hair and reviving her makeup; and, naturally, nothing happened. In the course of ten minutes of applying fresh eye shadow, blusher, and her ever-fading under-eye cover-up stick, not one of her features appeared to turn Colonial.

She smiled, content that she'd banished whatever burn-out-induced demons had risen up in her earlier. She would go off with her good friend Molly now and enjoy one of the delectable meals that this elegant setting seemed to promise. Then they'd probably take a leisurely walk around the block and simply soak in these restful eighteenth-century surroundings.

Just as Alison grew steady in the belief that she would not experience any illusions again, however, she heard a male voice groaning from somewhere behind her. She turned back, in an effort to discern precisely where it was coming from; but she had no luck. It could have been issuing from the now-closed armoire. Or from under the bed perhaps. Too scared by the eerie sound to stay and investigate it further, however, she snatched up her purse and suite key and rushed out into the hallway, slamming the door behind her!

Chapter Two

"What's the matter?" Molly greeted with a bewildered expression, as she responded to Alison's knocks at her door seconds later. "You look like you've just seen a ghost. But that's right," she added with a laugh, "according to the staff here, you might have. Right?"

Alison scowled, both annoyed and discomfited by the fact that her friend had so quickly pinpointed the apparent cause of her agitation. "Would you stop with that! Let's just go get some dinner. Mildred called a few minutes ago and as usual she's driven me to want to drink."

"Yeah. Okay," Molly replied, stepping back to where she'd left her purse on the bed. Then, stowing it under her right arm, she moved to exit with Alison—last-minute arrangements being her favorite variety.

In a glance, Alison had seen that her friend had yet to unpack her suitcase, though she'd had more than enough time to do so, given the waylaying call from Mrs. Kimball. But Molly was like that, claiming to hate too much regimentation in her personal life because of the constant demand her overloaded patient schedule made for it while she was on the job.

"Where to then?" Molly asked, rushing to keep up with Alison as she hurried on down the corridor.

The truth was that Alison didn't much care where they

ate, so long as she got as far away as possible from that vexing suite of hers. "Somewhere else," she replied, careful to keep her tone unreadable. "That is, I have a feeling we're going to be seeing enough of the Wetherby in the coming week, so let's venture out a bit. Be a little daring, as you're always encouraging."

Molly hesitated, obviously searching her memory for a suitable suggestion. "Hmm.... Oh, I know. The Regency Dining Room at Williamsburg Inn. That would be a great place to celebrate our first night here. Real *très, très* frou-frou, if you know what I mean."

"Real out of my price range, in other words," Alison grumbled.

Finally coming up along side her, as they reached the bottom of the stairs, Molly gave her back a pat. "Now, now. Nothing's too expensive for the next seven days, remember. This is our great escape for the year, after all."

They did, indeed, proceed to the Williamsburg Inn. It was an expansive three-story establishment with a façade of columns and arches which, to Alison's architecturally untrained eye, seemed to rival that of the White House. Once settled into the formal, white-linen-draped dining room, they sampled one another's entrées of chateaubriand and assorted Chesapeake Bay seafood—both of which were expertly arranged on the fine china plates, with artistically balanced scatterings of steamed vegetables and colorful splashes of savory sauces.

"I'm definitely going to gain weight on this vacation," Alison declared, as she finally reached her satiation point and began to inch her plate away from her.

"Yeah. Me, too," Molly agreed, drinking down the last of the pricey bottle of champagne they'd split. "But, look at it this way: it will be *quality* weight you're putting on. Cellulite created by some of the best damn food on the East Coast. None of that cheap, vending-machine-candy fat our bodies usually have to work with."

Alison laughed. "Always looking on the bright side, aren't you, Moll?"

"Yup. I've found it's the best way to be."

"Oh, you don't honestly think the human body can tell the difference between fat from prime rib and fat from a chocolate bar, do you?"

"Maybe. I don't know. Physiology is more up your alley than mine, Ms. R. N. All I'm sure of is that if we get some exercise on this vacation, we'll feel less guilty about these dinners. So, tomorrow—and I don't want to hear any argument on this—" she added, holding up a halting palm, "you and I are going to play some tennis."

"I haven't done that since the eighth grade, but, if you're up for chasing out-of-bounds balls around, you're on."

Molly smirked, then innocently batted her eyelashes. "Why, you know me. I'm always up for chasing balls."

"You and your one-track mind! Do you have any idea how obnoxious you can be sometimes?"

The psychologist leaned toward her with an analytical squint. "Why are you in such a critical frame of mind this evening? It was your chat with Mildred, wasn't it? I should have guessed. She always brings you down. I don't know why you told her where we were going."

"Well, for better or worse, Moll, my parents are my next of kin. So I thought they had the right to know."

"Okay. Now, having established that they've got your number, do yourself a favor and quit answering your phone. That's my advice. . . . Listen, I'd love to sit here for the rest of the night grousing about your mom, but I've got a hot date. So I think I better get out of here, before our waiter comes by with some irresistibly sinful dessert tray."

Alison furrowed her brow, as her companion set her dinner napkin on the table and pushed up to her feet. "A hot date? How is that possible? We've only been here for a couple hours! When did you have time to meet anyone?"

"Sam. The bellboy," she explained with a wink. "Well, you didn't seem to want him. God knows, I gave you more than enough opportunity to get his attention. So, I just called the front desk, once you left, and had him sent back up to help me with opening a stuck window."

Alison's mouth dropped open, the cause of her friend's still-unpacked case now apparent to her. "A stuck window? You said it yourself, the place is *air-conditioned*."

Molly shrugged, donning a somewhat sheepish smile. "Well, yes, but they sent him up anyway. I guess he just must have wanted to come. So, there you have it: my plans for the rest of the evening. But I promise not to desert you again tomorrow night. It's just that I haven't had a date in a coon's age and I'm dying for some foreplay. Besides, I'm sure I'll be much better company for you, once I've indulged in a little amorous activity," she concluded apologetically.

"Lord, I'm glad I'm not the slave to my hormones that you are," Alison fired up to her. If she were really being honest, however, she had to admit to herself that it was more fear of returning to the unearthly occurrences in her suite than her friend's sudden bow out that most bothered her.

"Well, if you're going to get huffy about it," Molly replied, sinking back down in her seat, "I'll stay and have coffee with you."

"Heck, don't linger on my account."

With her accustomed demonstrativeness, Molly reached across the table and gave Alison's hand a quick, consolatory squeeze. "No. I *want* to. I've still got some time before Sam's scheduled to come up for me, and I want to know what's eating you. You've been acting kind of oddly ever since you came to get me for dinner. What's the matter?"

"Nothing."

"Yes, there is. I know when people aren't telling me the truth, Alison. It's one of my specialties. Now, what's the matter? Are you sorry we came to Williamsburg? Don't you like it here?"

"Yeah. It's okay. It's just that . . . ," her words broke off as she searched her mind for some not-too-crazy way of explaining what had happened to her.

"Just that what? You don't like the furniture, right? Too uncomfortable? Look, a lot of people feel that way about Colonial pieces. It's no big deal."

Alison rolled her eyes and laughed to herself. "No, it's not about the inn's furniture."

"Well, what is it then?"

"Nothing. It's just that I was wondering if you've heard any strange noises in your suite at all."

"What kind of noises?"

"I don't know. Just strange ones."

"What? You mean, like creaking floorboards or something?"

"No. Much stranger than that."

"Look it's a big place. There are people in the suites on either side of ours and more people on the floor below. Naturally, you're going to hear some stirrings now and then."

"I'm not talking about stirrings," Alison snapped.

"Then what, in heaven's name, *are* you talking about?" Molly asked with equal annoyance. "I said I'd sit here and have coffee with you, but that doesn't mean I'm up for a game of twenty questions."

"Like—like groaning sounds," Alison choked out, not wanting to have to reveal this much about her rather embarrassing experiences, but knowing that her friend's time and patience were running short.

Molly looked befuddled. "Groaning?"

"Yes."

"What kind of groaning?"

"Well, how many kinds are there?"

"Lots, really. I mean, there's the sort that Lurch in the Addams' Family does—the world-weary kind. And there's the having-sex sort of groaning, of course. And then there's the tormented-spirit-in-a-haunted-house kind. *That's* not what you mean, is it?'' she inquired, a look of deep concern coming over her face.

"No," Alison quickly denied. "Actually, I don't think it was any of those, now that I recall."

"Well, what was it like then?"

"Um. . . . Like—like the suffering kind. The sort of sounds I hear from accident and assault victims in the E.R. sometimes. I mean, before anyone's had the chance to give them some painkiller."

"Whoa," Molly replied, her eyes growing round with interest. "That's weird all right. Where was it coming from?"

Alison swallowed dryly, ill at ease with having revealed so much.

"I couldn't tell exactly. From the armoire, maybe. But then I thought it might have been from under the bed."

"And you're absolutely sure it wasn't that haunted-house kind of groaning?"

"Yes. I'm telling you, I've heard this sort of sound before and it was definitely made by someone who was injured."

"Ooh, weird," Molly said again. "I think you should probably let the front-desk clerk know about it. Maybe something creepy happened in that suite, like someone was murdered there."

"God, Moll, that hadn't occurred to me, but thanks heaps for making me feel better about it!"

"Geez, I'm sorry. I guess that wasn't the best thing for me to say. It's just that I don't think I've ever heard this sort of complaint about a hotel room before. . . . Do you want to sleep in my suite instead? I'm sure Sam and I can leave for the night. He says he's staying at his brother's seaside cabin this summer, so I could probably talk him into taking me there for our little liaison. Would that help any?"

Although Alison had every intention of taking her up on this offer—given the fact that Molly was so abruptly abandoning her and it was her idiotic idea that they stay at a ''haunted'' inn in the first place—she knew that, in all good conscience, she should object to Molly's rather injudicious plans for the night. ''Do you really think it's smart to go off to a cabin with a guy you've only just met?''

''Why not? People do that sort of thing in singles' bars all the time.''

''Yeah, but, what if he's a serial killer or something? It's not as though you're on familiar turf here, after all. Don't you think it would be safer to stay in or around the Wetherby with him until the two of you get to know each other better?''

''Oh, God, Alison, you're turning into a mini-Mildred on me. If you knew how many credits of criminal psych I had to take in college, you'd realize what an expert judge of character I am and you'd stop fretting about my dating practices. Besides, I don't think I'll spend the whole night with him. Mornings-after are just too awkward, if you know what I mean. So I'll probably make him bring me back to the inn while it's still dark out and my mascara hasn't migrated to my cheekbones.''

''But, if I take your room, where will you sleep?''

''Next to you, of course. That bed is spacious enough for both of us, and I promise not to snore, if you don't,'' she concluded with a laugh. ''Then, in the morning, we'll have the management look into getting you moved to another suite. Sam mentioned something about them being full up for the night, but there should be some checkouts tomorrow.''

''Well, okay,'' Alison agreed, ''if you're sure you don't mind having a roommate for that long.''

''Not in the least.''

With that settled, they paid their dinner tab and headed back to the Wetherby together—Alison also having decided that skipping dessert was a pretty good idea.

''Go get what you'll need for the night and come back

here, okay?'' Molly directed, as they reached her suite a short time later.

Alison hesitated, as her companion rushed to unlock her door and get inside to start primping for her date. ''Will you come with me?'' she asked with a whimper, which was only half issued in jest.

Molly turned and scowled at her. ''You mean to tell me you're afraid to go back in there for just a minute or two?''

''Yup,'' she answered without hesitation.

''*You*? The all-time skeptic? The 'I-don't-believe-in-ghosts' queen of Minneapolis?''

''Look, don't rub it in. Isn't it sufficient that I was big enough to admit that I heard groaning in there?''

''Oh, Lord, all right,'' Molly returned with a weary sigh. ''But please don't take forever. Just grab a nightgown and your toothbrush and let's *move*. I'm down to just an hour before Sam calls for me, so I'm going to have to skip my oatmeal facial scrub and my waxing altogether.''

''Geez, you're worse than I am when it comes to getting ready to go out! An entire kabuki company could be ready for dress rehearsal in the time it takes you to just 'freshen up.' But, yeah, I'll hurry. Believe me, I don't want to spend any longer in there than is absolutely necessary. And neither would you, if you'd heard what I did.''

So, as Molly made a comical show of searching under the bed and yoo-hooing into the armoire for any groaning entities, Alison scurried around her suite, snatching up everything she thought she'd need before morning.

They were safely back in Molly's room in just under three minutes. While the psychologist began preparing for her evening of sexual dalliance, Alison kicked off her heeled sandals and sprawled upon the canopied bed to start scanning the TV's channels with the remote control she found on the right-side night table.

''How do I look?'' Molly whispered, before answering

Sam's knock at her door some fifty-five minutes later.

Alison shifted her gaze from the television to run her eyes over her friend's studied casualness. It was a style so windswept and incidental that it was almost impossible to believe it could have taken nearly an hour to achieve.

Molly could easily have been mistaken for a millionaire movie star who was just stepping off her private yacht for a day of sightseeing in some exotic port. She wore a softly tailored teal jumpsuit, which was trimmed with large, shimmering mother-of-pearl buttons, and her hair was swept back with a silky white scarf which lent her complexion an angelic glow.

"Wow! Great," Alison answered sincerely. "Kind of a Sharon Stone/Grace Kelly combo."

"Really?" Molly returned, fighting an immodest grin. "Yes."

The psychologist squealed with delight. "Fabulous! Don't wait up." After giving her slender hips a sexy shimmy, she rushed over to open the door to her date.

"Who were you talking to?" the bellboy inquired with a laugh, as Molly greeted him an instant later.

"Alison. She's not happy with her room, so she's sharing mine tonight."

Having exchanged his Colonial footman attire for a pair of Dockers and a casual short-sleeved shirt, Sam stepped farther inside and peered around at where Alison still lay on the bed. His clean-cut honey-colored hair, previously covered by a dark ponytail wig, receded now with his questioning expression. "Really? What's the matter with it? I don't believe we've had any complaints about Suite 37 before."

"She says—"

Given Alison's adamant claim earlier that she didn't believe in ghosts, she interrupted Molly before she could speak a word more to embarrass her. "It's just, um, just that I think there must have been a smoker in there right before me. I'm very sensitive to the lingering scent of burnt tobacco, you see. Allergies,'' she added for good measure.

"Hmm," he said in response. "Well, I suppose that's possible, though we do keep our smokin' guests in the opposite wing of the place as a rule."

"So, we'll see what the manager can do about moving her in the morning, right guys?" Molly interjected, sounding most anxious to be off for their date.

"Right," Alison replied.

"Listen, I feel kind of bad about this, Molly. I mean, goin' off and leavin' your friend alone on your first night here," Sam declared. He shifted his gaze to Alison. "Would you like to join us? We're just goin' down to the beach for a while."

In that same instant, the psychologist managed to step behind him just enough to offer Alison a warning glower at this potential threat to her evening of heavy petting with the hunky young Texan.

"Oh, no thank you," Alison answered, raising her right palm to cover a feigned yawn. "I just want to rest up tonight. Lots of sightseeing slated for tomorrow, you understand."

"Well, okay," he drawled, looking politely disappointed. He wrapped an arm about Molly's waist, as she straightened from retrieving her purse from the adjacent nightstand. "Just thought I'd ask."

"Yes. Thanks again, anyway," Alison replied. "And have a good time," she added, managing to flash her friend a teasing look as the two of them finally made their exit.

Alison truly was tired, she realized, as she heard their jocular small talk fading down the corridor seconds later. She rose, and, after making sure the door had locked behind them and the room's drapes were closed, she took off her dress and undergarments. Then she slipped into the silky peach nightgown she'd brought from her suite and settled back down on the bed to resume her TV viewing.

Though this was hardly how she'd pictured her first evening in Williamsburg, she had to admit to herself that she was finding it wonderfully mindless and relaxing. It seemed ages since her long hours at the hospital had allowed her time for much more than coming home to eat a microwaved freezer-case entrée and collapsing into bed. So simply having the leisure to lie about awake, with nothing in particular to attend to, seemed a marvelous luxury to her now.

Around eleven o'clock she shut off the television and the bedside lamp. Then she pulled her propped-up pillow down from the headboard and she reclined. Fearing that Molly might accidentally wake her by turning on a light upon her return, she rolled over onto her right side, facing away from the door, and began to drift off into one of the heaviest sleeps she'd experienced in months.

As illogical as it seemed, given that her own "haunted" suite was just yards away, she felt safe here, somehow out of reach of the spooky goings-on she'd witnessed next door. The silence, which always seemed to fall upon a room that had been darkened for the night, held such an inviting sense of calm that she was slowly but surely drawn into sweet slumber.

She was roused slightly sometime later by the shifting of the large mattress, as Molly finally returned and crawled into bed. Alison considered, in her half-conscious state, inquiring as to how the date had gone. But, instantly recalling the psychologist's tendency to crow rather ceaselessly about her sexual conquests, she decided to postpone the question until morning. Having been plagued by insomnia off and on since her split up with Stan, Alison had come to know what a fleeting thing sleep could be for her, so she thought she'd better not risk becoming too fully awakened by conversation.

Things probably hadn't gone too well, though, she concluded, since it seemed that only a couple of hours had passed since she'd fallen asleep. It was hardly the nearly all-nighter that Molly had claimed to be hoping for.

On the other hand, Alison couldn't help taking tremendous comfort in the fact that her friend had obviously avoided being kidnapped or murdered by the stranger; and this, in itself, seemed answer enough to satisfy her until the next day.

She shut her eyes and nuzzled back into her pillow, heaving a drowsy sigh of relief. In addition to Molly's safe return, it was also very comforting to know that she was no longer alone in this unsettling establishment. Between the psychologist's quick-wittedness and her own intermediate training in the martial arts, she felt fairly certain that no intruders, living or otherwise, could get the upper hand with them *both*.

So, once again, Alison slipped into a dream state, an unfamiliar tune filling her mind's ear like a kind of lullaby. It was a minuet, a voice within her acknowledged after several seconds. Dulcet and fluid, it was rendered on some sort of classical string instrument which was being plucked with such clarity that she could only conclude it was very nearby.

To this was gradually added what sounded like an oboe. And then, a violin—the musician's long, gliding bow work seeming to speak of the eternity of a cloudless sky and the flowing of a winding creek in a meadow far below. It was sound converted to color and graceful motion, and it brought her the thoroughly heart-warming sense that she was floating upon a summer breeze.

Her legs were slowly propelling her somehow, and she became aware that her arms were wrapped about a firm form which was encased in stiff fabric. Warm and seemingly as solid as a tree trunk, it led her about in a series of stately steps.

Dancing, some higher part of her mind realized. She was dancing with a handsome well-built young man and she was hugging his sturdy waist. She could feel his knee-length coat brushing against the flesh of her hands and forearms, as he continued to lead her effortlessly about in some sort of celestial pas de deux.

Dancing. It had been nearly a decade since she'd had the chance to do so with anyone—Stan never having been much of a fan of it, either slow or fast.

But this partner she had now seemed not only willing to dance but completely attuned to her movement within his reciprocal hold. The private parts of his anatomy were so well aligned with hers, in fact, that she began to realize, for what seemed the very first time, what an intimate activity dancing was.

As if able to read her mind, her companion let his large right palm travel down to her heavily draped bottom; and he brought it forward to cause her loins to press against his own—his rock-hard arousal telling her that he too knew what a perfect match they were for one another.

Instead of looking down to see herself wearing clunky white, rubber-soled shoes—the image of which had become seared upon her mind, year after year of patrolling her ward at the hospital—Alison realized that her slender ankles were now sheathed in silky hose and her feet shod in delicate heeled slippers, which were topped with what appeared to be jewel-lined buckles.

"Rose," she suddenly heard her partner whispering into her ear.

Rose. It was a single syllable, murmured with such yearning, such approbation that it felt as though she was being addressed by a guardian angel. His was a spirit so adoring of her, so cherishing that she instinctively knew that she had never been as treasured by anyone as she was now. Not by her overly protective parents nor by her doting aunts and uncles. And, most certainly, never by Stan—or any other male she'd dated in her lifetime.

How was it possible for one utterance, one simple word to tell her so much? she wondered. How was this stranger, who presently held her, capable of conveying such need, such longing that she was instantly aware that she was as vital to him as the air he breathed? And all with nothing more than a soft articulation.

Hot with urgency, the word "rose" streamed into her right ear once again as they continued their slow, rhythmic dance. And somewhere, in the ethereal midst of it, Alison became aware of a gently mischievous smirk upon her partner's lips. As she looked down once more, she saw the roguish secret he was hiding with the cloaking sides of his flared coat.

To her surprise, it appeared that they were joined in a great deal more than a dance. The highly raised hem of the ankle-length gown she wore was also serving to hide their impassioned union from view.

She *felt* him now. He was pressing more and more deeply into her with each squeeze of his cupping palm upon her posterior and every forward step of their measured dance.

Although none of the other couples, who were promenading about them, seemed likely to catch sight of this most intimate coupling, the two of them were, naturally, both acutely aware of it. And the urge to issue a pleasure-filled moan at his pulsating movement within her caused Alison to bite down upon her lower lip until it nearly bled with her determination to keep silent.

His eyes caught hers in that same instant. Large and blue, they met her gaze with a look that said he was every bit as tortured as she by the drive to give forth an ecstatic cry at the rapture their bodies were producing. But there was great stoicism in those cornflower orbs as well. It was a strength of spirit that said he would die before he would thusly dishonor her; and, all at once, she became aware that he was a soldier. The gold-edged white vest her arms encircled, as well as his brass-button-trimmed blue coat, were clearly part of some Revolutionary War officer's uniform.

"No, we mustn't do this," she heard herself exclaim. She knew she should pull away, yet she felt too transported by the hot throbbing length of him to even try to free herself. "We are not wed," she protested weakly.

"But we could be. If only you would find the courage to dash your father's plans for you and come away with me," he replied, the surging heat of his whisper against her ear causing her to grow weak in his strong embrace. "Besides, I swear that no one can see what we are doing at present. Beloved Rose, who, with the blades of your fan, did tell me to meet you thus at one hour past midnight upon this ground. You can no more withdraw your invitation now, than I can withdraw my—" He paused, seeming to be searching for a tasteful word, "my *love* from you," he concluded with a low, almost rakish chuckle. "Such is the plight of maidens who offer themselves with wavering intent. They do oft find themselves *taken*."

"But I'm not the flirt Molly is," Alison heard herself counter loudly.

"What was that?" another voice demanded.

Alison awoke with a start to see her friend standing, fully dressed, just inside the door of her suite.

"What? Was I in your dream just now or something?" Molly asked with amusement. "I heard you say my name."

Alison blinked against the light of dawn, which shone from between the edges of the room's closed drapes, and she saw in that instant that her friend was still wearing the outfit she'd had on for her date the night before. "What—what time is it?" she croaked in a sleep-hoarse voice.

The psychologist began unbuttoning her jumpsuit. "I don't know. About six, I guess. The sun's coming up, so it must be around that hour."

Continuing to squint in response to the early light, Alison struggled up to a sitting position. "Are you just getting in?" she asked in disbelief. This did strike her as a ridiculous question, considering that she'd felt Molly crawl into bed with her hours before. Yet, given the fact that her friend probably wouldn't have risen this early after a late-night date and redressed in precisely the same clothes she'd worn with Sam, Alison felt compelled to ask it.

"Yeah. Sorry I woke you. I was hoping to just creep in and catch a few winks before breakfast. Sam's car broke down on the way back here and we were stuck on some deserted road for over five hours! Lord, it was one of the worst nights of my life! Nothing but mosquito bites, sand in my shoes, and that godawful sticky heat out there. And," she added, crinkling her nose with repulsion, "I think I stepped in dog doo somewhere along the way." She leaned back against the door and raised her left foot in a clumsy effort to inspect the bottom of her espadrille.

Alison felt her heart begin to race with her gradual realization that it had not been Molly who was sleeping with her. "But I could have sworn I heard you come back and climb into bed sometime around one."

Molly shook her head and let her foot drop back to the floor with a snarl. "Oh, that I only could have! After a couple hours of listening to that cowboy trying to save my soul, I would have given *anything* to be back here with you. Just think of all the college guys I could have gone off with for some fun, and I had to get stuck with a backwater seminarian who's never even kissed a woman! Damn it, I thought I was a much better judge of character than that," she concluded, reaching up and pulling off her jeweled clip-on earrings with a grimace that said she'd been wearing them for far too long. "Nope. It wasn't me you heard, I'm afraid. You must have just been dreaming."

But, as Alison extended an arm to her left and felt for herself that Molly's vacant side of the bed was every bit as warm as her own—as her hand swept downward and stopped upon a small circle of wetness on the sheet which could only have been made by a couple's intimate joining, she knew that what she'd experienced was anything but a dream!

Chapter Three

"That's it!" Alison exclaimed. "I'm not staying here another day!" She sprang out of bed and made a beeline for one of the room's wing chairs. Upon reaching it, she curled into fetal position on its seat, her hands clasped tightly around her knees.

The psychologist looked dumbfounded. "Why? What's the matter?"

"As God is my witness, someone slept in that bed with me last night, Molly! And, if it wasn't you, *who* was it?"

"But the door was locked when I came back just now. How could anyone have gotten in here?"

"I—I'm not sure," Alison stammered, a renewed sense of terror running through her. "I only know that I wasn't alone. Someone slipped in between those sheets and made love to me!"

Molly looked altogether too intrigued with this revelation. "Really? How was it?"

Alison glowered at her. "What do you mean, 'How was it?' Are you out of your mind? I just told you that a total stranger got in here somehow and had his way with me!"

"Well, what did he look like?"

"I don't know exactly. I was sleeping at the time."

"So you were just dreaming then."

"*No.* I'm telling you, I think it really happened. Because I'm positive I felt someone get into bed with me around one o'clock.''

"Well, did you see him? When you were dreaming, I mean?''

"Um . . . yeah.''

"So what did he look like?''

Alison shook her head in confusion. "I don't know. Kinda like Mel Gibson, I guess. He had his eyes, anyway, and his dark hair. But, then again, maybe that was just the color of a wig he was wearing. It was long and tied back in one of those Colonial ponytails.''

"You mean to tell me that I risked life and limb to go off with a stranger for some mere foreplay and you, meanwhile, safe and free of bug bites, just lay here and found yourself being ravished by Mel Gibson?'' She rolled her eyes heavenward. "There's no justice!''

"I didn't say he *was* Mel Gibson, I just said he sort of looked like him. Ah, damn it, Moll, quit kidding around about this! What if he got me pregnant or something?''

"Oh, that's ridiculous. I don't know what they taught you in biology, but I'm relatively certain you can't get preggers from a dream. It was simply some kind of shock reaction. Just leftover trauma from what you experienced in your suite yesterday. You were probably sort of wakeful, fretting over when I'd get back, and it only *seemed* like it was actually occurring. Besides, if it was really so bad, why didn't you fight him off somehow? Why didn't you try to keep it from happening?''

"Because it didn't start out that way, see. He was just dancing with me was all. And then, suddenly, I looked down and we were—''

"Having sex?'' Molly supplied with her usual ready candor on the subject.

Alison felt her cheeks grow warm with embarrassment. "Right. And it was really weird, too, because we were both fully dressed. In late-eighteenth-century clothes, I mean. So, when I think about it, it would have been pretty impossible, right? With me wearing panties and all.''

"Oh, but Colonial women didn't wear underpants."

"They didn't?" Alison returned in amazement.

"Nope. There was no need for them, I guess. The hems of their long gowns were so weighted down, that it wasn't necessary to wear anything under them. It wasn't as if their skirts were apt to get swept up by a strong wind or anything. So, they used to make love with their clothes on now and then, somewhere other than in bed, I mean. It was known as 'taking a flier,' as I recall.''

Alison narrowed her eyes at her skeptically, anger again rising in her at Molly's apparent unwillingness to do anything but make light of her claim. " 'Taking a flier?' Lord, you're full of it! Where did you hear that?''

"I didn't hear it, I read it somewhere. Probably in one of the historical romance novels I'm always devouring in my free time. Honestly, it's amazing the things you learn from those stories. But I'm sure I've read about 'taking a flier' in more than one of them through the years, so it must be true. . . . Listen, though, if you really believe you were raped, maybe we should report it to someone,'' she added, growing commendably solemn.

"No," Alison replied, recalling the liaison now in all of its arousing detail. "It wasn't rape. Not by a long shot. In fact, it was one of the most wonderful experiences I've ever had. I mean, I felt totally adored by this guy. But then, too, I'm not entirely sure it was me he was making love to.''

Molly furrowed her brow. "Look, Alison, I haven't slept in nearly twenty-four hours and I've just come off one of the most miserable nights of my life, so would you please stop playing with my mind here? Now, either this guy made love to you or he didn't. So which is it?''

"He did," she maintained. "It's just that he kept calling me Rose the whole time.''

"*Rose?*" Molly repeated, her voice cracking with incredulity.

"Yes. You know, like the flower."

The psychologist was visibly shaken by this.

"What's the matter?" Alison inquired with a suspicious look.

"Oh, you talked to someone here, didn't you," she said knowingly after a moment, a salty grin coming to her lips. "Someone on the staff, right?"

"No. Why?"

Molly waved her off. "You're just putting me on to get back at me for giving you a hard time about not believing in ghosts."

Alison straightened in her chair, now hell-bent on finding out what her friend was talking about. "I most certainly am not. Now, tell me what's going on, Moll! Why did your face turn pale when I mentioned the name Rose?"

The psychologist shrugged, busying herself by again leaning against the door and slipping off her espadrilles. "Oh, it's nothing. Probably just a coincidence."

"*What*? . . . Look, I think I have the right to know, don't you, since you're the one who wanted to come to this house of horrors in the first place."

This guilt-invoking retort worked, apparently, because Molly met her gaze once more with a look that was unmistakably apologetic. "Well, okay. If you're going to grill me, I'll just go ahead and tell you. But I've got to warn you that you're probably not going to like it."

"Like *what*?"

"The fact that one of the ghosts here is supposedly that of a woman named Rose Rollins."

Alison gulped.

"Sam claimed that she lived during the time of the Revolutionary War and her father promised to marry her off to some guy, but she was in love with another. A colonel in the Virginia State Forces."

Instantly recalling that her dance partner had been wearing what appeared to be the uniform of an officer, Alison felt goose bumps rising on her back and shoulders. "So what happened?" she asked, her voice edged with far too much anxiousness. "Did they end up together? She and the officer, I mean."

"No. I guess she was so depressed by the fact that her father wouldn't let her marry him that she caught some sort of fever soon after and died."

"And what about the man she loved? What happened to him?"

"I don't know. He was pretty badly wounded by the redcoats, Sam said. So I suppose he died before his time, too."

Alison sat back in her chair, a sorrowful lump forming in her throat. "Wow, that's sad."

"Yeah it is, isn't it? I guess ghosts aren't so scary, once you find out who they were in life and what happened to them. Which is probably why the staff here doesn't mind spotting them once in a while. And you know what I think?" she continued, sitting down on the edge of the bed and pointing a finger at Alison.

"What?"

"I think what happened to you was nothing more than a case of mistaken identity. Because Sam mentioned that Rose had dark curly hair and a porcelain complexion, just like yours. So maybe this lover of hers, this officer, just got you confused with her somehow."

No, some irrational part of Alison wanted to cry out in response, *it was **me** he held with such adoration!* And all at once, she felt desperately jealous of this Rose Rollins. Wrenchingly envious of a *ghost,* for heavens' sake! . . . But it was just that she'd never felt such ardor from anyone. With a procession of self-serving men like Stan having stomped through her life since she'd started dating, she wasn't at all sure now that she'd ever been loved, in the romantic sense, a day in her life. "Just the same," she replied finally in a low voice, "I meant what I said earlier. I really do have to get out of this place. It's just too weird, being pulled into the personal lives of ghosts!"

"Yeah, all right." Molly nodded, yawning. "I guess I'd have to agree with that assessment. So, I promise you, just as soon as I've had the chance to get a few hours of sleep, we'll check into finding another hotel. Okay? I mean, now that I think about it, I'm probably not going to want to stay at the Wetherby either. Not with that Texan just waiting to corner me again and tell me how worried he is about my 'promiscuity' putting me 'beyond redemption.' "

"All right. But just what am *I* supposed to do while you're snoozing?"

She gave the opposite side of the bed a pat. "Come get some more sleep as well."

"Are you kidding? I'm not letting myself doze off in this place again!"

Molly rolled her eyes wearily. "Then get dressed, go downstairs, buy yourself a morning paper, and order some breakfast in the dining room. You know, have a leisurely read over some eggs and toast. There isn't a ghost on the planet who'll bother you in broad daylight with other people hanging around. And before you know it, I'll be rested up and be down to join you. How's that for an idea?"

"Oh, all right, I guess," Alison answered, slowly unfolding her legs and rising from the chair. "But I'm getting you up by ten, damn it! I'm not spending half the day sitting around drinking coffee when we could be out sightseeing. I could have saved myself the airfare and stayed in the hospital cafeteria, if that's all I wanted from my vacation," she concluded with a put-upon "humph."

"Okay. Ten bells it is. I'll even ask the front desk for a wake-up call, so I'm sure to be downstairs on time."

True to her word, Molly was redressed in jeans and a tank top and ready to tour Williamsburg by ten o'clock sharp. So, after making arrangements to move to a motel in nearby Yorktown and canceling their rooms at the Wetherby, the two women went off to see everything from the Governor's Palace to the Public Hospital of 1773—this last stop being of particular interest to Alison due to her nursing background.

At roughly two o'clock, they stopped at a local tavern for a light lunch. Then after taking a cab to the modern accommodations they'd arranged in Yorktown, they unpacked and went off to play tennis at an adjacent court—as during their fattening supper the previous evening Molly had insisted they should do.

"I'm not claiming to be any good at this, remember," Alison cautioned again, once they'd taken their places on either side of the net.

While Molly practiced her serve, Alison stood nervously turning her rented racquet's grip about in her hands. Then she assumed the ready stance she'd seen a few times on the televised games at Wimbledon.

"Well, the main thing is just to run around the court a lot," Molly called back. "That's how you burn the most calories." With that, the psychologist finally sent the ball sailing over the net; and Alison, in an attempt to intercept it with her racquet, leapt up, missed it entirely, and fell backward onto her well-rounded bottom.

"You're right," Molly said loudly, after Alison failed to return the next five serves with equal ineptitude, "you're *not* any good at this."

Alison mopped her forehead with the front hem of the T-shirt she wore. Although the court was pretty well shaded by the woodlands that stood to the west of it, Virginia's summer heat was beginning to make her feel boiled in her own perspiration. "Yes, well, croquet has always been more my game. So you just let me know if ever you're brave enough to take me on at that sport," she shot back with playful defiance.

"Okay. Now, you try to serve it to me. I mean, as it is, you're getting all the exercise and I'm just standing here laughing."

"Thanks, pal! I'm so glad I'm such a crack-up for you," Alison shouted, dashing to the back fence to again retrieve the ball. Then she returned to her former spot near the net and, with teeth-gritting determination, she whacked it over to her friend.

To her amazement, it not only cleared the net, but landed with a marked burst of sound—like a gunshot ringing out.

Molly froze in that same instant, making absolutely no effort to swing at the serve. "What was that?"

"What?"

"That bang."

Alison shrugged. "I don't know. Probably just a backfire from a car in the motel's parking lot. Or maybe more of the firecrackers we've been hearing since we got here. It's only a few days till the Fourth, after all."

These seemed like probable enough explanations to Alison. Yet, just as her opponent was fetching the fallen ball and turning to swat it back to her, the explosive sound was heard again; and this time it became apparent that it was emanating from somewhere very close by.

"Good God," Molly exclaimed, "someone's shooting at us!"

Astounded, Alison turned to look at the neighboring woods, the apparent source of the firing. "No," she gasped.

"Yes," Molly insisted, dropping to her stomach. "Get down, damn it. *Get down*, before you get hit!"

Thinking this sound advice in those panic-stricken seconds, Alison complied; and, as she lay with the length of her pressed to the hot court, her mother's warning about drive-by shootings flashed through her mind like a lightning bolt. Though she could scarcely believe it, she and Molly truly were being fired upon. That much was clear as a third shot rang out from the woods, and, then, about a minute later, a fourth.

"Dear Lord, we're in Iraq!" Alison cried out.

"Shh," Molly hissed back fiercely. "Act like you've already been shot and maybe whoever it is will go away."

Again Alison followed her friend's good counsel, pressing her left cheek, as well as the rest of herself, more firmly to the asphalt.

After a moment or two had passed in silence, Molly addressed her once more in a hushed voice. "I think it's over now. What do you think?"

"Yeah. Probably. But let's not just stand up and become easy targets again. Maybe, if we crawl over toward the mouth of the court very slowly, we'll escape the shooter's notice."

Molly still sounded breathless with terror as she replied. "All right. But you go first, since it's your idea."

"Okay."

"Okay," the psychologist echoed emphatically when, after several seconds, Alison failed to move an inch.

It was—or so Alison had thought—a pretty good plan when she'd proposed it, but running the risk of carrying it out was proving far more difficult than having come up with it. What was more, her eyes had just lit upon a strange object, which lay a couple feet beyond Molly's extended right hand, and she wanted very much to identify it before making any moves. "What's that?"

"What?"

"That shiny thing above where your racquet's lying."

Molly raised her head just enough to steal a glance at it. "I don't know. It looks kind of like a jawbreaker, doesn't it."

"Yeah. Except that they're not metallic."

"Right."

"Is it a bullet?"

The psychologist strained to get a better look. "I don't think so. It's too round, isn't it? Bullets are usually pointed, aren't they?"

"Yeah. So what is it then?"

Molly finally ran the risk of using her racquet to roll the mysterious ball over to her. Then she reached out her right hand and caught hold of it. "It—ooh, it's hot, whatever it is."

"Maybe just from the sun shining on it."

"No. Way hotter than that. Besides, it wasn't out here when we started playing. I'm sure I would have spotted it, if it had been. I'm a real stickler about not tripping over anything when I'm running around a court."

"Look," Alison exclaimed, pointing several feet farther to her friend's right, "there's another one." In that same instant, her eyes traveled yards beyond it and she saw that a large hole had been blown into the court's western fence.

"Dear God, they're *musket* balls," Molly declared, apparently spotting the damaged chain-link fence as well.

"Do you think so?"

"Yes. They look exactly like what I've seen in the Revolutionary War displays here. And you know as well as I do that a bullet couldn't have made a hole that big in the fence. That's why the thing was so hot when I touched it. Someone just fired at us with a musket, Alison! Can you believe it?"

"Oh, that's crazy. Who would want to do that?"

"You got me. But I think we'd better race out of here before the shooter gets a chance to reload."

"Well, he's had enough time to do that by now, hasn't he?"

"Who knows. Let's just get out of here! If it really was a musket, I can assure you it can't hit a moving target nearly as well as a still one."

Although Alison continued to have reservations, she decided that it would be preferable to be shot at with her friend than to be left behind to do so alone; and, without further hesitation, the two women were back on their feet and dashing off the court toward the back door of their motel.

Fortunately, there was no more shooting during their race for shelter. But, as Alison followed closely on the long-legged Molly's heels, her ears were suddenly besieged by the very same loud moaning that she'd heard back at the Wetherby. To her amazement, she went on hearing it, even after they'd succeeded in slipping safely into the building.

"What's that?" she asked Molly, as they stood just within the rear entrance, fighting for breath after their frantic run.

"What?"

"That moaning sound?"

Molly stopped gasping for air just long enough to listen intently. "I don't hear anything."

"Well, I do."

"Oh, it's just the blood rushing through your ears after that mad sprint. You probably haven't exerted yourself like that since college gym class. I know I haven't, in any case. It's surprising how fast you can run, though, when your life's on the line, isn't it?" she added with a rankled laugh.

"Yes," Alison agreed. In spite of her friend's claim that it was merely her own racing heart she was hearing, however, she knew full well it was something else. It was coming from someone very much separate from her, yet somehow capable of getting into her mind.

"Now who would have access to a musket?" Molly queried, narrowing her eyes like a sleuth who was hot on a trail. "That's what we've got to ask ourselves."

"I don't know. Those reenactment guys from the College of William and Mary you were talking about before we flew down here?"

"Yeah. They march with weapons sometimes. There's no doubt about it. So we'll just tell the cops what happened and let them sort it out."

"Yes, well, maybe it was simply some kind of target practice or an Independence Day rehearsal gone awry. Maybe whoever it was didn't mean to shoot at us, but we happened to get in the way. Muskets aren't very accurate, are they?"

Molly's semi-intrigued expression suddenly gave way to a pained one and she flung the back of her right hand to her forehead. "Lord, I don't know if I just didn't get enough sleep or if I'm still scared spitless or what. But I feel like I'm going to faint!''

Having heard this warning more than once in the course of her nursing career, Alison hurriedly tucked her racquet under her left arm, then reached out and firmly took hold of her friend's shoulders. ''It's probably heat exhaustion. Let's get you upstairs to bed and have you drink a couple glasses of water.''

Molly leaned heavily into her companion's supporting hold. ''All things considered, I think I'd much rather have vodka.''

''Nope,'' Alison said sternly, her head-nurse mentality coming to the fore. ''Booze is too dehydrating. It's water or fruit juice only, until you're feeling better. And that's final.''

''But what about the shooter?'' Molly pursued, as they slowly made their way to the lobby elevator and then up to their rooms.

''Don't worry. I'll take care of letting the police know. You just get some rest, so you don't end up in an E.R.''

After seeing her friend down two tall glasses of water, then tucking her into bed, Alison closed the room's drapes and left Molly to get some rest. Although she fully intended to phone the cops as she'd promised, the continued moaning she was hearing kept her from doing anything but returning to the motel's back door and staring, trancelike, out at the woods from which both the shooting and the groaning seemed to come.

There was a sniper out there, the still rational half of her reminded. Yet, watching some of the motel's other guests calmly walking to and from their cars unscathed now, she couldn't help but conclude that the danger had passed. And although she knew perfectly well that her first order of business should have been alerting the authorities to the potentially deadly incident, some other part of her felt driven to go back outside and bodily confront the apparent source of her continued haunting.

She instinctively knew that the attack had not been

directed at Molly—nor at any other visitor to or citizen of Virginia. It was *personal* somehow. It had been, indisputably, a summons to Alison Kimball, R. N., from the spirit world; and, rather than continuing to feel fear at the possibility of being shot, she found herself filled with rage at the fact that the musketeer had had the gall to involve anyone else in it.

Muttering a few choice swear words, she pulled the back door open and stormed off across the parking lot toward the expanse of trees beyond. "If you want to talk to me so badly, here I am," she declared in a hiss.

With that, she headed into the woods, only slowing her pace as she began to spot what looked to be a trail of blood on the well-worn footpath upon which she'd embarked.

Their assailant, or perhaps someone with him, was wounded, she realized. Just desserts, she supposed, for firing at her and her friend. But, as the groaning grew almost deafeningly loud, she somehow knew that her only hope for getting it to stop was to follow the red drops to wherever they led.

She strode on, finally reaching a clearing where she saw a man, in Colonial garb, sitting with his back up against the trunk of a huge oak.

She came to a halt and squinted, straining to get a good look at him amidst the shade of the tree.

Her mouth dropped open as she finally did. Dear God, he was the same guy who'd made love to her in her sleep the night before! Yet he appeared far too tangible to be either a ghost or the product of a dream. And, far from extending his open arms to her now, he took up the musket, which was leaning next to him against the oak, and leveled it at her with a snarl.

He was definitely wounded, she acknowledged in those horrendous seconds. His otherwise dark blue coat was stained with a large circle of crimson at roughly the level of his left shoulder; and, sensing that he was in no shape to get off a shot at her, she rushed at him and knocked the weapon from his hands.

"Rose," he said, an odd mix of astonishment and elation coming over his pale face as he slowly righted himself after her charge. "Alas, 'tis indeed Heaven which takes me, sending my beloved to usher me to Her gates!"

Having managed to kick the musket well out of his reach, Alison now stood with both of her feet planted upon its barrel. "I am *not* Rose, you maniac. My name is Alison, and I'll have you know that you nearly killed my friend and me back there at the tennis court! What on earth is the matter with you?" she demanded.

His eyes traveled up and focused upon her face with what seemed tremendous concentration. "So you are not my Rose, after all."

"Exactly. That's precisely what I'm saying. Now *who* are you and why did you shoot at us?"

He swallowed loudly, as though parched by the afternoon heat. "Madam, in spite of your claim, I will have you know that I, Colonel Richard Adams of the Virginia State Forces, have never fired upon a woman in my life, and, moreover, I never shall! I—I was simply crossing enemy-held ground and, sadly, as you can see, I was hit by one of Cornwallis' men."

Although Alison's gaze couldn't help but follow his nod toward his wounded shoulder as he concluded this claim, she somehow refrained from lunging to tend to his bleeding, as was her impulse. "What? Are you deranged? There haven't been any battles fought in this area since probably the Civil War."

He scowled in confusion. "Oh, pray do let me assure you, dear lady, that there is nothing in the least *civil* about a war. In truth, I loathe the fact that those two words are so oft uttered in the same breath." He punctuated this with a biting laugh, followed by a cough which Alison found disturbingly gurgly.

It was possible, she guessed, that his wound was low enough to have involved a lung. But she couldn't be certain of this, of course, without having a much better look at it.

"All right," she conceded after several seconds. "We'll play it your way. Let's just suppose you *were* shot by one of this Cornwallis person's men. Would he have been a Brit or an American?"

His big blue eyes grew larger still with obvious incredulity. "What manner of madness could cause you to think him anything but an Englishman?" he fired back.

He sounded so affronted that Alison felt a wave of guilt run through her at her ignorance of the Revolutionary War. Of course she'd studied it, somewhere back in her grade-school or junior-high years. But over two decades had passed since then and most of what she'd learned was long forgotten.

"Well, how should I know?" she returned defensively. "You rebels wore so many different colors of uniform that I can hardly be expected to recognize every one of them."

" 'We rebels?' " he repeated uneasily, drawing his long legs away from where she stood. "Am I to understand then that you are a Tory, Madam?"

"No. Don't you remember me? I'm the woman you made love to last night. Alison Kimball from Minnesota."

"I most certainly do *not* remember you. Nor have I heard of this place you come from. Pray you, where would it be?"

"Far to the north and west of here."

Again this response seemed to disconcert him. "Ah, from Canada, are you? Please do tell me then that you are of French loyalties."

She clucked with impatience, now determined to do what she could to stop his bleeding. "I'm an American, for heaven's sake," she declared, closing the gap between them and dropping to her knees to begin examining his wound. "Now quit worrying yourself about whose side I'm on. You're only making your heart pump faster by fretting.''

Although his sword was still in the scabbard he wore against his back, Richard Adams did not attempt to draw it upon this stranger, as she began unfastening the buckle of the cross-belts over his chest.

She was friend, not foe, he tried to assure himself, as the sweet scent of her long dark hair filled his nostrils and she gently peeled the blood-soaked left side of his coat away to reveal the equally drenched fabric of his white vest.

Even though he knew that her accusations that he'd bedded her and shot at her were insane, he somehow sensed that she meant him no harm, and he did his best to cooperate now, as her slender fingers worked to undo the many buttons of his waistcoat.

In spite of the fact that she was clearly being as careful as possible, her effort to disrobe him was naturally painful. So, in an effort to avoid the humiliation of groaning once more, he clenched his teeth and distracted himself by staring down at her bared thighs. They were protruding from the odd and disgracefully short breeches she wore. And this, as would have been true for any man he'd ever met, proved more than ample diversion from his discomfort.

"Alison," she'd said she was called. "Alison of the soft and *shaven* legs," his mind elaborated, as he studied them where her knees were pressed into the moist soil of the forest floor, amidst her endearing attempt to come to his aid.

No, he hadn't made love with her as she'd claimed, he silently acknowledged. No matter how fuddled his bleeding was causing him to become, he knew with all certainty that he'd never been intimate with this woman. For, if he had, he would surely remember those most inviting thighs—to say nothing of the well-endowed bosom which brushed against him now, as she removed the sheer white scarf from her swept-back hair and began using it to wipe the blood from his wound. He would, without doubt, recall the heavenly scent of her, the feel of her agile hands upon him, and the sympathetic sounds she was producing from somewhere deep in her throat.

Of a sudden, however, his reveling in her charms was shattered by unignorable pain, as her fingers began probing the area where he'd been shot.

He couldn't help letting a yelp escape his lips. "What, by Christ, are you doing?" he growled, reaching up and seizing both of her wrists.

Alison recoiled, surprised at the strength of his hold, given his disabled state. "Feeling for the bullet. Just checking to see if it's close enough to the surface to be easily removed."

"No. Fetch me no surgeon, woman! They are butchers all. I would prefer to die by God's Own Hand, if 'tis all the same to you."

Alison jerked her wrists free of him. "Well, it's not all the same to me. I've never turned my back on a bleeding patient in my life and I certainly don't intend to start with you."

"Patient?"

"I'm a nurse. A *medical* nurse," she added with a blush, recalling that somewhere in history the word nurse had applied strictly to one who went about breastfeeding other women's babies.

"A battlefield nurse?"

"Well, no," she admitted. "But certainly well trained enough to keep you alive until I can get you to a hospital." She eased her long scarf behind him and brought its ends forward to fashion it into a bandage about his shoulder. Then she folded his coat into quarters and slipped it in under the scarf's knot for greater absorption of his blood.

"Oh, let me die, my dear," he replied. "Let me leave the Yorktown battle to those who are yet able, and let me be reunited with my Rose in that peaceful Heaven above."

"Nonsense," Alison countered, slipping her arms under both of his and struggling to bring his heavy form upward with her as she began rising from her kneeling position.

To her dismay, however, she looked down to see his eyes drift shut and his head fall limply forward, and she realized in that instant what torment she must have brought him in trying to get him to his feet so they could go for help.

The Colonial colonel had lost consciousness. His shallow labored respiration seemed the only evidence that he was still alive. And, in the silence that followed, Alison suddenly became aware that the phantomish moaning, that had helped to lead her to him, had finally come to an end.

She was no longer being haunted. Indeed, the warm, weighty body, which she was now forced to return to its sitting position against the oak, was every bit as real and vital as she. And she knew that she'd have to call for an ambulance *immediately*, if she wished to keep it that way.

Chapter Four

Not wishing to involve any more people in the situation than were absolutely necessary, Alison refrained from informing the desk clerk of it and simply called 911 herself from the motel's lobby, as she reached it a few minutes later. She then dashed up to her room and retrieved her nightshirt from where she'd hung it in her closet.

The truth of the matter was that it wasn't actually *her* nightshirt, but Stan's—one of the few things she'd managed to take away with her when their marriage had ended. She'd always enjoyed wearing it on lazy weekend mornings. Voluminous and relatively shapeless, it had never made her feel remorse for any overindulgences of the night before. And, because it was long enough to reach down to just about any man's thighs, she knew that it was her only alternative to sending "Colonel Richard Adams," as he'd called himself, off to the hospital in an eighteenth-century uniform which would probably cause him a deluge of questions from the local authorities and the press.

Of course, being found seriously wounded in a nightshirt wasn't altogether normal either, she realized. But it did seem preferable to running the risk of having some police lab doing fabric-dating tests on his Colonial apparel. If he was indeed some sort of visitor to the present from the Revolutionary War, Alison thought it best that it remain a secret between the two of them. Given her own previous skepticism about ghosts and time travelers, she could only imagine that the real story behind his shooting might well land him in a psych ward; and she knew in her heart that, whomever he was, he didn't deserve such a fate.

With a continued calmness, which was purely the result of having tended to so many emergencies in her professional life, she made her way hurriedly back downstairs and out to the woods where she'd left her patient. Mercifully, he hadn't yet regained consciousness, and she was able to remove what remained of his uniform and redress him in the nightshirt in record time. She even got the chance to hide his blood-stained clothing and musket farther back in the woods, before the ambulance's siren was heard in the motel's parking lot a few minutes later.

Although she found it surprisingly wrenching, she had to leave Richard one more time in order to run back to the paramedics and lead them to him. As they bent to check his vital signs moments later, she realized what a mistake she'd made in thinking that he could possibly have walked with her to the motel for help. Some illogical part of her had simply wanted to believe, however, that she could handle the situation on her own.

Colonel Richard Adams of the Virginia State Forces was, once again, committed into his fair Virginia's hands, though; and, as Alison watched the ambulance attendants load his dead weight onto their wheeled stretcher, she became aware that this would probably be her last opportunity to extricate herself from him and the bizarre circumstances surrounding his wound.

She could simply claim that she'd been going for a stroll through the woods when she'd happened upon him, she supposed. She could say she'd never set eyes on him before that moment and had no idea how he'd come to be in such a grave condition. . . . If she admitted that they were acquainted, after all, maybe she herself would somehow be implicated in his shooting.

But, as his blue eyes fluttered open now, at the jarring movement of being transferred to the gurney—as he glanced about with a terror that only seemed quelled once he again caught sight of her standing at his right side, Alison realized that she would have to remain with him, no matter what the risks. It seemed inhuman to do anything else.

"You know this guy, lady?" one of the paramedics asked, apparently spotting the look of recognition on the colonel's face.

"Yes. We're engaged," Alison blurted out, knowing that claiming such a relationship was probably the only way to guarantee that she'd be able to stay with Richard throughout his hospitalization.

Although he looked surprised by this, their patient remained blessedly silent, seeming to somehow understand that his best course was to let Alison do the talking for him.

"So why was he out here in nothing but a pajama top?" the attendant pursued suspiciously.

"What are you? The *police*?" Alison snapped back at him, having had to face down more than one officious paramedic through the years. "He's shot, for God's sake! Just get him to the hospital and ask questions later!"

"Fine," he retorted with an angry harrumph; and Alison, having long since taken Richard's right hand in hers, had to travel double time, against the backward lashes of bush branches, to keep in step with the gurney as it was whisked down the narrow footpath toward the ambulance.

She was sadly aware that, from that point on, her moments with the Colonial officer largely would have to be stolen ones. Most of their conversations would need to be kept nearly inaudible, as they strove to avoid the overly curious ears of the hospital staff. And, after working in such a setting for nearly a decade, she was ruefully aware of just how overly curious such a staff could be.

"To hospital?" Richard whispered up to her, once they reached the parking lot and she was better able to flank him again.

She nodded and tried to produce a comforting smile.

"But I told you no surgeons, and I meant it!" He began straining against the stretcher's chest strap, which the ambulance crew had fastened over him.

She shushed him, reaching out and gently pressing him back down upon the gurney. "I know, but they are the only ones who can help you."

"What? Am I a *prisoner* that they should truss me thusly?" he demanded, his voice growing louder with rage.

"No. Heavens, no," she assured him. "They simply don't want to risk having you injured further en route. . . . We're all Americans here, Richard," she added in a voice too soft for anyone but him to hear. "I give you my solemn vow on that."

Although he appeared to take solace in this claim, his eyes again filled with alarm as the crew suddenly wheeled the gurney away from her and began loading it into the back of the ambulance.

"Alison," he cried out; and his tone was so piteous that it made her heart feel as if it were being torn from her chest.

"I'm here. I'm here," she called back, wasting no time in climbing into the vehicle and kneeling beside him.

"I must confess to being frightened," he murmured, doing an admirable job of trying to smile up at her, given the circumstances.

"Naturally," she said into his ear. "But I promise they won't hurt you. Even when they take the bullet out. You'll be asleep, you see."

"Rubbish! No one sleeps through such agony."

"Well, I swear that *you* will. You'll sleep like a baby, in fact. Now, just rest, please. The more you talk, the more you'll bleed, I'm afraid."

Although part of him knew her claims were too good to be true, Richard decided to comply, as the metal doors of this unworldly conveyance were slammed shut behind them. She was, after all, the only one who seemed the slightest bit familiar to him amidst this strange set of circumstances in which he had so suddenly found himself. It therefore struck him as unwise to cross her.

What was more, there was genuine concern and compassion for him in her eyes. It was a tenderness as unmistakable as that a mother holds for her newborn babe; and it had been a very long time indeed since any woman had been moved to bestow the like of it upon him. Not since his dear Rose had died, he recalled with a sorrowful swallow.

He suddenly felt the white-clad man at his other side prick the hollow of his left elbow. As Richard looked over and saw him suspending a pouch full of clear fluid from a silver hook which hung overhead, he couldn't help but conclude once more that he'd followed his deceased lover into the untold marvels of the afterlife.

"You will stay with me then?" he entreated, returning his gaze to Alison.

"Yes. Until you are completely healed," she promised, giving his right hand another squeeze.

In a saner moment, she would have realized that it sometimes took *months* to recover from wounds such as his. But she knew that both of them had slipped well past true sanity. And the only thing that mattered in Heaven or on Earth now was telling this handsome courageous man, with those heart-rending blue eyes, what he so desperately needed to hear.

"*Where* are you?" Molly demanded, her piercing tone on the other end of the pay phone reflecting great annoyance.

"Riverside Medical Center." Before Alison could say a word more, however, her friend was again interrupting, her tone continuing to sound testy.

"Yeah. I woke up when I heard that ambulance down in the parking lot about an hour ago. Then I walked over to the window and saw you getting into the back of it. But the people at the front desk here claimed to know nothing about what had happened. And, when I called the local hospitals, they couldn't seem to tell me anything either."

"Well, I'm fine," Alison assured. "Don't worry."

"Then why are you at a hospital?"

"Because I found a guy in the woods who had been shot and I—I felt sorry for him. I mean, being alone out there with a bullet in his shoulder. So I agreed to go into the E.R. with him."

"You went off to keep a strange man company? What's the deal, Kimball? Don't tell me I'm rubbing off on you."

"Never," Alison answered with a soft laugh.

"So what's the story then? Was he hit by the sniper who was shooting at us?"

"No. He said he was shot by Cornwallis' men. The English, you know. In the Battle of Yorktown."

"Oh, quit kidding around. What really happened?"

"But that *is* what happened, don't you see? He's the man in my dream, Moll. The one I told you about at the Wetherby. Remember?"

There was a disquieting silence on the other end of the phone.

"Molly? Are you still there?" Alison asked after several seconds.

"Yes."

"Well, why aren't you saying anything?"

"Because, simply put, I think you've flipped out, pal."

"But I haven't. He's real. And he was dressed in a Revolutionary War uniform when I found him, just like my dream. You can go have a look at it, in fact. I hid it, along with his musket and stuff, about ten yards from the clearing in the woods on the other side of the parking lot. All you have to do is follow the footpath in and it will lead you right to where I first spotted him.''

"You mean you packed him off to the hospital *in the nude*?''

Alison laughed again. She'd never provoked such a nonplussed state in her old friend before and some slightly retaliatory part of her was rather enjoying it now. "No. I redressed him in one of the nightshirts I got from Stan.''

"But why would you do that?''

"Because you know how the police are going to be about a case like this. It wouldn't take them long to realize that Richard's uniform dates back to the 1700s, and then he'd be made into some sort of carnival sideshow by the media. Nope,'' she added flatly, "you're the only one we can trust with this.''

Again the psychologist's silence was unsettling.

"Hello? Are you still there?''

"Look, Alison, I think you and I had better have a talk in person. Why don't you catch a cab and come back here?''

"Oh, but I can't. Richard's in surgery right now and I promised I'd be here when he comes out.''

"He told you his name is Richard?''

"Right. Colonel Richard Adams. Of 'the Virginia State Forces,' just like Sam said he was. And you were right about him getting me confused with his girlfriend Rose. You know, that female ghost Sam mentioned to you? Because he thought I was Rose when I first found him in the woods. It's the same guy, Molly. I'm telling you. I could never forget his face and eyes.''

"Okay,'' she replied sharply. "If you won't come back here, I'll come to you. Did they admit him under the name Richard Adams?''

"Yeah. I guess I should have come up with an alias for him. He was in such serious condition, though, that I just wasn't thinking clearly enough at the time. But you'll find me in the waiting room down the hall from the O.R. he's in. The front desk should be able to direct you."

"All right. I'll call a cab and be over in a little while. Don't wander off now, okay?"

"Okay. But, wait a minute, what about your dizzy spell earlier? Are you sure you're feeling well enough to make the trip?"

"I'm fine. I ordered up a sandwich and some orange juice about half an hour ago. And I'm managing to keep them down, so I think I've recovered."

"Good. See you in a bit, then."

"Yeah. See ya."

"And, Molly?" Alison said anxiously, as an afterthought.

"Yes?"

"I had to tell the staff here that Richard's my fiancé. It was the only way I could be sure they'd let me stay with him. So please don't slip up and blow my cover. Okay?"

She gasped. "Geez! You're *fiancé*? You're up to your eyeballs in this, aren't you."

"Yeah, well, it was the only thing I could think of. So just promise me you'll play along."

"All right. Okay. I promise I won't tell anyone otherwise."

"Thanks. See you in a little while then."

"Yeah. 'Bye."

Molly still thought she was crazy, Alison sadly acknowledged, as she hung up the receiver an instant later and started walking back to the waiting room. Despite the fact that she had told her where Richard's bloodstained uniform and Colonial weaponry could be found, the psychologist just wasn't buying the story.

But maybe things would be different once Molly had the chance to see Richard for herself. Perhaps when she heard how archaically he spoke and witnessed what a stranger he seemed to twentieth-century technology, she could be persuaded to lend her support to the cause of getting him back on his feet.

God knew there were going to be enormous hospital bills to pay on this completely uninsured man, to say nothing of countless problems in trying to acclimate him to this new time; and Alison was going to need all the help she could get.

"Alison Kimball?" a doctor in light-blue surgical scrubs queried, as he emerged from the O.R. a short time later.

She turned, amidst her nervous pacing about the corridor which led to the waiting room, and rushed over to the balding, gray-haired man. His middle-aged appearance seemed to indicate that he was a physician of considerable experience, and she instantly took comfort in this. "Yes. That's me," she replied.

"I'm Dr. Iverson, one of your fiancé's surgeons, and I'm happy to report that it looks like he's going to be fine. There was nothing vital hit."

She clapped a hand to her chest. "Oh, thank God!"

"There was some damage to the left scapula, but we got the bone fragments out and the muscles in that area are still pretty well intact, so he should recover full mobility. He's lost a fair amount of blood, though, so I think you can count on him having to remain hospitalized for the next few days."

"Yes. I expected that."

"They tell me you're a nurse."

"Yeah. A head nurse at a hospital in Minneapolis."

"Then I guess I can be straight with you."

She felt herself tense up, his tone seeming to suggest bad news, even though he'd just said the prognosis looked very good. "Yes, of course."

"Well, first of all, I think you should know that those weren't exactly bullets we removed from him."

"No?" she returned innocently.

He shook his head. "In fact, they weren't like anything I've seen before, and I've operated on many gunshot

cases. So, obviously, there will have to be more investigation into this matter. I mean, they were clearly pro-
jectiles of some sort, of course. His wound leaves no
question that they were blown into him by a firearm. And
from a good distance away, which seems to eliminate the
possibility that it was self-inflicted. But you know as well
as I do that he wasn't shot in that pajama top he was
wearing when he was brought in. No rips or tears in the
fabric of it. So you had better brace yourself for a lot of
questions from the police. I don't need to tell you that
we've got what looks like attempted murder here. And,
being that you're a nurse, you know that there's no way
around our filing a full report."

Alison dropped her gaze. "Right."

He lowered his voice to a whisper. "So your story is
still just that you found him shot in the woods near your
motel?"

She met his eyes once more with the quiet confidence
that always came with knowing she was being honest.
"That's right. I wish I could tell you more. But all I
know for sure is that there was a sniper out there around
the time Richard was hurt, because my friend Molly and
I were playing tennis nearby and we were shot at, too."

He looked somewhat relieved to hear this. "So then
you have a witness to it?"

Although she hadn't thought of Molly as such until
that moment, she certainly realized now what a crucial
role her friend would be asked to play in the matter.
"Yes," she answered, showing great relief as well.

The surgeon reached out and gave her back a pat.
"Good. I have a feeling you'll be needing one." His
attention suddenly shifted to the page that sounded overhead; and Alison realized it was for him, as she heard
the name "Iverson" spoken.

"Look, I'm needed in another O.R., so I've got to run.
But I'll be by to check on Richard later, once he's settled
into his room."

"May I go and stay in Recovery with him?" she asked anxiously.

An awkward flush came to his cheeks. "Well, I know you're a nurse and all, but I think that under the circumstances, it would be best to have you wait to see him until he's out of there."

"Yeah. Okay," she replied resignedly, reaching out and shaking the hand he extended to her in parting. "And thanks, doctor," she called after him as he rushed off down the corridor.

"You're welcome," he returned, before slipping through another pre-op door near the end of the hall.

She felt guilty, she realized, as she was again left to the lonely business of awaiting Richard's return to consciousness. But *why* should she? another part of her demanded. She'd told the truth. She really had simply come upon him in the woods in that state and had had nothing whatsoever to do with causing it. What was more, if pressed by the police, which she no doubt would be, she could claim that she found Richard wounded in the nude and, for the sake of his dignity, had redressed him in the nightshirt while they waited for the ambulance she'd called.

That was partially the truth, in any case. Having always before been the honest sort, however, she wasn't at all easy with this growing web of white lies which she was being forced to spin.

But whoever Richard was, he was worth it, she told herself. She didn't know how she could be sure of this— she, Alison Kimball, who had sworn off ever falling in love again, once she'd caught Stan cheating on her. Even so, she'd never felt as certain of anything in her life.

Chapter Five

Although Richard was still rather drowsy when they wheeled him into his room a while later, he seemed to recognize Alison. What was more, he looked very pleased to see her again, where she now sat at the right side of his bed.

"I did sleep through the surgery, even as you said I would," he declared, his speech somewhat slurred.

Alison reciprocated his smile. Then she pressed a silencing finger to her lips, doing her best to make her eyes warn him of the dangers of speaking too much in front of members of the hospital's staff. "Yes. Of course. We'll talk when you're feeling a little more awake, sweetheart."

" 'Sweetheart'?" he repeated in a whisper, once the orderlies had transferred him to his bed and left with the gurney.

"Yes. It's a term of affection. It means—"

A smirk tugged at one corner of his mouth. "I know well enough its meaning. In truth, I have used the word myself on occasion. Your English is not so very strange to me that I've no notion of it. Indeed, if I am not mistaken, I heard you tell my litter-bearers earlier that you and I are betrothed. Is that not so?"

Alison felt her face grow hot with embarrassment. "Well, yes," she admitted. "It was the only way they'd let me stay with you here in the hospital. I had to claim that you were related to me somehow.''

Although he was clearly still filled with stupefying painkillers, there was a slight sparkle in his eye which seemed to indicate a most resilient libido. ''Would not claiming me your brother or cousin have sufficed in such case, my lady?''

Alison couldn't help feeling defensive at his rather teasing tone. ''Well, they—they would be able to find some record of my siblings and cousins, you see. They'd discover, sooner or later, that you are neither. So my fiancé was the only relation I could think of.''

Although this seemed as innocent and plausible a response as any, he met it with a knowing expression which again inwardly ruffled her.

''Ah, yes. I will assume then that 'twas for no other reason you chose it . . . I am no longer in Yorktown, am I,'' he added, his sportive manner giving way to a solemnness which said he didn't really want to hear the answer to this.

Alison slid her chair up closer to his bed and took his right hand in hers.

''As skilled as the surgeons here seem, I do think them quite in error in believing my arm to be broken,'' he remarked, looking down at the sling which had prohibited her from taking hold of his left hand instead.

''Oh, no. They don't think it's broken. They know it's not. They just don't want you using it for a while.''

''But why not?''

''Because they want the muscles in that wounded shoulder to heal. And they won't do so as quickly if you keep trying to use them.''

His eyes shone with admiration. ''You truly are a medical nurse, aren't you.''

She nodded.

''Then, do you not think it unwise of them to bleed me clear this way?'' he asked in a conspiratorial hush, pointing to the intravenous tube that was attached to the hollow of his right elbow.

"Bleed you clear?" she repeated blankly.

"Yes. It was, without doubt, blood coursing through this siphon earlier. I saw it, crimson as a redcoat, when I woke from that sleeping potion they gave me. But do you not think me amply purged now, considering all of the bleeding I did by cause of Cornwallis' bullets?"

She bit her lower lip, doing her best not to seem amused at his misunderstanding of the situation. "Oh, no. That wasn't *your* blood you saw in that tube when you woke up."

"It wasn't?"

"No. It was someone else's and it was being put into you."

He looked plainly aghast. "Someone else's?"

"Yes. A donor's. In order to replace what you'd lost."

"But how is that possible?"

"It just is. They simply matched your blood type to someone else's and then put it into you."

"My blood type?" he echoed in amazement.

"Yes. Blood comes in different types, you see."

"Then, pray, what is this clear liquid which runs into me at present? Please do not tell me 'tis simply water, for I would gladly consent to drinking some, if offered, rather than having it stabbed into me thus." With that, to Alison's dismay, he moved to pull the IV needle out of him with his encumbered left hand.

"Richard, *no*! Leave that alone," she ordered. "It's not just water. It's a lot more. It contains painkillers and everything your body needs to sustain it right now."

Fortunately seeming to believe her, he let his left hand return to its hanging position in the sling. "Pain 'killers,' you say?"

"Right."

"Ah. So that is why I am scarcely aware that I have been both shot and sutured today."

She nodded again.

"In that case," he went on, thrusting out his chin as if he were in full control of his circumstances, "I shall let them administer it for as long as they wish."

Alison grinned. "Yes. I thought you'd feel that way. . . . Now, to answer the question you asked earlier," she began again gingerly, "the truth is you are still in Yorktown. It's just that it has changed quite a bit."

"Indeed! Beyond all recognition."

"Well, that's because, while you're in the same town, you seem to be in a different time."

"I fear I am failing to follow you."

"It's the year nineteen hundred and ninety-seven," she said gently.

His mouth dropped open with astoundment. "You mean to tell me that over two hundred and score years have passed since I was wounded? But how could that be?"

She shook her head, her vision blurring with sudden tearfulness at having had to break such devastating news to him. In essence it meant that everyone he'd ever known was long dead and gone; and quite probably, there was no hope of his returning to them.

Alison was his only acquaintance now, his only semblance of kith or kin, and she simply hadn't realized until that moment what a daunting responsibility it was. "I don't know," she answered. "I only know that it seems to be true, and that we must keep it a secret between us, unless you want far worse things to happen to you."

He swallowed uneasily. "What could be worse than finding myself cast to such a distant date with a mortal wound?"

"Well, first of all," she said hearteningly, "your wound is not mortal. One of the doctors told me that you will recover completely from it. And, secondly, you should know that there are many people in this century who would either put you into an insane asylum or study you half to death for telling them the truth about where you came from. That's why I hid your uniform and weap-

ons farther out in the woods before the ambulance crew—
er, the 'litter-bearers,' arrived,'' she amended, wanting to
make certain he understood.

He gave forth what seemed a mock gasp. ''You mean
to say that *you* are the one who put me into that long
white shirt?''

''Yes.''

''Madam, I am shocked and abashed at having been
laid bare by you!''

She fought her amusement, just as he was. ''Don't be.
I'm a nurse, remember. And, as I've said, it was strictly
in the line of duty.''

''Well, I do hope you did not find me disappointing.''

She finally gave in to the urge to chuckle. ''Not in the
least.''

He grew sober once more. ''That is good, for you truly
are, in every sense, my only confidant now.''

Alison felt a wave of hurt run through her at his discouraged tone. ''Yes. I'm sorry, Richard. . . . Maybe I
shouldn't have told them that I was engaged to you after
all. I guess I should have stayed behind at my motel when
they brought you here for surgery.''

He squeezed her hand with surprising firmness. ''Oh,
no. *No*. Because, without you, I would surely have bled
to death. You and you alone did give me the will to go
on drawing breath. But will you ever forgive my for-
wardness in admitting as much to you?''

He paused, his large eyes questioning, and it was clear
to her that he was actually making a much deeper inquiry
than the one he'd just voiced.

''Oh, yes. Of—of course,'' she stammered.

''In any case, I was too weak after being shot to return
to my men at our camp. 'Twas a very long way from
where I fell. And,'' he added, looking as though it was
his turn to bear any jocular remarks she might wish to
make about the undeniable attraction between them, ''I
do recall now having met you before today.''

''Where?''

"I know not. I merely know that we were doing the minuet. I thought you my dear Rose at first. But then I came to realize that you were someone else. Yet I went on dancing with you until—until it led to a great deal more," he concluded, sheepishly dropping his gaze to the bed's linens.

He hated confessing to the fact that he remembered having taken such liberties with her. It, nevertheless, seemed the only way to reveal that he now *knew* there was, and perhaps always had been, some intimate link between them. "Though I suppose it could have been the sleeping potion the surgeons gave me which made me simply dream such."

"No," Alison said emphatically, leaning over him, so she could look him squarely in the eye. "Because, don't you see? You remember that we danced together. The minuet. And I didn't tell you that part back in the woods. So you *must* have been there with me. Dancing, I mean."

He donned another chagrined smile. "And doing 'a great deal more.'"

"Yes, well, we needn't dwell on that, I guess, if it embarrasses you," she said clumsily. It had been years since she'd made love with anyone but Stan, and she was amazed at how awkward she felt about it now. It was as if she were back in junior high with the very first boy she'd ever held hands with; and she hated how readily this relative stranger was able to strip away from her every shred of the worldliness that society expected her to have amassed by her age.

She looked down and saw him lift her hand to his lips and press a kiss to the back of it.

"Oh, but I would never prove foolish enough to try to put it out of my mind, fair Alison," he said in an undertone. "In truth, 'twould be às a pirate spilling a chest full of treasure overboard. Only a madman would seek to rid himself of all memory of the feel of you."

The *feel* of her? Alison gulped. She'd never been exposed to such old-world charm as he clearly possessed, and part of her knew that she was utterly defenseless against it.

"Richard," she began again after several seconds, barely managing to tear her eyes from his melting azure gaze, "before we get too carried away here, there are a few things I think you should know."

"Of you, you mean? But, dearest, having traversed over two centuries to be with you, what barriers could you possibly tell me of now? That you are wed or betrothed to another? 'Twould be a child's game when held up to the wonders that Providence has already worked to bring us together. And, what with my Rose so long dead—"

Fearing that she might disturb his incision by giving in to the growing urge she felt to kiss him soundly, Alison reached up to press a silencing finger to his lips instead. Then she eased her other hand out of his grasp and rose to pace nervously beside the adjacent window. "Um, well, it's just that I think you should know that the doctors say you'll be able to move your left arm and shoulder fully again in a few weeks. And, um." She turned and ran the risk of meeting his eyes once more. "You won the war. You and all the men fighting with you. You really did succeed in winning independence from the English. As a matter of fact, in just a couple days, we'll be celebrating the two-hundred-twenty-second anniversary of you're having done so."

He looked very pleased. "So these United States of America truly did become ours?"

"Yes. 'From sea to shining sea,' as the song goes. Because there's an ocean far to the west of here," she explained. "That is, I don't know if you were aware of that."

He gave forth a soft laugh, as though sensing that it was little more than maidenly trepidation that had caused her to physically distance herself from him. "No. In very truth, my dear, I was not. But, of course, I am most glad to hear it." He gestured toward the chair she had just occupied. "Now, pray you, come and sit beside me once more. I know not how it is in this century, but in mine, a man could scarce be expected to become better acquainted with a lady from across a room."

Though she was very tempted to comply, Alison managed to stay where she was. "Well, now, this is really more complicated than it probably seems. I mean, while I'm not married or 'betrothed,' as you would put it, I do have my feelings to consider. And, having just had my heart broken by an ex-husband, I'm sure you can understand that I'm hesitant about plunging headlong into another relationship with a man."

"Yes. I do fathom you better than you know, dear lady, for I felt the very same at the death of my beloved Rose a few years past. Never again, I resolved, did I wish to risk feeling such loss. But now I find that *you* have nearly vanquished all such pain in me, just as your marvelous surgeons did remove the redcoats' bullets from my flesh." He extended his right hand to her once more. "So, pray, let me return the favor to you."

"Hi," a female voice suddenly hailed from the room's doorway.

Alison looked over and, to her great relief, saw that it was Molly who stood at the threshold. The psychologist had somehow managed to break Richard's almost hypnotically seductive power over her. Yet she wasn't sure if the gratefulness she felt for it now was due to the simple fact that she'd always been leery of sweet talk from men or if she was actually beginning to fear that the only reason why this handsome Colonial officer was being so solicitous was because he was aware that he would probably be in desperate need of her continued help in the weeks to come.

"Hi, Molly," she replied, rushing over to her as if this were the last person she'd expected to have stop in for a visit.

"Oh, is that him?" the psychologist whispered, as Alison came within a foot or two of her.

"Yes," she answered through closed teeth, her eyes warning her friend not to say anything that might embarrass either of them in his presence.

"God, is he cool," Molly mouthed. Then she leaned over to Alison's right ear and continued to speak under her breath. "He *does* look a little like Mel Gibson, doesn't he."

As Alison turned to flank her friend and walk her over to introduce her to the colonel, she took the added precaution of greatly tightening her grip upon Molly's closest forearm—another silent plea for discretion.

"Richard," Alison said, as they reached the left side of his bed, "I'd like you to meet my friend, Molly Miller. Molly, Colonel Richard Adams of the Virginia State Forces," she concluded, lowering her voice enough to ensure that no one passing by the room might overhear.

Molly thrust out a hand at him with such speed that he couldn't seem to help drawing back a bit. "A pleasure. *Really.*"

He donned an amused expression, as though finding her emphasis on the word "really" humorous. Then he gave the hand she'd offered an obligatory shake. "No. The pleasure is entirely mine, Madam."

Looking as if she were a child who'd just been let into Disneyland for the first time, Molly turned back to Alison. "Wow. He really does sound like he's not from this time!"

"I've told her our secret, Richard," Alison interjected, "because she is my closest friend and I know we can trust her."

"Oh, yeah," Molly assured, still looking gaga over him. "She and I tell each other everything. You know, about the men in our lives—"

"Would you excuse us?" Alison asked Richard by way of interruption. This seemed just about enough candor from the psychologist for one day. "I need to speak to Molly outside for a moment, if you don't mind." With that Alison wrapped an arm about her friend's shoulders and began steering her back towards the door.

"Very well," he replied. "But, pray, do not go far, my dear. Surely you must know by now my disposition toward you."

"Geez, what did that mean?" Molly asked in a hush, once they were well into the corridor. "What disposition?"

Alison kept her voice equally low as she answered. "Well, it's just like in that dream I told you about. I think he *loves* me or something."

"But that's great. Don't you think that's great?"

"Yeah. I guess so."

"God, what a hunk. You'd better *know* so, sweetie, or someone else is likely to snatch him out from under you! . . . What's the matter? Aren't you attracted to him?"

"Lord, yes! Way too attracted in fact. And after what I went through with Stan, I'm scared to death of falling in love again."

"So, you'll just take your time with this guy. Really get to know him first."

"Look, Moll, I think we'd better review what's happened here. I found him bleeding to death in the woods of a *musket* wound. He isn't just another hero in one of those historical romances you read. He's real! He's so real, in fact, that *I* might be the one who gets blamed for his shooting!" She reached out and took both of her friend's hands in hers. "Now, you've got to stick with me on this thing, okay? You have to tell the police that you and I were shot at with musket balls, too, out on the tennis court. You've got to be my alibi."

"Well, yeah. Of course I'll tell them that. It's the truth, after all. It's not as though you're asking me to lie."

"Yes, but you're going to have to do that, too, don't you see? You know he's not my fiancé, but, since that's what I had to tell them here in order to get them to let me stay with him, you've got to back me up on it."

"What are you so worked up about? It's not like I'm a stranger to police cases. The authorities come sniffing around psychologists' offices a lot in search of info on patients who've turned violent. So I know how to handle myself. And, the truth is, I kind of *like* cops,'' she added, with a telling rise of her right brow.

Although no assurance from Molly was ever overly comforting, Alison did find a degree of solace in this one. ''Well, okay. But just don't talk too much with anyone, all right? Not even Richard. I mean, it's easy to slip up and say more than you should when you start chatting with people, you know.''

Molly donned a hurt expression, which, fortunately, appeared only half genuine. ''Okay, then. Maybe I'll start by not talking too much to *you*. And that would be a damned shame,'' she continued, pulling a couple folded sheets of their motel's stationery out of her purse, ''since I went to all the trouble of taking down this information for you.''

''What information?''

''The facts about the battle of Yorktown, as you referred to it on the phone. Well, actually, it was called the Yorktown 'campaign'; but I think we're talking about the same thing here, because it was the time in the Revolutionary War when the English General Cornwallis was surrounded by our troops and forced to surrender. It was the final and decisive battle of the whole war. Dig that! And it all happened right here in Yorktown. Now, how's that for a coincidence?'' she concluded, handing the stationery to Alison.

''But you sounded like you didn't believe me on the phone. So why would you take the time to research Richard's claims?''

''Because I went and found his uniform and musket in the woods, like you suggested. And because I've known you practically your whole life and you've never seemed nuts before. In fact, you know my biggest criticism of you has always been that you're a little too sane for your own good. So I had to assume you hadn't lost your mind this late in the game. Besides, the whole thing has my curiosity piqued. I mean, as you just pointed out, you're not the only one who was having musket balls fired at her this afternoon. Anyway, as you can see from those notes I took, there's no specific reference to the Virginia State Forces being involved in the Yorktown campaign. The sources I checked just said that Cornwallis was surrounded by the troops of Lafayette, Washington, Steuben, and some guy named Rochambeau, who I guess was also on our side, since he had a French name. But, considering that this campaign occurred here in Virginia, it stands to reason that its state forces would take part in it. So now we have to figure out what role Richard might have been playing. Has he told you anything more about the circumstances of his shooting?''

Alison searched her memory, her thoughts still somewhat jumbled by his amorous conversation with her. ''Um. He just said that had I not come along and found him when I did, he would definitely have bled to death in those woods, because he was too far from his base camp to return to his men in that shape.''

''So he really was alone out there when Cornwallis' troops shot him?''

''Yeah. I guess so.''

''Hmm. I wonder—'' Molly's words broke off as a nurse, carrying a tray of food, swept past them and entered Richard's room.

''Oh, Lord,'' Alison said in a whisper, ''we'd better get back in there before he's given the chance to say too much.''

''Something light for you, Mr. Adams,'' the nurse was announcing, as Alison and Molly hurried in behind her.

''This is food, you mean?'' he inquired, staring down at what appeared to be a steaming bowl of broth, accompanied by a saucer full of wobbling green gelatin.

Giving forth an awkward laugh, the nurse pulled his wheeled bed tray up to his torso, then set the dishes down upon it. ''Oh, now, let's not criticize, until you've tried it. Hospital food isn't really that bad, after all.''

Having thusly defended her turf, she turned, and, with an exasperated roll of her eyes, walked past Alison and her friend and made a hasty exit.

"Hi, again. We're back," Alison declared, as she and Molly crossed to stand beside his bed.

His gaze remained, nevertheless, fixed upon the quivering gelatin. "Christ's Church, it yet moves, and I'm to understand that they wish me to eat it?" he asked with repulsion.

"Wow, he really *isn't* from this time, is he," the psychologist noted again with wonder.

"Oh, it's just Jell-O, Richard," Alison explained, reaching down and taking up the spoon which lay on his serving tray. She sliced off a piece of the gelatin. Then, with it resting in the bowl of the utensil, she raised it to the level of his eyes so he could view it more closely.

"I do not know that word. I only know that it is clear and green and somehow still alive!"

"See, it's a dessert that tastes like a lime," Molly put in. "A sweetened lime. You know, like a pudding type of dessert."

He continued to look as though he had great reservations, as Alison moved the spoon toward his mouth. "S'death, I fear I have never seen a lime of that hue."

"Well, no, because it just tastes like limes," Alison expounded. "But the color actually comes from dye."

He reached out and eased her hand away from his face.

"You eat dye in this century? Are you mad?"

Molly laughed. "But it's not the kind of dye that can hurt you."

"Nevertheless, I think I shall stay with the soup alone, ladies. This *is*, indeed, soup, is it not?" he pursued, pulling the bowl toward him and taking a cautious sniff of the steam which was rising from it.

"Yes," Alison assured. "Beef broth, I believe."

"May I?" he asked, reaching out to take the spoon from her.

She surrendered it to him; and, after letting the mouthful of gelatin slide back down to whence it came, he wiped the bowl of the utensil with the paper napkin the kitchen had provided, then dipped it into the broth.

"Hmm. Yes. Beef," he said, after swallowing his first mouthful of it. "Now that is a taste with which I am familiar. . . . But, pray, do tell me that this is not all you eat in this time," he began again, after consuming a few more spoonfuls.

Alison shook her head. "Oh, no. Not at all. We eat a lot more than you see here. It's just that, with the pain-killers they're pumping into you, they're probably afraid your stomach will be upset if you consume too much right now."

He picked up the tiny packet of soda crackers, which rested next to the broth, and studied it closely. "Biscuits?" he asked, extending them to Alison.

"Yes. Well, we call them crackers. But, yes, they'd probably be 'biscuits' to you. Salted ones. For your soup, you see," she continued, taking them from him just long enough to remove them from their cellophane packaging. "Should I crumble them into your bowl?"

"Yes, pray you. That would be good, I think."

"Oh, God," Molly said with a delighted squeal. "He's just adorable, Alison! All this business about not recognizing our food. Lord, I just want to *adopt* him, don't you?"

Richard met this question with an indignant expression. "I beg your pardon, Madam," he said, turning to glower at the psychologist, "but I will have you know that I am fully score and nine years of age and I am not now, nor have I ever been, tendered for adoption!"

Molly appeared amply rebuked by this. "My, my," she said with a note of surprise in her voice. "Well, I've certainly been put in my place, haven't I."

"He's right though," Alison noted, trying to sound as diplomatic as possible. "He's not a child. He's an officer in the U.S. Army, for heaven's sake. It's just that he's not yet acquainted with our time."

"Well, look, okay," Molly replied, throwing her palms up before her rather defensively. "I understand that. It's just that I think there are a few things *he* needs to understand, too. He really should know, for instance, the risks you've taken in coming to his rescue. I mean, does he have any idea, Alison, that you might be charged with attempted murder for his shooting?"

Richard turned and gaped at the psychologist.

"Shh," Alison hissed. "He just got out of surgery, for the love of God. Let's not go into all that right now!"

Molly shifted her gaze back to the colonel. "Well, it's true, though, Richard. She's really laying it on the line for you, so you had better not be playing some sort of sick game with us with this Battle of Yorktown business! Alison doesn't need her heart broken by another lying, manipulative sack of doody. So just you remember that, buster. Or you'll have me to deal with, and I'm not nearly as nice as she is!"

Although Alison hardly thought she could become more distressed in those seconds, she managed to, as she saw Richard grow pale and then *transparent* in response to her friend's denunciation.

"Molly," she exclaimed, "stop it! Look what you're doing to him!"

The psychologist saw it too, apparently, because she fell stone silent for a moment. "He almost disappeared!" She reached out and gave one of his fingers a squeeze as if to confirm that he was solid once more. "Lord, you know," she continued in an undertone, "I might have had my doubts about him being the same guy who came to you in your dream, Alison, but not after what just happened! He really is a time traveler or a ghost or something, because I've never seen anything like that! . . . What happened to you just now?" she asked Richard anxiously. "Were you aware of the fact that you were growing invisible?"

"I fear so, yes," he replied in a tremulous voice, "for

I just felt myself slip back to where I was shot, in the woods.''

Molly studied him pensively. "And were you still wounded?''

He furrowed his brow as though struggling to recapture that fateful instant. "No. That is, yes. I was wounded, and yet I was sutured and bandaged, even as I am now.''

The psychologist shifted her gaze back to Alison and shook her head with discouragement. "I might be wrong, kiddo, but I think we've got a paradox here, and, if so, he's bound to slip back to the Revolutionary War sooner or later.''

Although Alison still felt horrified by his near disappearance, she managed to choke out a response. "What's a paradox?''

"Well, he looks and feels way too substantial to be a ghost. Doctors can't perform surgery on apparitions, right? So that means he's got to be a time traveler. And, that being the case, we'll have to assume it's a paradox that made him start to vanish just now. You know, one of those occurrences in time that's crucial to all of the other events that follow. Richard must have done something very important during that war. Something that took place *after* he was shot in the woods.''

"But how is that possible?" Alison countered, her voice cracking with her growing fear of losing him. "Isn't it obvious that he would have died, if I hadn't come along when I did? He'd lost so much blood, Moll. How could anyone have helped him back in his own time? They didn't know how to do transfusions in the 1700s.''

Molly shrugged, then heaved a pained sigh. "Okay. Maybe you were his divine intervention. The guardian spirit who helped him through his crisis. But now he's got to go back and finish some other critical piece of business in the Yorktown campaign. So, what we've got to try to figure out is what that missing piece might have been.'' She returned her gaze to Richard. ''What were you doing out there all alone? Alison told me you were miles from your camp and your men. Why was that?''

''Because of the missive.''

''What missive?'' Alison asked, naturally even more anxious to get to the bottom of the matter than Molly was.

''There was a Whiggish spy bound for General Washington. He carried a message as to Cornwallis' precise position and the nature of the defensive he intended to execute. And, when this informant failed to report to Washington at the arranged time, I took it upon myself to go in search of him.''

''You? A colonel out scouting for a messenger?'' Molly queried. ''But weren't you a little too high-ranking for that?''

A sad smile played upon his lips, and he grimaced as he shifted against the pillows which the orderlies had propped up behind him.

''Perhaps. However, it was enemy-held ground and I would never have sent one of my men to do that which I myself would not brave. Then, too, they were husbands or affianced all, and I, with only my dear Rose's memory to cling to, had no one to leave behind, should the search end in my death. Indeed, I half hoped I would find my demise in the quest and thereby be allowed to return to my love, even as my men each hoped to return to theirs when the war was over. . . . So, I found our spy well enough,'' he continued bitterly. ''Floating facedown in a creek, not far from where sweet Alison came upon me. He had been shot to death, but the missive was yet in his cartridge box. Thus, I removed it and stowed it in my own. 'Twas my intention, of course, to carry it on to General Washington, when, alas, I too was shot en route.''

''That's got to be it, then,'' Molly declared. ''Washington needed the missive and Alison came along to save you so you could get back there and finish the job of delivering it to him. . . . Tell me, had Cornwallis' troops been surrounded by the American forces by the time you were shot?''

"Faith, no! You mean to say we had the devils surrounded in the end?''

"You bet you did,'' the psychologist returned proudly. "You forced Cornwallis to surrender and acknowledge America's independence from England on October 17, 1781.''

"Then that missive must have been of far more aid to Washington than any of us imagined.''

Molly nodded.

Richard stared up at her with an awed expression. "So you believe me fated to return to my time?''

"Unless we can figure out some way around it, yes I do. I'm sorry, you two, but I've read an awful lot of what physicists have written about time slips and paradoxes and stuff like that, and I'm sure any one of them would tell you pretty much the same thing.''

At this, Richard shifted his eyes to Alison and reached out to take her left hand in his. "But I do not want to go back, if it means being parted from you, my angel,'' he said in a whisper.

Alison bit her lower lip and nodded, her chin crinkling with the sudden urge to weep. She now realized that his affection for her was not solely based upon his need for her help in the twentieth century. Indeed, it seemed to be just *her* he sought, no matter what time he ended up in.

"This is a most wondrous day in which the pair of you live,'' he acknowledged. "But the greatest of its marvels stands here before me, warming my fingers in hers, and I would never again be separated from her.''

"Lord, Alison,'' Molly put in under her breath, "let me go get the hospital chaplain so he can marry you guys right now. You'd be a damn fool to let a heartthrob like this one get away!''

"Yeah,'' she agreed sadly, her hand tightening about Richard's. "But, as you just pointed out, I might not have any choice in the matter.''

Chapter Six

Within twenty-four hours, the police had stopped by the hospital to question both Alison and Richard about the shooting. Alison was careful to tell them exactly the same story she had the ambulance crew and hospital staff.

Richard, having rehearsed the details with Alison and Molly, accounted for his rather European accent and old-fashioned phraseology by claiming to be from England. Alison had traveled to Oxford two summers earlier to attend an international medical convention, and she instructed Richard to inform the authorities that that was where the two of them had met. Then he was to add that, after months of ardent correspondence, they had become engaged.

As for Richard's version of his shooting, Alison and Molly had coached him to claim that he'd been out jogging through the woods near the motel in nothing but swimming trunks when he'd been fired upon by an unseen gunman. Alison, meanwhile, had been off playing tennis with her friend Molly and had only discovered what had happened to Richard when she'd become worried that he'd fallen prey to the same sniper who'd been shooting at her and Ms. Miller. Well, lo and behold, so he had. And, once Alison found him, shivering due to blood loss, in the woods, she'd run back to the motel and called for an ambulance. Then she'd rushed up to her room and grabbed the pajama top, which the ambulance crew had found Richard in, in order to warm him. This then accounted for why there were no bullet holes in the garment.

With Alison thusly eliminated as a suspect in his shooting, Richard was released from the hospital into her care a couple of days later; and the two of them returned to her motel to share her room there. Although the threat of Alison being arrested in connection with the incident seemed to be behind them, another danger to their relationship remained. This was that Richard continued to periodically fade from view, and, sadly, the lengths of time during which he did so were increasing.

"It seems extraordinarily cruel, does it not," he asked her, where he now sat in one of the wing chairs near her room's large window, "that Heaven should bring us together this way, only to tear us asunder?"

Heaving a forlorn sigh, Alison sank down on the end of her bed and locked her gaze upon him. "It seems more than cruel, really. It's horrible. I mean, we've hardly even been given the chance to get to know each other."

He studied her in the bluish tone of that evening's twilight, a worshipful chill rushing through him at the rosy glow of her angular cheeks and the luminousness of her sapphire eyes. "But, my dear, I have *always* known you. Across the ages and through the mists of nightly dreams, my soul has been with yours. The heartless hand of fate shall never steal that from me. Nor, I pray, when I am finally swallowed back by this 'paradox' of which your friend keeps speaking, will all memory of me be taken from you, love."

She shook her head and did her best not to grow teary-eyed on him again. "No. I won't forget you. It's just not possible. You're the most exciting, life-affirming thing that's ever happened to me, Colonel Richard Adams. You can rest assured of that."

There was a sudden rumble outside the window and

Richard, thinking it some sort of canon fire, couldn't help giving a slight start.

"Fireworks," Alison explained, her voice assuaging. "They've already begun setting some off, I guess, since it's getting dark."

A melancholy smile came to his lips. "How odd that you should celebrate that war today by creating such explosions, when, in truth, we who fought it, wanted only for them to finally end."

"Well, it's not so much for the sound that we do it, as for the light and color. . . . See," she added after a few seconds, pointing out the window at the radiant red shower of a distant skyrocket, which could be seen far above the nearby treetops. "It's like painting the night with sparkles."

His smile broadened as he turned and caught sight of the tail end of the glimmering vermilion burst. This was immediately followed by a dazzling cascade of white and gold light. And then a breathtaking eruption of blue, which ended in whistling silver streamers which caused Richard to laugh a bit to himself. "Ah, yes. They are rather beautiful, when viewed from such a secure distance."

"I'm glad you approve, because Molly's insisting that we go out with her in a little while and watch the local display. It is the Fourth, after all."

"So the Fourth is the day on which Cornwallis finally surrendered?"

"No. It's the day of the adoption of the Declaration of Independence. July 4, 1776. Remember?"

He nodded, his expression brightening with sudden comprehension. "So it was. I suppose that, having not yet won the war in my day, we did not think that date as significant as you do now. . . . 'Tis strange, though," he continued, his features again sinking into the glumness that had darkened them off and on ever since he'd begun growing transparent, "that I should now know so very much about the future and yet so little of my own. . . .

Tell, me, my darling, would you dance with me? As we did in that dream in which we met.''

He was both surprised and pleased to see her blush at this request. ''Oh, God. I—I don't know how to do the minuet,'' she admitted.

''So then, I shall teach you,'' he declared, rising from the chair.

''But what about your sutures? And your arm? The doctors would have had the sling removed, you know, if they'd wanted you using it this soon.''

He crossed to her and extended his right hand to help her to her feet. ''But what good is their skill if they would mend a mere shoulder, yet let a heart remain broken?''

She fought a smirk and put her hand into the one he offered. ''You're a charmer. There's no denying that.'' She lowered her gaze a bit, looking up at him through a provocative fringe of dark lashes. ''But as your nurse, Colonel Adams, I feel I should warn you that I am not at all inclined to simply dance with you.''

''Nor am I with you,'' he confessed in a whisper, as she finally rose and he pulled her up against his torso in a heated embrace.

''Some of the dancing of our day is just like this,'' she said softly. ''Cheek to cheek.''

''Oh, yes? What an improvement then upon the censorious distance we Colonists were always taught to maintain from our partners.''

''But we need some music,'' Alison declared, breaking away from him just long enough to rush over to the night table on which she'd set her travel-sized clock radio. She kept turning the station dial until she caught a few notes of something which sounded suitably romantic. She realized after a couple seconds that it was a decades-old rendition of ''I Only Have Eyes For You.''

''Oh, I like that,'' Richard cooed as she hurried back to him and took up where they'd left off, her arms closing gently about his shoulders. ''The minstrel is wondering if there be stars out tonight, given that all he can see is his beloved. Is that not right?'' he whispered into her ear, as their bodies began swaying in unison to the tune.

''Exactly,'' she murmured back. Then she shut her eyes and did her best to relish every blissful second in his embrace. God only knew how much more time they'd be given together.

'' 'Tis a marvelous thing, my dear, that musical clock of yours.''

''But no where near as marvelous as what we're about to do, you sweet wonderful man,'' she replied, pressing her lips to the side of his warm, sturdy neck.

And, somewhere in the gloaming, in the blue hour of that celebrated night, the nurse's healing fingers found their way to the most private parts of him. And the soldier stabbed not into the flesh of the enemy, but into the welcoming and heavenly recesses of the one he now held most dear.

Somewhere, amidst the sparkling sky lights of that special evening, the year 1781 not only claimed the Colonial colonel, who was destined to help win the war the date commemorated, but the lovely nurse, who was equally fated to help him through the darkness, through the woods, to General Washington—who awaited the crucial message they'd been brought together to deliver.

SHOWERS AND SPARKS

Trana Mae Simmons

Chapter One

"Uh-oh. There she goes again!"

The red Mustang convertible whizzed by the intersection so fast it shimmered in the Texas heat rising from the asphalt. The woman driving either didn't see the Highway Patrol car preparing to turn onto the main road—or didn't give a darn. Hank pulled out from the stop sign in a shower of gravel and, despite being off duty, reached to flip on the siren.

Zach groaned. "Aw hell, Hank," he told his cousin. "Do you have to do this? I'm ready for a beer, and I didn't get any lunch either. Let's keep going, so you can change and we can get to the Hickory Smoke before it's too crowded."

Although he kept his foot jammed on the gas feed and the special-engine patrol car quickly shortened the distance between it and the Mustang, Hank hesitated over the siren toggle switch. Then he flipped the switch. The siren blared and Zach grimaced.

"Do you know who's in that car?" Hank asked. When Zach muttered a negative, Hank said, "That's Gerrie Jean Cartwright, and almost every time I see her, she's breaking the speed limit. Look how fast she's going right now, when I've already given her three tickets this year!"

"Shoot, out here on this flat highway anything under a hundred is slow driving, Hank. Seems like you're never gonna get anywhere even at that speed. And I've got no idea who Gerrie Jean Cartwright is, although the name sounds like she's one of those typical, double-named Texas sweethearts.''

"Condoning speeding is a fine thing for an officer of the court, Cousin, especially since I know for a fact you wouldn't any more go over the limit than you'd use a salad fork to eat your meat. And you don't know who a famous artist like Gerrie Jean Cartwright is? Naw, I guess you wouldn't. Her type of art wouldn't sell in your social circles.''

Hank had one thing right, Zach thought in semiannoyance. He'd only received one speeding ticket in his entire life, when he was sixteen. The remembered horror of facing his father back then kept him setting his cruise control exactly even today.

The Mustang's driver pulled to the side of the endless stretch of highway, and Hank followed. Zach eyed the back of the driver's blond head. Past those riotous curls, a set of bright green, extremely long fingernails tapped out an impatient cadence on the steering wheel, and what he could see of her face in the Mustang's rearview mirror looked interesting enough to keep his attention. But either those eyes were tilted a little or narrowed in warning as she waited for the inevitable ''License, insurance, and what's so darned important you have to drive like your tail's on fire to get there?''

Hell, Hank wouldn't use the word *tail*, would he? That would be something—a sexual harassment suit against a Highway Patrol by a ticketed driver. That one would end up in Zach's higher court. But why on earth did the double entendre leap into his mind just because he was trying to figure out what color those eyes were?

"She's an artist?" he asked Hank.

"Yeah, and well-known in her own way by the type of people who buy what she does. Look, I'll leave the air on and you can sit here in comfort. This won't take long.''

Hank unfolded from the patrol car, and Zach sighed in resignation. Hell, he wasn't even supposed to be in the car. Hank had talked him into it, saying they could get away with it this once, since Zach's Mercedes was in for its regular, semimonthly maintenance. All they had to do was stop and let Hank change and pick up his personal car. With Hank's wife and kids off visiting, he and his cousin could spend the evening eating melt-in-your-mouth barbecue and drinking cold longnecks at the Hickory Smoke Ice House and Barbecue Shack. They hadn't had a chance to do that since before they both got married within six weeks of the other. Even in his youth, Zach only went to the Hickory Smoke when his father was out of town.

But Miss Gerrie Jean Cartwright had to be speeding in front of his stickler-for-the-law cousin! Hell, even a federal judge like Zach knew to back off and put business aside for pleasure once in a while. Or, at least he was trying to learn how to do that the past couple years, since Amanda had accused him during the divorce of being so stodgy he creaked when he tried to unbend.

Later, he seemed to recall everything happening in slow motion, but it couldn't have. Hank stood in the open driver's door a moment, tucking his shirt neatly into his pants and readjusting the tie he'd loosened while he and Zach caught up on each other's lives on the drive from the courthouse. Ahead of them, those green-tipped fingers pattered more rapidly on the steering wheel, then the slender shoulders beneath the mane of wind-blown hair rose and fell as though in a sigh. Next, she leaned across the seat, one hand reaching for the glove box. Maneuvering a thumb topped with another vicious-looking nail, she pried at the glove box button.

Deciding she must be reaching for her insurance card— hell, this wasn't a high-risk type of stop for Hank to make because he obviously knew the woman—he nevertheless kept an eye on her. The glove box fairly burst open, papers raining to the floorboard and scattering on the seat. She tried to push some of them back into a space way too small to handle that flood, and suddenly Zach heard the *clunk* of the trunk latch releasing. Hank evidently heard the sound, too, and instinctively dropped behind the car door as he drew his pistol.

Zach caught a brief glimpse of her full face as she wrenched around in the seat and stared at the rising trunk lid, eyes wide and mouth open in consternation. *An extremely kissable mouth* flashed through his mind before he found himself wondering whether to duck beneath the dash in case she came up with a gun of her own or risk getting shot to watch the show.

"Freeze, Gerrie Jean!" Hank shouted.

Instead, she scrambled out of the car and stood on the longest, sexiest pair of legs Zach had ever seen in his thirty-five years of prowling the confines of his restricted life, not even realizing he was looking for those exact legs. The brief shorts gave him the perfect opportunity to scan every inch of them, too. To top that off, she wore a pair of nearly strapless sandals, the stiletto heels adding at least another four inches to her leg length. She lunged for the trunk lid, and Zach winced. That lid had to be burning hot in the Texas sun. It had been up near a hundred today, ever since noon.

She banged the lid shut and jerked her hands back.

"God, that woman nearly caused me to shoot her," Hank mumbled. He stood and shoved his pistol into the holster. Muttering something about brainless blondes, which Zach was sure could also get him into sexual harassment trouble, Hank slammed the car door and walked toward the Mustang. The culprit stood in front of the trunk now, arms crossed beneath a more than adequate set of breasts in a multicolored tank top and a look of defiance on her extremely beautiful face.

Deciding he needed a lot closer vantage point to watch this show, Zach opened the passenger door and stepped out.

"Why aren't you out chasing bad guys?" the culprit

asked in a defensive voice, though it was still as sticky sweet as warm honey oozing down a stack of hotcakes. One thing Zach had always had trouble with was controlling his between-the-legs response to a sexy Southern feminine drawl. In fact, the first thing that had drawn him to Amanda was her sultry, Southern nights voice.

"Come on, Gerrie Jean," Hank said. "You can do better than that. Why, I could retire if I had a dollar for every time someone made that comment to me. Now, let's open that trunk again."

She tilted her delicate chin up a notch. "No. First, let me see your warrant."

"I don't need a warrant when I have probable cause to search a car," Hank said. "And your acting so suspicious about me seeing what's in that trunk is definitely probable cause. Now, open it."

Without thinking, Zach propped his bare forearm on the patrol car's roof, then drew it back with a curse when the hot metal burned his arm. Wrapping his fingers around the pain, he glanced up into a pair of brown eyes, which for some reason fit that mane of blond hair better than typical blues ones would have.

"Do you need help to catch us poor li'l ole heavy-footed females these days, Hank?" she oozed. As she spoke, she gave Zach a brief once-over that sent another charge of heat right where he didn't need it on such a hot day.

Shaking his head, Hank walked around her and headed for the passenger side of the Mustang. She'd left the glove box open, but when he reached toward it, Gerrie Jean shrieked in outrage, rushing after him in a surprisingly steady gait, given her dangerous-looking shoes. She grabbed for Hank's arm, and as he held her off, he used his other hand to punch the trunk release.

Reacting spontaneously, Zach lunged past the patrol car door and headed for the Mustang to assist Hank. He wrapped his arms around the little hellion's small waist and easily pulled her away. She wiggled and pried at his fingers, but her words were for Hank.

"Damn you, Henry Allen Tagglebond! You have no right to search my car!"

"I have every right in the world," Hank said around a huff of impatience. "And if you think I don't, sue me."

"Ohhhhhh!"

Just as Zach decided he could safely release her, she gave a more emphatic twist. Awkward without his support, she staggered against him, and somehow Zach's right hand slipped beneath her tube top. A soft, bare boob landed in his hand, and he could no more pull back from the contact than conjure up a snowstorm right then to cool his even more heated response. She froze, and the nipple beneath his thumb pebbled into a hard knot. His damned thumb knew from years of experience just what to do, and it swept back and forth across the nipple at least three times before she stomped one of those stiletto heels right through the Italian leather on his right foot.

Howling with pain, Zach tossed Gerrie Jean to Hank and lifted his foot. When he tried to brace himself for balance, his hand landed on the metal of the car's fender, and he ended up with another burn. He swiveled and propped his rear against the fender instead, raising his leg and jerking off his shoe. Blood spattered his light tan sock.

"Now you've done it," he heard Hank tell that feminine piece of menace looking for a place to happen. "You've gone and assaulted a judge—an officer of the law!"

"Uh-oh," was her response.

Considering the nearly debilitating pain in his foot, there wasn't nearly enough fear or trepidation in her voice to satisfy Zach.

Gerrie Jean drew in a breath and stood her ground. Well, so what if that sexy hunk of masculinity was a judge? He'd deliberately fondled her breast, and she sure as shooting didn't have to allow that! But she couldn't quite stifle the thought that, had she known him a little better, fondling might be an option.

A judge, huh? Seemed a shame for a black robe to cover up all that muscle and sinew each day. Even in his casual tan Dockers and cream knit shirt he looked like he'd just stepped out of the pages of *GQ*. If he sat on that high bench in a tight T-shirt and jeans, every woman in Bexar County would be committing crimes to get a look at him.

"Uh . . . what sort of offense do you have to commit to get in front of *him*?" she asked Hank, tilting her head to indicate Zach.

Instead of Hank answering, the judge's dark brown bottomless eyes speared her like a kabob for a barbecue grill. "You need to worry more about what sort of mood the judge who's going to hear your assault case is going to be in, Miss Long Legs," he snarled.

"Why, you lecherous case of walking sexual harassment!" she threw back at him. Propping her hands on her hips, she walked closer, so he could clearly understand every word. "On top of that sexual name you just used about my legs, *you* put your dirty hands on *my* breast! I've got every right in the world to defend my body from your filthy paws!"

"All I was doing was assisting Hank—keeping you from assaulting him. Every citizen in the United States has the right—the *duty*—to assist law enforcement personnel!"

Gasping with outrage, she inched her nose closer to him. She didn't want him to miss even one tiny syllable of her next remark. "Your hand slipping under my tube top when we were struggling might have been construed as an accident. Your hand staying there long enough to rub your thumb back and forth across my nipple three times was deliberate!"

"You counted, too, huh?" he replied.

With an extreme effort—to the point of biting down

hard on the inside of her cheek—she choked back the
laugh that bubbled up and surprised her. He looked like
he wished he'd bitten his cheek, too, rather than let that
comment loose. Feeling a movement on her stomach, she
glanced down to see his toes pressed against her. They
wiggled again.

"Ohhhhh!" She flew backwards, saved from tumbling
to the gravelly roadside only by Hank catching her this
time. He released her the very instant she caught her balance, holding his hands far out to his sides when she
turned on him.

"I didn't touch you any longer than it took me to make
sure you weren't going to fall, Gerrie Jean," Hank said.
"Now, sit your butt down in that car and wait until I
make sure I don't have to run Zach to the hospital for
stitches before we look in that trunk."

Evidently to drive his point home more emphatically,
Hank reached inside the Mustang and grabbed the keys
she'd left dangling in the ignition. Shoving them into his
pants pocket, he walked past her to the judge—Zach, she
guessed his name was, since they hadn't been formally
introduced.

They would be soon, she supposed, hanging her head
and shaking it back and forth in resignation. What the
hell had she done? She'd probably have had a defense if
it had just been her and Hank on the highway. But with
a judge—a male judge—for Hank's compadre in the
Texas Good Ole Boys Club, she didn't stand a chance.
And she didn't even know why she'd tried to keep Hank
from examining the stuff in the trunk, unless it was because she hadn't had time to look at it herself. More
probably, she didn't like the violation of her space—her
car. And Cool Hand wouldn't have brought anything illegal back from Missouri. Would he?

A tiny voice tried to caution that she could possibly
be wrong, but she mentally shooed it away.

"I'm going to get the first-aid kit out of the patrol car,
Gerrie Jean," Hank broke into her thoughts, his voice

continuing to hold a warning tone. "Don't try to go any-where."

"You've got my keys," she reminded him. She started to lift her head, but her gaze caught on a bare male foot propped against the opposite leg. The pale skin should have turned off her response, but those long toes seemed to strike something in her, especially when she remembered them stroking her stomach. Then the blood seeping into the trouser material registered on her mind, as well as the strip of skin hanging from the largest toe. Her emotions flipflopped as the sight made her stomach boil with nausea.

She clapped a hand over her mouth, all the while knowing it was no use. Swiveling, she grabbed the mirror on the side of her car for support and leaned forward, emptying her stomach with sounds so wretched they spurred her upchucking. The bitter bile spattered when it hit the pebbly ground, soaking her bare legs. That feeling, too, heightened her heaves of misery, until she could barely keep from collapsing into the mess at her feet.

Fortunately, a pair of strong arms wrapped around her just as her leg muscles turned cooked-spaghetti weak.

Chapter Two

W hen she could straighten again, Gerrie Jean saw a handkerchief under her nose. The fine linen look told her the judge had to be making the offer since, knowing Hank, he probably carried a red bandanna. The judge kept his arm around her waist in a gesture she found both comforting and soothing—definitely not sexual this time. But then, what man in his right mind would come on to a woman puking her guts out on the ground? Rather than hang around while she heaved, most of them would get a fair distance away at the first hint of a preliminary burp or green-tinged face.

Thinking he was going to wipe her face, Gerrie Jean grabbed the handkerchief and did that herself, then swiped her legs. Bending pressed her rear against his semi-hard erection, but she was much too nauseous for it to bother her. He grunted a dismayed sound and stepped away, probably thinking she was going to turn on him and continue their shouting match and threats of a harassment suit. She was too sick for that, too, and the illness wasn't totally centered in her stomach.

It was going to take a good long time before she got over the mental guilt of what she'd done to him, even though he deserved it for not pulling his hand back immediately. But hell—she could have jerked away. Why hadn't she?

She couldn't ever recall hurting another person or animal in her life. Shoot, she even put the fish she caught on ice and let them die before she cleaned them! The vision of the damage her heel had done—the blood and loose flap of skin—made her want to heave again.

Tears blurring her vision, she turned toward Zach. "I'm very, very sorry for what happened. I'll pay any doctor's bills you have."

For just an instant, she thought she saw a look of hunger on his face, but his eyes immediately softened and one corner of his mouth lifted slightly. He raised a hand toward her cheek, as though to wipe away the tear that trembled on her lower lash briefly, then tumbled free. But Hank interrupted.

"You bet your boots you will, Gerrie Jean," the Highway Patrolman said sternly. "You'll pay doctor bills and you'll face assault charges if Zach wants to press them. And I might even add resisting arrest to whatever I can come up with over those illegal fireworks in your trunk."

"Hell, Hank," Zach growled. "Shut up already about the assault charges and doctor bills. This incident was as much yours and my fault as anything. I'd bristle some, too, if a couple bullies twice as big as me tried to push me around."

Surprised at his defense of her, Gerrie Jean caught Zach's eye just as he slipped her a surreptitious wink. The tone of his voice made her wish she could crawl into his arms and let him take care of her troubles, but Hank wasn't about to let her get by with that.

"Look, Zach," he said. "You haven't had to deal with her every time you turn around. It's your call on what you want to do about her peeling half your foot off with that sharp-as-switchblade heel of hers, but I'm not about to forget those illegal fireworks. We've had a drought this year that rivals Death Valley, and there's a reason some of these things have been banned. More than one person could get hurt if they started a fire."

Right now Gerrie Jean was out of anger to use to defend herself. She sighed and said to Hank, "I don't suppose you'd believe me if I told you I had no idea any of those fireworks were illegal. A friend brought them back from Missouri for me just today, and I haven't even gone through those boxes yet. Anyway, when did you look at them?"

Hank handed Zach a red and white metal first-aid kit as he replied, "On the way back over to your car with the first-aid kit. Not everything in there is illegal, unless I catch you setting them off somewhere they've been prohibited, but those M-80s right on top are. They're definitely outlawed in Texas, as well as every other state. Plus the aerial stuff has been banned in Bexar County this year, because of the drought."

Suddenly something flickered in his eyes, and Hank narrowed his gaze. "You say these came back from Missouri with some friend of yours? That's interstate transport of illegal fireworks, and it's a federal charge. Who bought them for you?"

Oh, God! That's all she needed, for Cool Hand to end up in trouble for doing her a favor. "The responsibility for them ending up in Texas is mine," she evaded Hank. "I asked for them to be brought here."

"Fine. Then you can appear on the charges."

She shrugged. "Whatever. Just tell me when to be in court." Hank reacted with a narrowed gaze, as though he didn't trust her sudden submissiveness. She ignored him and opened the car door. "If you'll sit down," she told Zach, "I'll see what I can do with your toe. I can at least bandage it until you get to the doctor."

"You sure you've got the stomach for it?" he asked as he slid into the seat.

"I'll manage. It's the least I can do, since you so graciously admitted this was partly your fault."

He propped his ankle on the opposite knee and opened the first-aid kit on his lap. Selecting a cottonball and bottle of peroxide, she went to work. Moments later, with him only giving one gasp as the peroxide bubbles cleaned the wound, she finished a neat bandage over the toe.

Closing the first-aid kit, she handed it to Hank, then wiped the tingles on her fingers against her bare thighs. Who would have thought a man's foot could cause a reaction in her? She hadn't felt the type of turn on simmering just below the surface of her emotions in years. And it started when the judge got out of the car. She was definitely going to have to quit watching those Patrick Swayze movies before bed.

Suddenly realizing he hadn't said a word to her all during the time she took care of his wound, she slowly inched her gaze up to meet Zach's. Sweat plastered a silky black curl to his forehead, and she instinctively reached to push it back in place. He jerked his head away sharply.

"I have a bit of a problem with those wicked-looking nails," he explained with a chuckle. "In fact, I don't see how you do anything at all with them on your fingers, yet you managed that bandage perfectly well. It's fascinating how you maneuver with them."

She smiled slightly and shook her head. "It's just practice. You should see me wield a paintbrush. Do you want me to help you get your sock back on, or are you going to go barefoot?"

"I'll take care of it."

She picked up his shoe while he slid on the sock, rubbing her index finger back and forth over the hole her heel punched in it. "You should at least let me pay for a new pair of shoes."

"I doubt I'm going to need to go to the doctor at all, since you did a very adequate job bandaging my toe. And let's just say the shoe damage was also partly my own fault and call it even." His eyes twinkled, and she saw a flash of dimple in his right cheek when he grinned at her. "You only damaged *one* shoe, so you shouldn't have to buy me two. And a new pair of shoes will be cheaper than an attorney to defend me for not keeping control of my hands."

"I know that wasn't deliberate," Gerrie Jean admitted, savoring the little curl of pleasure twisting through her. Darn, she'd always been sucker for dimples in a man.

"Well, truthfully, as you so astutely pointed out, part of it *was* deliberate," Zach murmured. "And I apologize for that part, although I can't bring myself to admit I'm sorry for it."

"If you two are done flirting," Hank said, "I've loaded the fireworks into the patrol car. You'll get back whatever isn't illegal after I impound the rest, Gerrie Jean. And now I need to see your insurance card."

"Flirting?" Zach mused. "Hell, Hank, I haven't even gotten around to asking for her phone number yet."

"Well, she's in the book," Hank told him. "Hog Heaven Bikes out in Cibilo, that eastern suburb of San Antonio. Now, the insurance card, Gerrie Jean?"

She tightened her lips, Hank's dictator tone poking leaks in her composure. The insurance card was somewhere in that mess on the floorboard, with the hundred and eighty pounds of masculinity sitting sideways in the passenger seat blocking her from searching for it.

"It's the same insurance I've had all year, and you've already seen it three times," she reminded Hank. "Just write up the ticket, and I'll sign it."

"If I don't actually see the card, I'll also be writing up a ticket for no proof of insurance," he told her. "You'll have to bring your insurance policy to court to get that one dismissed, and pay court costs even then."

"Ohhhh!" He'd finally managed to spark her anger again. She glared at him, then before she could change her mind, she leaned past Zach and scooped up the entire mess of papers on the floorboard. That brief few seconds of contact against him made her nipples pebble, and she silently cursed her body as she stood. She'd always known her nipples were longer than a lot of other women's, and she damned sure wouldn't have worn that tube top if she'd thought she'd be placed in a situation where she'd get sexually charged.

Resolutely not looking down at her chest, she leafed through the papers. Once, twice. "It's not here," she muttered.

Zach reached out and picked up the top piece of paper from the pile in her hand. "Isn't this it?"

Biting her lip in humiliation, she nodded her head. Zach handed the insurance card to Hank, and he fastened it to his clipboard as he wrote out her speeding ticket. Then he handed the ticket to her to sign. She didn't protest. All she wanted to do was get out of there. Preferably five minutes ago.

"Now," Hank said. "I'll let you know when you have to appear on the fireworks violation charge. In fact, you'll be hearing from the Bureau of Alcohol, Tobacco and Firearms folks on that. And since this is your fourth speeding ticket this year, you're going to have to appear in court on that, also, instead of just paying the fine. There's a good possibility you'll lose your license for ninety days."

"I can't!" she gasped. "How will I get back and forth to my dealership? And take care of all my volunteer work?"

"You should have thought of that when you kept breaking the law," Hank said with a shrug. "You ready to go, Zach?"

"Wait a minute!" Gerrie Jean said in horror. "Back up and repeat what you said about the Bureau of Whatever and the fireworks charges."

"They're federal folks," Hank said. "I think I'll let them explain your troubles to you."

Zach stood, and Hank ambled away, tucking his clipboard beneath his arm. Just before Zach started after him, he murmured, "Hog Heaven out in Cibilo, huh?"

That little curl turned into a full-blown corkscrew in her stomach as Zach's words slithered through her senses. But almost immediately she felt debilitating fear replace her craving to get to know the sexy judge better as Hank's warning came to the forefront. Why on earth would a few little fireworks end her up in trouble with the federal people like that? And wasn't that the department involved in that horrible debacle in Waco a couple years ago, where so many innocent women and children were burned to death?

Chapter Three

Cool Hand propped one battered leather boot on the chopper's gas tank and took a deep drag on his cigarette. "Well, la-di-da di-da," he muttered, undaunted by Gerrie Jean's reproving look. "So I brought a few M-80s back with me. Hell, I didn't know us little Texas boys weren't allowed to play with such dangerous toys."

"I'm not mad, Cool Hand," Gerrie Jean denied. "I really appreciate your getting these fireworks for me. They're a lot cheaper than what we could've got them for here in Texas, plus we couldn't even buy them for another couple weeks, since the stands are only allowed to sell them for two weeks prior to the Fourth each year. That wouldn't have given me enough time to design and paint the gas tank for the raffle. I was just warning you, in case you kept a few of those M-80s or aerial fireworks for yourself. You know they routinely search your bike's saddlebags whenever you get stopped."

"Yeah," Cool Hand sneered. "Well, what's the deal? You say you have to go to court over it? What'd ole Hank do? Write you some little bitty ole ticket?"

"Uh . . . well, no. I mean, I did get a speeding ticket. But I left the sales receipt for the fireworks in the box. So on them, there's a small matter of transporting them illegally across state lines—from Missouri to Texas. And I was served a warrant from a federal marshal earlier today—on behalf of the Bureau of Alcohol, Tobacco and Firearms.''

Cool Hand stood so fast his chopper teetered, and he grabbed it to keep it from falling to the concrete shop floor and scratching the beautiful gas tank Gerrie Jean had painted for him. ''For crying out loud, G J! You ended up in *federal* court because of this? Jesus. You could've told them *I* was the one who brought them back here.''

Her shoulders heaved. ''You did it because I asked you to when you said you were going to visit your brother, Cool Hand. That makes it totally my fault. Besides, you'd have three strikes against you already in that court.''

''Yeah, it sure as hell didn't do no good that time to gripe about my civil rights being violated over them searching my bike. Not with Society Zach on the bench. It came right down to it, Zach'd probably say it was all right for the cops to search Hoedown's wheelchair, 'cause he might just be faking not being able to move his legs. That way, he could get some sympathy and the cops would overlook the fact he might be hiding something illegal beneath his chair cushion!''

Something thudded into Gerrie Jean's stomach, and she stared at Cool Hand in dawning dread. ''Who did you say was on the bench?''

''What? You mean the federal bench when my case got tossed out last year? That damned judge said the cops had a right to strip-search me, just 'cause they smelled pot on my clothes! Only reason they smelled it was 'cause I'd just come from a Guns 'N Roses concert and the whole damned arena had pockets of pot smokers in it! They'd've had a riot on their hands, they tried to arrest everyone smoking a joint in there.''

''I know all about your case, Cool Hand.'' Gerrie Jean stifled a sigh. ''I was asking what the name of your judge was.''

''Oh. That was good ole Judge Zachariah Edward Brenham, Mr. High Society himself. His daddy was a judge before him, and his granddaddy, too, and rumor is they're some blood kin all the way back to ole Judge Roy Bean. 'Course they'd never claim that ole pervert these days, the circles they travel in.''

Good God, it had to be! How many judges named Zach could there be in San Antonio? She didn't know that much about the court system—her appearance on the speeding charge was the first time she hadn't managed to wiggle out of having to go to court by just taking defensive driving or paying her speeding fines. Try as she might, she couldn't seem to remember to use her cruise control. And when she got to fantasizing about her next art project, she forgot to pay attention to her speed.

The fireworks in the trunk were what had caused it all. She'd been imagining designs for the motorcycle gas tank she would prepare for the raffle to benefit Hoedown. Hopefully, they would raise enough funds to buy a computer for the biker, who was paralyzed from the waist down because of the motorcycle wreck two years ago. Hoedown's wife could sure use some help supporting their three children, and Texas Rehab had paid for some classes for Hoedown.

Federal court—her second court appearance—had an ominous ring and had her duly scared to death. She hadn't really sympathized with Cool Hand's story that much when he hired a lawyer to go after what he thought was going to be a few easy bucks for his civil rights violation. Far as she had always been concerned, law enforcement personnel had a right to check things out. But that was before Hank had treated her like a low-class criminal last week and demanded to search her car.

He wouldn't have demanded that if you hadn't acted so suspicious, her mind told her. She grimaced as her thoughts tracked over that day in split-second flashes, ending up on the vision of the blood-smeared toe. The guilt once again escalated.

She'd thought maybe she'd have a chance to alleviate that guilt when Zach called her, but evidently she'd totally misinterpreted his interest in her. Of course, now she understood why, even though for a while she'd considered buying a cellular phone so she wouldn't take a chance on missing his call. He'd had fun flirting with her, but Federal Judge Zachariah Edward Brenham darned sure wouldn't date Miss Geralyn Jean Cartwright, the owner of a motorcycle dealership in Cibilo, Texas, and an accused federal felon.

And she didn't give a rat's butt, either. She nodded her head for emphasis. She preferred ginger ale over champagne, and her idea of fun was cruising around Lake McQueeney in her brother's boat—or going with him when he ran his trotline, hoping he'd pull in enough catfish for a fish fry. Federal Judge Zachariah Edward Brenham probably ate trout amandine instead of deep-fried catfish and got his jollies by beating a buddy on a handball court at his health club. Hadn't his feet been so white they looked like they'd hidden inside his pants legs every time there was danger of a sunbeam hitting them?

But damn it, she'd always wondered if trout tasted better than catfish. . . .

Well, her summons, or whatever they called that stupid piece of paper full of unreadable, supposed English, had said she'd be going in front of something called a magistrate, not a full-blown judge. She probably wouldn't even see Zach. But maybe she should have contacted a lawyer instead of just figuring she'd go in there and tell them she was guilty. Let them do whatever they wanted to her and take her medicine.

"You want to do what?" Magistrate Thomas gaped at Zach in disbelief.

"Take your caseload this afternoon," Zach repeated. "I'm between trials, since I scheduled these next couple weeks for vacation, and I'd like to get a taste of some other facets of the bench for once."

"Well, you're sure as hell qualified to sit over my cases, Zach. And I'd be glad to have the afternoon off, although I'd like to be a fly on the wall when a full-blown chief judge walks into my little courtroom. But have at it.''

The magistrate waved a hand and hurried off, as though he was afraid Zach might change his mind. Fat chance. He'd been waiting two weeks for Gerrie Jean's name to come up on the magistrate's docket. He knew it would be as soon as possible, since Hank had remained fairly hot over the situation all during dinner that evening at the Hickory Smoke.

Whistling—something he hadn't done since child-hood—he headed for the judge's chambers behind the other courtroom. Fifteen minutes later, he scanned a mea-ger courtroom galley as he strode to the dais, his black robe flapping around his legs. As soon as the attorneys recognized him, the proverbial pin dropping in that court-room would have made a loud enough explosion to reg-ister on the Richter scale. His years on the bench allowed him to control his urge to smile, but he silently admitted to a stab of satisfaction at the reverence in the courtroom. In his regular court, some of the attorneys were high-dollar, jaded old-timers, who barely covered up their in-solence as they played out their role of the best damned legal counsel their client's laundered money could buy.

He heard a Motion first, barely paying any attention to the convoluted reasoning the attorney presented in his brief before dismissing the asinine suggestion and order-ing the attorney to quit delaying the case. Had the losing attorney had a tail, it would have been tucked between his legs as he slunk off. The young prosecutor hadn't been around long enough to know he should cover up his emotions, and Zach had to hide his smile behind his hand when the prosecutor smirked at the opposing attor-ney's loss.

But where the hell was the case he'd come here to handle?

The courtroom door flew open and a figure rushed through. Ah, there she was. God, he loved the short hem lengths that had come back into style. She wore a different pair of sandals—red, white, and blue today—but the heels were every bit as high, although more chunky than those stiletto ones which had injured him. She probably thought that loose, flowing white blouse was antisexy, but the sensuous fabric clung in the appropriate places.

"Your honor!"

"Huh?" Zach said, realizing at the same instant that the bailiff had repeated the words at least three times. Just then, Gerrie Jean skidded to a wobbling stop in the middle of the aisle, her eyes on his face and her jaw dropping. He couldn't keep from giving her a slight nod, and she shook her head in denial. He heard a snort of derision from the female court reporter, and gave her a warning glare.

Gerrie Jean bent and whispered something in the ear of the man nearest her. Hell, she could have had her pick of any man in the courtroom to talk to! Every male eye was trained on her, and he heard a door squeak. The rear courtroom door opened again and some pimply faced teenage boy stuck his head in, his eyes unerringly centering on Gerrie Jean. Zach swore he saw a shimmering line of drool running down the punk's chin.

"Miss Cartwright!" he called, putting all the green rancor clouding his emotions into his voice. "Take a seat until your name is called! And bailiff, post someone back there to keep interruptions out of this courtroom. This isn't traffic court!"

Suitably chastised, the bailiff headed for the back of the room. He carried his copy of the docket with him so he could call the cases from back there—the docket on which Zach had rearranged the numbered order of the cases.

"Miss Cartwright," Zach repeated.

"Uh . . . I . . . must have the wrong courtroom," she sputtered. "But the clerk told me this was where I should come."

"You're in the right court, Miss Cartwright." He felt a stab of uneasiness when her face paled, then realized the problem. "You're in the Magistrate Court, which handles lesser charges, not in the full Federal Court. I'm filling in here this afternoon."

If anything, her face grew paler. She wilted onto the hard wooden bench beside her, sending the man she'd whispered to scooting sideways to give her room. But Zach noticed the slimy bastard didn't move too far away. Huh. He wondered which case on the docket belonged to that piece of scum with the thousand-dollar snakeskins, which he could see from his position as soon as the man resettled himself and crossed his legs. Gerrie Jean turned and whispered to the snakeskin-boot man again, and for good measure, Zach grabbed his gavel and slammed it on his dais.

"Quiet in the court!" he ordered, then felt his stomach go even more hollow when Gerrie Jean gave him a frightened look and hunched her shoulders, scooting down in her seat.

He felt guilty as hell making her wait, but what he had in mind made it necessary for her to be the last case he heard that day. It chafed his ass that the snakeskin-boot attorney had a good argument and he had to rule for him instead of against him, but he gritted his teeth and did the fair, honest, and just thing. At one point, the bailiff strolled down the aisle and held a short discussion with Gerrie Jean, then went back and delivered some message to whoever was waiting on the other side of the courtroom door.

Finally no one was left in the courtroom except him, the bailiff, the court reporter, the young prosecutor, and the woman with the million-dollar legs. At least the snakeskin-boot attorney wasn't her lawyer, but it looked like neither was anyone else. The bailiff called her case, and Gerrie Jean stood. He watched her take a deep breath, then tilt that chin up to where it looked like it would be a perfect fit in the palm of his hand and resolutely walk to stand in front of his dais. The prosecutor approached her and whispered that she should go over to the defendant's table, but Zach waved him off.

"Miss Cartwright," he said formally. "Don't you have an attorney?"

"I didn't think I needed to waste my money on one if I planned to plead guilty, Za . . . uh . . . your Honor."

Leaning back in his chair and playing with the pencil between his fingers, Zach frowned at her. "You didn't even need to appear in court if you planned on pleading guilty, Gerrie Jean. Why did you?"

An endearing mixture of surprise and confusion filled those brown eyes. "But . . . but on TV they always have to get up and say they're guilty. And Hank told me I had to actually appear in traffic court, not just pay my fine this time. I figured this was even more serious."

When the prosecutor cleared his throat, Zach covered up a sigh. "Mr. Covington, I realize you have a part in this, although it's a small part now that the defendant has indicated she's going to plead out. I'll allow you to speak in a minute. All right?"

"Oh, yes, Your Honor. Of course, Your Honor." The young man's head bobbed and he backed away. Since the man had actually proven to be a fairly competent prosecutor, Zach didn't follow up on his chastisement.

"What happened in traffic court?" he continued to Gerrie Jean.

Her lower lip protruded, and the huskiness in her voice could have been from the sulkiness he sensed. "I lost my license for thirty days. I had to get Becky Rose to give me a ride here today."

Becky Rose, huh? Another double-named Texas sweetheart. "You could have lost it for up to ninety days, you know."

"I know." She released a sigh and pulled that delectable lip back into place. "Well, I'm pleading guilty here, so just tell me what my punishment will be."

He managed to control his evil grin. "That's still to

be determined. It could be anything from jail time to probation with deferred adjudication.''

"J . . . jail time?'' She took a step backwards, then clasped her hands in front of her and stood as stiff as though she were a soldier at parade attention. "I . . . I hope you'll at least let me make a phone call first.''

He nearly had to put the pencil in his mouth and bite down on it to keep his laughter back, but he managed. "As I said, your punishment is still to be determined. I need to ask you a few questions first. Are you sure you don't want an attorney?''

"No, I still don't want an attorney! What sort of questions? I thought if I admitted I was guilty, that was it.''

Her defensiveness raised suspicious hackles in Zach's mind. He'd watched way too many *real* criminals try to outsmart him over the years to not know Gerrie Jean was hiding something. Protecting someone? Leaning on the dais surface, he opened the file labeled "Cartwright" in front of him, studying the sales slip Hank had kept for evidence. Then he peered at her again.

"Who's Alex Hilton?'' he asked, carefully watching her expression as he read off the name of the customer who had signed the sales slip. She didn't let him down, dropping her gaze and biting the side of her cheek.

"He's a friend of mine,'' she admitted after a few seconds, then hurriedly continued, "but he has nothing to do with this. Well, almost nothing. Nothing to be punished for. This is all my fault, and I'm ready to pay for my crime.''

Zach had to admire her. She didn't want to lie in court, but she didn't want to involve her friend, either. Her *male* friend, he reminded himself, not an Alexandria, since she called the friend 'he.' She'd done a fairly admirable job of not actually telling the truth but not lying either.

"What sort of friend?'' Zach hadn't even realized he was going to ask that question, but he fairly held his breath waiting for her answer. Again, she didn't satisfy his curiosity.

"A longtime friend," she grumbled. "Look, I really am getting more and more worried the longer you put off telling me what you're going to do to me."

"The court's not obligated to lessen the stress you're going through, Gerrie Jean. You're here at the court's convenience, not vice versa."

"Yes, Your Honor." She caught her lower lip between her teeth and reluctantly nodded her head, suitably rebuked—only for the moment, he was sure.

"Tell me why you had those illegal fireworks, Gerrie Jean."

"Why am I the only person in your court you're calling by a first name?" she asked.

Yep, she hadn't remained chastised very long.

"Is it some sort of lack of respect for me on your part? Because I wasn't smart enough to bring an attorney with me?"

"Tell me why you had those illegal fireworks, Miss Cartwright," he corrected himself.

She dropped her gaze again. "For the raffle."

He waited, but she didn't expand on her answer so he prodded some more. "Intending to sell illegal fireworks in Texas calls for a more severe sentence than just having them in your possession, Miss Cartwright."

That finally got to her.

"No!" she blurted. "Oh, no, that's not what I meant by the raffle. We weren't going to sell them. I did need to set them off, but I was going to do that out at my brother's place on the lake—over the water. I needed them for inspiration. You see, I was going to paint a motorcycle gas tank with a Fourth of July theme to raffle off. That's where my mind was when Hank caught me speeding—trying to imagine how the fireworks in the trunk would look exploding over the water. I mean, I've seen fireworks displays before, but not over water. I thought the reflection would make a wonderfully different type of scene than just a regular nighttime display in the air. I. . . ."

"Miss Cartwright!" She clamped her mouth shut immediately. "What was the raffle for?"

"For Hoedown. To get him a computer. He's got three kids and. . . ."

"Miss Cartwright!"

She heaved her shoulders and glared at him. "Now what? Darn it, Zach! I can't tell you what it's all about if you keep interrupting me!"

The bailiff's stifled gasp at her audacity in addressing him by name and in such a confrontational fashion carried all the way from the rear of the room, and he saw a look of total awe on the prosecutor's face. Zach bit back his threatening laugh, ignoring the disgruntled huff of the court reporter.

"Uh. . . ." Gerrie Jean glanced over her nicely turned shoulder at the bailiff. "Uh . . . Your Honor," she said.

He leaned back in his chair again. "Why don't you start at the beginning, Gerrie Jean? But keep it as short as you can. I'd like to get out of here sometime today before dark."

Over the next few minutes, he found out about the paralyzed biker—Hoedown—but she never told him how the man got his name. He had three children and a wife who worked for some catering service to help support the family. But if Hoedown could get a computer, Gerrie Jean said, he could do some desktop publishing and help them make ends meet. He'd already taken classes at the adult education center, and they'd been trying to save up on their own. Joshua, though, their youngest, had been born with a heart murmur, and he was born after Hoedown's medical insurance had lapsed because of course he couldn't go back to work at his construction job after the accident. So they were still paying for that operation.

"And I assume this Hoedown is another friend of yours?" Zach finally got a chance to ask.

"Yes, but he was closer to my mother and father," Gerrie Jean said. "He's sort of like an older brother to me, and he was the president of the Weekend Rovers before he got hurt. That's the club my mother and father started twenty years ago.''

''Weekend Rovers?''

''It's a family-style bikers club,'' she explained. ''They go camping together on their bikes. The club is involved in a lot of community efforts, too. They're helping sponsor the big Fourth of July picnic for the children's wing at the charity hospital. That's when we'll have the raffle.''

The rear courtroom door opened again, but Zach didn't pay any attention. At least, not until he heard footsteps coming down the aisle and glanced up to give the bailiff another put-down for allowing the interruption. His stomach tightened instead, and he forced back his terse comment. Retired Federal Judge Hamilton Edward Brenham—his father—slid into the first bench inside the spectator's galley and crossed his arms over his chest, propped one ankle on the other knee. Damn, his father had on a pair of snakeskin boots just like those on that smarmy lawyer who'd almost plastered himself against Gerrie Jean earlier!

And how the hell had his father found him here, unless the fast-paced rumor mill in the courthouse had already spread the news that he'd taken over a session of the Magistrate Court for the afternoon. Hell, one of dear old dad's buddies might even have called and told him that his son had gone over the border into state-hospital-candidate land. Well, this time Zach wasn't going back into the mold. This time, something was stronger than his thirty-five years of training on how to follow in the exalted footsteps of his predecessors. And a deep, gut instinct told him this *something* was a lot more than just testosterone foaming for release.

He hadn't realized the silence had stretched that long until Gerrie Jean looked over her shoulder at his father, then quirked a feathery brow as she gave him her attention again.

''Please approach the bench closer,'' Zach told her.

She frowned, glancing at the wooden benches in the jury section, and he smiled at her bewilderment. "That's court slang for approaching me, Miss Cartwright," he said.

"Slang?" She walked up to within a foot of his dais. "I didn't think something as revered as our court system would use slang."

"Maybe I should have said it's vernacular," he corrected himself. "But for now, I want to tell you what I've decided."

The court reporter's fingers paused over her stenotype machine, and she gave Gerrie Jean a smirk. If he'd known how to operate that damned machine himself, Zach would have sent her packing. As it was, he made a mental note to leave word to never assign her to his courtroom. That would cause some juicy gossip as the rumor mongers wondered what it was all about, but it would also administer a silent reprimand to the woman.

"I'm going to take into consideration your purpose for having those fireworks, Gerrie . . . uh . . . Miss Cartwright." Zach noticed his father leaning forward somewhat, and smiled inwardly when he realized his ploy at moving Gerrie Jean closer had worked. His father couldn't hear what he was saying. Of course, he could get the transcripts later, but he wouldn't be able to determine the tone of voice from them.

Then Zach grew furious at himself, chaining in his anger when he saw that Gerrie Jean had evidently noticed his face tensing up. He couldn't tell her right then that his ire was directed at himself, for hedging against what he supposed would be his father's irritation. Instead, he lifted his voice to carry throughout the courtroom.

"I'm going to leave the charges against you as they are right now, Miss Cartwright. Is that all right with you, Mr. Covington?"

The prosecutor nodded affirmatively so violently his hair fell over his forehead. Zach made a mental note to praise the young man at the same time he chastised the court reporter's reputation.

He turned back to Gerrie Jean, who had a questioning frown on her face. "What that means," he explained, "is that I'm not going to make a ruling on your guilt at this time. My final decision will be made after I see how you perform your duties."

"What duties?"

"I'm going to assign you to one hundred hours of community service, the organization you will serve to be decided upon."

"And if I do my good works?"

"If you perform your 'good works' satisfactorily, without getting into any more trouble during that time, I have the power to completely drop these charges against you. You won't go through the rest of your life with the stigma of a felony charge on your record."

He saw by her deathly white face that she hadn't really taken in the significance of what this entire mess meant in terms of a record against her. Her whisper confirming his thought barely reached his ears.

"Oh, my God. I didn't realize."

Zach's sharp gaze told him immediately that those million-dollar legs were losing the battle to hold her upright. Long, black-robed skirts be damned. Zach made a flying leap over his dais that could possibly have qualified him for some sort of Olympic competition.

Chapter Four

R ight before total blackness caved in, Gerrie Jean had
two quick thoughts. *I've never hyperventilated in my
life!* Then: *This isn't so bad, almost like flying.* The soar-
ing sensation chased the darkness away, but the debilitating fear she'd felt when she heard Zach mention that
she could possibly carry the stigma of a felony criminal
the rest of her life lingered on the edge of her mind. Still,
the cozy strength around her kept the fear at bay, and
even appeared to have it on the run.

Funny, the hard muscular sensation was the total opposite of what she'd expect to soothe a woman's fear.
Brick-hard comfort with rippling planes and valleys lay
beneath her cheek. Sinewy bands held her close. And the
smell. She'd never thought comfort could smell like a
fresh-from-the-shower male.

She stiffened, her mind clearing swiftly. Garbled
words quickly became intelligible.

"I've had CPR training, Judge. Let me see her." *The
bailiff's voice.*

"Get your hands off her! Get a real doctor in here!"
Zach.

"Son, sit down here. Bailiff, go call a paramedic." *A
strange voice. Maybe that man who came in later. Son?
Ohmigod! Hopefully, that man was just a fatherly friend
of Zach's.*

She felt Zach obey the one directive and sit. Stirring, she marshalled her willpower and pushed against his chest. "Please. I'm fine now. Let me up."

He allowed her to sit up, but he wouldn't release her. "We're going to have someone look you over, Gerrie Jean. No way are you going out of here until I'm sure you're all right."

"I told you, I'm fine. I just had a reaction to being labeled a criminal for the rest of my life. You'd have felt the same way if someone had told you that you'd be an ex-con from now on!"

"Sweetheart, all you've got to do is. . . ."

"Sweetheart?" that strange voice repeated. "Zach, my boy, you do know that you have to be very careful as to ethics in making a ruling on someone you know."

Gerrie Jean glanced up into an older version of Zach's face, still heartbreakingly handsome with the added years. Oh, God, it had to be his father. She couldn't quite read the message in those eyes, but his cleaned-and-pressed, everything-matching-because-I-paid-highly-to-make-it-that-way appearance registered. Men like him always sneered at the bike riders they encountered.

"She's not someone I know," Zach denied, drawing Gerrie Jean's attention back to his face. His gaze was on her, not his father. "But she's someone I've got every intention of getting to know."

"Huh!" a feminine voice muttered, and Zach glared at the court reporter.

"It's one minute before five, Miss Hardesty," he muttered. "You've got sixty seconds to get clocked out, because I won't authorize a minute's overtime for you."

The woman gasped, then whirled and grabbed her machine. Gerrie Jean didn't understand how the woman made it out of the courtroom with her nose so defiantly in the air, but she managed. Zach waited until the door swung shut behind her before he started to speak again. The paramedics burst into the room instead, and Gerrie Jean groaned under her breath.

It took her all of ten minutes to convince both the paramedics and Zach that she didn't need to go to the hospital—ten full minutes on Zach's lap, because he refused to let her go while the paramedics examined her. They stuck a thermometer in her mouth at one point, which she thought was probably to still her tongue rather than check her temperature. They wound a blood pressure cuff around her arm, and one of them peered into her ears and eyes with a bright light. When that one started to stick his stethoscope inside her blouse, Zach grabbed it away from him and did that himself.

He also struck the other paramedic's hands away when he reached for her legs.

"I need her to cross her legs, Judge Brenham," the paramedic said sternly. "I have to check her reflexes."

"Cross your legs, Gerrie Jean," Zach ordered, and she complied. The paramedic struck her lightly with a rubber-headed hammer, and her leg kicked out. The paramedic nodded and pulled the thermometer out of her mouth.

"Well," he said after he read the thermometer, "I don't see anything wrong here. But if you have any more dizzy spells, I'd advise you to get to your own doctor."

Any more dizzy spells? Hell, she'd have plenty of them if she didn't get off Zach's lap! But she didn't think those sort of dizzy spells called for a doctor's care.

"I will," she said firmly. "Now." She gave Zach her sternest obey-me look. "Let . . . me . . . up."

"I might as well carry you on out to the car," he said nonchalantly as he rose. "You need a ride home, don't you?"

"The lady waiting for her already left," the bailiff put in, dashing Gerrie Jean's slight hope of insinuating she already had a ride. "Said she had to pick her kids up from school, but that Miss Cartwright was to call her if she needed her."

"Son, I'd like a minute with you before you go," the other man said.

Zach's arms tightened around her before he made a

perceptible effort to relax. Turning slightly, he faced the older man. "Gerrie Jean Cartwright, this is my father, Judge Hamilton Edward Brenham. And whatever it is you need to discuss will have to wait, Dad. I have to take Gerrie Jean home, since she doesn't have her car."

"Or a license to drive it if I did have it," Gerrie Jean admitted in a grudging voice. She kept her gaze on Zach's father until she nodded an acknowledgment of the introduction. With a closed, enigmatic look on his face, Judge Brenham studied her extremely closely in return, his concluding opinion of her never showing in his expression.

"Don't you think it would be more seemly if you allowed her to walk?" Judge Brenham asked.

"No," Zach replied flatly. "I'll see you at dinner on Sunday."

Zach strode away, and Gerrie Jean peered over his shoulder. She still couldn't tell a thing about Judge Brenham's feelings toward her. For all she knew, he could have been holding back boiling anger at seeing a criminal who had just appeared in front of his son being borne out of the courtroom in his son's arms. In fact, she caught some sort of spark in Judge Brenham's brown eyes, but the straight line of his lips didn't give her a hint of a clue as to whether it was anger or something else. Thinking back on the impression she had formed of the Brenham family while talking with Cool Hand, Gerrie Jean decided he was probably already formulating plans to counteract the slur on his family name resulting from Zach's unseemly actions. For now, however, she couldn't summon enough willpower to deny herself this ride in the arms of a man who had shadowed her thoughts for the last two weeks.

Instead of heading to the parking lot, Zach passed right by the hallway leading outside. He carried her into the office where she'd asked directions earlier that day, already knowing she was late for her court date, since Becky Rose had been held up by the semicrisis of a crying child who didn't want his mother to leave. The same elderly lady who had been so nice to her then peered at them anxiously.

"Oh my, Judge Brenham," she said. "I heard you'd had a defendant pass out in the courtroom. Is there anything I can do to help? Maybe get her some water?"

"Word sure does travel fast in this building," Zach muttered. Then he continued in a louder voice, "No. Or at least, I don't think so. Do you want some water, Gerrie Jean?"

She shook her head, a warm, cozy feeling crawling through her at the concern in his voice. Deciding to take complete advantage of this amazing and delicious situation, she snuggled her head against his shoulder. "Ummmm, what are we doing here?"

"I'm supposed to pick up a permit here. Did the State Fire Marshal's Office send it down from Austin, Mabel?"

"Sure did, Judge Brenham. Here it is."

She handed him a brown envelope, which Zach somehow managed to accept and tuck on Gerrie Jean's stomach even with his arms full. Thanking Mabel, he left the office, not stopping again until they were outside in the parking lot beside a black Mercedes. At the passenger door, he rather reluctantly let her slide to the ground, catching the envelope as it fell.

"What's in there?" Gerrie Jean asked.

"I'll tell you in a minute. Right now, do you want to go straight home, or would you like to get something to drink? Or eat? I don't want you to push yourself, if you need to rest after that fainting spell."

"It wasn't really a fainting spell. I hyperventilated—from fear, I guess. And I would like to get a burger or something. Or . . ." She studied him contemplatively for an instant. "Or do you know somewhere that has good trout amandine?"

"Funny," Zach said with a chuckle. "I was going to ask you if you knew anywhere that had great fried catfish.

But if trout is what you want, we'll go that route.''

"I should probably go home and change first.''

"That won't be necessary.'' He opened the door, then told her to wait before she got in, until he cooled the car off a little. Striding around the front, he got in the driver's side and started the engine, turning on the air. In far less time than it would have taken her Mustang to cool off, Zach murmured for her to slide on in. As soon as he got out onto the street, he picked up his car phone. A few seconds into the overheard conversation, she deduced that he was talking to his housekeeper, and her eyes widened.

"Yes, that would be great, Mrs. Philistine,'' he said finally. "We'll be there in a half hour or so and have drinks before dinner. Yes, that's right. The trout I caught out in Colorado this spring. Uh-huh. In the game freezer. Fine. Thanks so much for doing this for me on such short notice. You're a love.''

He hung up, and Gerrie Jean gaped at him. "We're going to your house and you've just called your house-keeper to fix trout for us? And she's willing to do that on such short notice?''

"She likes me,'' Zach said with a charming grin. "And she knows I'll slip something extra in her pay envelope for this. Her husband has Alzheimer's and is in a home. Her son-in-law was killed in a car wreck, and she's helping her daughter raise her two grandchildren. Every little bit helps.''

"How sad,'' Gerrie Jean mused. "But she sounds like a wonderful person.''

Zach headed north out of town and they made innocuous small talk while he drove. Once Gerrie Jean glanced pointedly at the brown envelope on the seat between them, but Zach didn't take the hint and explain it. Soon she was caught by the beautiful scenery on the drive into the fringes of the Texas Hill Country and amused herself by trying to guess where he was heading. Zach's masculine chuckles each time she guessed wrong sent quivers of sensation through her, making the game that much more delicious.

Finally he turned off onto a farm-to-market road, then shortly onto another road, this one with a gravel surface. It wound along a surprisingly wide creek lined with cottonwoods, climbing as it went. The huge log cabin burst on them around the last bend, and Gerrie Jean sighed in awe.

"It's gorgeous! Look at all the windows. No wonder you need a housekeeper. But it's not what. . . ." She bit her lip to cut off her words.

"Not what you'd expect me to live in?" Zach finished for her, with another of those delicious, gravelly chuckles. "Amanda got our house in the divorce."

"You're divorced?"

"For a couple years now. And to answer your next question, no, we didn't have any children. And the next question, no, it wasn't a real bitter divorce. Afterwards, I decided to move into this place, since I'd always loved it and there wasn't really anyone else to do anything with it. The original portion of it's way over a hundred years old, but over time, the various women in the family demanded remodeling and a few modern things. There is actually inside plumbing now. It's really very comfortable, although any entertaining I do, I do in San Antonio at Dad's place."

"I'd want to keep this place special, too," Gerrie Jean mused, although she knew immediately that wasn't exactly what Zach meant.

He searched her face for a moment, then nodded. "Yeah, special," he said.

He parked in the driveway instead of driving into the garage and was out of the car and around to her door before she could get out. He held out a hand, and she noticed the brown envelope in his other hand. Zach led her to the front door, surprising her by saying that he helped Mrs. Philistine take care of the multitude of flowers in the yard because he thoroughly enjoyed gardening and landscaping.

Inside, he gave her a leisurely tour of the house, upstairs first: four huge bedrooms, each with its own bath and a large library/sitting room off the master bedroom. Downstairs, he showed her around, then led her into the kitchen to introduce her to Mrs. Philistine. Gerrie Jean immediately fell in love with the grandmotherly woman when she whacked Zach's fingers with a wooden spoon as he reached to steal a bite of fresh salad.

"You two go on out to the deck," she ordered. "And if you'd rather have something nonalcoholic, Gerrie Jean, I've got fresh lemonade."

"Oh, that's what I'd rather have," Gerrie Jean admitted. A moment later, she settled into a cushioned chair on the deck running along the entire back side of the house and propped her feet up on a wooden bench. "I could get used to this," she said with a huge sigh. A cool breeze soughed through the large jack pines and cottonwoods. She could see the creek from here and imagine hill country deer drinking there in the late evening.

"I might just be able to get used to you being here," Zach mused, and she gave him a startled look.

"No, no, you couldn't," she insisted. "Look, I know you're just feeling guilty because you scared me in the courtroom. That's why you brought me here and are feeding me. I know who you are and where you come from, and I wouldn't presume for one moment to think that there'd ever be any sort of man-woman relationship between us."

"What do you know about me?" Zach asked. He leaned against the deck railing and crossed his ankles, sipping his own lemonade to which he'd added a jigger of bourbon.

"Cool Hand told me. . . ."

"Cool Hand?"

"Cool Hand appeared in front of you in court last year. And Cool Hand's the nickname for the Alex Hilton you

were asking about," Gerrie Jean admitted, then gasped.
"That can't get him into trouble with me on those
fireworks now, can it? After I've confessed it's all my
fault?"

Instead of answering, Zach lifted the brown envelope
he'd carried with him and handed it to Gerrie Jean. She
unclasped it and frowned as she read the piece of paper.
"It says this is a fire permit. Are you planning to build
a fire out here?"

"It's a permit to allow me to set off some fireworks,"
Zach corrected. "I have a confession of my own to make.
The reason I haven't contacted you the last couple weeks
is because I was covered up in a nasty racketeering trial.
I wanted to get it over with, so I could enjoy my vacation
the next two weeks. But I did have a friend of mine find
out about you."

She leapt to her feet, spilling lemonade all down the
front of her skirt and legs. "You had me investigated?
How dare you?" The endearing look of confusion on his
face made her have to harden her heart, but her outrage
overrode her other emotions. "I'm not some damned
common criminal, Zach Brenham! How dare you treat
me like one? And how dare you act like you didn't already know everything I told you today in court? You
knew the whole damned story, didn't you?"

"I needed your story on the record, Gerrie Jean," Zach
said in exasperation. "For your information, I could be
reprimanded and possibly even stripped of my position
if it were proven I gave anyone special consideration,
instead of making sure adequate justice was done."

"And to that end, you had to *investigate* me?" She
gripped her glass tightly in an effort not to fling the re-
maining dregs of lemonade into his face, then set it on a
nearby table. "I want to go home. Will you take me, or
will I walk?"

Zach straightened and held out his free hand. "Will
you listen to me for just a minute? Please?" Setting his
own glass beside hers, he stepped in front of her and

placed his hands on her shoulders. "Please?" he almost whispered, and she felt her legs wobble.

"N . . . no." It came out weak, as weak as a newborn puppy's whimper. The pleading look in his eyes deepened and he raised one thumb, softly caressing her chin as he repeated the word. "Please?" She couldn't look away from him, and she clenched her fingers in the front of his shirt, inanely realizing she didn't even recall putting her hands on his chest. His breath feathered across her face, and his eyes were bottomless, beckoning her to drown in them. Bedroom eyes, she thought.

She shook her head in denial, the effort costing her willpower she had to draw from some depth she didn't even know she had. Zach's lower lip protruded just a tiny, almost imperceptible bit, and she was lost. "O . . . okay," she whimpered. "I'll listen."

"After I kiss you, all right?" he growled in a barely audible voice.

"Oh, yes. Yes."

He groaned as he bent his head to close the distance between their mouths, the vibration of that sound lingering on his lips as he kissed her—and rumbling in his chest beneath her fingertips. She only *thought* she'd been kissed before. Zach Brenham's kiss zapped through her body from head to toe with a killer intensity. From the way his hand burrowed into her hair and his arm tightened around her waist, the way he deepened the kiss almost immediately, it hit him just as hard. She'd never felt such instant desire before, and she instinctively moved against him, finding the hardness her body cried for just where it should be. His moan of frustration mingled with hers, but it was Zach who mustered the fortitude to break the kiss, not her.

He leaned his forehead against hers, his heart thundering beneath her fingers. "I want you more than I've ever wanted a woman in my entire life, sweetheart," he growled. He lifted his head and cupped her chin, gazing into her eyes. "But I want more than just you in my bed.

There's something else here. Something I want to learn about slow and easy—some kind of possibly forever thing.''

Her heart thudded to her feet and she shook her head, stepping back without him trying to stop her. "No, you're wrong, Zach. They say opposites attract, but that doesn't mean a relationship between opposites would ever work permanently. I'll admit, I've thought about you a lot the last couple weeks. The conclusion I came to is that I'm down home and you're society. We're from two different worlds, and I have absolutely no desire to always have to be on my best behavior, so I won't end up in one of the scandal sheets and cause you problems. I prefer my Mustang, but a few times a year, I go camping with my parents and their motorcycle gang. I've got my own Harley, and I can handle it. It wouldn't work, Zach. Heck, I'll even be a convicted felon if I screw up my probation. I'm definitely not a suitable date for a federal judge.''

Instead of pushing her, he gave her a wry grin. "I'll let you get by with that for now. But over the next couple weeks, I'm going to be trying to change your mind.''

"Next two weeks?''

"Uh huh. I'm on vacation, and you're without a driver's license. I intend to be your chauffeur. I also intend to take you somewhere and let you set off your fireworks over a lake, since that's what this permit is for. You'll be able to get your inspiration and do your painting. But I warn you. The permit comes attached to me.''

Why didn't that caveat bother her?

Chapter Five

The minute she reached for the phone, her lips started to tingle. He hadn't kissed her again last night, although she'd done everything to tease him into it except rip open her blouse and offer herself to him when they were standing on her door stoop saying good night. The control he had was amazing. Not that she fell into bed with every man who made her insides tingle, but she had never, *ever* wanted to make love with a man as badly as she'd wanted Zach Brenham ever since he'd kissed her. Judge Zach Brenham, she told herself. Maybe attorneys and judges were taught "poker face how-to's" in law school. At the very least, they were taught acting skills, from what she'd seen in a few movies she'd been to on dates. She didn't much care for those John Grisham–type films, but sometimes she'd give in to placate her escort for the evening.

He told you to call him and let him know what time to pick you up, she reminded herself. *You even have his very private, personal phone number.* She glanced at the slip of paper in her hand, although she'd had the darned phone number memorized by the time she got from her front door to her bedroom last night. She needed to see the fireworks display he had arranged for her inspiration. She'd already sanded the gas tank and watched every video she could think of with a fireworks display in it—

and there had only been one film with an over-the-water display, a scene all of thirty seconds long. She always painted better, in her opinion, with an actual experience of her own to build on, so her work wouldn't be the same if she didn't actually see a live display. One time she'd driven all the way to South Dakota to see Mount Rushmore and the site of the yearly Sturgis Bike Run, when the Harley-Davidson publicity people asked her to design one of their T-shirts.

With a gulp for courage that quickly turned into bubbling anticipation, she picked up the phone, frowning and replacing the receiver when she heard a car horn blow out front. She walked to the window and saw a black Mercedes in her driveway. Shaking her head in wonder and a smile curving her lips, she hurried to open the front door and step outside.

He stood leaning against the driver's door, one hand inside the open window on the horn. "Come on in," she called. "I thought you were going to wait until I phoned you."

"I've been waiting all day," he said, sauntering toward her. The shadowy predatory look in his eyes matched the low growl of his voice, and her stomach quivered like a mass of gelatin. "You told me you had to work at your dealership, but I figured you'd call some time during the day. When you didn't, I thought maybe you'd decided to break our date."

"I didn't," she denied. He stopped in front of her, still on the sidewalk, which left her on the step and her eyes level with his. "I mean, I hadn't exactly decided for sure, until a minute ago. But I was picking up the phone just now."

"I'm glad," he murmured. "So have you decided where we can go?"

"My brother lives on Lake McQueeney. I did call him earlier, and he said we could use his dock. He has two nine-year-old boys, and they'd love to watch the display, also. So, you see, I intended to go all along."

"You could have called your brother and canceled," he said with a shrug. "I've got the fireworks in my trunk."

"Did you . . . uh . . . want to come in and have a drink or something before we leave?"

"I don't think that would be a good idea. You said for it to do you any good time-wise, you needed to see this display by this weekend. Being alone with you inside four private walls . . . you *do* live alone, don't you?"

Her head wobbled up and down, although she had no idea how she controlled her feeble muscles enough to make them move. "Ever since my parents retired and started traveling," she managed to say. Visions of her own idea of exactly what could happen in the privacy of her house churned through her mind, deliriously clear since the other half of her fantasy stood within kissing distance.

"I'll wait in the car while you get a light jacket. It might cool off over the lake in the evening. On the way to your brother's, we can notify whatever authorities we have to about our plans and show them our permit."

"I keep clothes out at my brother's," she said.

"Then we might as well go."

"Yeah." She pulled the door closed behind her, and he stepped back to let her precede him to the car. She started to step down, suddenly remembering halfway through her motion that she wasn't entirely ready to leave after all. "Oh!" She teetered, one foot planted firmly on the stoop and the other one reaching for the sidewalk, then wavering in uncertainty. She probably looked like an incompetent ballerina!

Zach leapt forward, but she wobbled backward and crashed into the door before he could grab her. The latch must not have caught well, because the door burst open and she tumbled to the floor, saved from any real injury by the carpet with thick padding beneath it in the entry-way.

"My God! Are you hurt?" Zach knelt beside her, his

face reflecting his strong anxiety. She stared up at him in surprise at her quick change of position for a moment, then burst into giggles.

"I . . . my purse," she said around her giggles. "I forgot it."

"Well, hell," he muttered, the concern on his face fading to relief. "I would've waited for you. You didn't have to make such a big production out of it."

He actually waggled his eyebrows, and she erupted into full-fledged laughter. Joining her hilarity, Zach stretched out beside her, propping his head on his hand and gazing down at her as he chuckled. After a few seconds, he reached out a finger and traced her chin. "Are you sure you didn't get hurt? Isn't there somewhere I should kiss it and make it well?"

She damned sure wasn't going to miss this opportunity! "Here," she said pointing at her lips. "I have a terrible ache right here."

He soothed that ache completely. His lips fit hers so perfectly it was scary. She threaded her fingers in his hair, returning his kiss with every bit of the longing she'd kept bottled up all day. A real ache grew now, in the spot between her legs where it could be soothed only by complete lovemaking. Groaning in the sensuous way now familiar to her, Zach pulled her along the length of his body and ravaged her mouth.

A long, long time later—or it could have been only a few seconds, she had no idea—Zach drew back far enough to look into her eyes. "Gerrie Jean. . . ."

"Ahem!"

Her gaze flew past Zach's shoulder to see Cool Hand standing slouched on her sidewalk, fingertips in the back pockets of his black leathers and a smile on his face.

"You didn't look like you were fighting him, G J," Cool Hand mused. "So I didn't play knight in shining armor and drag him off you."

Zach groaned a different sound and flipped over. "Who the hell are you?"

Cool Hand's mouth dropped open. "What the hell are *you* doing making love to G J right in front of God and everyone on this street?" he growled in response, then glared at Gerrie Jean. "I can't believe you're messing around with *him*, G J!"

Gerrie Jean scrambled to her feet a half second behind Zach—he already had a grip on the neck of Cool Hand's black T-shirt and a fist drawn back. She flew off the step and foolishly jammed herself between the two men, nearly getting crushed for her trouble. But at least it separated them before any further damage was done.

"Now stop it! Both of you. . . ."

Cool Hand grabbed one of her arms. "I didn't realize he really was attacking you, G J. . . ."

Zach wrapped an arm around her waist. "Let go of her, you Neanderthal, or I'll call the cops!"

"Get *your* hands off her, you son of a bitch!" Cool Hand pulled on Gerrie Jean's arm, and Zach held on tighter.

Gerrie Jean screamed as loud as she could and both men dropped their holds. Little old Miss Betsy from next door came toddling out of her house with a huge black umbrella in her hands and tottered across the yard. "I've called 911, Geralyn!" she said in a cracked voice. "They're on their way. You monsters get away from her!"

Mouth open in astonishment, Gerrie Jean watched Miss Betsy first whack Cool Hand, then Zach over the head. The men threw up their arms to try to protect themselves, but Miss Betsy found an opening on both of them. They staggered backwards, away from Gerrie Jean . . . and away from Miss Betsy's umbrella. Suddenly Gerrie Jean heard a siren in the distance and while Miss Betsy planted herself in front of her, umbrella at the ready with the vicious long steel point on the end outward now, a police car sped down the street and screeched to a halt in Gerrie Jean's driveway. Two policemen flung open the patrol car's doors and knelt behind them, guns drawn.

"Freeze!" one of them shouted. Gerrie Jean hid her face in her hands and groaned in dismay.

"There, there, dear." Miss Betsy turned and put her frail arms around Gerrie Jean's shoulders. "Are you hurt? Everything will be all right now. The police will arrest these horrible men."

Thank God one of the cops who showed up was a close friend of his father's, Zach thought as the patrol car left a while later. He promised to keep this comedy of errors out of the papers if at all possible. And he had to admit, at least once—well, maybe twice—during the last ten minutes, he'd recalled Gerrie Jean's words from the previous evening. Maybe they were way too different to ever make a go of a relationship. She sure enough had a completely different circle of friends than he had. Still, he wouldn't know unless he tried. He damned sure had enough wanting left in him to give it a little more time.

Gerrie Jean, on the other hand, looked so woebegone he almost thought the best thing to do would be get in his car and quickly drive out of her life. She needed those fireworks set off, however, and his influence would make it easier to get the authorities on the lake to accept the permit without giving her the runaround. He went to meet her as she came back across the yard from walking that firebrand little old umbrella lady home.

"Is your neighbor lady all right?"

"Uh-huh." A blond curl fell across her cheek, and she negligently brushed it back as she looked at him. "Oh! Oh, no. Look at you. There's a big bruise on your forehead."

"From Miss Betsy's umbrella," he said solemnly. "That little old lady doesn't mess around. I guess it's like they tell people in firearms training. If you pull a gun on someone, be ready to kill them. Only she feels that way about her umbrella."

She laughed half-heartedly at his attempt to cheer her. "We better go in and put some ice on that bruise."

"Nah. It's fine. Let's get on out to the lake. I'm ready to relax."

He hadn't forgotten about the Neanderthal he recognized from court last year, but Zach sort of hoped Gerrie Jean would. No such luck. She heaved a sigh and gazed around until she saw the biker waiting for her by the garage.

"What did you come over for, Cool Hand?" she asked as she walked toward him. "I'm getting ready to leave."

"I wanted to see if I could borrow your bike," Cool Hand said. "My starter went out, and we don't have one in stock at the dealership. Blackie had to order one for me, and it won't be in until Monday."

"Sure," she said. "Let me get her for you. I haven't started her for a couple weeks, and you know she doesn't like to start up after being idle that long for anyone but me."

She walked over to raise the garage door, and Zach said without thinking, "She sounds like that bike is a human being."

Cool Hand snorted in disbelief. "Shows what you know. Bikes are more important than a lot of humans!"

Zach ignored him as he watched Gerrie Jean straddle a wicked-looking motorcycle with the most beautiful gas tank Zach had ever seen. About the only thing he could tell about the bike was that it looked like a Harley, and that deduction came partially from the emblem he vaguely recognized in the center of the front wire wheel. If the gas tank was her creation, his opinion of her talent as an artist rose sky high. She'd painted an eagle flowing into a rider on a bike, both flying down the road. The words "Free Spirits" inscribed beneath the picture didn't even begin to describe the impact the scene made.

Gerrie Jean was only able to touch the ground on either side of the bike because the seat was slung so low there was barely any clearance between it and the concrete garage floor. She twisted the throttle, then patted the gas tank as she pushed the starter button. The engine turned over, then over some more, but didn't rumble to life. Gerrie Jean stood and pulled the kickstart lever out. She jumped on it twice with no results. Sitting back on the seat again, she lovingly stroked the gas tank, then pushed the starter button again.

Zach jumped as the deep roar of the engine blasted his ears. Gerrie Jean twisted the throttle a few times, revving the engine even higher and sending clouds of exhaust spewing from the tailpipe. Finally she allowed the engine to settle into a smooth, throaty rumble and stuck a toe on the gearshift lever. Zach heard a muffled *thunk,* and the monstrous bike slowly moved toward them, with Gerrie Jean looking like a child on its back. Stopping beside Cool Hand, Gerrie Jean got off the bike as the biker traded places with her.

"She'll start fine for you now, as long as you ride her every day," she told Cool Hand. "Keep her as long as you need to. I won't be allowed to ride again for a while."

"Thanks, G J," Cool Hand said. He glanced at Zach and frowned. "Wish I could say it's been nice seeing you again, but I don't much care for telling lies." He dropped the bike into gear again and smoothly pulled out of the driveway. Within seconds, he had disappeared down the street, but the rumble of the powerful engine lingered in the air.

Surprisingly, Zach felt a primitive urge to be in Cool Hand's place on the back of that enormous machine. Hell, he'd never even had a bicycle while he grew up. Instead, a chauffeur drove him until he was old enough for a license. For fun, he rode horses and played polo. He had snuck off to a rodeo to watch Hank ride bulls a few times, but he'd never felt even an inkling of desire to see how long he could stay on the back of one of those dangerous beasts before he plowed a path through an acre of dirt with his mouth. The longing to feel that motorcycle rumbling between his legs, though, was almost as strong as the desire to bed a woman. Well, except for the woman who murmured she'd be right back as soon as she got her purse. That desire was a constant crackling fire, which roared into a full-blown blaze whenever he kissed her.

He waited at the passenger door until she returned, helped her in the car, and got into the driver's seat. Evidently by mutual consent, they didn't discuss what had happened. Instead, Gerrie Jean rather desperately chattered about the easiest route to take to her brother's house. After stopping to notify both the local fire marshal and sheriff, they arrived at a pretty cedar-sided A-frame on the lake. A fantastic sunset lit the western sky, and Zach assisted Gerrie Jean out of the car, then paused to enjoy it.

"Beautiful here," he mused. "I do prefer living out in the woods rather than in town."

Gerrie Jean stood beside him, obviously taken also with the wonderful colors in the sky. "Bobby Joe always says I can come out any time, but I don't like to intrude. My parents owned this lake lot and we camped out here growing up. When Bobby Joe got married, they deeded it to him to build a house on."

"And you got the house in Cibilo? And the dealership?"

"Bobby Joe is a civil engineer. He has his own company, and he prefers that to selling motorcycles. He still loves to ride, though."

A set of whoops split the air, and two little sandy-haired boys skidded around the edge of the house, barreling straight for them. "Aunt G J! Aunt G J!" they both shouted. "Did you bring the fireworks?"

Unfortunately, the huge Great Dane lumbering after the boys reached Zach and Aunt G J first. The dog's "whoof" of doggie breath hit Zach full force in the face, without the dog even having to stand on his hind legs. He froze, but the dog completely ignored him after it made his stomach roil. A split second later, there was a pile of madly thrashing dog legs, little boy legs, and million-dollar legs at his feet. The shrieks and shouts made it impossible for him to hear whatever the man strolling toward them was saying. Finally the man gave up and motioned for Zach to come with him. When they were close enough, he handed Zach a can of beer with water rivulets running down it and slices of ice still clinging. A safe distance from the clamor, Zach lifted the can to his mouth and took a long swallow, then saluted his host with it.

"Thanks. In the last couple hours, I've come close to having a biker knock my teeth down my throat, been assaulted by a little old lady who wields a mean umbrella, almost arrested by the cops, and so scared by a monster dog I nearly had to go home and change my underwear. I need about a half dozen of these."

"Of course," the man said with a laugh. "You've been with G J, who is fully capable of driving a man to drink at times. And don't worry about Monster Mash." When Zach frowned in confusion, he added, "The Great Dane. That's what the kids named him." Then he stuck out his hand. "Bobby Joe Cartwright. You gotta be Judge Brenham."

"Zach, please," Zach insisted as he clasped the extended hand. "When I'm with Gerrie Jean, I damned sure don't feel like a federal judge."

"That's probably good for you," Bobby Joe said with a nod.

"It is. Very good."

The two men's eyes met in complete understanding. "G J's special," Bobby Joe informed Zach. "She thinks being tied down with a family would make her give up a lot of the things she enjoys in life, like her bike and that blasted car she drives, as well as her art. I keep telling her that she can do most of that stuff, especially her art, just as easily being barefoot and pregnant. Except for riding the bike, of course. But hell, soon as she dropped each kid, she could bundle them all into a side-

car and bring them along on the bike runs, like some of
the other families do.''

Zach blanched at the thought of a nine-month-pregnant
Gerrie Jean on that monstrous bike he had so recently
seen. Surely she would take her brother's advice not to
ride until after she'd given birth, wouldn't she? And why
the hell had he centered in on that pregnancy comment,
out of all the other things Bobby Joe had said? He could
almost imagine a sidecar on that huge bike, with stair-
step little bodies yelling their excitement over the ride.

Right before they went around the edge of the house,
he paused and turned. She was still on the ground, and
just then Monster Mash slurped her face. One boy burrowed under each arm, both chattering to try to get her
attention. She stood out against the backdrop of the vi-
brant sunset, and he wished desperately he had a camera.
Hearing a click, he glanced aside to see a petite woman
using a very professional-looking camera with a tele-
photo lens on it.

She lowered the camera and stuck out a hand. ''I'm
Belle, G J's sister-in-law. If you'll give me your address,
I'll see that you get a print of that picture I just took. I
do some freelance photography, and I always have my
camera ready when G J's around. She's very photo-
genic.'' She winked. ''Plus you never know what sort of
shot you'll get of her.''

Zach agreed, and a moment later she had one of his
business cards stuck in the back pocket of her cutoff
bluejean shorts. They continued on to the back of the
house. She led him up a rear staircase, which ended at
the second story of the house, then back around to the
deck on the lake side. Gerrie Jean was sitting on the
ground chatting with the twins, heedless of the sandy soil.

Chapter Six

"Huh-uh, Billy," Gerrie Jean cautioned one twin. "You only get to set those off with an adult supervising you."

Zach slapped a mosquito drawn by the light over the dock and muttered, "How do you tell them apart? I can't tell Billy from Brad."

Her eyes twinkled, and she laid a finger on her lips, leaning close to his ear. "Shhhh. Don't tell them my secret, because they still try to fool me now and then. But Brad has more freckles on his nose than his cheeks, and vice versa for Billy."

Fighting against the urge to pull her into his arms and see if she tasted as sweet as she smelled—wouldn't that be a good example for the twins?—he curled his fingers into his palms. "What if you can't see their faces?"

She shrugged. "I guess I just know their personalities well enough to figure out which one of them would be doing what. Billy isn't afraid of the devil himself, but Brad's a little more cautious. Billy would stand out in plain sight watching to see what my reaction would be when my feet hit the slimy frog he'd stuck in my bed, while Brad would be sneaking a peek around the door-jamb. And believe me, I know this from experience."

Zach eyed the two boys warily, but Gerrie Jean laughed. "Oh, they obey well enough, so don't worry

about them not minding us. Bobby Joe and Belle were
only teasing when they said they'd wait on the deck for
us because they valued their hides too much to be in close
proximity to their twins and a dangerous box of
fireworks. You've just got to stay a step ahead of them
as to what they might come up with that we haven't
actually forbidden them to do.''

She knelt on the dock to lay out the rules to the boys,
and Zach propped his rear against the railing, waiting.
He liked Gerrie Jean's brother and Belle. They'd appeared to enjoy his company, too, over burgers and
grilled corn while they waited for full darkness to fall.
Funny. He'd never known a burger could taste like that.
Every barbecue he'd attended served either steaks or bris-
ket, sausage, and chicken. He'd already asked Bobby Joe
for his mop sauce recipe and been told with a wink that
the Cartwright barbecue sauce recipe only went to family
members. No way had he been able to keep his eyes from
going directly to Gerrie Jean after that comment, and she
had blushed so bright she rivaled the deep tone of the
delicious sauce.

Damn, he was falling for her fast. He felt like he was
on a runaway downhill slide, something like that movie
he'd seen where the hero slid down the mountain of mud
and ended up with his face right on the heroine's stomach. Well, a little lower, if he remembered his movie
right. But that hinted at strictly a sexual urge to possess
Gerrie Jean, and what he'd told her last night was the
truth. The relationship terrain he wanted to explore with
Gerrie Jean Cartwright had suggestions of forever inter-
woven into the landscape. Perhaps it was far too soon for
him to be feeling this way, but he had to honestly admit
the truth to himself.

She finished explaining the rules to the twins and
stood. Zach probably could have obtained the release of
the fireworks they'd found in her trunk, except for the
strictly illegal M-80s, but instead he'd gotten an entire
new batch from one of his father's associates. With all

the money he contributed to charities, he'd only had to ask Matt Peters to give him part of the display planned for the hospital's Fourth of July extravaganza and have Matt replace them before he needed the stuff. There were some beauties in the box, and he'd agreed when both the fire marshal and sheriff asked if he minded if they let the people around the lake know to watch for the display. Already, a few boats were meandering around aimlessly nearby.

"Shoot," Gerrie Jean murmured. "I didn't bring any matches down."

"I'll get some for you!"

The twin she called Billy took off at a dead run up the stairs from the dock. Gerrie Jean yelled after him, "You ask your mother for matches and you bring them straight back here!"

Belle stood up from her chair on the deck and waved at Gerrie Jean, indicating she'd heard the caution. Within a minute, Billy was racing back toward them, barreling onto the dock and tripping over the Monster Mash when the dog raised its head to greet him. Zach caught Billy by the shorts right before he tumbled into the water. He gathered him into his arms, surprised at how chunky and good he felt there.

"Thanks!" Billy said, giving Zach a hug around his neck. "Brad would've laughed at me from now on 'til next Sunday if I'd've ended up in the water."

"You looked just as funny dangling by the seat of your pants, Billy Butt!" the other twin said with a chortle. When Zach set Billy down, he lunged at Brad, but Gerrie Jean grabbed an ear on each twin.

"You know what to do," she said to them.

"Owww! I'm sorry I called you Billy Butt," Brad said.

"Ouch, ouch, ouch!" Billy hollered. "I'm sorry I was gonna attack you, Brad!"

Gerrie Jean released the two of them, and they crouched beside the box of fireworks, heads together and chattering as though they weren't just at each other's throats. Zach shook his head and joined them. Soon they had the fireworks arranged in an order of presentation that satisfied everyone. Gerrie Jean lit a punk for each twin, cautioning them once again not to do anything with them until an adult gave them permission.

Zach had also asked Matt to throw in the appropriate safety equipment to launch the fireworks, and for the next half hour, they set off sky rockets and roman candles. They interspersed them with a few fireworks that would explode even under water, and some smoke bombs, which skittered around on the dock and made them high-step to avoid them as they laughed at each other's antics. At first, Monster Mash only covered his ears with his paws when the fireworks exploded in the sky, but he left the dock in a lope after the first smoke bomb tank headed for him, spewing its noxious odor.

"At least we shouldn't have to worry about mosquitoes with all this smoke," Zach said with a laugh. "And I bet I'll have to air my car out after we ride home in it tonight." Funny, though, he didn't care if it took a month to get the smell out of the Mercedes. The memories brought on, if the smoke odor did linger, would be a lot more pleasant than the smell of expensive leather. The pleasure he saw on the twins' faces—and the face of the woman he was quickly falling in love with—was well worth it.

When they got to the final, more extravagant aerial displays, Zach told the twins how much more dangerous these rockets could be and admonished them to wait patiently until he was completely ready for them to help set them off. In fact, he insisted he would light the first couple of rockets alone, so he could adequately supervise the twins on the rest.

He carefully fastened the rocket in the launcher, then waited until Gerrie Jean lit a punk for him. Separating the wick from the body of the rocket, he lit the end of it and stepped way back. After a few seconds of sputtering sparks, it flew into the air with a whoosh, echoed by the twins' awestruck gasps. It went up, up, up, and for a brief instant, it appeared it was a dud, as the sky remained dark. The twins and Gerrie Jean groaned, and Zach stifled his assertion for them to wait. Suddenly the rocket exploded in a shower of red, green, yellow, and white sparks, covering a huge area of the black sky. The look of wonder and enjoyment in Gerrie Jean's eyes was worth every bit of the trouble Zach had gone to in order to get the fireworks.

She turned to him, the last fading sparks of the rocket mirrored in her beautiful brown eyes. Half open in awe, her lips tempted him with a pull so strong he almost gave in. But the twins clamored for the next rocket, and he sighed in resignation.

The second rocket actually exploded into a picture of an American flag. The twins whooped in wonder, and Zach heard Bobby Joe and Belle clapping from up on the deck. He, however, was watching the display in Gerrie Jean's eyes instead of the sky. And when she glanced at him this time, he decided he absolutely had to sneak at least a tiny kiss.

He should have known. None of his kisses with Gerrie Jean had been tiny. She exploded on his senses with the same impact as one of those overhead rockets. He clenched his fingers in the back of her blouse, holding her close yet at the same time holding her away. Somewhere on the edge of his mind, he heard more clapping and had an inkling it hadn't resulted from the rocket exploding. He pulled his lips free, unable to completely leave her without at least rubbing the tip of her nose with his in a brief caress.

"Zach, I. . . ."

"Aunt G J!"

Zach could have cheerfully strangled the little whelp, or at the very least, growled at him. His reward for restraint was Aunt G J ignoring the interruption for a good, long instant, while her eyes promised him that she wouldn't forget whatever she'd meant to say. *Later*, her eyes assured him. *Later*.

"What, Brad?" she asked.

"We's s'posed to get to set off the rest of the rockets," the little imp told her in a self-important voice. "Your boyfriend promised! And since I'm fifty seconds older than Billy, I get to be first!"

"All right, all right," Zach yielded. "Let me get another rocket ready, while your aunt lights a couple more punks for you two."

He cheated a little on the next rocket, choosing one out of line—one that would last a longer time in the air, with its variegated timings for explosions. With a freshly lit punk in his hand, Brad stepped forward, waiting impatiently while Zach inspected the rocket before he allowed the boy to light it. Finally, Zach nodded and Brad pressed his punk to the fuse.

Suddenly Gerrie Jean screamed. "No! Oh, God, Billy! Everyone! Everyone in the water!"

She followed her warning with action, grabbing Billy and tearing to the side of the dock opposite the box of fireworks to jump into the lake. One brief glance was all Zach needed to seize Brad and follow her. The rocket whooshed into the air about the same time the cold water hit Zach full force. It was fairly deep, but he managed to get to his feet and wrap Brad's hands on the edge of the dock, ordering him to hang on there. The child obeyed, and Zach pulled himself back onto the dock.

"No!" Gerrie Jean yelled again. "It'll explode!"

Ignoring her, Zach grabbed a dip net he'd noticed leaning against the dock railing and pushed the burning box of fireworks into the lake on the other side of the dock. The odiferous smoke and flames from the burning box sizzled in the water, and there were a couple muffled explosions, but the entire mess was safely out within a few seconds.

The second explosion went off overhead, and Zach looked up, then shrugged. He jumped back into the water with Gerrie Jean and the twins, wrapping his arms around Gerrie Jean's waist and tilting his head to the sky as the third explosion sounded. The waves of different-colored sparks formed a rainbow effect, beautiful in the night sky.

"You shouldn't have taken a chance like that," Gerrie Jean said, twisting in his arms. "That box of stuff could have exploded in your face."

"We took all the rockets out of it and lined them up on the bench beneath the launcher, remember?" he assured her. "All that was left in the box were some smoke bombs and a couple packs of firecrackers."

"The firecrackers could have been dangerous."

"Not as dangerous as letting that box burn where it was. It could've caught the dock on fire."

"Oh. By the way, why are we still in the water?"

"I'm in here because you are," he said with a laugh.

"We can't lit off the rest of the fireworks from here," Brad said logically, swinging one leg onto the dock and following it.

"Light off, not lit," Gerrie Jean corrected him. Billy lunged onto the dock, also, in time to collect a towel Bobby Joe handed him.

"Belle sent down towels for all of you," he said, chuckling. "And it's only fair to warn you, she had the video camera out filming this entire scramble that ended with everyone in the lake."

"Oh, no," one of the twins groaned. "Mom better not show it to our friends when they come over for our Fourth of July barbecue!"

"Maybe you could be real good little boys and get her to edit that part onto another tape," Bobby Joe suggested. "But I believe you'd have to be real, real good." As the twins stared up the bank at the deck where their mother sat, he continued to Gerrie Jean and Zach, "Thanks, both of you, for taking care of the kids. I didn't even notice Billy holding his punk too near that box until the flames had already flared. I'm glad you kept your head enough to shove the box into the water, Zach."

"Instinct," Zach admitted with a slight lift of one shoulder.

Bobby Joe nodded. "Yeah, it does seem to be a male instinct to protect the people we care for, even at a risk to ourselves."

Zach paused in wiping at water dripping down his neck, turning to Gerrie Jean. She gazed back at him, appreciation for his heroic actions clear on her face. He could get used to that look from her.

Chapter Seven

Two days later, Gerrie Jean exited the children's hospital to find Zach leaning against the Mercedes, ankles and arms crossed as he glared at her. He wore faded jeans, which clung to his thighs and slim hips, and a T-shirt that looked fairly new. She chewed her bottom lip for a second, then lifted her chin and approached him. She could read the saying on the shirt as she got near: YOU MIGHT BE A REDNECK IF. . . . Probably the rest was on the back.

"I would think hot metal would be uncomfortable to lean against," she said.

He didn't bother to respond to that comment. "I left you several messages. I said I'd take you to the probation office and help you get things set up. Reminded you that I was on vacation and would be glad to drive you around, since I knew you didn't have a license this month."

"I'm not a child, Zach. I made this mess myself, and I can handle things." He straightened, and she managed to keep her eyes on his face, rather than give in to the pull to scan the muscular chest beneath that almost-too-small T-shirt. Still, her mind sighed in appreciation. When he opened his mouth to say something else, she held out her hand in protest. "I got Becky Rose to bring me here, and now I'm going over to her house to watch the kids for a while so she can do some errands. Hoedown's at therapy, but he'll probably be back by the time Becky Rose gets done shopping, and then she can take me home without having to drag the kids out in the heat.''

Zach gazed around. "So where's Becky Rose now?"

"Well . . . uh . . . I obviously didn't want her to have to wait here with all three kids while I set things up with the volunteer office for my community service. It's way too hot, and she didn't really want to bring the kids into the hospital and wait for me. I told her to go on home.''

"So how are you getting to her house?''

"I'd planned on a cab, but . . . oh, all right. You can take me!''

"Well, golly gee, ma'am," Zach mocked. "It would be an honor to drive you somewhere.'' He opened the passenger door and swept out his arm, motioning her into the car. Clutching the packet of paperwork to her breast, she scooted by him and slid into the seat. He closed the door, was around the car and inside with the air conditioning running before she much more than broke a sweat on her forehead from the hot air in the car. But instead of slipping the car into gear and leaving the parking lot, he turned and put his arm on the back of her seat.

"Why didn't you return my calls? Saturday night was very special, and I didn't push you when I took you home because you were dead on your feet. I did tell you that I'd promised to have dinner with my father on Sunday, but I'd call you later that evening. I called at least a half-dozen times, and when you didn't answer, I even drove by your house like some moonstruck teenager. The lights were on, but I lost my nerve before I got out of the car and came to the door. The lights were on in the house where that little old lady with the umbrella lives, too, and I figured maybe she might assault me again if I pounded on your door and you wouldn't answer it.''

She gazed into his hurt and troubled eyes, feeling her determination to end it with him slide away with the drop of sweat easing downward between her breasts. God, if he only knew how she'd sat on the floor last night, staring at the phone—listening to his voice on her answering machine and forcing herself not to pick up that receiver. If anything, knowing what today had in store for her had shown her there was absolutely no future for the two of them. She could just imagine Zach Brenham escorting one of the criminals from his court to a probation officer and to the hospital to set up her community service, where probably every person on the hospital staff knew of the Brenham family's huge charitable contributions. She'd already suffered through the embarrassment of the volunteer coordinator's recognition of Zach's name on the paperwork she had to turn in to satisfy the court requirements.

Zach's eyes narrowed. "I could have made it a lot easier for you, you know. I could have handled all this for you, and you wouldn't even have had to let anyone know you were fulfilling a probation requirement. You could have just continued to do your regular volunteer hours."

"I suppose you found out about that during your *investigation* of me."

"Yeah," he admitted. "Gerrie Jean. . . ." He cupped her face, rubbing his thumb back and forth across her cheek bone. "I can't change who I am. I understand that who I am will probably embarrass the hell out of you. . . ."

"What?" she gasped. "*You* embarrass *me*? Zach, I didn't let you know what my schedule was today because I thought you'd find it awfully difficult being seen with *me*."

"Why?" he asked in a puzzled voice. Then, "Oh. Because you appeared in my court? For crying out loud, Gerrie Jean, you were there on a stupid fireworks charge that I couldn't talk Hank into dropping. My damned cousin probably would have dropped that charge if it had been any other judge except me ordering him to do it, but he knows me too well to be afraid of my influence.

Not that I'd do anything drastic to family anyway, but it was asinine for Hank to pursue this. Since it's so unfair, I don't feel guilty about helping you get through it any way I can.''

She sighed in resignation, leaning into his palm and wishing he would kiss her. "It's because I've mouthed off to Hank a time or two when he's stopped me," she admitted. "I normally am not like that with law officials, but Hank rubs me the wrong way for some reason."

"Yeah, he does that to me sometimes, too, but he's a damned good patrolman. He's even been offered a position in the Texas Rangers, so you won't have to worry much longer about him stopping you for speeding."

The way she felt now, she'd never speed again. She wanted her entire life to slow down—to never go forward—to stay at this very point forever. She wanted his thumb to keep caressing her cheekbone. She wanted him to keep looking at her like she was the only other person on earth who mattered. She wanted him to kiss her. And he did.

His groan rumbled deliciously against her lips, his fingers threaded in her hair, and his muscles beneath that tight T-shirt were every bit as firm as she remembered. She smoothed her hands up his chest and around his neck. He deepened the kiss, fulfilling a desire she hadn't realized she felt until he licked his tongue around her lips and then past her teeth to taste inside her mouth. She tasted him in return—the Zach taste, the mint and man and masculinity. The love she had felt growing beyond her control as she stared at the phone and listened to his voice last night burst into her consciousness with a power she was helpless to deny.

He drew back far enough to see into her face. The hunger in his eyes made the warmth in her belly and between her legs spiral into an inferno. Had he wanted to strip her right there and settle her onto his lap, join her to him, she could not have resisted. The windows were tinted limousine dark anyway. . . .

"I want you," he growled, as though she needed to hear the spoken words to confirm what she already knew. "I want your body, but I also want you, the Gerrie Jean I'm getting to know. The Gerrie Jean who's hair is like tangled silk I'd like to wind around me. The Gerrie Jean who's eyes are a velvet brown as smooth and deep as fine brandy."

He unbuttoned one blouse button, the next, and another. She somehow managed to stay upright in the seat by clinging to the support of his neck, but she felt her insides melting—and definitely not from the Texas heat. "I want to feel your breasts again, and kiss them this time," he murmured, and she could only nod helplessly. He tenderly lifted her breast free of the wisp of mint green bra she'd put on this morning—had she maybe hoped he'd find her somewhere along the path of her busy day? Bending his head, he sipped her nipple into his mouth and she arched against him, almost climaxing right there in the bucket seat.

Lifting his head, he murmured, "Come home with me tonight."

"Okay," she squeaked.

He nodded, then kissed her again, his lips clinging and finally parting from hers reluctantly. Gently he tugged her bra back into place and rebuttoned her blouse. He pushed her back into her own seat and lovingly fastened her seatbelt. After a deep, dark look of promise, he sat back and buckled his own seatbelt. Blowing out a breath she took for a final effort at control, he reached for the gearshift.

"Which way?" he asked when he stopped before pulling out onto the street.

"Huh? Oh, left. She lives on Cimarron Drive. Do you know where that is?"

"Vaguely," he replied. "If I go the wrong way, let me know."

She tried, but she was so distracted she let him make a total of three wrong turns, only becoming aware of her lack of proper directions each time when she drew herself back to reality and realized she didn't recognize the surroundings. Shoot, she'd been to Becky Rose and Hoedown's house a million times. But never riding with a man she cared so desperately about and one she wanted so badly to have hold her. Finally, Zach reached over and took her hand, settling it beneath his palm on his thigh. She let him make one final wrong turn that time, then was able to direct him to the small, neat frame house on Cimarron Drive.

He captured her hand again on the walk up to the front door, and she decided not to protest. Huh. As if she could have anyway. Her fingers curled around his as though it was the only proper place for them to reside, and her mind assured her it was.

Becky Rose barely took time to show her surprise at the identity of her escort, but Gerrie Jean knew darned well she'd get the third-degree later on. Right now, Becky Rose was too excited about going on one of her rare excursions into the outside world without three tagalong rug rats demanding candy, ice cream, or a bathroom break.

Within a few minutes, Gerrie Jean found herself desperately glad she had someone to help her with the rambunctious kids. But then, she wouldn't have been so spacey and distracted, so unable to cope with the kids today, if she hadn't had this particular escort, so she didn't feel too guilty.

The oldest child, Benjie, took to Zach immediately. Six years old, he had lorded it over his two brothers long enough to feel confident of his position as leader of the pack. The five-year-old, Archie, was just coming into his assertiveness, so Gerrie Jean figured Benjie wouldn't be unchallenged for long. Both of the older boys loved to wrestle, and Zach evidently decided to revert to his own childhood ways and fulfill their desire.

Gerrie Jean's favorite was the child Becky Rose called her surprise—the one she got pregnant with after Hoedown became paralyzed. Sometimes Becky Rose called year-old Scooter her celebration child, also. The designation was always accompanied with a sly wink that brought tears to Gerrie Jean's eyes rather than embarrassment that Becky Rose was letting her know she and Hoedown could still make love, despite his partial paralysis.

Scooter, able to walk at the tender age of nine months, normally strutted around with all the confidence of a spoiled brat, but today Gerrie Jean noticed he was somewhat quieter than usual. The reason became obvious after she took him into the bedroom when he tugged at his diaper, indicating a need for a change. Red spots speckled his little bottom, and when she drew his shirt up to examine him, she found more on his chest. Uh oh. They looked suspiciously like the chicken pox spots she'd seen recently on the child of one of her and Becky Rose's mutual friends.

While Zach continued to entertain Benjie and Archie, she kept Scooter quiet and fed him liquids. Hoedown arrived home a few minutes before Becky Rose, the handicap van driver walking up to the front door with the biker and opening it for him so he could roll his wheelchair inside. She decided to wait for Becky Rose to mention the chicken pox, since Hoedown was always tired after his therapy. Surprising her, Zach and the biker hit it off immediately and were sharing a couple of beers when Becky Rose hurried in. Gerrie Jean motioned her friend into the bedroom, where Scooter slept restlessly.

"Oh, no!" Becky Rose gasped as soon as Gerrie Jean explained what she thought was wrong. "I'll call the doctor right away. And I guess this means I can't earn the money for Benjie's bicycle for his birthday after all."

"What do you mean?" Gerrie Jean asked.

"There's a charity supper tomorrow night," Becky Rose said with a sigh. "You remember I've been helping my friend Mary Beth with her catering service and earning a little extra money to supplement Zach's disability check. This account is so important to Mary Beth, too, that when I let her down, she'll probably never give me the opportunity to work for her again. The job was perfect for me, too, because the boys would usually be in bed before I left, and Hoedown wouldn't have so much trouble with them.''

"I'll fill in for you while the chicken pox are running their course, Becky Rose. Just tell me when and where. That way, Mary Beth will keep the job for you."

"Oh, G J! Would you? It's horrible of me to even consider taking you up on your offer, but. . . .''

"Don't even think about turning me down. We'll get Cool Hand or someone to drive me, so you can nurse your kids.''

"Thanks so much, G J. Hopefully, they'll all come down with the pox within a few days of each other and get over it all at once. They were all three exposed at the same time. Remember?''

"Uh-huh. When we were at that birthday party a couple of weeks ago.''

Just then Benjie wandered into the room, his cheeks bright and flushed. "Ma,'' he said. "I don't feel so well.'' Becky Rose stood up and went to him.

The log house looked beautiful in the moonlight, sprawling over the landscape the way a lover would lay bonelessly across a huge bed after satisfaction—satisfaction Gerrie Jean had no doubt wasn't that far off for both her and Zach. He didn't speak. He didn't need to. He took her hand and led her into the house, up the stairwell and into the master bedroom. He flung the wide French doors across one wall open, leaving the screen in place to block the mosquitoes. Outside, silvery moonlight filtered through the tall, spiraling jack pines, casting the landscape into grays and blacks, lights and darks.

"A lover's moon,'' he murmured as he returned to her. "For lovers. I want to be your lover, Gerrie Jean.''

"Please,'' she breathed.

He kissed her, a bare hint of a caress. When she yearned after his lips as he lifted his head, he tenderly placed a finger on her mouth. She lapped his finger, a throaty purr rumbling from her throat and the salty-sweet taste of him exploding on her senses with much more impact than if he'd been a bowl of honey-laced cream and she a spoiled cat. He gasped, whatever he'd started to say lost in the rumbling growl of desire mingling with her feline hum.

Languidly, she opened her eyes halfway, and his pent-up breath whispered across her face with the banked force of a rising evening breeze as he said, "I want you to be sure. I want you to tell me you want me for a lover and mean it."

"I want you for my lover, Zach," she said with a whimper of surrender. "I want you for my lover, my man, and my soul mate. Make love to me, Zach. Love me."

"Oh God, Gerrie Jean," he groaned. "I do."

His kiss ravaged her this time, satisfying her need to be ravaged. In her last brief glimmer of sanity, she felt surprise flicker across her mind—something to do with a deep joy at whatever he had said. But before she could zero on complete understanding, she lost the thought in the inferno of desire.

In turn soft and frenzied, banked and out of control, they helped each other out of the irksome clothing. Naked at last, Zach halted her long enough to reach inside the drawer on the bedside table. The foil packet rustled, and she could see the reluctance on his face, but she put her hands over his to help him guide the only barrier they would have between them into place.

Then Zach folded backwards onto the bed, pulling her with him and sliding every inch of her over every wonderful naked inch of him. His lips and hands sought her yearning places, her private places, the places she had never even known were erotic until Zach touched them. She strove to give as much in return, because there was so much more here than physical striving for release. When he finally slipped inside her long, untold moments later, she knew a deep, incredulous feeling of oneness— something she had thought only a figment of an author's imagination in a book somewhere. She tumbled with him into the moonlit night, crying his name.

Their next time was slower, more tender, more laughing and teasing. Sometime during the night they fell asleep, and she woke the next morning immediately aware of where she was—who lay at her side—who held her securely, lovingly. He'd closed the sliding doors before they slept, when the air conditioning had labored and they'd started to get too sticky. She felt cool, yet at the same time warm and feminine, satisfied and coddled.

"Morning, lover," Zach whispered.

"Ummmmm. You forgot to say 'good' with the morning. Or maybe 'wonderful.' "

"Wonderful morning, lover," he corrected, and she giggled with extreme feminine contentment. "What shall we do today?"

Gerrie Jean shifted to sit up, stretching and gazing down at him in sorrow. "I know you're on vacation, but I have to be at the shop—and also do an hour or two of community service every day. Maybe I can talk to Cool Hand about putting in some extra hours after today."

"Tonight, then," Zach murmured. "We'll go to this fund-raiser I should make an appearance at, then cut out early and go do our own thing."

She shook her head. "I can't. I promised Becky Rose I'd work in her place tonight at her part-time job while she takes care of the kids. Hoedown will help her, but if the kids get real feverish and fussy, he'll have a hard time handling them in his wheelchair."

"How late will you be? I'll pick you up."

"I don't know. Tomorrow night?"

"You better believe it," Zach promised. "And maybe

even tonight. I'll drive by your house after this damned engagement I have to attend is over and see if you're home yet.''

''I'd like that,'' she admitted.

Chapter Eight

She was ready to drop, but Gerrie Jean pasted on a smile and passed around a silver-coated tray of after-dinner mints and nuts. Becky Rose had failed to mention the party that evening was at the mayor's house until right before she hung up the phone after giving Gerrie Jean the address. She'd ranted and raved to Cool Hand all the way to the grand mansion, riding in her own Mustang and gritting her teeth every time Cool Hand shot out from a stoplight with a heavy foot on the gas pedal. But hell, she couldn't have arrived at such a prestigious address on the back of the bike, could she?

The day had proven to have far too few hours in it. With her mind on all the other variables which had recently entered her life, paperwork at the dealership—something both she and Cool Hand despised—was piling up. Zach had called twice, just in case she'd changed her mind about the party. She'd spent her two hours at the children's hospital, then sprayed a coat of primer on the gas tank to prepare it for painting. As usual, she got caught up in envisioning the finished work and barely managed to shower and dress before Cool Hand showed up to chauffeur her.

The party was huge. At first, she helped in the kitchen, since one of the caterer's staff assigned there failed to appear. Even knowing the culprit would be fired—at least according to the manager—didn't help as the temperature climbed due to the cooking and rush of scurrying bodies. Just when she thought she'd be able to call Cool Hand and have him pick her up—the manager had assured Gerrie Jean that her duties didn't include cleanup—one of the waitstaff women doubled over in pain. Murmuring something about her period being especially bad this month, the poor woman stumbled to a chair.

A quick perusal revealed Gerrie Jean was the only one available who would fit the uniform, and after a quick change of clothing and repair job on her makeup, she headed for the party outside the kitchen. Feet throbbing, she carried the tray around, smiling and being totally ignored except by one overweight, half-drunk man, who almost tipped the entire tray when he snared a double fist of mints and nuts. Most of the rest of the people treated her as invisible, although a couple of women sort of waved a hand in the air when she approached, as though shooing a pesky fly. She gritted her teeth, wondering how the hell the catering manager ever kept a full staff when they were treated about as welcome as cow shit on an evening gown.

One man finally heeded her. She rounded a huge plant beside the sparkling pool and skidded to a halt. It took Zach a minute, since he had a blond vamp wrapped around him, bare leg clear of the slit in her gown and knee rubbing Zach's crotch, but some instinct seemed to prod him. He lifted his head from only about a half inch from the bimbo's lips, unerringly spearing Gerrie Jean with his gaze. His drink glass shattered on the concrete, and the woman's head snapped on her neck as he unpeeled her from him.

Gerrie Jean didn't hang around to see what happened next. Whirling, she raced through the crowd and into the kitchen, scattering nuts and mints behind her. She covered up her shattered emotions well, or else the manager was too busy to notice the threatening tears. Dismissed with a vague "thank you," she headed for the half-bath assigned to change clothes and called Cool Hand on the convenient phone in there.

Even given his heavy foot, Cool Hand seemed to arrive in no time, although Gerrie Jean had no idea how much time had truly passed while she adamantly held the pain at bay. As the Mustang slid to a stop, she hurried out the back entrance, and a man stepped out of the bushes as though he'd been waiting for her. Zach. Wearing tennis shoes now, she evaded him and made it to the Mustang. He caught her hand as she tried to open the passenger door.

"I can explain that," he said as Cool Hand threw the driver's door open and crawled out, then glared across the car roof at them. "She was someone who doesn't understand 'no' or 'goodbye.' But her family is important enough that. . . ."

"Everything all right, G J?" Cool Hand snarled. "You want me to come around there and play valet and help you in the car?"

"No!" she told the biker. Raising her head, she glared at Zach. "You've got two seconds to let go of me before I give you a jolt with *my* knee right where that bimbo's knee was. Only my knee's not going to be *stroking* your precious family jewels!"

He dropped her hand as though it had turned into the hot Texas sun, then growled, "I can't believe you're not even giving me a chance to explain!"

Shaking her head, she sneered at him. "There's no explanation needed. I saw with my own eyes what the idea of morality is in your social stratosphere. You let that vamp crawl all over you the day after you made love to me! It's like I thought all along—you're cognac and I'm Pearl Beer. Now step the hell out of the way of the car door!"

He complied, holding his hands out to his sides to indicate she was free from any interference. The thunder on his face only made her own anger flare higher, and the grimness of his lips made her wonder how on earth they could have ever felt so soft and sexy on hers. She yanked the door open, barely noticing Cool Hand sliding into his seat at the same time she did. From the way Cool Hand tore out of the parking lot, she supposed Zach probably ended up with gravel in his eyes. Recalling again the bimbo's pythonlike pose and vulgar knee between Zach's legs, she couldn't bring herself to feel even a slight pang of sympathy for him.

Cool Hand waited several minutes before he spoke. "You all right?" he repeated.

"No," she admitted. "But I'll get over it. I knew all along it would end, but I didn't think it would be this fast." She shuddered a shaky laugh. "Guess all I can say is that it was fun while it lasted."

Cool Hand slid her a contemplative look. "He wasn't that bad, once you got to know him. He could've made big trouble for me when the cops showed up at your house the other night. And those two rug-rat hellions your brother's raisin' were by the shop today after you left to play nursie maid. They said he put on a real kick-ass show for them at the lake. Kids usually know about people."

She shoved her fingertips into her jeans pockets and ducked her head into her shoulders. He didn't understand. *He* hadn't seen that bimbo practically eating Zach alive right out there in front of everyone.

"You wanna talk about it?" Cool Hand asked.

She chewed her lip. "I don't know. I don't even like remembering it right now."

"I got sort of an idea of what went on from what you two said to each other. But I can't figure out if it was something that would've happened no matter if you'd been with your beer-drinking buddies or those Dom Perignon high hats."

After a few seconds' silence, Gerrie Jean said, "We've got lawyers, bankers, and corporate presidents riding with the Weekend Rovers some weekends, Cool Hand. Sure, some of them prefer imported beer to the kegs we take

up a collection and buy, but we don't razz them about
that. They unroll their sleeping bags in tents just like we
do and take their turn at the cooking pots. It was . . . it
was. . . ."

"Sounds to me like it could've happened whether
you'd been at a campfire around the lake with the gang
or at the Governor's Ball."

"Probably," she admitted. "But he could have tried a
little harder to explain."

Cool Hand snorted in disbelief. "Spoken like a true
dame. Baby, you had your claws out and your tongue
sharpened. Ain't no man on earth would've risked the
layin' into you were fixin' to give him. I didn't blame
ole Society Zach one bit for backing off."

Knowing her as well as he did, Zach didn't really expect
her to take his calls. But he called once a day anyway,
leaving the same message on the answering machine.
"Call me, please." Torn between his aching heart and
his anger at her judging him without even listening to his
defense, he refused to make any sort of further attempt—
like giving in to the urge to drive over there and shake
her until she listened. Or kiss her silly and make love to
her until she laid there so out of it with boneless fulfillment she couldn't gather enough energy to walk away
while he told her the blonde didn't mean a thing. That
he'd been trying to pry her off him before he gave in to
the desire to shove her into the pool. That would've been
a clearly wrong move, since she was the granddaughter
of the judge who helped his father put Zach on the bench.

By Sunday, when he was expected to dine with his
father and had planned to take Gerrie Jean with him, she
still hadn't called back. Usually he enjoyed Sundays with
his father, because with both their busy schedules, they
almost had to make appointments to see each other. But
they worked in Sunday brunch or dinner at least a couple
times a month.

Drinks in the library before dinner were customary and

a time to catch up on each other's lives. Recently, they'd both leaned more and more often to mineral water rather than the fine old bourbon Hamilton Brenham kept in stock, although they usually sampled it after their meal. Tradition also came into play when Zach's father got right to the point of what he wanted to talk about that day, rather than lead up to it with polite, innocuous conversation.

"Why didn't you bring Miss Cartwright with you? I told the cook to prepare for three people, even though you didn't say you were bringing her."

In the process of settling deeply into one of the cushioned chairs in front of the unlit fireplace, Zach reversed himself. He stood and walked back over to the bar, setting down his glass of mineral water and lime and picking up an empty glass. When he returned to his seat, the new glass contained dark, smoky bourbon on the rocks.

"I suppose you know all about Gerrie Jean by now, don't you, Dad?" he said before taking a deep swallow. "You know, I don't appreciate your checking up on my dates, especially a woman I've known for so brief a time."

"I didn't check on this one," Hamilton denied. "I didn't have to. The courthouse was buzzing with the whole story last week after you flaunted protocol and took over Magistrate's Court." When Zach glared at him and started to speak again, Hamilton hurried to continue. "And let me assure you, I and anyone else interested could see that the rumors had a basis in fact. You never once looked at Amanda the way you looked at Geralyn Cartwright."

"Gerrie Jean," Zach corrected before he finished his drink in one more gulp and rose for another one. As he passed his father's chair, Hamilton held out his nearly full glass of mineral water, and Zach knew he didn't want a refill of the same thing.

"Gerrie Jean?" Hamilton mused as Zach fixed them each a bourbon.

"Yeah, that's what she goes by rather than Geralyn. Or G J is what a lot of her friends and her relatives call her." Returning to the chair, he handed his father his drink and took his seat again. "She's definitely not a Geralyn, just like Amanda could never had been a Mandy."

"I think Amanda would have liked to have had a try at being a Mandy," Hamilton mused. "She wouldn't have been happy staying a Mandy, but you never gave her a chance to realize that. I guess you and I are destined to make similar mistakes in our lives. But you've still got time to correct one of yours, if you want."

"What do you mean?"

Hamilton propped his ankle on the opposite knee and pondered Zach for a while. Then he said, "I loved your mother an awful lot, but over the years I came to understand part of that love came from us being a matched set. You know, similar backgrounds, similar goals, similar tastes."

He sipped his drink. "Once, when I was wild and young, and before I met your mother, I came close to breaking away from all that. I met a young girl who grabbed my heart so fast and so tight it hurt. But I was terribly immature, and I'd been indoctrinated all my life as to what was expected of me. I can still remember the horrible pain I felt the day she climbed onto the back of her brother's motorcycle and rode off with him—to camp across the United States and then decide what they wanted to do with their lives on a permanent basis. I could have gone with them. I could have had one year of freedom then gone back into the fold. But I didn't have the nerve to face your grandfather if I did that."

Zach chuckled wryly. "Well, I'm a little too old to kidnap Gerrie Jean and take her across the country on the back of a bike. And she's got a business to run. Besides, she hates me now. She came on Pamela Rathbone trying to seduce me at the fund-raiser the other night."

"Wouldn't let you explain, huh? Hurting too bad herself?"

"I suppose. But damn it, Dad, I was hurting, too. Hurting that she wouldn't give me a chance to tell her what was going on before she slammed the car door in my face and took off with that damned biker buddy of hers!"

"If she was hurt that bad, she must love you a lot." Hamilton finished off his drink and stood up. "It's time for dinner. We better go on in." As they walked out of the library, Hamilton said, "Seems to me a woman would have to listen to a man if he kidnapped her and took her off somewhere she couldn't leave him until he got done talking to her."

"Jesus, Dad. I could get thrown off the bench in a second if anyone found out I was even thinking about kidnapping a woman."

"For the right woman, the scandal might be worth it," Hamilton mused.

Zach stopped so fast his father was in the dining room before he realized he was alone. When Hamilton turned with a questioning look on his face, Zach motioned him on. "I'll be in after I make a phone call."

In the end, it took him three calls—one to the motorcycle dealership, which he should have realized was closed on Sunday. One to Gerrie Jean's brother out at the lake, who promised in man-to-man fashion to keep his mouth shut about the call. And one to the biker, who surprised him and didn't hold him up for a ransom amount in order to fulfill Zach's request.

Chapter Nine

Someone ought to change Independence Day to wintertime, Gerrie Jean mused. No one should have to endure the Texas heat in July. Yep, it would be much better to have the outdoor activities in, say, November or December. Shoot, maybe even January, when once in a thousand years even San Antonio, Texas, experienced snow. Her heat-activated deodorant had lost the battle twice today, and she fought the urge to lift her arm and sniff to see if she needed to replenish it again.

At least the sun had finally made it to the horizon. They could have the raffle now, and within another hour, set off the fireworks. Even some of the more ill patients had been brought out into the less thick evening air, and she caught a snicker from a ten-year-old boy Billy was visiting with.

"Yeah, I can't help it," Billy told the little bald-headed guy, who was spending the night at the hospital after a chemo treatment. "She's family, and we don't get no choice 'bout who we get borned into."

Gerrie Jean propped her hands on her hips and glared at Billy. "Was that remark about me?"

"Uh-huh," Billy said with a sad nod of his head. "I just can't get away from it, Aunt G J. Everyone here knows who you are and laughs at me soon's I tell them my own name. I don't s'pose you could find somethin'

else to wear, could you? Them there red, white, and blue
striped shorts is bad enough, lookin' like men's underwear like they do. And that blue star-spangled blouse is
so tight, you must be awful hot. I think you're gonna
have a problem tomorrow, too, with them shoes bein'
laced up your legs. You're gonna have a striped sunburn.
Plus you wobble so bad on them high heels that your . . .
uh . . . you wobble in front, too.''

"Billy!"

His lower lip pouted outward. "Well, it's true."

Gerrie Jean sighed dramatically. "I was asked to dress
like this by the celebration committee, Billy. They
thought it would be nice to have a few of us in costume
today."

"Mostly they done that to the women, tho', didn't
they?" Billy replied astutely. "Mom said she was gonna
tell you to tell them to shove it next year. That they was
s'poit . . . exploi . . . well, when I asked her, she said the
word meant taking advantage of the pretty women on the
committee."

Gerrie Jean pursed her lips in thought. "You're right,"
she said at last. "And so is your mother. I'm going to
change, and the hell with what the mayor and his cronies
have to say!"

Before she could get a half dozen feet, the loudspeaker
over her head blared. "Ladies and gentlemen! May I
have your attention, please? The moment you've all been
waiting for has arrived—we're going to draw the winning raffle ticket for the motorcycle gas tank our own,
lovely Miss Fourth of July, Gerrie Jean Cartwright, do-
nated and decorated with one of her wonderful paintings!"

"The mayor could've left off the *lovely*," Gerrie Jean
muttered to herself. But it was too late now. Next year,
she would have a say in how the announcements came
off.

She made her way to the platform as the mayor explained what had gone into planning today's celebration.

How the Weekend Rovers had adopted the children's wing of this hospital. How on certain holidays during the year—Easter, Fourth of July, Thanksgiving, and Christmas—the club raised funds and sponsored a party for the children separated from their families on those special days. How this year, they'd even gone a step further, raising funds for the father of one of the children who had been treated in the hospital, a man who had been partially paralyzed in a motorcycle accident, but who was determined to take over the support of his family again.

Gerrie Jean paused at the bottom of the stairs to the speaker's platform while the mayor introduced Hoedown and his family. She'd had such different plans for this day. Although, looking back, she had seen the looming signs of failure in her relationship with Zach all along, she had dreamed of having him by her side today. Of their two worlds combining at a charity function, proving they did indeed have a few things in common.

Her heart still felt as though the shattered pieces were crawling around inside her chest, looking for each other so they could form a whole heart for her again. He quit calling after those first few days, and he hadn't shown up in person. She'd gotten so down and depressed one day that she sought out Cool Hand, willing to discuss the situation now. Ready to admit she needed a friendly shoulder to cry on. Cool Hand waved her off, adamant he didn't have time right then for a confidence, since summer was a busy time at a bike dealership. He at least promised to see if he could fit her in for a heart-to-heart after the Fourth of July celebration.

Fit her in! Who the hell had ever heard of a biker you had to make an appointment with like some big corporate executive? Especially a biker who worked for her!

Someone nudged her from behind, and Gerrie Jean glanced up to see the mayor motioning to her impatiently. Tugging down the billowing hem of her shorts—and up the top of the blue lamé halter top—she teetered up the steps on her high-heeled sandals. Tomorrow, she was go-

ing through her closet and throw out every damned pair
of heels over half an inch high!

She clamped her lips when the hoots and hollers of
several hundred redneck and biker men sounded in appreciation of her brief outfit. Damn, at least she hadn't
agreed to help at Easter next year. They'd probably try
to put her in a Playboy Bunny costume! Just for the hell
of it, she strutted across the platform, then happened to
glance down and see Billy's pained face. Caving in on
herself—both physically and emotionally—she walked
on over to the mayor.

At first they drew for the lesser prizes: a pair of boots,
a set of leathers, and a year's worth of gas for a bike.
For some reason, every winner came from far back in
the rear of the crowd. Then the mayor turned the tumbler
several more times to totally mix up the ticket stubs and
paused dramatically.

"Ladies and gentlemen! It's my great honor and priv-
ilege to be a part of this charity celebration. I'm sure you
know how strongly the mayor's office supports events
such as these."

"Cut to the chase," Gerrie Jean ordered out of the side
of her mouth. "This isn't the place for you to campaign.
It's for the kids and Hoedown. Get on with it, or I'm
gonna start doing a strip-tease and embarrass the hell out
of your prim and proper office!"

The mayor gulped and his eyes widened. For a moment, Gerrie Jean thought he would take her up on her
offer, but he finally turned back to the crowd. "This final
drawing is for our grand prize, the motorcycle gas tank
with the valuable G J Cartwright painting on it! Everyone, please look at your tickets carefully!"

Gerrie Jean heard a little grumbling, but couldn't make
any sense out of it. She did notice, however, that no one
near the platform appeared to have a ticket, since no one
held any in their hands. Or else, they all had their numbers memorized, which she doubted. She dug into the

wire tumbler and pulled out a ticket stub, handing it to the mayor.

"And the winner is!" He paused dramatically, milking the eyes on him for all he was worth. "Number six-five-nine-nine-zero-two!"

"He got it!" Bobby Joe hollered, raising a fist in the air. "That's one of Zach Brenham's numbers!"

"Huh?" Gerrie Jean's mouth dropped open as she stared down at her brother in stunned amazement. How did Bobby Joe know that? Then she sensed Hoedown creeping up on her in his wheelchair and turned to him. The biker winked at her, then reached out and gave her a shove—right off the side of the platform. Even above her own scream, she heard the deep-throated growl of a Harley approaching through the crowd.

Someone caught her before she hit the ground, and she looked up into her brother's face. Bobby Joe grinned evilly at her, and Belle pushed up to his side. Her sister-in-law at least winked and placed a comforting hand on her arm.

"It's all right," Belle said. "Truly."

The bike motor idled to a stop beside Bobby Joe, and Gerrie Jean glanced over to see a vaguely familiar masculine body sitting on it. The black helmet and tinted visor kept her from identifying the rider. He nodded, and Bobby Joe swiveled to place Gerry Jean on the back of the bike. Before she could blink, Bobby Joe grabbed a helmet the bike rider handed him and plopped it over Gerrie Jean's head, fastening it securely.

The bike immediately took off, the crowd parting as though it had been warned this would happen and never giving her a chance to spring free. Her only option, other than a clumsy dump off the back fender, was to wrap her arms around the muscular chest and hold on.

She knew immediately who it was. Zach. She knew his feel even without being able to see his face. She'd felt it over and over every night in her dreams since the night of that damned party. She even knew his smell, and she laid her helmeted-head sideways against his back, breathing in and curling her fingers into his chest.

He rode out of town and kept going until she realized he was headed for his house. She never struggled—she couldn't dredge up the willpower to do that. Besides, he wasn't that adept on the bike and wobbled a time or two on the curves. Given her scant attire, she didn't need to take a chance on making him wreck and suffer a severe case of road rash all over her body!

Cool Hand probably taught Zach to ride, she pondered as she clung to him. That's what kept him so busy. Plus, she recognized the bike as one from her own showroom. That's why Zach stopped calling—he was planning this way to get her attention again. Who would have ever thought a federal judge would risk his reputation by kidnapping Miss Fourth of July right in front of half of San Antonio's elite? She daringly unsnapped the helmet and took it off, keeping it at the ready in case the bike wobbled and she needed to jam it back on. Then she snuggled her head against his back and purred. She'd bet her ass that bimbo she'd seen in his arms at the party had never driven Zach to such lengths to get a few minutes alone with *her!*

He pulled the bike to a stop in his driveway and waited until she dismounted first. She tried—hard—to keep a proper frown of fear on her face, but when he took his helmet off, she gave up the unfair battle and tossed her helmet aside, flung herself into his arms. To her utter relief, he dropped his helmet with a thud and pulled her close.

"She was the granddaughter of one of Dad's friends," he said in a desperate voice. "I was trying to get her off me without causing a big scene."

"I understand," she murmured. "I'm sorry I didn't let you explain. How . . ." She leaned back to look into his face. "How on earth did you manage to win the gas tank?"

"I bought every damned ticket I could find. Still, there

were a few floating around out there. I was afraid one of
those would win, but I'd have still found some way to
grab you up.''

''But other people won the rest of the prizes.''

''I handed people near me the winning tickets and let
them go up and claim those prizes,'' Zach admitted.

''Why?'' she asked with her heart in an uproar of ap-
prehension. ''I . . . acted like a fool.''

His brows rose, and she wasn't able to decide if the
sparkle in his eyes was amusement or anger until he
spoke in a teasing voice. ''Maybe I was just giving you
a chance to make up for your error in judgment.'' When
she dropped her head in embarrassment, he chucked her
under the chin and lifted her gaze to his again. ''It was
just as much my fault, darling. And since I'm desperately
hoping that you'll say yes when I ask you to marry me
in a few seconds, I hope we can decide that we'll follow
that rule of never going to bed angry.''

''M . . . marry you?'' she gasped. Then a thought
crossed her mind, and she narrowed her eyes. ''Can I ask
you one thing?''

''Of course.''

''Why did you hide your face with a helmet? It seems
like if you truly loved me, you wouldn't have cared if
everyone in that entire crowd knew who you were when
you kidnapped me.''

''It's against the law to ride without a helmet,'' Zach
reminded her. ''But you didn't see this, did you?''

He led her over to the back of the bike and pointed.
She gasped and covered her mouth when she saw the
wide sign with neon letters on it: ZACH LOVES GERRIE
JEAN!!! Tears filling her eyes, she stepped back into his
arms.

''I love you,'' he whispered.

''Oh, Zach, I love you, too.''

She lifted her face for his kiss, but the sudden uproar
sent her jumping against him. They both hit the bike and
it crashed to the ground. Somehow Zach managed to

twist them so they didn't land on top of the bike's hot muffler, but they hit the dirt hard with a twin set of "oomphs," firecrackers and something louder exploding nearby. Zach flipped her over and covered her with his body, his head going up and a feral growl emanating from his throat.

"Whoever the hell's responsible for this is going to be dead meat in just about ten seconds!"

"Why, son," a voice said. "Would you commit patricide? And what do you think he would call killing you, Mrs. Philistine? Housekeeper-cide?"

Zach scrambled to his feet and pulled Gerrie Jean up. "Dad! What the hell's going on?"

"Mrs. Philistine and I are just preparing to head over to Miss Cartwright's brother's place and get to know the rest of the family," Hamilton said with a shrug. "I came to pick her up and take her over to Bobby Joe's house for a late cookout and fireworks show. When we saw you and my future daughter-in-law in the driveway, we couldn't resist giving her a welcome to our side of the family with some of the fireworks we'd bought for those little scamps who'll be my great-nephews before long."

Gerrie Jean stared from one man to the other. "When did you meet my brother and his family?"

Hamilton waved a negligent hand. "Oh, we've been conniving for quite some time now. I do like your free-spirited family. Might I now call you Gerrie Jean?"

"Of . . . course. But I haven't said yes to Zach yet," she squeaked. When Hamilton Edward Brenham cocked his head questioningly, she said, "But of course that *is* the answer I'm going to give him. I'd sort of like a proper proposal though, if you both don't mind."

Hamilton nodded his head. "Say, Mrs. Philistine. Have you ever ridden on a motorcycle before? I used to ride one."

"Then shall we proceed?" the housekeeper said, holding out her hand.

Gerrie Jean didn't see them leave the driveway. Zach

carried her toward the house, and just inside the door, he set her down and turned the deadbolt lock with a satisfying clunk. Then he dropped to one knee.

"There. No one will interrupt us again. I love you, Gerrie Jean Cartwright. Will you marry me?"

"Yes. Yes, yes, yes."

She was going to have to stop jumping on Zach, she thought a few seconds later. He really didn't seem able to brace himself against the thrust of her weight. But another thrust they managed together later was satisfying to both of them.

If you crave romance and can't resist chocolate, you'll adore this tantalizing assortment of unexpected encounters, witty flirtation, forbidden love, and tender rediscovered passion...

MARGARET BROWNLEY's straight-laced gray-suited insurance detective is a bull in a whimsical Los Angeles chocolate shop and its beautiful, nutty owner wants him out—until she discovers his surprisingly soft center.

RAINE CANTRELL carries you back to the Old West, where men were men and candy was scarce...and a cowboy with the devil's own good looks succumbs to a sassy and sensual lady's special confectionary.

In NADINE CRENSHAW's London of 1660, a reckless Puritan maid's life is changed forever by a decadent brew of frothy hot chocolate and the dashing owner of a sweetshop.

SANDRA KITT follows a Chicago child's search for a box of Sweet Dreams that brings together a tall, handsome engineer and a tough single mother with eyes like chocolate drops.

For
The Love
of
Chocolate

YOU CAN'T RESIST IT!

ANITA MILLS
ARNETTE LAMB
ROSANNE BITTNER

*Join three of your favorite storytellers
on a tender journey of the heart...*

Cherished Moments is an extraordinary collection of breathtaking novellas woven around the theme of motherhood. Before you turn the last page you will have been swept from the storm-tossed coast of a Scottish isle to the fury of the American frontier, and you will have lived the lives and loves of three indomitable women, as they experience their most passionate moments.

THE NATIONAL BESTSELLER

CHERISHED MOMENTS
Anita Mills, Arnette Lamb, Rosanne Bittner
_____ 95473-5 $4.99 U.S./$5.99 Can.

No one believes in ghosts anymore, not even in Salem, Massachusetts. And especially not sensible Helen Evett, a widow who lives for her two teenaged kids and who runs the best preschool in town. But when little Katie Byrne enters her school, strange things begin to happen. Katie's widowed father, Nat, begins to awaken feelings in Helen that she had counted as dead. But why does Helen get the feeling that Linda, Katie's mother, is reaching beyond the grave to tell her something?

As Helen and Nat each explore the pain of their losses and the joy of their newfound love, Linda Byrne's ghost plays a bold hand, beseeching Helen to uncover the mystery of her death. But what Helen finds could make her the target of a jealous killer and a modern Salem witch-hunt that threatens her, her family...and the magical second-time-around love that's taking her and Nat by storm.

BESTSELLING, AWARD-WINNING AUTHOR

ANTOINETTE STOCKENBERG

Beyond Midnight

Three breathtaking novellas by these acclaimed authors celebrate the warmth of family, the challenges of the frontier and the power of love...

ROSANNE BITTNER
DENISE DOMNING
VIVIAN VAUGHAN

CHERISHED LOVE

CHERISHED LOVE
Rosanne Bittner, Denise Domning, Vivian Vaughan
_____ 96171-5 $5.99 U.S./$7.99 CAN.